COURTNEY MILAN

Unraveled

For DKH and KG, who don't deserve the mention.

And for RG, who does.

Chapter One

Bristol. October 1843.

"WELL, BILLY CROGGINS, WHY are you here again?"

The petty sessions had already started when Miranda Darling slipped into the dingy hearing room. She ducked her head and contemplated the floor, trying not to attract attention. She was playing a young lady today: posture erect, eyes cast demurely down, elbows at her sides. A young lady wouldn't fuss with her hair. Especially not to scratch where her wig drove an errant pin into her scalp. Today, her future rested on her performance.

Nothing new in that. The future was a perpetual burden, weighing her down. Sometimes she felt like one of the acrobats her father had taken her to see at Astley's as a child, dancing atop a bareback horse. One foot put false on a backflip, and she was like to come crashing to the ground. Like the acrobat, she could only pretend her footing was secure, do her best, and smile for the audience no matter what came.

There was a bit of a crowd today, maybe ten or fifteen men and women seated on the wooden benches of the hearing room. Her palms prickled with an edgy energy. She smoothed her hands against the fine muslin of her borrowed gown and counted breaths until the tension inside her faded to a passive lump of nerves.

The white-haired man at the front of the room—Billy Croggins, he'd been called—didn't seem nervous at all. His face was red, and he shrugged, unembarrassed, at the question that had been put to him.

"Why, Your Worships, I'm here for the same reason I'm always here. I had myself a little bit to drink." He raised his hand, miming. "I ended up a bit disorderly. You heard what my daughter had to say." Croggins flashed an ingratiating grin.

He had nice teeth for a drunkard. Miranda sidled down the aisle and slipped into an empty spot in the front. Billy Croggins had a nice nose, too. His white, disordered hair gave him an air of respectable eccentricity. Useful, if you were a layabout.

Nobody noticed her as she arranged her skirts. All eyes were trained on the unfolding drama, insignificant though it was.

These weren't the quarter sessions, where murderers and burglars would be sentenced to death or transportation. The magistrates here judged little thefts, brawls gone bad, acts of public lewdness. Fines were levied; men were imprisoned for a few days. The stakes were low, and the crimes were interesting only because a neighbor had committed them.

She'd not yet allowed herself to look in the direction of the magistrates. Old superstition, that—one didn't peek through the curtains at an audience before a performance. That spelled ill luck.

The austere white walls seemed to magnify the autumn chill, but Miranda slipped out of her worn cloak and removed her straw bonnet, taking care not to disturb the blond wig she'd donned that morning.

"What is this?" one of the magistrates asked. "The fifth time you've appeared before us?" His voice was familiar. *Too* familiar.

She mustn't look up at him in betraying consternation. Miranda's hand clenched around the wool of her cloak instead; she forced it open before the gesture could betray her.

"Correct as always, Your Worship," came Croggins's cheery reply.

At her immediate right, the clerk sat, his pen arrested over the inkwell. He hadn't written a thing in minutes.

Miranda leaned over and spoke in an urgent whisper. "Sir. I happened to witness one of the crimes today. The accused is a boy, perhaps twelve years of age—"

He glanced at her, frowning, and then looked away. "Tell me when he's up," he whispered gruffly. "I'm busy now."

He didn't look busy. The register before him read only: *Drunk. Admits he did it. Convicted.* Billy Croggins hadn't been convicted yet, but she couldn't blame the man for prematurely recording the result.

"If we keep convicting you, why do you keep at it?" This voice, thin and reedy, came from the left. "Turner—what is the punishment, again?"

Turner. So she *had* recognized that earlier voice. Another flash of nervousness traveled through her, this one tinged with a hint of fear. Still, she kept her gaze trained on Croggins.

The defendant grinned unabashedly. "I wager I know the punishment by now. Ten pounds for the repeat offense, which I haven't got—and so six hours in the stocks instead."

"Don't worry, Billy," someone called from the audience. "We'll make sure all the turnips are nice and rotten before we throw them, so they don't scratch your pretty face."

The room erupted into laughter.

"Gentlemen," another voice said, "it's a conviction, then?"

Everyone else shifted to look at the magistrates to the left of the room. It would seem out of place if she didn't follow their lead, and so Miranda raised her head. The three men tasked to hear the sessions today sat behind a heavy oak bench. They were dressed identically: curled, white-powdered horsehair wigs atop, and heavy black robes beneath. The man in the center with the red face was the mayor. On his left sat a fellow she'd never seen before. That man's wig was askew.

"Indeed," Croggins was saying, "what's another conviction amongst friends?"

On the right, sitting a good two feet from his compatriots... "Perhaps," this last magistrate said, "I might ask a few questions before we rush to judgment."

Miranda swallowed. *He* was Magistrate Turner—better known as Lord Justice.

His face wasn't red. His wig was straight. And while the other magistrates were smiling at Croggins's antics, Lord Justice looked as somber as a crow in his black robes, stern and implacable. She could almost believe the stories that were told about him.

"Always covering the ground, Turner," the mayor said in exasperated tones. "Very well. I suppose you must have your way. But I hardly see the point, as the man has admitted his guilt."

Compared with his colleagues, Lord Justice looked like the statue of a magistrate instead of irresolute flesh and blood. He fit the name he'd been given. Justice made her think of hard lines and inflexible resolve. Lord Justice scanned the room with sharp, mobile eyes, which seemed to take in everything all at once.

Lord Justice, everyone said, could smell a lie at twenty paces. Miranda sat no more than fifteen from him.

Just looking at the man gave her gooseflesh. She'd appeared before him once. Even thinking of the questions he'd asked, the way his eyes had pierced her, made the skin on the back of her neck prickle. And *that* time, she'd been telling the truth.

"Perhaps," Lord Justice said, "you could help me understand the events of last night. I've heard the testimony from your daughter. But I wish to hear it in your words. How did the fire start?"

"Ah," Billy Croggins said, "that would be the *drunk* part of drunk and disorderly." He smiled winningly.

Lord Justice was not so easily won. He steepled his fingers. "Were you voluntarily drunk? Or did you have your drink forced upon you?"

"I'd be much obliged, Your Worship, if people forced drink upon me. As it were, I had to purchase it like a regular booby."

The only response to that witticism was a thinning of the magistrate's lips. "When you were inebriated, you went to your daughter's house?"

"Yes, and can you believe my own child wouldn't open her door for me? Told me to go away and come back sober. If I waited for that, I'd never see my grandchildren at all, not 'til Gabriel sounded his trump at the last."

A woman in the crowd let out a harsh bark of laughter at that, and the mayor hid a smile behind his sleeve.

Lord Justice still found no amusement in the proceedings. He tapped his fingers against the bench. "Was it then you threw the lantern into the woodshed and threatened to burn her out?"

The smile on Croggins's face fixed in place. "Might have done, might have done. Wasn't thinking so clearly at that point. I didn't *actually* burn her woodshed down—just wanted to scare her a little, so she'd show some respect for her father. Besides, it seemed like a good idea. At the time."

Lord Justice sighed and leaned back. "You see, Billy Croggins, this is what has me worried. Everyone in this courtroom seems to think you're a jolly old fellow. Everyone thinks you're amusing. Everyone is laughing. Everyone, that is, except your daughter. Why do you suppose that is?"

"She's got no sense of humor."

A few chuckles rose from the audience, but they were weaker, and held a nervous edge.

"Here's my theory: her two infants were in the house when you tried to burn her out. Maybe she didn't see the joke in putting their lives at risk."

"Aw, it was just the woodshed!"

"It was an outbuilding, within the curtilage and attached to the dwelling-house," Lord Justice said. His gaze focused on some point in the distance, as if he were reading those words off some page that only he could see. "According to the Statute of George, that's arson."

"Arson! But the wood scarcely even caught!"

Lord Justice leaned over the bench. "Arson," he repeated firmly. "As you didn't succeed, attempted arson, and as such, punishable by one year's hard labor. Do you think that might dry you out?"

"Your Worship, I was drunk. I didn't know what I was doing."

"Under the rule of Lord Hale, a man who becomes voluntarily drunk is responsible for his actions, the same as if he was sober."

Croggins glanced about. There was no laughter in the courtroom now. Lord Justice had emptied it of all humor. This little display, after all, was just another demonstration of how Magistrate Turner had come by his name.

Miranda clenched her hands together and bit her lip. She could only hope he would not examine her so closely.

"Turner," the mayor said, "this is the petty sessions. We've no authority to consider a charge of arson at a summary conviction."

"Quite right," Lord Justice said. "Nor was arson charged in the indictment. But we can dismiss the case and commit him until the Assizes. I've heard enough testimony to have him charged when next the grand jury meets."

It wasn't Magistrate Turner's looks that had earned him the sobriquet "Lord Justice." In the two years before he'd become a magistrate, the petty sessions had convicted every man but one who had stood before them. In Turner's first six months in office, he'd let more than a dozen people go, claiming the crimes had been unproven. But he wasn't kind; far from it. He punished the guilty with harsh efficiency.

The *Lord* part came about because his brother was a duke. But they called him *Justice* because he was as cruel—and as kind—as the weather. You never knew what you were going to get, and no complaint would change the result.

Billy Croggins licked his lips. "Lord Justice. Please. Have mercy."

The man shook his head. "The proper form of address is 'Your Worship.'"

Croggins frowned.

"In any event," Lord Justice continued, "if the house had truly caught fire, you might have killed your daughter and your grandchildren." He paused and looked round the room.

He stole the breath from his audience, packed a thousand years of expectation into those bare seconds. If this had been a performance, Miranda would have applauded the perfection of his timing. But this was no play, put on for public amusement. This was real.

Lord Justice looked back at the defendant. He spoke quietly, but his words carried in the waiting silence. "I *am* having mercy, Mr. Croggins. Just not on you. Not on you."

Miranda shut her eyes. She'd done this before—stolen down to the hearings at the Patron's behest and delivered testimony designed to prevent the conviction of a particular defendant. The other magistrates never doubted the testimony of a genteel young lady.

But Turner asked questions. He listened. He heard the things you didn't intend to say. She'd spoken before him only once—the first time she'd testified, well over a year ago. It was the only time she had actually witnessed the crime in question. He'd wrung every last drop of truth from her then.

She surely couldn't afford Magistrate Turner's brand of mercy today.

"I'll conduct the examination," Turner said. "Palter—hold Mr. Croggins."

A blighted silence reigned in the hearing room, broken only by the shuffling of feet.

"Call the next case," the mayor muttered.

Beside her, the clerk began to speak. As he did, Lord Justice's gaze traveled over the spectators. His eyes briefly rested on Miranda. It was only in her imagination that they narrowed. Still, she shivered.

Under Lord Justice's voluminous black robes, he might have been fat or slender. He might have had tentacles like a cuttlefish, for all she knew. His long white wig made his features seem thin and severe. Perversely, all that black and white made him appear almost young. That couldn't be the case. A man had to be ancient to deal justice as he did without flinching.

Don't lie to this man. The instinct seemed as deep as hunger, as fierce as cold. But if she walked away now, she'd lose the protection she so desperately needed. And Robbie... It didn't bear thinking about. One didn't say *no* to the Patron's requests. Not even when justice threatened.

She'd received her orders less than two hours before. She was to speak on Widdy's behalf, to make sure that he wasn't convicted.

She didn't know *why*. She was never told why. But she'd asked, once, in a fit of lunacy, and she'd never forgotten the answer the Patron's man had given her.

In Temple Parish, justice belongs to the Patron, not the magistrates.

An officer was shuffling about, bringing to the front... Oh, yes. It was Widdy this time.

At the front of the room, the boy looked fragile and scared. The harsh life of a street-urchin in Temple Parish had broken him long ago. She doubted Widdy's release mattered except as a symbol, proof that the Patron was more powerful than the law.

She listened attentively as the baker who was prosecuting the case—a florid-faced gentleman by the name of Pathington—railed against Widdy specifically, and all small scourges upon honest sellers in general. The urchin looked confused and desperate against that onslaught.

When the baker had completed an exaggerated recounting of crime, infamy, and a missing half-loaf of bread, it was Lord Justice who turned to Widdy. "What is your name, young master?"

Widdy swallowed. "Widdy."

There was a pause. The clerk next to Miranda wrote the word, then looked up. "I beg your pardon, Your Worships. Is that his Christian name or his surname?"

Widdy looked beleaguered.

"Well?" the mayor said. "Speak up. Is that short for something?"

"Yes?" Widdy shifted his feet uneasily.

A faint chuckle rose from the onlookers.

"Well, what for?"

"I don't know. Me mam called me Widdy, back when."

"And what is your mother's name?"

Widdy looked away.

"Well, boy," the magistrate in the lopsided wig thundered, "what is your mother's name?"

Widdy shrunk in on himself. "People called her 'Spanky.'"

The laughter rang out again, darker and just a little more cruel.

Lord Justice cast a quelling glance over the room. "What did she do?"

"She's dead," Widdy replied earnestly. "But she used to drink gin."

The hearing room erupted at that. Lord Justice didn't even crack a smile. "Do you have work? A place to stay?"

"I sweep streets, sometimes. I hold horses, when gentlemen go into the shops. That's my favorite. Sometimes, I deliver billy-dos."

"Billy-dos?" The mayor's mouth quirked up.

"For ladies," Widdy explained earnestly. "When they don't want their words to be seen."

Skew-wig reached over and nudged the mayor's elbow. "I believe the boy is referring to *billets-doux.*" His mouth twitched in a self-satisfied smile.

Lord Justice cut his eyes briefly in their direction, and did not join in their merriment. "Did you take the bread?"

"No, sir. It wasn't mine."

"That's what they all say," Skew-wig said, shaking his head. "It's his word against a respectable business-owner. I believe the man who *doesn't* carry billy-dos about."

That was as good an entry cue as any. Miranda took a deep breath, expelling all her fears. Then she reached out and tapped the clerk again. The man jumped, spattering ink, and then caught her eye. She pointed at Widdy, and the man coughed once more.

"Your Worships," the clerk said, "there is a lady here who claims to have witnessed the whole affair."

"Where is she?" the mayor asked.

The clerk jerked his head at Miranda. She felt as if she'd been thrust onstage: every eye in the room trained on her. She went from cold to too-hot. Still, as she pushed to her feet, she also felt a hint of excitement for the performance.

"Your Worships." The girl she was playing might have that slight tremor to her hands. She would drop her eyes from the intensity of Lord Justice's gaze. "I saw the events in question. This boy merely watched." Her words felt almost mushy in her mouth. She pitched her accent somewhere between aristocratically smooth and street-wary, with an added touch of broad country. She needed to hover on the brink of respectability. In this gown, she'd never manage wealthy.

Nobody said anything, so she kept her eyes on the floor. How many people had stood here like this, hoping for the best? A bead of sweat collected on her forehead. After a few moments—seconds really, although it felt an age—she dared to lift her eyes.

Lord Justice watched her, unblinking, one hand on his chin. If there'd been a hint of softness in his manner toward Widdy, it had evaporated at her appearance. Next to him, his colleague frowned in puzzlement.

It would be a mistake to let the stretching silence drive her to speak. That way lay babbling, and too much revelation altogether. She dropped her chin and contemplated the floor instead.

Lord Justice spoke first. "You saw the entire thing." It wasn't quite a question, the way he said it. Still, she bobbed her head in response.

Beside her, the clerk shuffled his feet. "Should she be sworn in?"

Lord Justice gave a negative wave of his hand. "What is your name?"

"Whitaker," Miranda said. "Miss Daisy Whitaker."

Her day-gown was serviceable muslin, one that a countrified girl might wear. He'd already taken note of her accent. He glanced to either side of her, and then scanned the room before raising one eyebrow.

"You are here unaccompanied," he commented.

"My father is a farmer. A gentleman farmer. He's here for market, and brought me along to town. It's my first time." Miranda ducked her head. "I didn't think it was wrong to come. Was it?" She glanced up once more through darkened lashes, and willed him to see a headstrong girl from Somerset. Someone not used to being chaperoned at all times. Someone who might walk through fields by herself at home. She wanted him to see a foolish chit, so innocent that she believed going out alone in the city was no different than traipsing down a dusty lane.

"I had to come," she added softly. "He was just a child, Your Worship."

Lord Justice examined her a minute longer—as if she were a mouse, and he the owl about to swoop down and gobble her whole. "Where do you and your father stay?"

"The Lamb Inn."

His gaze cut away from her. "Mr. Pathington, in what manner did Master Widdy remove the loaf of bread from your premises?"

The baker who'd made the accusation jerked his head up. "I—well—that is to say, I did not precisely *see* him take it. But there was no one else about. I saw him; I turned away for the barest of instants. I turned back, and the loaf was gone. Who else could it have been?"

Lord Justice tapped his fingers against the bench. "Precisely how bare was your instant?"

"Pardon?"

"Estimate how long you stood with your back turned. What were you doing?"

"Counting change for a half-crown, Your Worship."

Magistrate Turner looked up and away, as if in calculation. "As much as a half-minute, then. You want me to punish this boy, who had no bread on him when he was apprehended, because you did not watch your storefront?"

Pathington flushed red. "Well, Your Worship, I wouldn't put it precisely like that—"

Lord Justice turned to face the other magistrates. "In my opinion, the charges have not been proven. Gentlemen?"

"Here now," the mayor said, "Miss…uh, the miss over here has not delivered her testimony."

Turner's lips compressed. "No," he said shortly. "But there is no need to hear it, as it is duplicative of what we can determine by reason. The lady—" he glanced sharply at Miranda "—need not expose herself."

"You cannot be serious, Turner. Maybe the boy didn't steal this particular loaf of bread," the mayor said. "But surely he is guilty of *something*. Skulking about bakeries, carrying billy-dos. We can't just let him go."

Lord Justice turned to the mayor. Miranda had that sensation once again—that he could have been on a stage, so clever was his timing.

"How curious," he finally offered. "Here I thought our duty was to decide if the charges before us could be proven. I recall the indictment most particularly, and yet I don't remember seeing this boy charged with the illegal carrying of letters."

The mayor flushed and looked away. "Suit yourself, Turner. If you insist on letting the rabble run free, I suppose I can't stop you."

A small smile touched Lord Justice's lips. "You heard the man. Master Widdy, you are free to go."

Miranda held her shoulders high, not daring to gasp. Still, relief flooded through her. Thank God. He'd not seen through her. This time, she'd scarcely had to talk with him. She'd survived. She felt as if she'd landed that double backflip atop a moving horse, and she could not keep from grinning.

But just as the babble in the room was beginning to grow, Lord Justice held up one hand.

"Miss…" He paused. "Whitaker, you said?" His lip curled.

Miranda's apprehension returned in full force. "Yes, Your Worship?"

"The Lamb Inn is through the market. A woman shouldn't walk down those mobbed streets unaccompanied. There are cutpurses loose. And worse."

"If I leave now, Your Worship, I'll be back before my father returns."

He drummed his fingers against the oak bench. "I'll see you to your lodgings, if you'll wait a few minutes in the anteroom."

Oh God. What a ghastly proposition. "Your Worship. I sh-shouldn't take you from your duties."

He sighed. "We are in complete accord on that point. Nevertheless."

Before she had a chance to argue, he signaled and the clerk struck the gavel. The waiting crowd rose to its feet, and the magistrates stood as well. Miranda wanted to run. She wanted to shriek. But she didn't dare draw attention to herself—not here, not with constables and magistrates both close by.

The clerk hopped to his feet and ran to open the rear door. The other judges turned and marched out of the room, one in front of the other.

Turner was the last of the three to leave, his black robe swirling about him as if he were some kind of dark angel. But the clerk held the door open even after Lord Justice passed through, as if waiting for one last judge. And sure enough, from under the bench, a dog pushed to its feet and headed for the door. Miranda hadn't seen it before; it must have lain quietly on the floor for the duration of the session.

The animal, a bit higher than her knee, was a mass of gray-and-white fur. It followed on Turner's heels, as stately and ageless as its master. It paused when it reached the doorway, and looked back. She couldn't even see its eyes through all that fur. Still, it felt as if the creature were marking Miranda, ordering her to wait until Lord Justice could see to her. She shivered, once, and the creature turned away.

Just her imagination.

And just her luck that His Worship had chosen today to show a gallant streak. She could not let him accompany her. There was no gentleman farmer, no comfortable inn. There was nothing but her cold garret waiting, and if he knew that the shining blond ringlets on her head were a wig, and her gown a costume...

Miranda swallowed. She didn't need justice. She needed to get out of the room—and fast.

Chapter Two

THERE WERE TIMES WHEN Smite Turner disliked his Christian name. And then there were times when it felt all too appropriate. Today, it seemed, was one of the latter occasions. As soon as the door shut on the hearing room, he sprang into action. Step one was to divest himself of his robe; that was accomplished in one fluid motion. After all, if his suspicions were correct—and they usually were—he had only seconds to act. He threw the dark, heavy wool in a careless heap to the side, and spun around.

His coat wasn't on his desk where he'd left it.

"Palter," he swore, "What have you done with my greatcoat? I've got to get out of here now."

"See?" the mayor muttered to Clark, the other magistrate, in tones not quite low enough to escape Smite's notice. " *Now* he's in a tearing hurry. I'll never make sense of the man."

Smite ignored his colleagues, and instead removed his uncomfortable wig. Palter appeared behind him, advancing at a rate that would have been better suited to an octogenarian on the brink of permanent decline rather than a spry young clerk in his thirties.

"Your Worship," the man said. He spoke as slowly as he walked. "I was brushing your coat. It was covered in dog fur." Palter cast an accusing glance behind Smite as he spoke. But the object of Palter's scorn had embarked on a vigorous campaign of ear-scratching, and took no notice.

"Never mind that." Smite held out his hand. "I need it. Now."

She'd called herself Daisy Whitaker this time. Nobody else would have made the connection—they'd have been blinded by the perfectly arranged blond hair, the well-made walking dress. But when she'd stood, she'd glanced warily from side to side as if she felt unsafe in her surroundings. Her eyelashes had been darkened.

And her wrists... No gentleman farmer's daughter had wrists so thin. Poor fare at the dinner table showed first on the wrists.

"You know how I feel about your going out covered in gray hairs." The man's eyes narrowed as he took in Smite's shirtsleeves. "Your Worship. Never tell me you went out in the hearing room, not wearing a coat under your robe."

Smite simply stared at him. "That robe is blazing hot," he said. "Nobody can see beneath it. And my attire really is my own concern, and none of yours. Now where is my greatcoat?"

Palter was supposed to be just his clerk—a fellow who looked up legal precedents, when such were needed, who took dictation and handled the more laborious paperwork that arose. But within a few days of work, he'd appointed himself Smite's valet-in-residence at the Council House. He'd made himself utterly indispensable on all fronts. That only meant that when Smite wanted him dispensed with, he was damned inconvenient.

"I heard what you said out there." Palter strolled to the far side of the room once more, leisurely as you please. "Think about the dignity of your station. You ought to wear a coat to talk to an innocent miss."

Innocent. Ha.

Everyone else had been fooled. But for years, Smite had been blessed with a superior memory. He had an eye for face and color, an ear for words. He remembered conversations that had taken place decades in the past. He could recall the precise shape of the brooch his mother had worn to his sister's funeral.

And so it had taken only a few seconds to recognize the supposed Miss Whitaker. The last time he'd seen her, she'd had orange hair and freckles. She'd been wearing a simple frock of dark green, matching brilliant eyes that she had been unable to conceal now. She'd given a different name, too. It had been a year since that first encounter, but he'd thought he'd seen her more than once, dressed differently each time.

He didn't know what she was up to, but he didn't like it, and he was going to make her stop.

Across the room, his man opened a wardrobe and pulled out the missing coat.

"I see no reason to elevate my dignity to the level of pomposity." Smite crossed the room in three quick strides, and took the garment. "In my experience, dignity naturally follows competence. I'll look after my work, and trust my dignity to take care of itself."

"Your Worship, you've got powder on the coat now," Palter accused. "You could spare a half-minute for dignity. The girl will wait." His clerk handed over a pair of gloves, which Smite jammed in his coat pocket.

A liar who had been prepared to commit bald-faced perjury? Unlikely she'd still be around. Smite simply shook his head and strode to the door. But retrieving the coat had been a cue: Ghost instantly perked up and moved to the door, a silent shadow. The dog looked up in entreaty. Liquid brown eyes begged: *Take me with you. I'll be good.*

Oh, the lies that dogs told.

"Ghost," Smite commanded, "you will stay."

The dog let out a faint huff of protest. Palter, by contrast, made a muffled, choking sound in response.

Smite turned and raised an eyebrow. "Do cheer up, Palter. I took him for a long walk this morning. He shouldn't careen off the walls more than five, six..." Smite paused and looked at Ghost. The dog watched, his paws practically quivering in frustrated want. "Maybe seven thousand times," he finished.

Ghost sat as still as an animal scarcely out of puppyhood could manage. The expression on his face was deeply earnest.

"Ghost. Do listen. In the event that I need a squirrel brought to justice, I will go to you first. Until then..." He adopted his harshest tone. "Behave in my absence, or you will pay the consequences when I return."

"Your Worship." Palter's voice trailed off plaintively.

"Keep the dog in," Smite advised. "I don't need him following me." The last thing he saw as he stepped outside was Palter ducking his head in acquiescence.

Turner pulled the door shut behind him, stepping out into a larger hall. His footsteps echoed on the wood floor. A few laborers were dawdling in the antechamber, but Miss Whitaker—or Miss Darling, as she'd called herself the first time he'd seen her—was not present in any of her incarnations. Damn Palter, for robbing him of those extra seconds. Still, it had not been so long. She couldn't have gone far.

Smite headed out the main door.

The Council House stood just behind him. High Street was crowded, faces shielded from view by hats and umbrellas and cloaks drawn tight about figures. It was, after all, raining. Nothing but a determined drizzle, but still, it was enough that he tamped down a frisson of unease.

Stop coddling yourself, Turner. Sugar melts; you'll survive.

Instead, he crossed the street to stand in front of All Saints Church, and concentrated on the crowds about him. He was looking for a young woman, and he couldn't depend upon the color of her hair or the style of her gown. She'd been disguised in the courtroom; she could be again. He was looking for *how*, not *what*.

He found his *how* a few seconds later. She ducked out of an alley, now dressed in a shabby cloak more appropriate to a serving girl. She glanced from one end of the street to the other with that telltale wariness.

He couldn't say what it was about her that made him know she was the one. Her hair, whatever color it actually was, was hidden beneath a massive straw bonnet. She started down the street, and then glanced over her shoulder, toward the building beside the Council House. Where Smite was supposed to have met her.

She didn't see him standing across the street.

He began to walk toward her. He'd left his hat—Palter would rant about it when he returned—and the rain plastered his hair uncomfortably to his head.

But before he reached her, she started off, her strides now swift and purposeful. He was taller, but he made little headway. She darted through the crowds with a determined agility. He followed her down one crowded cobblestone street, past a market and then another church. Buildings loomed, dark gray stone streaked by the rain. Smite's cuffs became damp, and he pulled the gloves Palter had shoved at him from his pocket.

She was making her way to the Floating Harbour. Just beyond the crowds, he could see the stone wall that bounded the water. Masts of ships stretched skyward. Gulls circled and called as he pushed through the waterfront crowds. He could hear timbers creaking in the wind, the shout of men, and the shrieking complaint of a winch—the all-too-familiar sounds of Bristol's lifeblood, trade and transportation. In the distance, he could see the high topmasts of the *S.S. Great Britain* where she waited, silent and lifeless, in the docks. Her funnel, a dark, imposing chimney against the sky, was cold. No smoke issued from it; no boilers worked below. She was the largest steamship ever built, and she was imprisoned where she stood.

He felt an odd sort of sympathy with the ship. They'd neither of them been served well by water.

He shook his head, dispelling the sentiment. Her straw bonnet bobbed down the street some fifteen yards in front of him, and she darted across the Bristol Bridge.

She'd crossed to the other side by the time Smite reached the edge. He came to a stop.

There was nothing odd about this slow-moving body of water—it was a bit of liquid, nothing more. He was perfectly safe. The solid stones of the bridge had withstood the traffic of heavy-laden carts for almost a century. Its span stretched twenty feet above the level of the water. On a clear, sunny day, he could cross with only the slightest twist to his stomach.

Today, though, the waters were gray-green from a week's worth of hard rains. They seemed closer than usual, and, as they slapped against the stones of the channel, they spoke a language all of their own. In Smite's ear, the sound whispered of dark cellars and the rising tide of a flood.

Nonsense. He snorted. It wasn't even a river. Besides, the level of the Floating Harbour never rose—it was regulated by locks.

"Don't be an ass," he advised himself aloud.

And she—whoever *she* was—was disappearing down the street. If he didn't follow now, he'd lose her. With a deep breath, Smite looked forward. He set his gaze on the street across the bridge, where a team and horses stood, men loading goods into the cart. So long as he didn't think of the water at all, it couldn't bother him.

Smite looked at the solid ground on the far side and stepped forward. He had more important things to concern himself with today.

THERE WEREN'T MANY PEOPLE who felt easier in the dark corners of the slums than in the wide streets of the city center. But Miranda had lived in Temple Parish for three years. She knew the backstreets, the people. She knew the alleyways she shouldn't visit, and the ones where she'd be watched by unseen eyes and kept safe. Here, she was free from the harshness of sanctioned order, arbitrarily enforced by constables in blue tailcoats. She'd paid for her freedom; she might as well enjoy it.

Still, she'd felt her skin prickle the entire journey back, as if the long arm of the law still hovered over her.

That, she told herself briskly, was merely the last remnant of her conscience speaking. She leaned against the brick at the mouth of the alley where she lived and pulled off the bonnet she'd been wearing, and then the wig. Her hairpins underneath caught; she wiggled them free carefully, counting as she removed them. She couldn't afford to lose a one.

Her own hair—a too-recognizable orange—spilled over her shoulder as she stuffed the weight of that blond wig into a sack she pulled from her skirt-pocket.

Lord Justice obviously had his suspicions about the fresh-faced Miss Daisy Whitaker. But he'd be looking for a young, golden-haired girl staying at the Lamb Inn, not a redheaded seamstress, a sometime wig-maker who lived in a garret beside a glassworks. She was safe once again. At least for today.

Miranda shut her eyes and raised her face to the rain. It felt freeing to have her skin washed clean of its suffocating layer of rice powder and rouge. She pulled a handkerchief from her basket and wiped her brows, her cheeks. The remains of Daisy Whitaker disappeared in a smear of rouge and the coal dust she'd used to darken her lashes.

She let her handkerchief fall, opened her eyes—and jumped back. A man was standing directly in front of her. She hadn't even heard him approach.

"I do beg your pardon," the man—the *gentle*man, by that haughty accent—said.

He didn't sound as if he was begging her anything. From the proper tone of his speech, he'd never had to beg at all—just buy. There was something familiar about his voice, though. As if to reinforce that sense of familiarity, he reached out and placed a gloved hand on her wrist.

She sized him up in one instant, taking in the thick, fine wool of his greatcoat and the snow-white of his cuffs, peeking out beneath well-made sleeves. His shoes were polished black, with no creases worn in the leather. His cravat had been fastidiously starched. She couldn't find even a solitary piece of lint on his clothing, a surer sign of wealth than even his shiny brass buttons.

He was handsome in an austere sort of way, his features sharp, his eyes clear and blue in contrast with the ebony of his hair. Incongruously, a dusting of white powder touched the shoulders of his coat.

He wore no hat, which didn't fit at all.

Still, she had his measure. Rich. Handsome. And not very intelligent, if he'd ventured into an alley in Temple Parish wearing shoes like *that*.

No doubt he was looking to buy himself a little pleasure. Pleasure often made men stupid.

"Let go of me." She let her own accent creep toward the common—consonants sliding together, vowels eliding.

The stranger relinquished his hold on her wrist and stepped into a doorway, just out of the rain. He didn't take his eyes off her, though. There was something arrogantly peremptory about the way he perused her from head down to toe, and then back again.

She raised her chin. "The whores are all back by the Floating Harbour. I'm not for sale, and so I'll thank you not to eye me like a piece of flesh."

He did not appear the least put off by her vulgarity. "I'm not looking for a whore from the harbor."

"Well, I'm not like to take you." She snorted. "What's wrong with you, then? Must be something dreadful, if a pretty thing like yourself is forced to pay for a tumble."

"Pretty?" He shook his head in bemusement. "I haven't been called pretty in years. I'm afraid you have the matter entirely backward. I came here looking for you, darling."

"Darling?" Miranda bristled. "I've not given you leave to address me by something so familiar."

"If ever I address you with an intimacy, you'll know it. Darling is your name, is it not?"

Her face was turned toward the glassworks, where heat radiated out the open door. Still, she felt suddenly cold all over. How did he know her? What did he want?

And there was the indisputable fact that he was taller than her. Bigger. Stronger. She had safe passage from the thieves and the bullyboys, but the Patron had no control over gentlemen.

Miranda took a step backward. "I don't know what you're talking about, mister."

"Mister." A half-smile crossed his face, and he took a step toward her. Up close, that grin looked like the self-satisfied expression of a shark closing in on a hapless fish.

The smattering of powder on his greatcoat was too evenly distributed to be dandruff. She of all people should have recognized it: it was wig-powder. But the only people who powdered their wigs these days were actors. Actors and—

Miranda felt the blood run from her face. He reached out and took hold of her wrist again, and this time, he drew her close.

"It's simple," he said, "Miranda Darling is the first name you gave me, and it would be best for you if that much turned out to be true. You're certainly not Daisy Whitaker, no matter what you claimed today."

He was supposed be fat. He was supposed be old. He was supposed to be back at the bleeding Council House.

"And as we're establishing what we call one another," he continued, "the proper form of address for me is not *mister*. It's 'Your Worship.'"

"Lord Justice," Miranda heard herself say. "Oh, *shite.*"

Chapter Three

SMITE HAD ASSUMED THAT Miss Miranda Darling was young—no more than the fifteen or so years of age that she'd acted earlier in the morning. Impressionable enough that he might frighten her into compliance with a stern little speech. But up close, he could see that she was not coltishly slender, just undernourished. Not desperately so—she wasn't starving—but he very much doubted she ever ate to her satisfaction.

Aside from that one expletive, she had a presence to her, a self-possession that young girls lacked. He could feel the pulse in her wrist hammering against his grip, but she raised bright green eyes to him with just a hint of defiance…and something else.

If one judged age by the eyes, she was ancient.

One could never determine age properly in the more squalid districts. She might have been anywhere from nineteen to nine-and-twenty.

Her eyes widened; her pupils dilated. But she merely tossed her head, and the bright mass of reddish-orange hair slipped down her shoulder.

Most women in her situation would have lied, never mind that the falsehood would have been transparent.

She simply shifted her stance, angling away from him. "Well. What do you want?"

"You can start by thanking me."

She glanced at his hand on her wrist, and curled her lip. "Am I supposed to thank you in some particular fashion?" Her gaze fell to his trousers.

"No." He dropped her hand. "That's appalling."

"I hadn't realized I was entirely repellent."

"I'm not that sort," he countered. "I wouldn't take advantage."

But he could see why others might. Objectively, she wasn't pretty. She was too thin, and it pinched her features: her cheeks were a touch on the hollow side, her hands too scrawny for real elegance. A smattering of freckles covered her nose, and a flush rose over her skin—not pink and demure, but red and angry.

Not that plainness would have mattered. In the back slums, it would only have mattered that she was female and alone.

She wasn't beautiful, but she had a vast store of defiant vitality that was all too attractive. He grimaced, and filed that observation away in the back of his mind.

"Let me spell matters out for you," he said slowly. "You came into my courtroom in disguise, bearing a false name. There is only one reason you aren't languishing in custody at the moment."

"Your forbearance?"

"My interference. I didn't let them swear you in. As it is, you merely told lies. Perjury, by contrast, is punishable by six months in prison."

She went utterly still.

"If you had actually committed that crime, it would have been my duty to act on the matter."

Miss Darling licked her lips and looked away. "Thank you, then." She glanced down the alleyway. "I can explain."

Smite cut her off with a chop of his hand. "You can *excuse.* I've heard it all before. You didn't have a choice. You did it for the common good." As he spoke, he ticked off fingers. "You were hungry." He shook his head. "I'm not interested in your pathetic reasons. This isn't a hearing."

"What is it, then?"

"A warning. Don't tell tales in my presence. Don't disguise yourself in my court. If ever I see you before me again, dressed as someone else and spouting falsehoods, I will have you arrested on the spot. And I won't give this—" he snapped his fingers "—for your *excuses.*"

She took a deep breath and eyed him. It was a canny look, that, one that sized him up and found him wanting all at once.

"Ah." He took a step closer to her. "You think you can fool me. That you need only don the right disguise and I'll look right past you. You're wrong."

She didn't say anything.

"I saw you first on October the twelfth, a little more than one year past. You spoke on behalf of Eric Armstrong, a thirteen-year-old boy accused of striking a patrolman. I actually think you were telling the truth then. You were wearing a gown of dark crepe."

Her mouth fell open.

"I glimpsed you in the hall eight months later. Then, you were dressed as a boy. I checked the records after; I believe you testified that one Tom Arkin was *not* the same boy who served as an apprentice to the chimney sweep."

He could see her swallow, could trace the contraction down her throat.

"I remember you precisely," he told her. "I'll be looking for you. You can't disguise yourself from me. Don't even try."

This time when she looked at him, he finally saw what he'd been waiting for. Fear. Real fear.

"You are inhumanly precise," she finally said.

"Yes." No point in quarreling over the truth. What did it matter, how inhuman his memory was, if it served his purpose? He'd scared her, and she would stay away. If he was successful, he'd never see her name on the gaol delivery lists. His inhumanity was a small price to pay for that.

"Enjoy the rest of your day, Miss Darling." He reached up to tip his hat to her, but then remembered that he hadn't brought one. He converted the gesture into a meaningful tap of his forehead and turned to leave.

He had taken four steps away when she spoke again. "Do you recall all your witnesses in such vivid detail, Your Worship?"

He paused, not looking back at her. "Yes," he said. "I remember everything." It was close enough to the truth to serve. His memory felt like dry leaves, pressed flat between the pages of some heavy book. The essence was preserved, but what remained was a poor facsimile for reality. He never could recall scents, and without those nothing seemed real.

He glanced at her over his shoulder. "I particularly remember you, Miss Darling." He met her eyes.

He hadn't meant it *that* way, but she raised her fingers to her lips, and a different sort of flush pinked her cheeks.

Nobody would call her beautiful, but she was striking. And perhaps some dormant part of him belatedly decided to notice that she'd called him pretty before she'd known who he was.

A woman. Wouldn't that be nice?

No. Not this one. And definitely not now.

He shook his head, more at himself than to her, and left before his imagination could cause him any more trouble.

OLD BLAZER WASN'T IN. Miranda could tell in one breath when she opened the door to the little shop on Temple Street. No heavy pipe smoke greeted her. Only a faint, lingering bitterness, hours old.

Old Blazer was in less and less these days.

Miranda sidled past the secondhand gowns that hung on pegs, waiting for new owners. Spools of cheap ribbon and bolts of middling quality calico were displayed atop barrels and boxes.

She did not look to her left. If she did not see how she had fared, she couldn't get any bad news.

She wasn't sure if she should be happy about the old man's absence. Only a faint, sour hint of pipe smoke remained to remind her of his presence. The two customers who were in the store were silent, looking through the wares. That, most of all, made the shop seem smaller and gloomier than usual. Usually, Old Blazer was chattering away. And unless he'd been set off on one of his famous rages, someone would have been laughing in response.

Miranda clutched her basket to her chest and tiptoed to the back of the store. The counter there, usually stacked with goods, had been cleared of everything but a red pincushion.

Jeremy Blasseur—Old Blazer's grandson—was sitting on a stool, needle in hand. He was slender, and had a shock of sandy brown hair that curled of its own accord. He was frowning at a seam, which gave him a somewhat abstracted expression. It almost made her want to laugh, which would have been very wrong, because Jeremy was one of the most intensely sober individuals she had met. Especially these days.

He looked up at her approach, and his face lit. "Miss Darling. You survived. How did it go?"

"As well as you might expect." And that was all he was going to get from her. "I do hope that Old Blazer is well."

Jeremy gave a halfhearted shrug. "He's got a bit of a head-cold. Or, at least, that's what he said. Mama says he's just malingering. But you haven't told me anything. I worry about you."

Old Blazer wouldn't have worried about her. He would have been worried about the gown she'd borrowed, and he'd have been grumbling already about the length of time she'd had it.

But Jeremy was so serious, so intent on doing everything right. Nothing made an easy friendship more awkward than a man who wanted to *help*.

"Don't," Miranda said. "Nothing happened."

He had enough to worry about as it was. The last thing he needed to hear, after that unfortunate business with George, was that Miranda had found herself hip-deep in trouble with a magistrate.

He gave her a sad-puppy look. "If you really don't want to talk of it…"

"It's over," she said shortly. "I survived. I'd rather forget it all."

It was impossible to forget. When Lord Justice had taken hold of her today, he'd not caviled about the matter. He'd grabbed her wrist with a firm, strong grip. She could still feel the warmth and pressure of his hand.

In contrast to Lord Justice's dark, fine coat, Jeremy was dressed in serviceable—but fading—brown. He didn't frighten her. He hadn't threatened to toss her in gaol.

"Did you like the gown?" he asked.

"It suited the occasion." She dipped into her skirt pocket and slid a half-shilling across the counter. That practically gutted her remaining stash of coins.

"No, no." He shook his head. "I can't possibly charge you for the loan. It was just a few hours that you had it."

"You're running a business, Jeremy. I'm a customer. I have to pay you, or you don't make any money."

"But I know how much you needed it."

"When a customer needs something, good business sense requires you to charge him *more*, not *less*." Equal in importance was the fact that Miranda owed enough favors. Owing favors had landed her in this tangle in the first place.

"But…" He sighed and ignored the coin. "You're a friend. You don't need to be a customer. I have few enough friends as it is."

"We'll be better friends if I act like a customer when I'm a customer. I don't want to impose on anyone. You, least of all."

"It's not—" He cut himself off, shook his head. "Bother. You don't have to trade for everything."

She ignored this. "We still have business to do, Jeremy." She reached into her basket. "I've brought another wig."

He drooped. "Um...we haven't sold the last two yet."

"This one is the best so far." How she managed to speak so calmly, Miranda didn't know. The payment for Robbie's schooling would be due in a few weeks. Shortly after that, she'd need to hand over the rents. Dread coiled inside of her, but she refused to let it show. Instead, she reached into her basket and pulled out her latest creation. "The hair is blond. It's long, and it's got the loveliest curls. I've fixed the hair up, but I can redo the style." She held it out to him. "Some vain, elderly lady will want to reclaim her youth with this."

Jeremy didn't reach for the wig. "I...well, there's no way to say this. Old Blazer is talking about getting rid of the wigs altogether. If they're not going to sell, he says there's no point in giving them valuable room in the store."

"They'll sell," Miranda said airily, even though her breath jarred from her. *Smile, and make it look easy.* "And what's more, they sell the hats. I should charge you a commission on the hats your customers purchase—they're so much more appealing atop a head of hair, don't you think? The instant a woman walks in the shop, she can imagine what the hat will look like on. Once you have a customer thinking of what she'll look like in an article of clothing, you're that much closer to a sale."

"That's true."

Miranda stifled a sigh. Old Blazer would never have admitted that. He'd have bargained to the end.

"I'll just set this one up, then, next to the others."

Jeremy didn't object to this piece of importunity, and so she arranged the wig—her third unsold wig. Her arrangement with Old Blazer paid her a percentage of each sale. Well enough in good months—more than she'd get selling her wares directly to shopkeepers. But in bad times... She had enough sewing work that they wouldn't starve. And Robbie made a few pennies—that would pay for coal.

But they were looking at lean weeks ahead. Lean weeks, with winter coming on. If her luck didn't turn, they might get down to thinning out the gruel until it was more water than sustenance.

In response to that, her stomach growled.

Behind her, Jeremy cleared his throat. "It's been weeks since your last sale. You...you don't need money, do you?"

She set a bonnet atop the golden hair. "You're a shopkeeper, Jeremy, not a moneylender."

"I wasn't offering to *lend* you anything." He swallowed. "We...we're doing quite well, and—"

"I'm not comfortable with anything else. I don't need a loan."

"Miranda." Jeremy set his hand over hers. "Listen to me. I don't care if you *need* a loan." He sighed. "George was supposed to be released today, did you know that?"

"Oh?" That should have been good news, but by the set of his jaw, it was not.

"I went to the gaol to inquire, but he wasn't on the list of men who were set free."

Miranda stared at Jeremy. "I can't imagine George making trouble, getting additional time."

"It's worse. I made them check—he wasn't inside the gaol, either. He's gone."

No wonder Jeremy looked so serious. Miranda shook her head in confusion. "How is that possible?"

"It's this place." Jeremy looked straight ahead. "It eats good people and spits out monsters. George didn't even do anything, and he was tossed in prison. Now he's disappeared. Mother—"

He stopped himself, shook his head, and looked up at Miranda. His pale eyes pierced her. And maybe they were done being shopkeeper and supplier, now, and were ready to move back to being friends. She closed her hand around his.

"Shh," she said softly. She couldn't bring herself to say that all would be well. Chances were, it wouldn't.

"I'm losing everything I care about," he said thickly. "I just want a normal life. Is that so much to ask?"

"Shh," she repeated.

He pulled his hand away from hers and pushed her coin across the table. "Take it." His face was stony. "And promise me that you'll come to me if you need anything else. I can't lose you, too."

Miranda owed enough favors as it was. Still, she couldn't turn him down—not with that look of stony certainty in his face. And so she picked up the small coin and slipped it back into her pocket.

It was just a little debt—a half-shilling's worth. It couldn't be too hard to make it up to him. She'd manage it somehow. And soon.

THE SUN HAD ALMOST retired when Miranda ducked out of Blasseur's Trade Goods & More. It was early yet; the clocks had not yet struck five. Still, she pulled her cloak around her against the chill of the oncoming night. A lamplighter across the street had lit half the lamps on Temple Street; they cast a dim glow down the thoroughfare. But the road was unlit in the direction Miranda headed.

The coming darkness lent urgency to this last errand. Robbie would still be at the glassworks where he worked in the afternoon, but it was not long until evensong. Miranda still had to make one last perilous visit. No point postponing it, except to coddle her nerves.

She darted across the street, and then down a short, dark lane. The buildings blocked all light, before giving way to a wide space, framed by a forbidding gate. After the bustle of the gloomy streets, the fog covered the churchyard like a cold, clammy blanket. The edges ruffled in a small breeze. Out of that sea of mist rose the dark silhouette of Temple Church.

To her eye, the church seemed a bit sad. After its construction, one side of the bell tower had begun to sink. At this point, hundreds of years later, the tower had tilted so much that it had actually separated from the church building; gray fog swirled through the gap. One day, the tower would come crashing down.

Miranda shook her head. "Not your problem, girl," she muttered. With any luck, by the time the whole thing fell to pieces, she and Robbie would be long gone. But for now...

She gathered up her skirts and trotted through the mist, around to the front of the church and up the steps. She paused before the doors, and dug in her pockets until she found what she needed. It was a black stone, with red wax dripped on one side— the sigil of the Patron. When she found it outside her door, it told her that she was needed. She set the stone just outside the church doors, signaling that she was inside and waiting.

It was colder inside the church than out, but the interior showed no signs of the decay that afflicted the tower. Lush paintings hung over the altar, and the benches shone with polish. The nave echoed with her footsteps. The church was empty at this hour. It was almost always empty. Nobody came here unless there was business to do.

Miranda pulled her cloak about her. It was just the chill, surely, that brought gooseflesh to her arms.

No one came to greet her. No bustling rector asked what she was doing. The church held only ghosts and memories, as far as she could see. She kept her eyes on the dark flagstones beneath her feet. They were cut in diamond shapes, and she followed their line diagonally to the side of the room.

There was no required confession in the Church of England. Confession, she had been told once by a gentle-faced curate, was a papist affliction. True confession, he'd said, was between herself and God.

But Temple Church had been built before there was a Church of England. While confession had been stamped out, the architecture was not so easily changed. Miranda glanced about her once more—she truly was alone—found her way to the third pew on the right, and then identified the place she needed, where the wall was overhung with heavy, forbidding curtains.

It was the work of a moment to slide them aside and enter.

The onetime confessional had long since been converted to a closet. In the dark alcove that waited stood a broom, a bucket, a cracked bar of harsh soap, and a three-legged stool. One wall was partially blocked by a rosewood screen—the last remnants of Catholicism in this ancient church. She pulled the curtains back, plunging herself into darkness. Then she sat on the stool, folded her hands carefully, and waited.

She never knew whom she would talk to. Sometimes it was a man. Once, she thought the voice she heard had belonged to a woman. She doubted she'd had any conversation with the Patron himself; whoever he was, his identity was a closely guarded secret. Unsurprising; if Bristol had a thieves' guild, the Patron was the undisputed head.

But the Patron was more than that. The constables kept order in the prosperous parts of Bristol; the Patron had taken charge of those places where constables didn't dare patrol. If Miranda walked undisturbed on the streets at night, it was because he granted her safe passage, and the lesser bullyboys didn't dare risk his wrath. If he refused to allow Robbie to get involved with the other street boys...well, she'd bargained for that, too.

She was mired deep in his debt.

The bargain had seemed so simple, on that fateful night when she'd begged for his help. She received the Patron's protection in exchange for one favor granted every month. Without the bargain, a woman and a boy living alone in the slums would never have survived.

But with every passing month, the value of that favor seemed to escalate. And now...

However pretty he had been, Lord Justice had promised to put her in gaol. In gaol, like George Patten. Who had disappeared. The room was cold, indeed.

Perched on that too-short stool, she felt her calves begin to ache. Finally, a soft rustle announced that someone had arrived on the other side of the screen.

The voice that addressed her today was a tenor with a bit of a rasp. She wasn't even sure it was a man. She detected the faint scent of tobacco from the other side of the screen. Still, she formed a picture in her mind—some hulking, brutish thing lurking in the old confessional.

"Have you come to confess?" the voice asked.

"I have." She reached out and snapped a straw from the broom, playing it between her fingers.

"The Patron will hear what you have to say, my child." The voice always started with that, no matter who spoke to her.

"I did as the Patron asked," she said. "I went to the hearing. I volunteered to speak on behalf of Widdy. The charges were dismissed as unproven, and he went free."

Her simple report was met with a brooding silence. Then: "Lying is a sin, child. And so is omission. What is it you aren't telling the Patron?"

Of course. The Patron had likely had a man in the hearing room. "I only volunteered, sir. I was not asked to speak by the magistrates."

Perhaps the Patron would claim that this favor didn't count, that it didn't clear her debt for the month. Miranda's stomach churned.

But instead of disputing the point, the voice simply said, "Tell me about Lord Justice."

"He offered to accompany me back to my inn. I mean, he offered to accompany Daisy Whitaker. I slipped away before he found me after the hearing." No point in giving more information than requested. The Patron hardly needed *more* of a hold on her.

The voice didn't remark on her second omission. The Patron probably didn't know about her second interaction with Lord Justice.

"Hmm," that raspy voice said. "Do you think that he might have a prurient interest in Miss Whitaker? That might be useful."

She could call to mind the turn of his shoulder, the quarter profile he'd given her. *I particularly remember you, Miss Darling.* She'd felt the most absurd curl of heat run through her at that, so much that she shivered now in recollection.

"No," she said forcefully. "I'm fairly certain that he recognized me. He was suspicious, not lustful. I don't think he believed me." She shook her head, and then blurted out the words that danced on the tip of her tongue. "I can't do this anymore."

Silence met this pronouncement. Her pulse beat. More dangerous than working for the Patron was *refusing* to work for him. One didn't say *can't* to a representative of the Patron.

But it was either that or cross paths with Lord Justice once more. Miranda clenched the broom straw in her fingers, waiting.

A sigh came from the other side of the screen. "Then your association with the Patron is at an end. You're not a slave, child. You have always been free to make your own choices."

"Th-that's it?"

"Of course. Consider the old arrangement dissolved, if that is what you wish."

"I do." Her words were quiet, but she almost swayed on the stool, dizzy with blossoming hope.

"The Patron's blessings upon you, child."

She stared at the rosewood screen, waiting for some signal. But a minute passed without any more word. For all she knew, the figure who'd spoken had stolen away in the silence. She couldn't quite believe that everything had worked out so easily. She *had* landed that backflip for a second time, and she felt suddenly warm, despite the draft that fluttered the curtain. She stood and patted her dress into place.

And that was when the voice spoke again. "Of course," came those whispered words, "if you are not bound by any agreement, neither is the Patron."

Miranda shivered. The straw snapped between her fingers.

"Robbie is…your brother, is he? He is so *eager* to help. So *interested,* when his little friend Joseph shows him the treasures that he's obtained by offering me his scant assistance. He chafes, making a mere pittance as a runner."

Robbie wasn't her brother; he was something akin to her ward. They had a long and complicated relationship. But she was responsible for him, and had been for years. She couldn't walk away from that kind of a threat. Miranda sat back on the stool.

The voice continued in singsong tones. "He would leap at the chance to be included in one of the finer opportunities the Patron offers. There's a house that needs burgling, and he's just the fellow to do it."

"He's never done anything like that."

"The Patron is aware of his history."

"He'll get caught," Miranda said miserably.

"Most likely."

"They'll hang him for burglary."

"It seems probable," the voice agreed carelessly.

"Then why have him do it? There's no profit in it for you."

"The Patron has little interest in Robbie's death. But he takes a great deal of interest in you, Miss Darling."

If she could just go back to the moment when she'd first struck this bargain… She'd been seventeen and new to Bristol, with a nine-year-old boy in tow. She had thought she had no choice at the time. It had been either the Patron, or…

She'd been raised in a troupe of traveling players. She could sew any costume, take on any disguise. She could change her voice until she hardly recognized it herself. She'd thought herself very clever, offering those services. So sure that the Patron would see her value.

He had. Unfortunately.

"If Lord Justice has me imprisoned, I'll not be of much use," she essayed.

"The Patron will take your protest under advisement. For now, it is important to determine what Lord Justice truly wants of you. To that end, tomorrow you will go back to the records room at the Council House, and ask to see the papers on—"

" *Tomorrow?*" Miranda echoed in shock. "But we had an agreement—I was to owe you a favor no more than once a month, and nothing dangerous or so unsavory as to—"

"Child," the voice interjected, "you *had* an agreement with the Patron. You dissolved it. This is the new bargain."

She stared at the screen, her hands cold. She could protest. She could argue. She wanted to scream and run away. But there was no need to force the Patron to repeat his threat toward Robbie. He could make good on it.

Robbie was twelve, now—headstrong and growing, believing he knew what was best for himself without understanding how vulnerable he was.

Well. She had no choice. There was nothing to do but smile, and hope she could make the landing instead of breaking her back.

"Very well, then," she said. Her voice didn't quiver. She refused to show the fear that welled up inside of her. "Tell me what I must do."

Chapter Four

"WHAT IN BLAZES IS this thing?" The voice, haughty and arrogant, came out of the records room.

Smite paused in the hall of the Council House. Beside him, Ghost skittered to a halt.

He should just walk on. He didn't need to intervene; in fact, the men who worked here were quite adept at explaining the necessary procedures to difficult fellows.

But he recognized that voice—that spoiled drawl, from a man who'd never worked a day in his life. A regular plague, he was.

Paper rustled in the room beyond the open doors, and the voice of the harried clerk sounded. "My good man, I—"

"My good man?" the voice demanded. "Are visitors to this city always addressed in so cavalier a fashion?"

Some things never changed. The man Smite heard was still as annoyingly determined on receiving his due as ever, no matter that the last years had changed his fortune entirely.

A pause. "Sir," he heard the clerk continue in a more placating tone of voice, "I should think the summons was perfectly clear. You are to appear on Tuesday next, at one of the clock, before—"

"Yes, but I don't *wish* to make a public appearance. What must I do to avoid that?"

Smite sighed, and stepped through the door. The clerk saw him and let out a deep breath in relief. The visitor towered over the other man, and brandished a familiar paper: a printed form, the blank spaces filled in with handwriting. Smite had seen a hundred like it in the course of his work.

"It goes away like most legal paperwork," Smite heard himself say. "By proper attention to the rule of law. You weren't trying to browbeat the clerk to escape a summons, were you?"

The man drew himself up and turned. Even knowing beforehand who the fellow was, it still felt like a punch to the gut when Smite looked him in the eyes. Smite knew Richard Dalrymple all too well, although he wished he could forget him.

The feeling, obviously, was mutual. Dalrymple froze. His mouth opened once, and then shut. He drew himself up very carefully.

"Turner," he said. "I—uh—this was not how I intended us to meet. You see, I just arrived last night, and I've been having the most dreadful difficulties."

"I know you used to have problems with Latin," Smite said with feigned carelessness, "but this is written in English." He reached out and took the paper from Dalrymple's fingers.

"I understand perfectly what it says." Dalrymple pinched the bridge of his nose between two fingers. "I don't understand why I received it."

"Let me explain." Smite scanned the paper. "You, the said Richard Dalrymple, et cetera et cetera, did leave a team and carriage stationed in the street for two hours—two hours, Dalrymple, really?"

"I told you I've been having difficulties," the man replied. "The solicitor I used before seems to have disappeared entirely. Besides, I had no idea the team was in the street, my tiger having abandoned them to, um, *other* entertainments the instant he arrived in the city."

"You admit it was in the street."

"Yes, but I'm telling you, it wasn't my fault."

"You left your carriage blocking the way, contrary to the statute passed in the third year of the Reign of Her Majesty Queen Victoria, entitled—"

Dalrymple snatched the paper from Smite's hand. "I can read, damn it." He scrubbed his hand through his hair. "Must you always be so condescending? I didn't come here to argue with you."

"Well." Smite snorted. "That's new."

Dalrymple grimaced, but ignored that gibe. "We'll get to that in just a bit. It says I'm supposed to appear before Her Majesty's Justices of the Peace."

"Yes."

"You're one of them. You know how the public has been these last years—looking for any sign to point to, some signal of my dissolute decay."

Smite knew it quite well. Dalrymple had been born a duke's heir, but a few years ago it had come out that his father was a bigamist—and he was a bastard. He'd weathered quite a bit of criticism in the years since—so much that he'd abandoned one attempt to buy himself a title.

But habits of birth never faded. Dalrymple didn't need to hold a title to act entitled. He raised his eyebrows at Smite significantly. "Is there any way we might settle this quietly?"

Smite tapped the paper. "It says to appear before any two magistrates. I am singular."

Dalrymple rolled his eyes. "Indeed. I've always said so."

"In addition, I make it a habit to recuse myself from hearing cases where one of the parties is known to me. It is my duty to be impartial."

Dalrymple looked honestly shocked at that. "You're not going to do anything?"

Smite shrugged. "If you're particularly hard up, I can loan you forty shillings."

"I don't need more Turner money, damn it. I'm telling you it wasn't my fault."

"Of course it wasn't. Your team ought to have put itself away. What you really mean, Dalrymple, is that because your father was a duke, you don't believe you should be subject to laws like everyone else. Blame the horses. Blame the tiger. Blame *me*. It's always everyone's fault but yours, isn't it?"

Dalrymple let out a sigh. "This is not how I envisioned this conversation proceeding. I'm here in Bristol to talk with you, Turner. I owe you an apology."

Smite had waited too many years to hear those words—almost two decades, now—for them to have any meaning.

He turned away. "If you're looking to kiss and be friends, Dalrymple, I suggest you start with your horse. I'm surely not interested."

"Fuck you," Dalrymple snapped.

"No, thank you," Smite heard himself say, his tone casually polite. *But,* some wayward part of his brain added, *try your horse again. You'll probably have better luck.*

Even though he'd left off half the thought, Smite almost expected Dalrymple to strike out at him under such provocation. Instead, the other man simply rubbed his forehead.

"Very well," Dalrymple muttered. "I suppose I deserved that. Old habits die hard." He let out a bit of a laugh. "You always do manage to get under my skin. I'm sorry. For all of it. I just want to talk to you. Give me half an hour."

Smite didn't trust himself to answer. Instead, he simply said, "Go to the hearing. Being a duke's brother makes you *more* obligated to uphold the laws, not less so."

"And the rest?"

"I'll think on it."

Dalrymple left, one backward glance over his shoulder. Smite gathered up Ghost's lead. He would have left, too, but he didn't want Dalrymple to think he was following him. Whatever game his brother-in-law was playing now, Smite wanted no part of it.

"You know him?" the clerk asked.

He had thought he did, long ago. He'd once believed that he'd known Dalrymple better than anyone. Smite stared after the man, a host of unwelcome memories stirring inside him. He'd hidden them away carefully, but he still felt the sting of that betrayal.

"Yes," he finally answered. "I knew him."

"Is he a...?" The clerk trailed off, obviously at a loss to characterize what he'd seen.

"An enemy. A friend." Smite shrugged. "A brother." That last, twice over.

The clerk was watching him curiously, and he hadn't intended to be so cryptic. Mystery, after all, invited questions, and questions led to inquiry.

"We were friends at Eton," he finally said. "But our brothers did not get along, and when circumstances forced us to take sides, the friendship crumbled. Years later, my elder brother married his sister. We manage to keep to common courtesies, so long as we stay out of each other's way."

Long ago, they'd sworn to treat each other as brothers. That obviously hadn't lasted. Dalrymple had no doubt decided that it was in his best interests to try to mend their old friendship.

Alas. Smite knew him rather too well to be taken in.

He shook his head, signaling the end of the conversation, and gathered up the lead.

That was when a woman turned the corner into the records room. She stopped at the sight of him.

Not just any woman. It was Miss Darling. She was dressed as herself—no wig, no fashionable gown, just a frock of faded blue cotton and her own too-bright hair.

She stared into his eyes in shock.

"Ma'am." The clerk rose behind Smite. "Might I help you?"

She turned on her heel and disappeared.

Smite handed Ghost's lead to the puzzled clerk. "Hold him," he said. "Hold him fast. He'll track me otherwise."

"What?"

No time for explanation. Smite started after her. She was nearly to the front entrance, walking so swiftly she was almost running.

"Hold there," he called. "Ahoy, *you.*"

She broke into a run, slapping open the front doors of the Council House. And he pursued. He was yards behind her when he came down the front steps. He could hear Ghost, yelping behind him, before the doors swung shut on his dog's protest.

She'd turned down Corn Street. He followed. Running outright, she wasn't a match for him. He was taller and swifter. But she didn't realize the inevitability of her capture. She kept running, dodging down one street, and then another, scarcely staying ahead of him.

His lungs burned, but she was only two strides in front of him. He was almost close enough to grab her. A few seconds and—

And she turned right, so abruptly that he stumbled trying to follow her. He brought his hands up just in time to keep himself from careening face-first into a wall.

His hands skittered across rough granite. He swiveled to track his quarry—and he swore. She'd turned onto Queen Street. It was scarcely a street; instead, it was closer to a narrow alley. It rose at an angle so sharp that the paving stones had been set as steps, not as a smooth incline. The public house on the corner was serving, and a crowd had gathered for the midday meal. Because carts could not negotiate the steps, the merchants along either side had partially spilled into the street, hawking their wares from tables and stools. They'd half blocked the way through, and what little space remained was crowded with customers. The air was thick with the scent of boiled fish and bread and fresh-brewed beer.

She was ten feet away now, but it might as well have been ten yards. She was darting and ducking through the crowd, and here his size was a curse, not a benefit. She squeezed between two passersby, finding gaps where he would never fit. By the time she got to the top of the steps, he wouldn't be able to see her. In the warren of streets on the hill above, she'd escape.

If he yelled, "Stop, thief!" now, the crowd might catch hold of her.

But she wasn't a thief, and he wasn't a liar. "Stop, attempted perjurer!" didn't have the same ring. He stared after her. But the baleful frustration didn't last long.

It didn't matter. If his legs wouldn't do the trick, he'd have to use his mind.

BY THE TIME MIRANDA found her way back to the tilted bell tower of Temple Church, she'd managed to catch her breath. Her pulse, on the other hand, was still racing.

She stormed into the building—empty, still, as it was hours before evensong—and pushed aside the curtain that shielded the closet-cum-confessional.

She was too outraged to sit. Instead she paced—two steps forward, a turn, two steps back, over and over, back and forth, and then forth and back once more. She wasn't sure when she became aware that she wasn't alone. The fury of her exercise had masked any of the usual betraying sounds. Only the slow prickle at the back of her neck informed her that someone had arrived.

"I didn't get the list," she said. "And in case you were wondering, Lord Justice saw me. He took one look at me and said, 'You there—what do you think you're doing?' He chased me over half of Bristol. I scarcely escaped."

"And yet you did." The voice that came out of the darkness was the same as the one she'd heard yesterday—dark and raspy, and more than slightly forbidding. "Why was it that he chased you?"

Miranda remembered belatedly that she'd not recounted her entire history with Lord Justice. "He recognized me. From yesterday."

"Useful," the representative remarked, "that he should have paid so marked attention. It might be advantageous to have someone who's caught the eye of a man like Lord Justice."

"No. If he had some sort of lustful interest in me, I should think he'd have tried a more gentle tactic than shouting 'Ahoy, you!' Not unless he's particularly inept with women."

He had many faults, she was sure, but somehow over the course of their short, dismal acquaintance, she'd gleaned enough to guess that ineptitude with women was not one of them.

"So there it is," she said. "No papers. I doubt I'll be of further use to you. I don't dare go near the Council House again." And how she was to keep Robbie safe, if she had nothing to bargain with, she didn't know. She wasn't sure if she should weep at what would become of them or rejoice at her freedom.

"The Patron didn't want the list," the voice said.

Miranda stared at the curtain, her fists balling. "Pardon?"

"It would have been convenient if you had been able to wield some influence over Lord Justice as well, but the Patron has no real interest in him, either."

Miranda stared at the rosewood screen. "Then…then why have me take so large a risk? I might have been caught. Arrested." She tried to keep all hint of anger from her voice. She didn't succeed.

"The Patron wanted information," the voice said. "And now he has received it. You will be informed when you are required again."

"What? What did he want to know? I haven't told you anything!"

She waited, but only silence met her. She sat on the stool and peered as best as she could through the grate, but she could see nothing. She waited until she was ready to poke the broom through the holes in the screen, just so she could have some kind of response. *Any* kind of response.

But there was nothing. The audience was over.

What had the Patron learned? She pondered the question as she left the church and crept back down the alley. He'd learned that she could outrun Lord Justice—or at least, out-dodge him, with a little luck. But what use was that?

He'd learned that Lord Justice would give chase. She glanced to either side when she reached the main thoroughfare, waited until a brewer's dray passed by, and then zagged across the street to the alley on the other side. This one was scarcely wide enough for her, little more than a gap between buildings, but at the moment, she didn't want to talk to people. She didn't have much friendliness in her.

None of the things she came up with seemed the sort of information that would justify the smug tone the voice had used.

Perhaps it was simply that. If you were a shadowy, anonymous figure, it made sense to pretend everything had gone according to some diabolical plan. Never mind if it hadn't. Maybe it was all just for show. Miranda understood *show*.

Thomas Street was clotted with slow-moving carts. It took her a few minutes to jog down to her alley.

She might have negotiated Temple Parish by scent alone. The wealthy might choose their abodes by view—did one want a panorama that included the cathedral, or a look at Brandon Hill?

The poor chose by smell. At Miranda's home, the scent of the coal burned by the glassblowers predominated during the day. At night, the breeze off the Floating Harbour brought in the smell from the starch works a few buildings over—a scent that put her in mind of clean laundry and boiling wheat. Far better than what she'd have endured with the stockyard as neighbor.

She shut her eyes and inhaled. And just as she did so, it came to her—the information the Patron had received.

"He wanted to know if I was willing to put myself in real danger after all this time being careful." She spoke aloud. "And I let him know I was. I'm *such* a fool."

Before she could do anything more, though, an arm snaked around her from behind—a strong, solid arm. She opened her eyes and tried to turn, tried to fight, but whoever had her took hold of her wrist and held it in such a way that she could scarcely wriggle without pain shooting down her arm. She hadn't a chance to feel fear—not until she looked down and saw that the arm holding her was clothed in unwrinkled superfine wool.

Of course. Lord Justice knew where she lived.

"I'm *such* a fool," she repeated.

"Would you know," a familiar voice said in her ear, "I quite agree."

WITH HIS ARM AROUND Miss Darling and his hand on her wrist, Smite could tell how thin she was. He could feel her pulse hammering against his grip.

"I'm going to turn you to face me," he said, "as this is no way to conduct a conversation, but I'm not about to let go. I've chased you three miles already, and I'm not interested in starting over."

"I didn't offer false testimony today." She struggled against him, but he held fast. "Ask anyone you like. Check the records if you wish. The clerk can tell you."

He already knew that. He'd been there, after all. He took his arm from around her, but did not let go of her wrist.

She turned to face him. "I haven't done anything wrong."

"Then why did you run?"

"You said you'd have me arrested if you saw me again."

His eyes narrowed. "I never said any such thing."

"You did."

He stared at her, searched his memory. And then—"I said, 'If ever I see you before me again, dressed as someone else and spouting falsehoods, I will have you arrested on the spot.' I can't have you arrested merely because I catch sight of you in a public building."

She yanked her hand from his grasp. "Begging your pardon, Your Worship, but you could have me arrested for breathing. Who would gainsay you?"

"If you wouldn't *act* guilty, I wouldn't—"

"*Act* guilty?" she cried. "I'm poor. My mother was an actress; my father the manager of a traveling troupe of players. I sew some for a living, and when I've got the wherewithal, I make wigs. I don't have to do anything to be guilty. I'm guilty the instant a constable lays eyes on me and decides I appear out of place." Her hands balled into fists at her side. "It doesn't matter what I've done or what I say. Who would listen to me?"

"I would." He glared at her. "I do listen to people like you. Every day." He took a step closer, and she shrank against the wall. "If you're so innocent," he pressed, "why were you there?"

But her gaze fixed on something just beyond him. Her mouth rounded. "Look out," she called. "Behind you."

He didn't take his eyes from her. "A feeble attempt. There's nobody there. You won't be evading me so easily."

And that was when something struck him from behind. He experienced a sharp, splintering pain in his head—a savage sense of disbelief—and then, the sure knowledge that his knees were giving way beneath him.

Darkness flooded his vision before he hit the ground.

Chapter Five

SMITE WOKE TO HEAD-POUNDING confusion. A twisting burn of pain at the back of his skull warred with the dryness of his mouth. Straws poked his back; a warm, wet cloth lay on his forehead. The air around him was thick with a perplexing mixture of smells: heavy coal smoke, overboiled wheat, lye soap, and over everything, a heavy, distasteful scent that put him in mind of the worst of the street's refuse.

Gradually, memory returned. He'd chased after Miss Darling in the gloom of a cloudy afternoon, ducking through the alleys of Temple Parish. He'd put his arm around her. She'd yelled at him. And then, the last thing he could bring to mind: her eyes cutting up and to the right, widening at what she saw behind him.

So. Her surprise hadn't been a ruse.

That explained the knot of hurt at the back of his head. Someone had struck him from behind.

And now he didn't know where he was or who held him. The thought of moving made his head whirl. He wasn't precisely in a position to fight his way to safety.

"Wash your hands," a voice said, not so far away. "It's time to eat." Not just a voice; it was Miss Darling. Rather a relief; he didn't think she intended him any harm.

Smite also didn't think that a bare nod to hygiene would make any difference, not with that scent of sewage so prominent. An unfortunate consequence of living in the poorer areas. No matter how the authorities tried to stamp out the practice, people would toss the contents of their chamber pots in the streets.

"I don't want to." *That* voice was unfamiliar. Flat and monotone, it hovered just barely above baritone range.

Miss Darling sighed. "Don't be difficult."

"You're not my mother." There were clinking sounds—dishes being moved, perhaps? He tried slitting his eyes open, but his head was turned full toward a window, and the red rays of sunlight left him temporarily blind.

"What does it matter, Robbie?" Miss Darling said. "I'm trying to do what's best for you. Can't you see that?"

"Ha," came the morose response from the other occupant.

Smite couldn't see him, but he could form an image in his mind of this *Robbie*. Young and hulking, if one trusted that voice. Muscular. A sweetheart, perhaps? He found himself vaguely annoyed by the thought of Miss Darling entertaining so boorish a lover.

"I can't believe you hit him," Miss Darling said.

"Huh," came the man's brilliantly articulate reply.

Wood scraped against wood. Smite moved his head a fraction, angling it away from the window, and slitted his eyes open again. From beneath his eyelashes, he could make out silhouettes against the light.

By the voice, Smite had expected Robbie to be a large, surly fellow, barely into manhood. But Robbie was a thin reed of a child, his voice desperately outsized in a scrawny body. Miss Darling, not precisely tall herself, towered a good six inches over him.

"You don't let me do anything," Robbie rumbled. Or rather, he attempted to rumble. His voice quavered on the last syllable, hanging on the verge of breaking until he cleared his throat and deliberately dropped it a handful of notes. "Can't take work at the mills. And now Joey says I'm not to be allowed to work with him either. That's ready money you're stopping me from getting, to be had for the taking."

"We both know how Joey gets his money. He's working with the Patron. I don't want to see you hanged."

"Ha," Robbie repeated.

Smite was unsure what Robbie was, but he was fast building up a list of things that he was *not*. He was not an adult. He was not Miss Darling's lover. He was not a stunning conversationalist.

"If you go to work for the Patron, Robbie, so help me I will toss you out on your ear. It is not safe. Now promise me you won't even try."

Sullen silence. Then—"What, I'm not even allowed to try a little dipping, but you can do whatever you wish?"

"What do you mean?"

"Why else would you be so angry when I hit that cove? You were planning to sell it to him."

Miss Darling gasped, and a slap echoed. That sound made the silence that followed all the more pressing. Smite could barely make out the details of the scene—Miss Darling, holding one hand in the other, looking down at her fingers as if she couldn't believe what she'd done, and Robbie, his own hand rubbing his cheek.

"Right, then," Robbie rumbled. He shoved away from the table and opened the door. Smite felt a breath of cool air against his face. "Charge him double. After all, he brought company."

"Where are you going? You haven't eaten."

Smite turned his face toward the draft, but his head throbbed and he shut his eyes, dizzy once more.

"Going to smoke with Joey," Robbie said. "And don't give me that look—at least smoking's healthful. Everyone says so."

The door slammed, and the reverberation echoed through Smite's throbbing head. But pain or no, he could reconstruct what had happened. Robbie had come upon Smite accosting Miss Darling, and had struck him a blow from behind. Presumably, the two of them had brought him up here, rather than leaving him facedown in the streets. Whoever Robbie was, he was looking for trouble…and dragging Miss Darling into it, right alongside him.

A mess, and Smite had landed himself squarely in the middle of it. He exhaled covertly.

Miss Darling was alone now. Her hair caught the last rays of the sun through what appeared to be a garret window. It seemed to catch into a brilliant orange—like a stack of foolscap thrown on the fire, bursting into flame.

She covered her face with her hands. "Oh, God," she moaned. "What am I going to do?" Her body curled in on itself. She brought her knees up on the seat beside her and hugged them close, rocking back and forth. It was still impossible to judge her age. She looked young now. Alone and unprotected.

Not a comfortable realization, that. She hid her vulnerability so well that his discovery felt curiously intrusive. As if he'd seen her stripped to her chemise, and she hadn't yet realized he was looking. He shut his eyes, giving her the privacy she thought she had.

He didn't think she would want him to watch her weep.

Instead, she sighed and he heard the rustle of fabric, the sound of steam being released, and the dull clank of wood on metal. Stirring the pot on the hob, he guessed.

"No," she said aloud. "You can't have any. I've already got laundry to send out because of you."

Another poor choice on her part. She had to eat. It was a foolish economy to skimp on her own meals to feed her surly charge; if she wasn't eating, it was hardly surprising that she made bad decisions.

"You really don't want any," she continued. "Don't give me that look. Dogs don't eat gruel."

Dogs?

His eyes flew all the way open and he half sat up. From this new vantage point, he could see everything: the carpets on the floor, so worn he could see the wood beneath them; the whitewash flaking from the walls. What furniture there was consisted of old trunks and barrels with blankets tossed over them. Miss Darling stood at the hob, spooning something white and porridge-looking into a bowl.

And yes, a dog sat next to her, watching with a hopeful expression that Smite knew all too well. Not that he could see it at this distance. But he recognized that expectant quiver in the dog's haunches.

Of course, it was not just *a* dog; it was *his* dog. Suddenly Robbie's line about bringing company made sense. Ghost had tracked him down. Smite's eyesight blurred, and then focused on the creature's silhouette. Gray muzzle. Gray chest. Paws... Damn. No longer white and pristine.

That smell he'd dismissed as a consequence of living in the slums? It wasn't caused by poor sanitation. It was his dog. His own disgustingly filthy animal. Ghost appeared to have found every pile of horse manure between here and the Council House.

"Ghost!" Smite said sharply. "Get away from there. Stop your begging this instant." His own voice sent a pulse of pain through his head.

Ghost turned, saw Smite sitting up on his elbow, and launched across the room. His paws were positively black, his chest spattered with drying mud—yes, Smite was going to call that dark filth *mud* out of grim optimism. Ghost, of course, had no idea that he was in disgrace, and so gave him a delighted bark, beating the air enthusiastically with his tail.

Turner shook his head. "What did you do with yourself? Drag yourself through a tour of the middens of Bristol?"

Ghost made an abortive attempt to leap onto him—the better to share the smell of those middens—and Smite made a sharp gesture, sending the dog to his haunches.

"You're a disgusting animal," Smite said, "and I'll most likely rid myself of you in the morning. Now behave yourself. I've got someone I need to talk to." He pushed himself up to a sit. His head spun dizzily, but so long as he balanced himself on his arms, he could hold himself upright and look over at Miss Darling.

Ghost danced around again, spinning in circles—

"You're making me dizzy," Smite told him. "Lie down and wait."

There were a great many complaints one could make about Ghost. Palter, in fact, had made most of them. But when the animal was given a direct command, he obeyed. On that, he lowered himself to the floor and fixed his gaze on Smite.

Miss Darling was watching him, too, and unlike Ghost, she did not seem overjoyed to see him. Her eyes were red but dry.

"Are you going to arrest me, Your Worship?" she asked directly.

"No." He rubbed his head and looked up. "My head is pounding too much to consider it."

She walked to him. As she came closer, Ghost stood up and crossed to investigate her, gray head lifted, sniffing gently. She didn't seem to notice the dog; instead, she sat on the straw tick beside him.

"You shouldn't be sitting up, you know. You've had a head injury, and they can be quite perilous." She was inches from him.

"I'm perfectly well," he said.

She frowned dubiously at that. "You can never be sure. I knew someone who hit his head and then dropped dead the next day."

She reached to touch his cheek, and he grabbed her hand.

"I said, I'm perfectly well."

But he wasn't. A flutter of…of *something* passed through him. Something barely recognizable. His hand fit around hers. She was warm, and he could feel calluses on her fingertips. She wasn't a lady, no matter how exalted her accent at the moment; he could feel the evidence against his palm. Her rough hands should have reminded him of the gulf between them.

There were too many differences: he was wealthy; she was not. She'd appeared in his courtroom; he might have to see her again.

But when he took hold of her hand, he was most aware of the other sharp distinction between them. He was a man. And she was, undoubtedly, a woman.

She looked down at him, at his grip on her, and slowly, he let her fingers loose.

She pulled away. "Well. My apologies for interfering."

His hand still tingled where he'd touched her; he made a fist of it. "If I'm going to drop dead, I'll do so regardless of whether you prod at me."

"Yes, but if you drop dead *here,* I'll be stuck disposing of your body." She narrowed her eyes at him. "I have enough to worry about."

It hurt to smile, so much so that he winced when he tried. "Well, then. I'll do my best to drag my sorry carcass away if I feel the sudden urge to keel over." He ran his hand over his face. "Why did you go to the records room?"

"Looking for records," she muttered evasively.

"What sort of records?"

She paused and looked up to her right. "I have a friend," she said slowly. "George Patten. He was put away two months ago, and due to be released yesterday, yet he's disappeared entirely. He wasn't let go. He's not in gaol. I don't know where he is." There was a twitch in her cheek.

"Those records would be kept at the gaol," Smite said. "You don't imagine that the records of daily dealings at the gaol would find their way to the Council House a mere day after the events in question. Tell me the truth, Miss Darling."

She raised her eyes and let out a long exhale. "Someone asked me to get a list of all the men employed by the police force," she said quickly.

Likely, that was the truth.

"I don't think you should have anything to do with *someone,*" he said.

"Of course I shouldn't." She stood up and paced away. "Especially as he didn't even want the list. I don't like having games played with my safety. But—"

"But you're in over your head, and you've someone else to watch over. It's not easy surviving by yourself."

"I—yes." She looked at him, her eyes crinkled in puzzlement. "I wouldn't have imagined you would understand. It is, after all, just one of those excuses that you decried the last time we spoke."

Smite had his own experience of Bristol life, decades old now. But he simply shook his head. "It's always difficult when responsibilities tug you in different directions."

"Difficult." She let out a sigh. "I feel like Antigone, operating under two incompatible directives."

Smite froze. "Antigone." He glanced up at her. "How do you know Antigone?"

She waved a hand. "I was raised by actors. You shouldn't be shocked that I have some passing familiarity with plays."

"Passing familiarity, yes, but... *Antigone* has not yet been translated from the Greek."

"One of the members of our troupe was translating it." She delivered this airily, with no sense of how remarkable that might have been.

There were only a handful of scholars who could have even attempted such a thing. Men who translated ancient Greek were fellows at Oxford. They didn't traipse about the countryside putting on performances for rural audiences.

It wasn't often that Smite was rendered stupid. "But... You were truly raised by actors?" It didn't come out as quite a question. He'd already noticed that over the course of their conversation, her accent had drifted toward the learned tones of an Oxonian. Her vocabulary was far beyond what he would have expected from a poor seamstress.

"It's not so hard to understand." She peered at him. "Are you sure you're well?" Before he realized what she was doing, she reached out and set her hand against his forehead. A brief flicker of her fingers against his temple—nothing more—and he was transported to a darker place. He was spitting out cold water, his hands rigid and aching from holding fast to wood. The light above him danced and dazzled—

"Ouch!"

Her cry brought him back to the present. He was warm and dry, no matter how quickly his heart raced. He wasn't *there*. He was in a garret room, sitting next to Miss Darling. She'd touched his face, and he'd grabbed her hand. He hadn't squeezed too hard, thank God. She was breathing quickly and looking at him as if he had perhaps passed over into lunacy.

He let go. "Don't fuss over me."

She flexed her hand gingerly.

"Will you be back, then, looking for records?"

She shook her head surely—but stopped halfway, her eyes focusing elsewhere. "Actually," she said, "I *will* need to find out what happened with George Patten. The gaol—how would one go about getting the records there?"

"One needs to be a man of some standing in the community," Smite said dryly. "Or one has the portcullis shut in one's face."

Instead of looking disheartened, Miss Darling simply nodded. As if she were contemplating—

Smite narrowed his eyes. "Thinking that you could pretend to be yet another person? No. I don't think so. Consider the improvidence of committing fraud while you are inside a gaol."

"Of course," she said, all too obediently. "You're quite right."

He'd bet Ghost a romp through a manure pile, that she was making plans at this very moment. But what was to be done? He couldn't watch the gaol himself. He *could* send warning.

But there was another option.

An odd impulse, nothing more. It had absolutely nothing to do with that wretched awareness of her that kept creeping out at the most inopportune moments—at least, he hoped it didn't. If he was going to exert himself on her behalf, he might as well choose the option that *didn't* end with her in prison. More efficient for everyone involved.

That was it. Efficiency. Nothing else.

"I have an idea," he heard himself say. "I'll take you there myself."

AFTER LORD JUSTICE AND his dog took their leave, Miranda negotiated the rickety steps of the narrow staircase down a level, until she heard the faint sound of boys talking. Robbie's deep rumble contrasted with Joey's higher treble.

She paused on the third-floor landing and shivered. The window was half open, and cold night air poured in. Robbie and his friend were on the other side. They'd leapt the foot-wide gap between upper window and gables, and she could see them perched on the flat roof of the neighboring building. They leaned against one of the chimney flues for warmth.

Joey passed Robbie a bottle, and Robbie lifted it to his lips. Moonlight glinted on amber glass, and Miranda's heart contracted.

Gin. At least Robbie was fake-swallowing, just as she'd told him. If you only took a little in your mouth…

She turned and flattened herself against the wall. Half of her wanted to storm out onto the roof, threatening bloody murder.

But she'd tried screaming. She'd tried punishments. She'd tried gentle affection and love. She'd tried everything in turn, until she'd come to the end of her wits. It all came down to the same thing: she was scarcely eight years older than he was. She simply wasn't adequate to the task of raising a twelve-year-old boy.

All she could do was watch him fall from her grasp.

Her eyes stung, and she wrapped her arms about herself to ward off the cold.

Miranda tried to be optimistic. Her future was spread out before her. She had good friends. When her wigs sold, she had more funds than most solitary women her age. She'd made do so far.

But she felt like a juggler tossing torches into the air. The circus-master kept throwing more in. Sooner or later, one would fall, and the life she'd built would burn to cinders.

No wonder Robbie never minded her. What did he have to look forward to? A life of hard labor where, honest or not, he could still end up in gaol. Like George. Her fingers dug into her arm, stinging.

Miranda gave her head a short shake. No. Down that road lay surrender and despair. She'd seen it before, and she wasn't going to succumb. Defeat might be inevitable, but she hadn't dropped her torches yet, and she wasn't going to stop trying.

Miranda straightened her spine, turned to the window, and wrestled it all the way open.

Out on the rooftop, Robbie jumped guiltily at the horrid creak it made. He shoved the bottle he was holding behind his back.

But all he said was, "What?" in a surly growl.

"I'm going dancing down at Pete's," Miranda called. "Want to come?"

Light. Heat. A fast country reel, and enough exertion that she could push aside the impossibility of her life.

"Dancing?" Robbie rumbled.

She could hear the distant sound of the fiddle a few streets over. The music reached out to her across the cold night. It was the sound of a few hours of forgetfulness—cheaper than gin and twice as warming.

"I'm getting my cloak. I'll be leaving in a few minutes." She paused, then offered, "Come along. You'll have fun." It wasn't an olive branch she held out; more like a twig stolen from some similar tree.

Robbie stood. "I guess." He shoved something at Joey—the bottle, Miranda supposed—and crossed the roof to the window. He didn't even look down at the gap between the buildings before he jumped inside.

"Do you want something to eat before we go?"

He smelled of gin, but he wasn't unsteady on his legs. She really should scold him. Or maybe she should apologize. But as she watched Robbie climb the stairs ahead of her, what she breathed instead was a whispered promise.

"I'm going to keep juggling," she said.

"Huh?" Robbie asked ahead of her.

She shook her head. "Nothing. It's nothing."

Chapter Six

THIS TIME, THE WATER in Smite's dreams was boiling hot and there was nothing to hold—no ladder, no stairs: nothing but rough walls that tore at his fingers. When he opened his mouth to scream, water bubbled in, stifling his voice to nothingness. He clawed for the surface, but it had ceased to exist. There was nothing but liquid surrounding him, nothing but this hot, filthy effluent stretching in all directions. No matter how he fought, there was no end to it.

It filled his lungs, caustic as lye soap, and he swallowed it, choking, burning—

Smite woke, jerking upright, swallowing a shout on his lips. He could hear it ringing around him, and he felt that old sense of embarrassment. Not that it mattered; there was nobody else about. What servants he employed lived outside his home; he'd arranged matters that way for this very reason. He gulped breath and urged his heart to cease racing.

There was a rustle in the dark, and then, against the palm of his hand, a cold nose.

So maybe there was someone around.

"Come on up." Smite's throat seemed sore. He *had* been shouting, then.

The bed swayed as Ghost jumped on it. His fur was still slightly damp; Smite had washed him on his return home last night. He gathered the animal to him.

Long, soft fur met his fingers. He breathed in and willed his heart to slow. He commanded the nauseating cramp in his stomach to relax. After a few minutes, his body obeyed.

Just the usual evening specter, then, although the heat of the water was an interesting twist. There had been no smell. There were never smells in his dreams.

When he was younger, his dreams had been a cause for consternation. He'd tried everything to rid himself of them. Hot milk. Exercise. Women. Laudanum.

Some afflictions, he'd concluded, weren't worth fighting. Not at that cost. He'd accepted the nightmares as a fact of his existence, no more debilitating than, say, a scar that restricted movement. Scars were manly. He'd won this one fair and square.

Of course, as afflictions went, this one was rather more like the gout than a scar. Made worse by alcohol; brought on by rain. No point in deluding himself.

He smiled into Ghost's fur and felt the tension slowly ease from him.

He'd long since stopped seeing the nightmares as a cause for complaint. They were more like a call to arms. They were a reminder of what had transpired. Of what it *meant* for him to do his job, to listen carefully to those who came before him. Of what might happen if he turned a blind eye.

When he woke on odd nights, he lulled himself back to sleep by reciting names as another man might count sheep. *Mrs. Wexforth. Jack Bloomsmith. Davy Duglett.* On down a parade of people he had seen during his days as magistrate. Ghost leaned against him as their faces danced through his memory.

His brother had obtained Ghost from a shepherd back in Shepton Mallet. Ghost had been the progeny of one of the most renowned sheepdogs in all of Somerset and some unknown stray. When they'd tested his instinct for herding as a small puppy, the little dog had shown an unsavory interest in the sheep's leavings and no interest at all in the sheep. And so he'd been passed on to Smite—a tiny bundle of gray-and-white fur. Eight weeks old, and already marked a failure.

In tonight's darkness, Ghost leaned against him.

He came to the end of his list.

When they needed someone, I was there. I listened. I acted. What happened to me won't happen to them. Not while I can prevent it.

Then there was Miss Darling.

God, what a conundrum she posed. Any pretense of impartiality had vanished when he'd seen her with Robbie. The boy reminded him all too much of what it had been like, taking charge of Mark, when they'd roamed Bristol's streets. He wasn't exactly thinking of her with the requisite disinterest. He knew all too well what it was like to be saddled with a charge, with no way to make good.

And as for Miss Darling herself... Smite had long ago resigned himself to the fact that he felt more alone around others than he did by himself. Any woman with a hint of education could never comprehend what Smite had been through; anyone who could fathom his childhood could never understand what he'd made of himself. It didn't matter how he yearned for companionship; there was none to be had. He'd resigned himself to short, lonely encounters.

But Miss Darling... damn. Apparently all it took was a combined knowledge of Sophocles and the streets. He was *susceptible* to her. If he wasn't careful, he might end up nursing a full-blown interest. Not a good idea. He had too much else to do.

In the dark of night, it was impossible to shove aside his memory of the canny flash of her smile, the turn of her profile. In some faraway world, their journey tomorrow might end, improbably, in some secluded park instead of at the gaol. She might call him Turner instead of Lord Justice. She might open up when he touched her...

Foolish fantasies, those. His cock didn't think so; it had grown hard and erect in anticipation. He gave it a thump in protest and leaned back against the pillow. Beside him, Ghost curled up. The animal let out a doggy sigh.

"Well," he said to Ghost. He could imagine the animal's ears flicking back toward him in the darkness, turning ever so slightly to catch his words. "I suppose we'll have to find something else for you to do tomorrow. I have a woman to see."

He wished he didn't sound so eager.

A SHADOW FELL ACROSS Smite's desk.

He was scheduled to meet Miss Darling in a few hours, and so he had rather more work than usual to cram into his foreshortened working hours. The shadow was an annoyance. He moved the report he was reading over a few inches to fall into the sunlight.

The shadow moved. Smite looked up, and his annoyance froze into something harder.

"Look," Richard Dalrymple said. "I know this is a bit much to ask. But do you suppose we can start over?"

"Start what over?" The lack of sleep during the previous evening made him feel as if a gritty veil had been cast over his eyes. It left him rather more cross than usual.

"Um." Dalrymple shifted uncomfortably. "Everything?" The man was dressed perfectly, his trousers creased with edges so sharp that they could have cut someone. He'd tied his cravat in some complicated knot. He could strangle on his neckcloth, for all Smite cared. Still, he hunched uneasily, not meeting Smite's eyes. "Everything since that first year and a half at Eton," he added.

"You want me to simply discard the last nineteen and a half years."

Dalrymple hunched further. "Yes," he said. "That would be lovely."

"And just be friends again, as if nothing had transpired."

"Please?"

Smite opened a drawer in his desk and slid his papers inside. "Have you any notion—" But that question answered itself as easily. "No. You haven't an inkling. One doesn't simply pick up a friendship again after all that you've done."

Dalrymple licked his lips uneasily. "I can understand that. But in the name of what we once had, and what we have now, could you not at least listen to me? For God's sake, the last time we were both at Parford Manor, it was a disaster. For the sake of our families, this can't continue."

"What am I supposed to say? 'Let's shake hands, old chap, and let bygones be bygones'?"

Dalrymple's shoulders sagged ever so slightly. "I'm relieved to hear you agree. Can we?"

Smite snorted, wishing he could stuff Dalrymple in the drawer alongside his papers. If only he could put him off, to be examined at some other time. Instead, he pushed the drawer closed. "I didn't agree. And there's a problem with what you propose. I can't forget."

Dalrymple flinched.

"What does an apology mean?" Smite pushed back his chair and stood. "I look at you and I remember the day you told the headmaster at Eton that I'd cheated on my examination."

A wince in response. "I'm sorry."

"You had my quarters searched when we were at Oxford, claiming that I had stolen from you. Am I supposed to forget that, too?"

Dalrymple shut his eyes. "I know. I'm sorry."

"And then there was that rumor you started a handful of years ago."

Dalrymple bit his lip.

"Ah." Smite set his hands on the desk, leaning forward. "Even you can't forget that one."

"I am," Dalrymple said, "most especially sorry for that. More than you can realize. But..."

"Here it comes. You haven't forgotten any of this at all." Smite leaned back against the wall. "Go on, Dalrymple. Tell me how you justified your lies."

The other man shook his head.

Smite smiled grimly. "Then let me advocate on your behalf. You *had* to do all those things—accuse me of cheating, lying, stealing, and buggery—because you feared that I would tell your secrets. You thought I would tell the world that you were a bastard. You feared that I would tell everyone that you—"

Dalrymple stepped forward, hands outstretched.

Smite snorted. "Ah, yes. It was that last one, wasn't it? You thought I would tell the truth, and so you spread lies about me to discredit my character. Before I'd even done anything wrong."

"Turner," Dalrymple said. There was a pleading note in his voice.

Smite ignored it. "There's a difference between the two of us. I promised you I wouldn't tell. And unlike you, I remember my promises. So, no, Dalrymple. I don't think I'm about to forget the last couple of decades. I'm not so foolish as to turn my back on you once more."

Dalrymple's features were frozen. He stared ahead, his arms straightening into ramrods at his side.

"God," he said. "That's it, then. No mercy. No forgiveness. There's nothing I can do to make matters right between us."

Smite shook his head.

"Not even..." He blinked, licked his lips. "Not even for our family? For Margaret and Ash?"

"I care for Margaret," Smite said carefully. "I don't want her unhappy. But given what I know of you, it seems unlikely that

you'll bring her happiness. All you have ever done, so far as
Margaret is concerned, is put yourself first."

Years ago, Dalrymple would have swelled up in indignation at
that accusation. It had always been too easy to bait him into
displaying his temper. Instead, he bit his lip and looked away, and
some small, neglected part of Smite's sympathies tugged in
response. Once, this man had been his friend.

He shoved the thought away.

"Yes," Dalrymple finally said. "You're right. You're completely
right. But maybe I want to do better."

People always claimed to want such things when they faced the
harsh light of judgment. With the prospect of punishment looming
over their heads, they would promise anything.

Sometimes people changed. Mostly, though, they forgot their
fine resolutions within a week. Smite didn't give Dalrymple that
long.

"You've always wanted to do better," Smite said. "I know you
too well to believe in it."

Dalrymple simply looked at him. "You will," he finally said.
"You will."

"I THINK," MIRANDA SAID, "I am about to do something
foolish this afternoon."

It was just past noon, and Blasseur's Trade Goods & More was
bustling with customers. Old Blazer was holding court in the front
of the shop, entertaining a crowd of people while measuring out
fabric. Jeremy, as usual, was ensconced at the table in the back and
occupied with the mending. The shop was so crowded they might
as well have been alone. Nobody paid them the least attention.

Miranda twirled a bit of ribbon about her finger and let it go,
before looking up. "Tell me I mustn't do it."

Jeremy sat on a stool, his lips clenched in concentration as he
carefully matched two broken ends of lace together. "Don't do it,"
he said absently, reaching for his needle.

"Are you listening? It might prove dangerous. Very dangerous."

"Mmm." He started in on careful stitches, lashing the lace
together. "Stop being so dramatic and spit out what it is."

Miranda expelled a breath and looked away.

"Ah." Jeremy set another precise stitch in the lace, and still
didn't glance at her. "I see. You *want* to do it. You just came here
to get my permission. So what is it?"

"I'm going—" She cut herself off, remembering what the journey was really about. Jeremy was fragile enough on the question of George; she didn't want to get his hopes up, only to have to dash them. "I'm going somewhere with a man," she tried instead. "I'm not sure why he asked me. Maybe he was just being nice." She frowned. *Nice* didn't seem to be part of Lord Justice's vocabulary.

"Maybe he wants to get you alone and have his wicked way with you." Jeremy raised an eyebrow at her.

Actually, she'd been thinking that maybe he'd arranged to have her come by the Council House and accompany him to the gaol to save him the trouble of marching her there himself. That possibility lent a certain piquancy to the afternoon's activity.

"Maybe," Jeremy surmised, his smile stretching to the sly, "you *want* him to have his wicked way."

She leaned her head back to contemplate the ceiling. "He's not very wicked."

"And you're still interested?" He pulled back in surprise.

So maybe she did have a preference for wicked men. She tried not to act on it anymore—not if she thought it would endanger her. Lord Justice hardly fit her usual mold. And she was far too canny to be *interested* in Lord Justice. But even if her mind knew that, it had not quite convinced her body. A little frisson went through her, just thinking of meeting him.

"Is this man you're meeting affiliated with the Patron?" Jeremy asked calmly.

Miranda choked. "What do you know of the Patron?"

"Shh!" Jeremy cast a baleful glance at her. "You don't have any idea who's listening."

"Don't be ridiculous." She glanced behind her. "Old Blazer is showing off the tweed. Nobody's listening to us."

And indeed, his grandfather had the group quite enraptured. She could only see the back of him, stooped with age, hair a tumbling mass down his shoulders. But his hands gestured wildly, and she could hear the sonorous cadences of his voice.

"Better safe than sorry," Jeremy whispered. "I dislike the notion of finding out that you've had your throat slit, or that you've been sent to the gallows. Tell me this has nothing to do with the Patron."

"The only reason I'm safe on the streets is because of the Patron," Miranda whispered back.

Jeremy dropped his eyes. "Don't you believe that. Don't you *ever* believe that. George thought he was safe, too."

Miranda swallowed and looked away. "I'm sure that George is…safe. Somewhere. He'll be back soon. You know it must be the case." She set her hand atop his.

Jeremy simply looked at her fingers. "I have no faith in any such thing." He pulled away from her and picked up his scissors, turning to the next gown in need of mending with a vengeance.

"If it sets your mind at ease, this man has nothing to do with the Patron," Miranda said. "In fact, he is about as exactly opposite the Patron as you can get. I'm afraid I might make a fool of myself over him. I'm not even sure he would notice if I did."

"Oh, Miranda!" The voice came from her left. Miranda jumped, and then let out a sigh of relief as Mrs. Blasseur pushed through the curtain at the very back. Jeremy's mother was carrying a basket filled with laundry; she set it down on the counter with a resounding thump, and paused to catch her breath. Her hair was tied up in a knot, but strands escaped from it and curled about her cheeks.

Once, those cheeks had been pleasantly plump. But recent illness had stripped Mrs. Blasseur of all excess flesh. Her clothing hung loosely on her too-thin frame. She was pale; her skin had a sickly, bluish cast to it. But her eyes were quick, darting about intelligently, and her smile was warm and welcoming.

"What's this about making a fool of yourself over a man?"

"Um." Miranda pressed her lips together.

"I do wish you'd choose Jeremy," Mrs. Blasseur continued brazenly. "He doesn't talk of any other girls but you."

The tips of Jeremy's ears turned bright red. "Mama."

"No, truly!" Mrs. Blasseur ignored her son. "I want to see him settled before I—before, well. I don't have *time* to be polite any longer."

Jeremy put his head in his hands. It didn't hide the mortified scarlet of his cheeks.

"I think he's in love with you," Mrs. Blasseur continued sincerely. "He's a good boy. He'd do anything for you."

Jeremy peered at her through his fingers and grimaced in silent apology. He was most definitely not in love with Miranda; in fact,

Jeremy was very much in love with someone else, and he'd thank her not to mention the matter to his mother, of all people.

"Mama," Jeremy muttered, "I know you want everything to be settled before…well, soon at any rate. But Miranda has nothing to do with this. I'm not in love with her."

"Am I meddling too much? I'm meddling too much. But, Jeremy…"

It was impossible to dislike the woman, no matter how interfering she seemed. She'd been afflicted by consumption for over a year. She was so thin now; her breath had grown labored.

A wealthy family might have taken her to the seaside, in hopes that gentler weather would allow her to recuperate. But Mrs. Blasseur stayed in the depths of Bristol, breathing coal-smoke all day. She kept to her daily tasks, doing laundry and tending the shop when she should have been in bed. Only her strength of will kept her going.

By the way she doubled over with the next cough, even her will couldn't overcome her body.

"I'm not in love with Miranda," Jeremy repeated. "Besides, she's going to meet a man just now. I'm happy for her. Really."

"Oh." Mrs. Blasseur's face fell. Then she turned to Miranda and impulsively took her hand. "But you'd give him up, wouldn't you? Whoever you're seeing. I'm sorry. I haven't time to be tactful any longer. You would make a lovely daughter, Miranda." Mrs. Blasseur sighed. "Wishful thinking, I suppose. I'm that hard up for help with the laundry."

Miranda couldn't help but smile. "My thanks, Mrs. Blasseur. But you persist in this notion that I'm a nice girl, and we all know I was raised by actors."

The older woman pulled a towel from the basket and snapped it straight before folding it. "Well, that hardly signifies," she said. "You'd fit right in. After all, Jeremy was raised by monkeys."

"Mama!"

"At least I assume that to be the case." She folded the fabric in her hands, and then reached into the basket once more. "He surely didn't acquire his manners from me."

"He's a nice boy."

"I suppose." His mother frowned. "Still, there was that one time, when he got snails and—"

"Mother, *please.*" Jeremy waved a hand. "I was three."

"Proper disclosure, dear. I wouldn't want a daughter-in-law claiming I brought her in under false pretenses. She'd find out the truth soon enough."

As she spoke, she doubled over and coughed once more. Miranda met Jeremy's eyes over her bent form. He looked absolutely stricken. He reached one hand out to her.

But Mrs. Blasseur straightened before he touched her. She tucked away the handkerchief she'd whisked out. And before Miranda could venture to ask if she needed assistance, she delivered a sunny smile. "I suppose there's this to say for Jeremy: he'll never do anything wrong."

"No," Jeremy said, setting his jaw. "I won't."

"And *that,*" Mrs. Blasseur said, thumping him on the collar, "is why Miranda is meeting another man. You're neat and tidy and orderly, and you never cause me any problems. But...you're neat and tidy and orderly, and you never cause anyone problems. Women want men with problems. We need something to fix."

There was not the least chance that Jeremy would fall in love with her, nor she with him. He met her eyes in quiet apology. Miranda shook her head. No need for him to be sorry. It was heartbreaking to watch Mrs. Blasseur fade away. All that exuberant wit and energy and charm seemed to compress in these final weeks. For all her physical weakness, she radiated frustration. She was leaving her life incomplete, too many things undone.

"Leave off Miranda," Jeremy said, his voice weary. "Or I'll..."

"You'll what?" Mrs. Blasseur's fingers slid across the counter. She took the lace that Jeremy had just mended from his hands, scanning it with a practiced eye. Mrs. Blasseur always wanted to fix everything. She found nothing to quibble about, though, and laid it aside.

"I haven't got forever," Mrs. Blasseur said. "You'd best act quickly. You know what will happen if I have to take matters into my own hands."

Jeremy set his jaw.

Miranda couldn't imagine how intensely frustrating it would be for Mrs. Blasseur, to have all of her thwarted ambition run aground on something as impossible as her own mortality.

But Jeremy simply shook his head. "It won't be happening," he said. "Not even to please you. And besides, I think Miranda has an appointment with a man." He gave her a shrug.

It was not just apology she saw in his eyes. Sorrow, resignation, bitterness, and more than a little anger. His father had died years before; his mother had practically raised him. Jeremy had watched her die for close to a year. No wonder he was bitter.

She reached out to him, but he jerked away. "You'd best be off, Miranda, unless you plan to be late."

Chapter Seven

THE CLOCK STRUCK TWO as Miranda arrived at the Council House. Overhead, clouds obscured the sun. Still, even the midday gloom could not hide the empty steps of the building. Magistrate Turner wasn't here.

She had imagined he would be punctual. He seemed the sort to be precise about—well, everything.

She waited for a minute, until she heard a faint mewing sound emanating from a nearby alleyway. Curious, she stepped back and peered around the corner.

Ah. *Here* was the reason Magistrate Turner wasn't standing on the stairs.

He had squeezed in that small gap between the buildings. His face was set in grim concentration, as if he were listening to a prisoner's speech. But he was sitting in judgment over a pair of cats—one small and orange, the other large and white.

One meowed again, and he broke off a piece from what appeared to be a meat pie, and tossed it to them.

He was dressed in sand-colored wool. Up until now, she'd only seen him in dark colors—black robes, navy jackets. The light color of his coat made his hair seem all the blacker. It brought out a warmth in his skin that she'd not seen before.

And when he looked up from the cats and met her gaze, she realized for the first time how intensely blue his eyes were— emphasis on *intense*. He seemed to see straight through her, right through her threadbare cloak and her nondescript dress, through her flesh, straight into her heart. That unruly organ thumped heavily in her chest.

She raised her hand to give him an awkward wave. Her pulse beat, and an unexpected thrill ran through her at the sight of him.

The sensation spilled through her body in little shocks, like a harpist strumming out an arpeggio against her ribs.

Oh, drat. She *was* attracted to him.

"Magistrate Turner," she said.

His eyes narrowed. "Turner," he corrected her.

"That's what I said, isn't it?"

"You called me Magistrate." His nostrils flared. "Magistrates decide cases and issue warrants for arrests. They don't go on walks with intriguing women, no matter what the destination might be. I must make it clear that I'm helping you in my private capacity. If you call me Magistrate Turner again, I'll turn around and walk away."

He made it sound so grim, the prospect of taking a walk with her. It took her a moment to hear that word— *intriguing.* But he wasn't smiling at her. That couldn't be an attempt at flirtation, could it?

Miranda shook her head slowly. "Good heavens. That's quite an act you put on."

He drew himself up haughtily. "I beg your pardon."

"An act," Miranda repeated. "Stand as tall as you like, and frown at me all you wish. I saw you just now. You were feeding cats."

"So I was. And do you make something of that?"

"You," Miranda said daringly, "have a kind heart."

He turned away from her, the tails of his greatcoat swirling about him. "Don't enlarge too much upon the matter. The cats were hungry. I had food. This seemed to be a problem with a ready solution. It's not kindness to solve problems; it's efficiency."

"I stand corrected. You have an efficient heart."

He turned to look at her, and the corner of his mouth quirked up. That half-smile sent another prickle down her spine.

"Also," he said, "I happen to like cats. They're aloof creatures that want nothing from me except a little food. Once they've had that, they walk away." He raised his chin. "I have a great deal of respect for creatures that walk away from me."

"Are you trying to intimidate me?" Miranda set one hand on her hip.

He simply gave her a level look.

"It won't work. I seek out frightening stories, just to send a shiver up my spine. I climb to the top of bell towers, just so I can look down at the ground. I *like* being scared. So please, give me that repressive look. Just once more."

She'd said it to tease him. But her stomach roiled as she spoke. It was true, all too true. He scared her with his curt speeches. He wielded extraordinary power, and he was willing to use it. He frightened her, and she liked it.

That hint of a smile flickered across his face once more. But all he said in response was, "I see. Shall we be off? It's a bit of a walk, and it looks like rain."

"You have an umbrella, Lord Justice."

He gave a deep sigh. "Don't call me that, either. Just a plain 'Turner' will do."

She trotted after him. "It's intended as a compliment. You're a stalwart defender of justice, and so forth."

"I suppose it started that way. When it was just the common people calling me that, I didn't mind. But my brother magistrates took up the cry as well." He stopped, took her elbow, and turned around, pointing back down the street. They'd scarcely gone twenty feet.

Miranda shook her head in confusion.

He touched her chin, tilted her head up—but he wasn't looking at her. Instead, he directed her attention to the roof of the Council House, still visible down the street. "Do you see that figure up there?"

It was hard to concentrate with his glove warm against her jaw. Still, she peered upward. There was a statue of a seated woman in flowing robes atop the Council House roof.

"That's Lady Justice," he explained.

"Isn't Justice supposed to be blindfolded?"

"No. In Bristol, Justice stares you straight in the face." He spoke matter-of-factly.

"Where are her scales? Has she misplaced them?"

"It would explain a great deal about my colleagues," he said dryly. "But never mind that. One of my fellow magistrates said that the common people call me by that unfortunate appellation because I was so dedicated to my work that I might as well be married to Lady Justice—hence the name. The jest has been played out all too often. Don't call me Lord Justice." He started off down the street once more.

Miranda followed. "That doesn't sound so awful as jokes go."

"I paraphrased only. He didn't imply actual *marriage.*"

"So circumspect, Mr. Turner." Miranda spread her hands. "You forget: I have no sensibilities to offend. I was raised by actors."

"Very well, then. He said I must be tumbling Lady Justice—'It would account for the hours, and would explain why you're cold as stone.' I can't hear the name now without calling to mind that ribald jest."

He cast a glance at her. Just a simple glance, but it reminded Miranda of a time she'd slipped in winter and slammed her palms on the ice to break her fall. Maybe he *was* cold, but sometimes ice burned.

He was walking at a good clip. His route dipped behind buildings, around squares, avoiding the crowds nearer the water's edge.

"You're not cold," Miranda offered. "You're...controlled. Besides, if you're a duke's brother, why aren't you Lord—um— Lord..." She trailed off. She didn't know his Christian name. There was a book somewhere that listed it, doubtless. She'd never seen it.

Little droplets of rain began misting down. Beside her, he swept up his umbrella and pushed it open.

"You mean, why am I not called Lord Andrew or Lord John, like a proper duke's son?"

She nodded.

"Simple. I'm not named John." He spared her another glance. "You'd better walk closer. No point in your getting wet."

She stepped toward him.

"No, all the way," he said. "If you keep your distance, I'm liable to poke your eye out with the ribs."

She stepped under his umbrella. No doubt it was her imagination, but it was warmer close to him. He smelled like clean, uncomplicated soap—just soap, no fussy perfumes or scents. The rain intensified, drumming into the fabric above.

"'It's efficient to feed the cats,'" she said, mimicking his gruff tone. "'If you don't share my umbrella, I might accidentally blind you.' I believe you're speaking English, Turner, but I'm not sure you're doing a good job of it. It makes a girl wonder what you meant by, 'Here, let me take you to gaol.'"

"I always mean precisely what I say, even if I don't say precisely what I mean."

She was trying to work that one out, when he continued.

"As for the other, I'm not a duke's son, which is the normal method of acquiring a courtesy title. My brother is a duke, but he took the title from a distant relation. I am just Mr. Turner."

They'd reached the Prince Street Bridge. He stopped at the edge of the water and rubbed his cheek.

From here, they could see the city's docks spread out before them. The harbor was full these days. A slim three-masted ship had been hoisted in the dry docks, and a crew scraped barnacles from her hull.

Beside her, Lord Justice— *Turner*—took a deep breath, and stared ahead.

"Are you much interested in ships?" she asked.

"Your pardon?"

"I ask only because you've stopped to look. I took Robbie to the launch of the *Great Britain* last summer." She frowned. "It's still in dock. I don't know why. It's been months."

He turned to where she was looking. "It won't fit out the locks." He started across the bridge, his pace even faster.

She jogged along beside him. "What do you mean?"

"It's the largest steamship ever built from iron. While she was being built, Bristol made some alterations to the locks that regulate the level of the Floating Harbour. Now the locks are too small—or the ship is too big—and she's trapped until the company can convince the harbormaster to widen the locks. It's an incredible waste."

They reached the other side of the river.

"Do you know much about ships, then? It's the only thing Robbie will talk about. I've tried to speak with him about them, but mostly, when I make an attempt, he rolls his eyes and says, 'That's not a *ship* you're pointing to; it's a boat.'"

"I know what is happening hereabouts, generally, and that means I occasionally know a tidbit about ships. I have a fair knowledge of watercraft." He cast her another glance. "I'm unlikely to board one, if that's what you're asking, and so all my understanding is theoretical."

"Oh."

They walked on in silence for a while, past dying weeds dripping rainwater along the footpath.

"So," Miranda finally said, "if you were to have a courtesy title, what would it be? Lord Andrew? Lord Robert?"

"No."

The street they were on was terribly muddy. The rain had only intensified, coming down in heavy sheets, but she was safe under his umbrella. He glanced sidelong at her. His eyes were blue— brighter than the stone-gray of the sky. It was only a few moments that he contemplated her, but still, she dropped her eyes in confusion. It didn't help; her gaze fixed on his hands, on long fingers encased in dark gloves. One of those fingers reached out and she held as still as she could, waiting…

But he only took her elbow and conducted her to the other side of the road.

"I don't like my Christian name," he said as they crossed to the other side. "I thank my lucky stars that I don't have to contend with it on a regular basis."

"It can't be that awful."

The path they were on dipped closer to the Avon. The water rushed through the channel, swirling in greenish-white rapids.

"Yes, it can." He took her elbow and guided her to the inside of the path. The gesture seemed almost sweet—as if she were a lady, and he a gentleman, protecting her from being splashed by puddles. He didn't even seem to have noticed that he'd done it.

"I knew a man named Defatigus once," she supplied. "He took the stage name of Robert Johns. He wasn't a pleasant fellow. Your name can't be much worse. I doubt you have any reason to mope about it."

He sighed. "You're indefatigable, did you know that? It's Smite."

"Smite? Your father named you Smite?"

"No. My mother named me. Also, she didn't name me 'Smite.' That's a short version of my real name, which is, 'The Lord said in his heart, I will not again curse the ground any more for man's sake; for the imagination of man's heart is evil from his youth; neither will I again smite any more every living thing, as I have done.'"

She stared at him.

"It's a verse from the Bible. Genesis. After Noah's flood, when God is promising that he'll never again punish all humankind by drowning them." He huffed, and waved a hand at her. "Stop looking at me that way. My mother wasn't well, and my father wasn't present. I trust you won't spread that about."

"Your mother named you after the rainbow?"

He winced. Around the corner, she could see the cold stones of New Gaol rising up.

"Oh, that's sweet. It makes me think of doves and olive branches and peace. I can't see why you don't use the name."

"For the love of all that is holy." His words would have been harsh, but his cheek twitched, ruining the delivery.

"I suspect," Miranda said, "that it has been a long time since anybody dared tease you."

He didn't deny it. He didn't tell her to stop. A few more steps. They reached the dripping front gate of the gaol. He stopped just outside the entrance. "Miranda Darling," he said in repressive tones that would brook no argument.

So why was it that she heard "Miranda, darling," instead? Maybe he paused for emphasis. Maybe he paused to indicate a comma. Never had one little punctuation mark mattered so much.

"Yes?" she answered breathlessly.

"We're looking for the records of George Patten, due to be released three days before. He was committed the twelfth of August. Yes?"

Ah. That had definitely *not* been a comma, then. "I told you all that?"

"No. You mentioned his name was George Patten. The rest I determined from our records, and interpolated as to the release date."

She swallowed. The conversation they'd just shared had verged on the intimate—she had thought. But perhaps he'd not felt the same.

He closed his umbrella. A shower of droplets spun out from it, and the warm cocoon of heat that had enveloped her disappeared. No sun was visible, and the rain had robbed the sky of most of the light. He rapped once on the wooden door, turning from her. The door swung open; he leaned forward and murmured something to the man behind it.

The fellow narrowed his eyes, casting Miranda a sullen glower. Still, he stepped aside and let them through. The heavy door closed behind them. It had seemed dark outside, with the rain clouds hiding the sun. But when the door shut, all the light seemed to vanish. Only a trickle of fitful illumination fell from the gaoler's lamp—not enough to light the way even ten feet in the damp corridor where they stood.

"Is there not more light than this?" Turner asked.

"No." The gaoler adjusted the hood on his lamp to demonstrate.

"I see."

Likely he couldn't see much. But no doubt he could smell. The gaol smelled of old things—sour sweat, years of mold that had never been scrubbed away, buckets of waste left to sit for weeks. It made her faintly ill.

Turner's nose twitched, but he showed no other sign of distress.

"Well?" he said. "Let's get on with it."

The records were in a dank room off the main hall. They were brought there by one of the gaolers, who stood in the corner. Turner ignored the man and took a dingy book from a shelf. "This," he said to Miranda, "is the record of arrivals and departures. If anything happened to your friend, it'll be listed here."

He opened the book and set it on the table. Miranda peered over his shoulder. He turned the pages, scanning them so quickly she wondered if he was even looking at the words.

"Hmm," he said, after he'd flipped through ten pages. "This is his arrival record." He tapped it. "I didn't see any record of his release. Or of a transfer. Curious." He didn't mention the possibility that he might have missed it.

"Is that bad?" Miranda asked.

He turned and plucked a more battered volume off the shelves. "The roll call," he explained without answering her question. He flipped through a handful of pages and then stopped. "He was here five days ago. He wasn't the day after."

"People don't just vanish into thin air."

"No." Turner frowned. "They do not. Maybe he escaped."

Miranda shook her head. "Not George. Why become a fugitive the day before he was to be set free? I find that unlikely."

He met her eyes. "I do, too. The most probable answer is that there has been an error. He was moved, or he was released, and it simply wasn't recorded. These things happen."

Miranda wasn't so sure. Accounting errors did happen. But if this was a simple failure to record, where was George?

Turner crossed to the gaoler, sketched out the situation in a few words. The man listened, and then shrugged.

"Sometimes," the gaoler said, "they disappear each other down there. Takes a while to notice it."

Miranda swallowed. But Turner simply nodded, as if such casual mention of murder meant nothing to him.

The gaoler continued with an indifferent shrug. "Only way to find out is to ask."

"Ah." Turner didn't move. He stood in the foul-smelling murk for a moment, staring straight ahead of him. "Of whom should I make these inquiries?"

"The prisoners," the gaoler said. "Who else?"

Turner had set his hat to the side of the book when he entered. He picked it up now and turned it over in his hands. "Is there some kind of an interview room up here? How does one go about having prisoners brought up?"

"Interview room? Brought up? What do you think this is?" The gaoler laughed. "No, you can talk to them right where they are. Don't worry; they're shackled. They'll be at the water wheel now, the ones this fellow would have been with. I'll take you down."

"We need to go down there," he repeated. If Miranda hadn't known better, she'd have thought Turner uneasy. His voice sounded sure. Something else in his face gave her that impression, but she couldn't have identified it. A trick of shadow, no doubt.

The gaoler shrugged again.

Turner set the hat down on the table, looked at Miranda once and then shook his head—a short, fast shake, as if he were shaking off raindrops. "Take us, then."

The gaoler led them back into the main hall, around a bend, and down a cramped staircase.

If it had been dim above, it was beyond black below. The darkness seemed to eat at the faint illumination from the lantern. Miranda could scarcely see the stone floor, strewn with straw; some feet away, she could make out the dim shape of thick iron bars. The scent of sewage grew heavier, almost overwhelming. Miranda slid a handkerchief in front of her nose, but it scarcely had any effect on the smell.

Somewhere in front of them, she heard the splash of water.

Turner stopped. "What is that? That noise."

"The water wheel. The prisoners that are here for hard labor, of course, need to—"

Water splashed again, this time in a louder rush.

"Never mind," Turner muttered beside her. "Not worth it." He turned in his tracks and started back up the stairs. Miranda stared at his retreating form. She couldn't believe it. He wasn't leaving. He couldn't be leaving.

She scampered after him. He mounted the steps so swiftly, she was out of breath by the time she caught him halfway up. "Wait. We haven't talked to anyone. Just a few people. A few minutes. Turner."

He said nothing; just turned into the hall.

"Is it the smell?" she asked. "You'll grow used to it, soon."

"It's not the smell."

She had to run to keep up; his long strides took the stairs two at a time, then three. But he didn't look at her when they came out into the dark corridor, didn't look as she came abreast of him.

"Listen to me," she started, reaching for him. "I'll ask all the questions. You don't even need to—"

He caught her hand. "I told you before." It came out almost as a snarl. "I'm not kind. I'm efficient." He pushed her away and turned down the hall. "Open the door," he called, and from down the corridor, a widening slit of gray daylight cut the darkness.

"I understand," she said, running to catch up with him. "It is a bit much to take in. But I promise, if you'll just stay—"

"You don't understand anything," he interrupted. His voice shook. She felt as if he'd slapped her.

"I don't believe you. You're acting like an unfeeling brute, and—"

"Believe it." The door opened to the day beyond. Clear air streamed through. He strode into the open gray of the rain outside. He kept walking, not looking to see if she followed.

Miranda darted in front and held up her hands to stop him. "No," she said. "If you think I'll allow you to walk off—it's my *friend* who's back there. My friend disappeared. How can you care about justice and not care about what happens once someone leaves your court?"

"Get out of my way." He spoke in an intimidating growl.

Miranda wasn't about to be intimidated. She set her hands on his chest. "Please. *Listen.*"

He put his hands about her shoulders. His face was white, his lips pressed together in tight resolve. For a second, Miranda thought he was actually going to shake her. Maybe even strike her. She felt an instant of real fear. Instead, his fingers bit into her flesh—hard. He lifted her up—she hadn't thought him so strong as to simply heft her in the air. And he set her down so roughly that she stumbled. Her arms stung where he'd held her.

"Don't you *dare* manhandle me," she hissed.

But he wasn't looking at her. He wasn't looking back at the gaol he'd quit so hastily. Instead, he doubled over as if in pain and fell to his knees.

And then, before she could quite comprehend what was happening, Lord Justice vomited into the bushes.

Chapter Eight

AFTER THE FIT OF retching passed, Smite became aware of two things. First, the mud was soaking through the knees of his trousers. And second, he'd just vomited in front of a woman. He was dirty and bedraggled. Miss Darling stood behind him, her breaths echoing amidst the sound of falling rain.

For a long second, he stared at the bushes in front of him, willing Miss Darling to disappear.

He had thought as long as it was dry and he wasn't alone, he could manage the darkness. But the smallest sound of liquid—the bare splash of water—and he'd been transported back. Back to that cellar. *He* had been the one shivering on the cold floor, the one who had felt the water seep through the one thin blanket that had been allotted him. In that moment, he'd been transported back to the truth of his past, and he'd felt all that old terror.

He took a deep breath of cleansing air and looked up at her. For one second, he hoped she had misconstrued what she'd seen.

Instead, her face was a mask of confused sympathy. She stood, staring at him, her lips pressed together. She appeared to be searching for something to say.

"Don't bother with platitudes. Don't ask after my health." He found a handkerchief in his pocket and wiped his mouth off. "I'm perfectly well," he added, feeling idiotic.

"Actually," she said, "what I was going to say was: I'm sorry."

He winced. "That's even worse. Don't *pity* me, for God's sake."

"I'm apologizing. I thought you were an unfeeling brute. But—you're not. Are you." It was not a question she was asking.

He spat again, his mouth sour. "Don't make too much of it. It was just bad fish, understand?"

Her clear green eyes bored into his.

"You're a terrible liar," she said. "That's as bad as your story about the cats."

He bowed his head, not wanting to acknowledge that. "I'll just need a moment." He coughed and planted one foot on the ground. "I'll go back." He curled his lip, and he attempted to stand. His muscles ached. Deep inside, that image swirled, floodwaters washing up.

"You're shaking." Her hand landed on his shoulder. "Was it...that wasn't the smell, was it?"

"Yes," he said, a moment too late for believability.

Her nose wrinkled.

"No," he amended softly. "It wasn't the smell. But I can return." He just wasn't sure what would happen if he did.

"No. George isn't there now. If he was killed by the other inmates, he won't be any less gone if we go back immediately. You shouldn't subject yourself to..." She trailed off, not knowing what it was.

He shouldn't have been so relieved at the reprieve. "I should have sent my clerk. If I'd been thinking clearly, I would have delegated the task. He's better at this sort of thing." He started to stand.

Her hand was surprisingly strong, driving him back to his knees. For one second, it seemed precisely right that he should be brought low before her. The rain fell around them. It dampened her hair into separate strings; in the uneven light, they seemed bright red against the dark color of her dress. He knelt before her, as if he were some kind of bedraggled knight, and the umbrella lying on the ground his sword.

A fanciful thought, rather belied by reality. The rain fell on his face, belled on his eyelashes. She seemed almost mystical, outlined by the water that stung his eyes. Before her, rain was just rain, washing everything away.

She reached into her own pocket and drew out a white scrap. And then she reached forward to wipe the rain from his forehead.

He snatched the fabric from her hand. "I can't abide being fussed over."

"Lord Justice," she said, "I think you should go home and rest."

"Thank you, but no. I've no need."

"What was that back there? It wasn't fish, and it wasn't the scent."

He stared mutely at her, and then held out her handkerchief in return.

She sighed and reached out to help him up. He was shaky enough that he took her arm, and he leaned on it. He let her open the umbrella.

"Is there anyone here to accompany you home?"

He glanced back at the gaol. Briefly, he considered lying. Only briefly. He shook his head.

"Will there be someone waiting for your arrival?"

His charwoman would be long gone; no other servants would be around today. No need for her to know that. "Yes," he said.

"Who?"

"My dog." He sighed and looked to the sky. "Don't look at me like that. He's very good company."

"You're trying to figure out how to rid yourself of me, aren't you?"

"Damn." The word had no rancor. "On this short an acquaintance, you should not know me so well."

She put her head to one side and considered him. So help him, if she spouted one word about what he *needed,* he was going to walk away and never speak to her again. He didn't want her bloody pity.

Maybe she saw the warning in his eyes, because she simply shrugged. "I'm the last one seen in your company, and it would be dreadfully inconvenient if I were to fall under suspicion. I just want to make sure that nobody kills you on your way home." Only the sparkle in her eyes suggested she was teasing.

That was the moment when he realized he was in trouble. She didn't insist on plying him with concern. In fact, she'd believed him when he said he didn't like fuss. Her hair was dripping from the rain; her gown was spattered.

He couldn't remember why he'd thought she wasn't pretty before. His elder brother would have had something brilliantly charming to say at the moment. Smite could think of nothing.

"Besides," she said, "I don't want to say farewell."

She couldn't mean what he'd heard. If her cheeks were pink, it was probably from the cold. But it was so much an echo of his own impulse that he set his hand over hers and squeezed her fingers.

"Then don't say it."

SMITE DIDN'T TELL LIES well, not even with his body. He walked back through the darkening streets, his steps this time more measured. She didn't say anything, thank God, on the return trip. He made his way to the small home where he lived near the edge of town.

He didn't have anything for her but silence.

He wasn't *good* with this sort of thing—with the back-and-forth dance between man and woman. He wasn't even sure if they were dancing, or if she was merely being polite.

"Thank you," he said when they reached his doorstep.

"That sounds suspiciously as if it's intended as a dismissal." She wrinkled her nose. "Do you really think I'm going to leave before I make sure that you eat?"

"Do I look so dire as to need all that attention?"

She studied him frankly. He could feel his hands trembling, and he folded his arms to hide the weakness.

"Yes," she said baldly. "You look awful."

Perhaps that simple honesty was why he didn't send her away. There was a little bit of fuss there, yes, but at least she hadn't called him a poor lamb. And maybe...maybe right now he wanted the company.

He shook his head and unlocked the door. A ball of gray-and-white fur launched itself into the rain, jumping and leaping and bludgeoning him with his tail. For a few minutes, amidst the wriggling and the barking, there was no conversation to be had. But eventually, Ghost managed to calm himself, and they entered.

Smite excused himself immediately to wash. It took too long to rid himself of the feeling of the prison. The oppressive stink had vanished, but still he scrubbed hard. He applied tooth powder and brushed out his mouth, and when that didn't seem strong enough, he used harsh soap. He scrubbed until he'd stripped away the layers of his weakness.

Only when his hands had grown steady did he return to the main room.

Miss Darling was examining the books on his shelves. She was... God, there were no words for her. She warmed up his dark room.

Maybe the effect came from the fire she'd started from the banked coals, or the lamps she'd lit. Maybe it was the absent wave she gave him when she heard his footsteps—or maybe, that curl of heat came when her expression froze in a half-smile as she took him in.

He'd stripped to his bare skin to wash, and had only donned his shirt again. The points of his collar were drooping, and the edges of his hair were damp. Her eyes drifted down and then up, and for the first time, she turned away, a faint blush touching her cheeks.

Ah. Maybe he'd let her come home with him for another reason entirely.

"Well," she said. "You should eat."

He shook his head, dispelling the prurient bent of his thoughts. He could smell the faint scent of roasted chicken. On the hob behind her, under a cover, lay the dinner his charwoman had left for him. He wasn't hungry. Not for *that,* at any rate. Still, he crossed the room and took a plate. Removing the cover, he heaped food onto it—a pile of new potatoes, peas, and a roasted breast of chicken. Ghost padded silently behind him, looking up in obvious entreaty.

Smite ignored him and crossed to the table. He set the plate down and then picked up a fork.

Miss Darling simply crossed her arms and gave him a look—the kind of look that said *get on with it.*

She shouldn't have been beautiful—she was too forward, too freckled, too thin. Still… Oh, to hell with it all. He wasn't hungry, anyway. He reached out and took her hand, drawing her to him. She drifted near, until she was close enough to kiss. Close enough for him to see the green of her eyes, widening as he turned her hand over, palm up.

"There's something I've wanted to do since the first moment I saw you," he said. It came out close to a whisper.

"Oh?" He could feel the puff of breath from that word against his nose.

"Don't even think of arguing."

She shook her head. Her lips opened, an impossible, inviting fraction.

He set the fork in the palm of her hand and closed his fingers tightly around hers. "I want you to eat," he said.

"But—"

"I've seen your wrists, Miss Darling. And your dinners. When I tell you to eat, damn it, you are going to do so. Now have a seat."

He turned and pulled a trunk from the wall, and shoved it up against the other side of the table to form a makeshift second seat. She did sit down, and as he went to pile a second plate high with more meat, she picked up a forkful of chicken.

When he returned, she glanced at his plate. "You should have peas, too."

"Hmm," was all he said in reply.

She had impeccable table manners for a woman who lived in the slums. Not for the first time, he found himself wondering about her. There was her accent, changing to match whoever was around her. And then there was Antigone. She was a conundrum, really.

He ripped a piece of chicken from the bone. She watched him curiously; her eyes narrowed as he held it out to his dog, who took it nimbly.

"Ghost doesn't like peas," he explained.

She didn't ask why a duke's brother had no servants, no long, splendid table set with silver. He didn't ask her where she'd acquired her manners. It would have broken the spell that seemed to enfold them.

If this was magic, magic was tiring. It drained him until he was bone-weary, until all that was left was a deep, empty ache, and a desire to belong to someone else, if only for a few moments.

He spoke as nonchalantly as he dared. "I suppose you're wondering about what happened. Back there. At the gaol."

She gave him a measured look and took a mouthful of potatoes. She chewed carefully and then shrugged. "I suppose I am."

He usually fobbed off such inquiries with frowns. But she wasn't looking at him. He wasn't likely to see her again, and so he'd not have to bear the burden of her pity. And so what came out was the truth. "When I was twelve, my mother locked me in the cellar. She kept me there for days. There was no light." He smiled faintly. "There were turnips. Beets. Also onions. A great many onions. I can't stand them anymore."

He leaned back on the trunk, looking up at the ceiling. The trunk was bound by metal straps; they were uncomfortable beneath him, and it was just as well, because the discomfort kept him firmly grounded in the present. "And then it began to rain. It was the worst rain that Shepton Mallet had experienced in living memory. The basement walls began to seep water, and then to fill. It came on terribly fast. The water crept to my ankles, and then before I knew it, it was up to my thighs. There were no stairs, just a wooden ladder descending into the cellar. So I clung to the top for hours, beating on the door and praying. If I let go, I would drown. Even if I held on, I had no escape, and the water was rising." He took a deep breath.

She set her fork down gently. But she didn't say anything.

"I was trapped. I was certain I would die." If he shut his eyes, he could still feel the cramp of his hands, clenched around the wood of the ladder. He'd been certain he'd not be able to hold on much longer.

"But you survived."

"My brother stole the key eventually."

"What did you do that warranted such treatment?"

"Hanging is fast," he snapped back. "You think leaving me to drown in freezing water was *warranted?*"

She held up her hands. "No. That's not what I meant."

It was all too easy to see everything as an attack when he thought of the cellar. He forced himself to breathe slowly. He could trace it back, step by step. Years ago, he'd questioned each decision, wondering if he could have averted calamity after all. Now, he simply accepted what it had made of him.

"The day before, I went to the town elders and told them my mother was mad. That if they didn't intervene, we would be in danger." He met her gaze. "They laughed at me, and scarcely listened to my tale. I went home. Someone informed her that I'd asked for help, and she flew into a fury. Hence the cellar." He ripped off another piece of chicken, and passed it under the table. "So I know what happens when justice lapses."

She nodded.

"It's why my duty is so important to me. When people come to me, I listen. So that what happened to me doesn't happen to anyone else. Don't feel sorry for me. Most people can't change their past. I change mine every day."

"I see," she said quietly.

"Sometimes," he continued, "rain and darkness and closed quarters have an odd effect on me. It passes quickly enough. All of which is to say, this is quite normal. I haven't any need for your company any longer."

An odd smile crossed her face. "How like you, to be arrogant even when you're vulnerable."

"I'm not vulnerable."

"Yes, you are," she contradicted. "You're looking at me as if I'm supposed to..."

His eyes riveted on her lips, and she stopped speaking. The heat in the room swirled about him, sinking beneath his skin. She blushed again. He stood. Two steps, and he was standing before her. She tilted her head back to look him in the face. Her eyes were wide and luminous, and he leaned down to her. She smelled softly, subtly sweet—like mint leaves, dried for tea.

"What is it you're supposed to do?" he asked.

"Kiss you. Kiss you and make it better."

"No." His voice rang hoarse. "I don't want that."

She drew back.

"I want you to kiss me and make it worse."

A little gasp escaped her. He touched his hand to the point of her chin, tilted her face up to his. Her skin was warm against his fingers, and she flushed under his touch. She looked utterly dazzled. Dangerous, that look, as if he'd hung the stars for her.

But he wanted to believe he could, so he kissed her.

As predicted, it made everything worse. Her kiss heightened the hunger for company that he'd long ignored. Her lips were slack in surprise at first, but then she came to life under him, kissing him back. That sparked a fierce, possessive desire. He wanted her. That want had the strength of years of loneliness behind it.

She reached up and twined her hands around the fabric of his shirt, pulling him down to her. She opened under his kiss, and then it was not just the softness of her lips, but that of her mouth, hot, melding with his. Their tongues touched; she made a little noise in the back of her throat—something fierce and needy.

He wrapped his arms around her, pulling her to him. She came easily, her hands sliding down his frame. She was so warm, so *present,* that she drove away all thoughts of the cold and distant past.

There was nothing but her—her kiss, her caress. Her breathy gasp of pleasure.

He courted that now, slowing the kiss so that he could slide his fingers up her waist, up the fabric of her dress to cup her breast. It was small in his hand, small but round and perfectly formed. Her gown fastened in the front; he undid a button. Then another. She ran her hands along his chest, urging him on. He, in turn, loosened the laces of her stays, and slipped his thumb under the fabric.

She moaned when he touched her nipple—not loud, but deep in her throat, a noise halfway to a purr that drove him mad. God, he wanted her. Wanted to wring more sounds from her, wanted to lose himself in her pleasure—and his own. He slid her loosened stays down and captured the pebbled tip of her breast between his lips.

She was sensitive—so damned sensitive and responsive to his touch. Her whole body arched against his. Her hand clenched around his arm.

He wanted to take her, to have her—not just her body, but her warmth, her smile, her presumptuous clever wit. He ran his other hand up her leg, sliding her skirts up to bare her knees.

The skin of her thighs was impossibly perfect—not just soft, but taut and supple. He slid his hand up her leg, so close…

She laid her hand over his. "No," she said distinctly.

He froze. He was inches from the juncture of her legs. He was burning for her. He was rock hard and ready; she was interested, too. His breath feathered against her nipple, erect in obvious arousal. "No?" he echoed in disbelief.

She struggled away from him and adjusted her stays. Her hands were unsteady, and tangled in the laces. "No," she repeated. "I can't do that." She gave a shaky laugh. "I have one child I can't manage. I hardly need another."

It was on his tongue to make promises to her—that he'd keep her, that he'd shoulder any burden that she might encounter. Or he might have simply leaned forward and taken her breast in his mouth again. He knew the sound of an objection that could be easily overridden with a bit of judicious action. It would be the easiest thing in the world to seduce her.

"I'm dreadfully sorry," she said earnestly. "But despite any appearances to the contrary, I'm not that kind of girl."

He took the edges of her corset in his hands and looked into her eyes.

What a damned joy it would be for her—a quick tumble with him. After he'd slaked himself on her warmth, her generosity, she would turn to him, expecting what he could never give. He wanted to rip her stays off altogether, to slide against her bare skin.

But there was no point in wallowing in what he wouldn't have. Instead, he pulled his hands away. "Lucky for you," he said softly. "I'm not that kind of man."

Nothing to do for it but tidy up her gown.

"I did want that kiss," she said earnestly. "It was a lovely kiss."

He tucked the ends of her laces in, before meeting her eyes. "Then here's another one."

This one was bitter in its sweetness. If the soft brush of her lips had driven away his loneliness before, her kiss now served only to remind him that this, too, was coming to an end. This kiss wasn't companionship or warmth. It didn't even encompass lust. It was farewell, and when it ended he'd be alone once more.

He pulled away before it could become anything else.

"Stay safe," he told her. "Eat well. I'll walk you back—and I'll hear no argument from you."

"You'll take me to the Bristol Bridge," she corrected. "It's dark. I won't be safe in your half of the city, but you'd not be safe in mine."

He leaned in and rested his forehead against hers.

"You won't see me in your hearing room again," she murmured. "I...you're right. You and Jeremy both. I have to walk away from that. And Robbie is old enough to make his own decisions."

"If I did see you again," he said, "I'd not render judgment. I believe I've misplaced my impartiality in regard to you."

"Will I see you at all?"

He shook his head. But he couldn't yet make himself move away. He was unwilling to relinquish his hold on her, unwilling to say that final good-bye. He held her for a minute, then two, then three, simply holding her and committing to memory what he could not have in life. There was a sweet, comforting scent to her.

His memory was very, very good, but she was better.

He only loosened his grip when he feared he might not be able to let go of her at all.

Chapter Nine

FOR ANOTHER MAN, THE memory of Miranda Darling might have faded over the days that passed.

But Smite's memories never faded, and he found himself strangely reluctant to push thoughts of her from his mind entirely. It was easy to withstand loneliness when the alternative was to saddle himself with some doe-eyed innocent who could not follow his conversation, and whose only experience in deprivation amounted to a few hours of boredom. It was harder to resist thoughts of a wary, green-eyed woman who knew Greek plays and made her own way on the streets.

He could call to mind what it felt like to have her walking next to him in the rain, her cheeks pink with exertion, that wide smile on her face as she teased him about his name. He woke some nights, not from one of his usual nightmares, but hard with want, the memory of her skin swimming through his mind.

No matter how he tried, he couldn't remember her scent—just that it had calmed him—and that failure was driving him wild.

He tried to tell himself it was nothing but lust. Except that he didn't only think of the heat of her mouth, her response to his kiss. He lusted after her smiles. After the easy way she teased him. It was deeply irrational, that want. But then, it had been a long while since a woman had laughed at him, and he couldn't help but treasure the memory.

There was nothing to do about such thoughts—nothing, that was, except to hope that she was eating well, and to send his clerk off to seek word of George Patten. But Palter had found nothing from the men in the gaol; days ago, he'd gone in search of those who'd been released since then. The inquiries were taking time.

This morning started as any other morning would. Palter brought him a summary of the prior day's dealings: licenses issued, hearings held.

Midway through the morning, a constable came in. "I'll need a warrant issued to hold a man until the Assizes," he said.

Across the room, Jamison, a fellow magistrate, spoke without looking up from his reading. "I'll sign," he offered. "Give the papers over."

"You can't just *sign,*" Smite interjected. "You haven't heard the evidence. The man hasn't even been charged, and besides, there's a bail hearing to be had." He was long past feeling appalled at the lax way in which weighty matters of law were decided. He wasn't past arguing, though.

"What's the point?" Jamison shrugged. "The constable wouldn't have brought the man in were he not guilty, and if he's guilty, he'll just run."

"It's almost an insult, sir," the constable said, nodding his head. "When you ask all those pointed questions. It's like saying that you don't trust my judgment."

Smite met the man's eyes. "This has nothing to do with your pride or your integrity or any of your finer personal feelings. It is not about you at all. It is about fidelity to the duty demanded by the laws that we have both sworn to honor. Adhering to the requirements of the law is *never* a personal slight."

"I see," the constable said with a frown, "but still, it's my judgment you're questioning."

Smite sighed and rubbed his forehead. "The law demands that an impartial observer consider the evidence."

Jamison exhaled noisily behind them. "Then *you* consider it," he said, turning a page of his newspaper. "I'm busy."

Smite had had similar conversations any number of times in his tenure as a magistrate in Bristol. He always felt as if he were fighting a losing battle with his colleagues. How hard was it to *listen?* To truly think of the requirements of justice, instead of mechanically signing whatever came their way?

Apparently, it was next to impossible.

"You haven't any family to speak of," Jamison continued. "If you did, you'd not be able to devote the hours you do. The rest of us, well, we've found it useful to accept that some of the legal technicalities can be set aside. No point in being slaves to formality."

"I have a family," Smite said quietly. The man who was being held out there might have one, too. "That's why I consider it imperative to discharge my duty to its utmost."

"Well then." The other magistrate waved his hand. "My sincerest compliments, *Lord Justice.*"

Smite gritted his teeth at that insult—at the implication that his duty was little more than a ribald commitment to a stone woman. This was how he ended up shouldering far more than his fair share of the work: nobody else would do it. Still, if he was the only one available... He stood.

"Well," he said, "let's see the fellow."

The constable shook his head. "Bloke's just this way."

He turned the corner...and his heart sank. It wasn't a *fellow* or a *bloke*. It was a boy.

To be more specific, it was a tiny rapscallion of a boy— scrawny, sullen, his hair mussed and standing up in untidy spikes. The tracks of fallen tears had wiped clean lines down his dirty cheeks. And when he saw Smite, his eyes widened in recognition.

Robbie.

Smite's thoughts turned instantly to Miss Darling. *I'm guilty the instant a constable lays eyes on me and decides I appear out of place,* she'd said. *Nobody listens.*

I do, he'd answered.

But he could already feel his emotions engaging, searching for an excuse on Robbie's behalf. He knew the boy. And he knew that if he authorized a grand jury to charge Robbie, Miranda would be devastated.

Smite took a deep breath. "Your full name, young master?"

"Robbie. I mean—Robert Barnstable."

He'd just lectured Jamison and the constable on fidelity and honor and duty. His duty in cases such as these was clear. With his emotions engaged, he had to step down and ask one of his brother magistrates to hear the evidence in his stead. The law required an impartial assessment, and Smite very much doubted that he could deliver.

"Are you going to hang me?" Robbie asked, his voice shaking.

But if he didn't act, who would? Jamison wouldn't listen; he had practically announced as much. He wouldn't think. He'd simply hold the boy for days until the grand jury laid an indictment.

There was no right choice. If Smite had any integrity, he'd walk away. If he cared at all about justice, he'd stay. But he couldn't sit here and dither over his options. And so Smite took a deep breath, checked his instinct, and came to a decision.

THE INSIDE STEPS UP to Miranda's rooms were always cold, but today the stairwell held a particularly drafty chill. She saw why when she came to the second-floor landing.

The window was ajar and Robbie sat on the sill, legs dangling out into open space as he stared at the city. Night had come on, and fog blanketed the buildings. A street away, a few lamps burned orange holes through the mist, but everything else was shadowed.

He wasn't smoking. He simply glanced at her as she walked by and then looked quickly away, his shoulders hunching in misery.

"What is it?" she asked.

"Nothing."

His chin fell, and he contemplated the top of the adjacent building, scarcely a foot away. But there was nothing there but coal-blackened brick and, far below, brown drifts of paper-dry leaves.

"Very well," Miranda said, and slid past him.

He let out a second, wearier sigh as she went by. Just a noisy exhalation—not even his usual handful of terse, disapproving syllables. Still, the sigh said it wasn't nothing, and at this point, Miranda would take any form of communication she could get from him.

She sat on the steps, just behind him.

"So tell me about this nothing."

He shrugged. "It's nothing."

She'd been looking after Robbie in some capacity for seven years. His mother had been an actress—and one of the flightier ones at that. She'd attached herself to Miranda's father's troupe just before everything had fallen to pieces. Robbie's mother had asked Miranda to take care of her son during the day, in exchange for a few pennies. For a few years, Miranda had watched Robbie. She'd not minded; they'd needed all the pennies she could find.

One day, long after the troupe had fallen apart, his mother had disappeared for good, leaving Robbie behind. For months, Miranda had tried to find someone—anyone—to take him. But nobody had wanted an abandoned eight-year-old child.

So Miranda had kept him. At first, she'd entertained hopes that the two of them might form a family of a sort. In books, women reduced to straitened circumstances always surrounded themselves with kind, adoring loved ones through pluck and determination.

The authors of heartwarming books apparently had no contact with actual adolescent boys. They weren't kind. They didn't know how to adore. They were just surly.

She'd hoped to mirror the laughing, tempestuous feel of her childhood, where family and friends merged. But instead of warmth and love, Robbie left Miranda in a constant state of near-terror. What was he going to do next? How was she to stop him?

He glanced over his shoulder at her. "What are you still doing here?" he growled. "I thought you'd finally decided to let me be."

"I'm no good at this, Robbie. If I were your mother, I'd know what to say. I'd make you laugh and feel better, and you'd never have need to complain."

"Sure," he agreed bitterly.

"But I'm not. I don't know how to be a mother. What role do you want me to play instead?"

Another shrug of his scrawny shoulders. "Nothing."

"Nothing?"

His shoulders stiffened. But he didn't look at her. After a few moments, he shrugged again. "I suppose," he said.

Oh, that hurt. To have all her care, all her work, tossed aside in one insouciant shrug of his shoulders. Years of looking after him had culminated in this bored rejection.

"Best to get on with it," Robbie said. But his voice broke on the last word, and his shoulders quivered. And that was when Miranda realized that he was crying—quietly, but crying nonetheless.

She stared at him, absolutely flummoxed. Surly, sullen, and...sad? What was she supposed to *do?*

She stood and walked down the steps to the window. "Hey, now," she whispered. "It's not so bad as that."

He wiped furiously at his eyes. "Sure. Wait 'til you hear."

"Hear what?"

"I was arrested today."

"What? Oh, no. But...but you didn't... Oh." A knot in her belly tightened. "You *did*, didn't you?"

"Maybe." He hunched. "Maybe I just tried. I did it wrong, in any event."

"And they brought you in."

"Made me talk to some fellow, who was supposed to determine if...um, something. It wasn't a trial. I wasn't really paying attention."

Wasn't really paying attention Miranda translated as *too scared to ask questions.*

"Was he a constable?" Miranda asked.

"I guess," Robbie said. "He let me go. But he yelled at me afterward."

"Yelled?" Miranda said. "What afterward?" Thank God the man he'd talked to had some compassion. It was a rare enough quality in the constables.

"He said, because I didn't actually manage to *steal* the watch, he couldn't prove what I meant to do, and he could treat it as...as something. I don't remember."

"What *do* you remember?" Miranda tried to ask the question as gently as she could.

"He said he could get me an apprenticeship at a shipwright."

Miranda held her breath, hardly daring to believe what she was hearing. It was more than she could have given him—a good start at life, a chance for solid work doing something Robbie enjoyed. It also cost more than she could imagine. That kind of favor, held over her head by some unknown person... "And what did you say? Did you accept?"

He shrugged. "I suppose. I didn't really have much choice. After this, you won't want anything to do with me, anyway."

His shoulders hunched even more, and Miranda stared at his back in puzzlement.

"Why wouldn't I want anything to do with you?"

"You always told me that if I ever risked hanging, you would never speak to me again. I know you never wanted me. You tried to get rid of me." His matter-of-fact tone broke her heart—as if he were recounting unalterable truths.

Maybe that's the way it had seemed to him. After his mother had disappeared, Miranda had tried to get someone—anyone—to take the boy. Of course she had. She'd been a child herself.

She hadn't wanted the responsibility. To Robbie, no doubt it had seemed that she hadn't wanted *him*.

"Oh," she breathed. She'd told a boy who'd been abandoned by his mother that she was going to leave him, too, unless he listened to her. He'd thought she'd *meant* it.

Slowly she set her hand on his shoulder.

He leaned away an inch and only gave one solitary half-hearted grunt in protest. It was practically encouragement. So she made a fist and rubbed his hair until it stood up on end.

"Stop that," he muttered, but he didn't pull away.

"Do you want to be a shipwright?"

Another shrug. "I guess."

"It's a good profession. And you're good at arithmetic. You were always good working with the carpenter when you were little." More practically, shipwrights could speak in two-word sentences and still get paid.

He slouched further. "You want me to go."

"I'd still get to see you sometimes, wouldn't I? On Sabbaths and holidays. I'd miss you the rest of the time, but I suppose I'd manage."

"You'd miss me?"

Miranda sighed, and dropped her voice into a gravelly imitation of his. "I guess," she intoned.

It took him a moment to realize she was mocking him, but he let out an exasperated sigh and punched her, lightly, on the arm. And then, leaving the rest unspoken, he pulled his legs in, slid off the sill, and started up the stairs.

Halfway to their garret, Robbie stopped. "Oh, I had a message for you. From the fellow who talked to me."

"A message? For me?"

"He said to meet him…um…somewhere. By a castle. Or a church. Something like that. Tomorrow at six in the morning."

"Why does a constable want to meet me at six in the morning? He doesn't even know who I am."

But as soon as she said the words, she knew the answer. Robbie turned to her, his eyes wide and innocent. "Didn't I say? It was that man—the one I hit over the head."

Chapter Ten

SMITE WAS NOT USED to indecision, but when the next morning dawned, he still had not determined whether he actually wanted to see Miss Darling again. He'd asked Robbie to convey the invitation on impulse—if one could call the product of long nights spent wanting an *impulse.* He crossed over to the green surrounding the old churchyard with Ghost tugging at the lead.

There was no question what he should do. He shouldn't want her at all. It had been foolish to ask, and even more foolish to pursue the...could he call what he'd planned an *acquaintance?*

He came to the stone walls of St. Philip's Church and slowly turned about. He was alone. She hadn't come.

Damn. The mist twined about the walls, turning the dawn to grayness. Regret was bitter.

Smite didn't believe in regret. He didn't need her. He'd only wanted her.

He stared into the slowly dissipating fog and willed it to show her form. But there was nobody about.

Apparently, he was lacking in all good sense. He slipped the lead from around Ghost's neck and gave him a pat. The animal darted off through the fog, in search of pigeons to chase.

The city was just coming to life. The brewery across the harbor had begun to belch smoke into the sky. Ghost came barreling back through the mist, a stick in his mouth. He tossed it on the ground before Smite and danced back, eagerly waiting.

"Very well, you wretched animal," Smite said. He picked it up and hurled it as far as it would go.

He was watching his dog run in great bounding leaps, when he heard a delighted laugh beside him.

"He led me to you, you know."

He turned.

Miranda Darling was standing behind him, one hand on the ruined stone wall. She was smiling at him.

"By Robbie's message, I thought you meant us to meet more by the bridge. Whatever you intended to say came somewhat garbled from the messenger." She gestured. "I was quite put out at having got up so early, only to be snubbed."

It was too early for sun, but her hair under her bonnet was as brilliant as a summer sunrise. She probably *wasn't* pretty, at least not in the classical sense of pristine English beauty. Her mouth was too wide; her nose too snub. And there was that profusion of freckles that covered her nose.

Classical English beauty could go hang, for all Smite cared. His mouth dried.

"And then I saw your dog bounding up out of the mist," she continued.

A ways off, Ghost pounced on the stick and shook it vigorously. "Good dog," Smite said approvingly.

"Robbie told me what you did for him. Thank—"

He cut her off with a decisive chop of his hand. "Don't thank me."

"But I must. It may have meant very little to you, but to me, to Robbie, it means everything." Her gown was tied with a simple fabric sash. She rubbed the ends between her fingers, not meeting his eyes.

"That was not a selfish attempt to coerce you into singing my praises. I shouldn't have done it. It was wrong for me to act in my capacity as magistrate when I knew my decision could be biased by personal inclination. I will not do it again."

"Oh," she said. "Then…I'm sorry?"

He leaned down, retrieved Ghost's stick, and threw it once more. "Don't apologize, either. I don't make a habit of fostering regrets."

She appeared to be only mildly taken aback, which seemed quite promising. His heart was laboring. His pulse beat heavily. There was no *right* way to proceed, and it seemed suddenly insupportable that this conversation would end any other way than what he'd envisioned last night.

"I surmised, based on our prior conversation, that Robbie might profit from an apprenticeship to a shipwright."

"I know. But the expense…"

"Is nothing. I've taken care of it."

She didn't burst into raptures, thank God. Instead, she stared at him suspiciously. "Why would you do that?" she asked. "I'm a little wary of accepting such a favor when I don't know how it can ever be repaid."

"This isn't commerce. I don't require payment, and I certainly don't expect it of you."

But she simply tapped her foot and glowered. "If you didn't expect anything of me, you'd have done it anonymously. You'd not have asked me to meet you. You expect something. What is it?"

He was a magistrate, and what's more, he had all the money. No wonder she was nervous.

He met her eyes once more. "If you insist on repaying me, I ask only that you hear my next proposition in its entirety before you slap my face."

She drew in a breath. "Am I going to *want* to slap your face?"

He rather hoped not. There had to be some way to put her at ease, but he didn't know it. Instead he shrugged.

"It's like this: I can't put you out of my mind."

She'd not been expecting that. Her eyes widened. To tell the truth, he hadn't expected to start that way, either.

"I think of you in my free moments," he said. The words came faster. "I think of you in moments that ought to be taken up by work. It's affecting my judgment—witness what happened with Robbie yesterday. I keep thinking of what I could do for you. No—I must be perfectly frank—what I want to do *to* you."

She hadn't moved. But at that, she wet her lips with her tongue. "To be clear," she said, "when you talk about what you want to do, you are talking about kissing me. You are not talking about throwing me in gaol."

"To be clear," Smite countered, "I am talking about having you as my mistress. About having you in every way possible."

She didn't slap his face or shriek in horror. Instead, she shook her head. "Then the answer is no. I've already said so. There's too much risk for me."

Ghost brought back the stick and dropped it once more. Smite ignored the dog. "I'm not proposing a one-time liaison. You'll have a house. Servants. New clothing."

She rolled her eyes. "Oh, Lord Justice, you do know how to woo a woman. Tell me more."

"Precisely," he agreed. "I'm not given to effusive sentiment. I'm not good at it, and you mustn't expect it. It's best we start as we mean to go on. I don't need false protestations of love. I ask only for fidelity for the term of the arrangement and basic honesty."

"And what *is* the term of the arrangement you're proposing?"

"One month." His pulse was beating more erratically than it ought. This was business—simple business. Not something to care about. No reason to watch her so carefully, to wonder what that flicker of her eyelashes might mean. No reason at all. He bent and retrieved Ghost's stick, to avoid looking in her eyes, and hurled it as far as he could. "In addition to what I mentioned before," he added, "I'll pay you a thousand pounds."

That got him an incredulous look. "One thousand pounds. Are you joking? Or are you mad?"

He'd decided on a few hundred last night. He wasn't sure where the new, vastly inflated number had come from. Perhaps because he feared that she might refuse two hundred.

"Neither," he said repressively.

"You drive a worse bargain than my friend Jeremy." She put her hand to her head. "I beg your pardon for not immediately snapping up the offer. My financial understanding stretches to shillings and pence in the quantities of ones and tens. I have never heard the word 'thousand' anywhere near the word 'pounds.' I am having difficulty comprehending what you mean. You had seemed a sensible man, but you cannot be one. That's an absurd amount for just that one thing."

"Yes," he snapped. "This entire endeavor is absurd. I don't know why I asked you to come, or why I could scarcely breathe this morning until I saw you. The only thing I know for certain is that I want more than *one* thing from you. I want forty or fifty. Most of all, I want this: when we are through, I want to be certain that I will not leave you in danger. This way, I'll know that you'll never find your way into my courtroom again—neither you nor Robbie—and I'll never have to compromise my judgment. I want you to be *safe*. I can't purchase that for a few pounds and a minute against a wall."

She was watching him. The bright green of her eyes bored into his. She raised one eyebrow at that, and he almost thought she might be laughing at him. But instead, she said, "That's four things you want. What are the other forty-something?"

He reached out and took her hand. She was wearing knit gloves; they thinned at the fingertips. He rolled the fabric off her hand, slowly, and then pressed his hand into hers. She stared down at their entwined fingers, and then looked up at him.

"There's really only the one other thing," he heard himself say. "But I imagine I'll want it more than once."

Her hand twitched in his.

"Also," he said, "to be quite truthful—I chose a thousand pounds because I don't want to risk the possibility of your saying no."

She gave him a little smile—as if she'd realized what he'd just said. He had the money, the power. And he'd practically admitted that she had him in the palm of her hand. She could have asked for two thousand pounds, and he'd have agreed. Ten.

But instead, she pulled back from him. Her nails trailed along the skin of his hand. "I have my own conditions," she said.

"Yes?"

"You can have my body. You can have my fidelity. You can even have my honesty—" this, with a little wayward smile "—but there is one thing you cannot ever buy from me, not with any coin you have."

"Oh?"

"You can't buy my affection."

It was not disappointment he felt. It would make matters easier. He should have been overjoyed.

"That hardly signifies." He jammed his hands in his pockets. "Affection is not one of the forty-four other things I want to have from you." He wouldn't know what to do with it, in any event. "I told you I have no desire for effusive sentiment."

She gave him a brisk nod. "There's something else you need to know."

"Oh?"

She cast her eyes down and then looked up at him through her lashes. "You're adorable when you're uncertain."

"Uncertain?" He drew himself up. "What makes you think I'm uncertain? I'm certain. I'm quite certain. I'm—"

He lost his words, the entire rest of his sputtering speech, when she stepped close to him, popped up onto her toes, and kissed him.

The feel of her was a cool, clean shock, as bracing as fresh morning air after a tortured night.

Smite remembered everything. He remembered every prisoner he'd thrown in gaol, and the ones he had let go. He remembered reports of crimes and the details of bloody history.

But when she kissed him, he forgot. He forgot everything in the world except the heady feel of her hands, resting against his lapels. For just that moment, he was nothing but an ordinary fellow out with his sweetheart. When she kissed him, she made him feel like a man—just a man, not a burdened magistrate responsible for the fate of half of Bristol.

And so he deepened the kiss, sliding his tongue between her lips. He set his hands on her hips and pulled her close, and she didn't resist. She nestled against him, sighing deep in her throat. He kissed her until the rumble of a cart intruded on the quiet fog shielding their tryst.

She drew back. He felt almost unsteady on his feet. He was drunk on the taste of her. He'd been knocked off balance, and he wouldn't be able to walk a straight line for years.

No, he definitely wasn't going to miss his thousand pounds. He'd got the better end of that bargain. Even if she never gave him one scrap of affection.

But what he said instead was, "So that's a yes, then."

"It's a yes."

The sun wasn't coming up yet, but it ought to have done. It felt like dawn, warm and red, arriving on the heels of a very dark night.

"About your other concern," he heard himself say. "Do you know how to avoid pregnancy?"

She hadn't stopped smiling at him. "I was raised by actors," she said archly. "And if those measures prove ineffective... Well, there is that thousand pounds."

If they proved ineffective, there'd be more than a thousand pounds, but he saw no need to spell that out. All he said was, "Good. Then I'll be in contact to arrange further particulars." He cast her one last look. "Don't expect to wait long."

"JEREMY," MIRANDA WHISPERED, "NOW I *know* I've done something foolish. Tell me I mustn't go through with it."

It was a scant few hours since her assignation with Lord Justice, and Miranda was still reeling. She'd wandered about in a daze after, watching the city come fully to life. She'd waited until the shops opened—and as soon as she'd been able, she'd come to see Jeremy.

Jeremy dropped his thimble and leaned in. "What? Oh God. Don't tell me. You—"

"I just agreed to be a man's mistress."

"What?!" His eyes widened.

"Shh!" Miranda glanced across the shop, searching out Old Blazer. He sat in his place at the front, watching the passersby through the window. He nodded and waved at acquaintances as he smoked his pipe.

Jeremy obligingly dropped his voice. "Why?"

"Because he's going to put me up in a nice house. And pay me a tidy sum." Because he'd *wanted* her, so damned badly he couldn't stop thinking of her. Because he'd made her think she was worth a thousand pounds—that, in fact, he was getting the better end of the deal.

Jeremy must have caught the dazed look in her eyes. "You know," he said cautiously, "whatever he's said, he doesn't love you."

"I'm not stupid," Miranda scoffed. A bit impulsive, yes. "He said he didn't want affection." She believed that story as much as that tale he'd spun about the cats. "And if you must know, he kisses like the devil. I want him, and he wants me. It's horribly wrong of me. I can't stop thinking how wicked it is, how much of a risk, how it's not too late to back out and tell him I've changed my mind—"

"But you don't want to," Jeremy finished softly.

"There's that, and…" She ran her hands along the countertop, not sure how to express her other reason.

"You don't think he'll hurt you," Jeremy finished.

Miranda nodded. Impulsive girls with a taste for wicked men…well, it didn't always turn out so well for them. It wouldn't have made sense if she'd explained it to anyone else.

"Besides," Jeremy said, "I always thought you were more likely to be a mistress than a wife."

"Raised by actors," Miranda said, mock-mournfully. "My morals have never been what they should."

"No." Jeremy frowned at his hands. "You're happier when your relationships can be framed in terms of commerce. You never accept help from anyone."

"I'm not so bad as that!"

"As you say," Jeremy said, which was his way of disagreeing without arguing. "Is this going to get you away from the Patron?"

"With what he's paying me? It'll get me out for good. Me *and* Robbie."

Jeremy leaned toward her, his pale eyes intense. "Do it," he said. "Do it. Go. Get out."

"I won't be living in Temple Parish any longer. I...I might not ever come back."

Jeremy didn't flinch. "Well, don't look back at me."

Miranda had always known that Jeremy was a good friend. But she hadn't quite realized how good until now. She'd just told him that she might never see him again, and he'd told her to grab hold with both hands.

Footsteps sounded behind her. And then a gruff voice spoke. "What are you two whispering about?"

"Becoming a mi—" Jeremy stopped, and blushed red hot, as if suddenly realizing what he'd been about to disclose to his grandfather. "A muh," he sputtered. "A mah."

"A magistrate," Miranda filled in smoothly, turning to Old Blazer. "We're talking about how one becomes a magistrate."

Jeremy screwed up his face in a grimace and gave her a short shake of his head. But it was too late. Old Blazer's eyes snapped, and he thumped his fists onto the table in front of them.

"A magistrate!" Old Blazer said. "It takes nothing to become a magistrate but lily-livered idiocy, that's what. They don't do any good, magistrates. Do you know what they've done?"

She'd seen Old Blazer run off on a tirade before—usually about workmanship and machine-knit cloth. She'd not known he put magistrates in the same category.

"Yes," Jeremy was saying soothingly. "I know." He shrugged hopelessly at Miranda.

Old Blazer would not be calmed. "Back in '31, it was, when they sent that nasty piece of work Wetherell down for the Assizes. City broke out in riots. And what did the magistrates do, Jeremy?"

"Nothing, Old Blazer." Jeremy spoke like a child repeating a lesson learned long before.

"Quite right. They did nothing. They hid in their homes like rabbits. Didn't bother to muster the militia. Not even when the rioters broke open the gaol and let the criminals free. The whole thing went on for days. And then, because the bloody magistrates had let the whole thing explode beyond fixing, what had to happen?"

"They called in the dragoons," Jeremy intoned dutifully.

Old Blazer's eyes swept the room. "They called in the dragoons. Opened fire on innocent men. Killed quite a few. Including my son—your father." By now, Old Blazer was practically spitting with rage. "So don't talk to me about magistrates. Those useless bastards killed my boy." He drew a deep breath, and then another.

"Blazer," said a voice behind them, "are you fretting again?"

Miranda breathed a sigh of subtle relief as Mrs. Blasseur stepped out from the back room.

"You know it's not good for you." She took his arm and gently led him to the back.

Miranda could hear her humming, could hear Old Blazer's raspy protests, muffled by the curtain. Finally, Mrs. Blasseur came back through.

"I'm sorry, Mama," Jeremy said.

"It's my fault," Miranda added. "I didn't know it would set him off. Truly."

Mrs. Blasseur simply shook her head. "He's a strong man, Old Blazer. But the older he gets, the angrier he becomes. Sometimes, it simply can't all be contained."

"He's not unwell, is he?"

As if in counterpoint, the smell of pipe smoke drifted into the room.

Mrs. Blasseur rolled her eyes. "No. He'll be perfectly well in a few minutes. It's just better that he not fuss at the customers while he's in this state. He *does* take it personally."

"But his son died."

"My husband." Mrs. Blasseur sighed. "Jeremy's father. That's the way these things go. Only lawlessness and chaos can be born out of lawlessness and chaos. No point getting angry when it happens, no matter whom you might lose. All you can do is try to make things better. Old Blazer has yet to learn that." She reached for a pair of scissors, and began to cut up bits of foolscap with a vengeance. The little slips of paper would be adorned with prices, and pinned to goods.

"But so solemn a subject, and on such a gloomy day. Tell me, Miss Darling—what's this I hear about Robbie and a shipyard?"

There were some details one divulged to one's best friend's mother. And then, there were some things one lied about. Doubly true when one's friend's mother wanted one to marry her son.

"A friend of my father's was recently in town," Miranda said smoothly. "My father left me a little bit of money after all. We've used it to apprentice Robbie to a shipwright."

Mrs. Blasseur looked suitably impressed. "A lucky chance, there. Jeremy, isn't that lovely?"

"Yes, Mama." Jeremy didn't sound so dutiful, though, whatever his words. "It's wonderful for Robbie."

"It's so lovely that he'll not be spending his afternoons with those wretched boys," Mrs. Blasseur continued.

"Yes."

Was that *anger* in his voice? Anger, from even-keeled Jeremy?

"I'm always happy when someone escapes Temple Parish," Jeremy added stiffly. "This place kills."

As if to underscore that, Mrs. Blasseur coughed twice. Jeremy met Miranda's eyes, his gaze communicating what he did not need to say any longer.

Get out. Get out, if you can.

Chapter Eleven

AS IT TURNED OUT, Turner settled the details that very morning.

It was scarcely ten when a runner came by. Robbie was to report to the shipwright for his apprenticeship in a handful of hours. Miranda helped him pack his things, and hugged him good-bye. He harrumphed at this treatment, and pulled away. But before he left, he stopped in front of her.

"Miranda?"

"Yes?"

"I'll still see you on Sundays, won't I? You'll want me to come over?" His voice had grown so deep that it almost disguised the querulous note to his inquiry.

"I'd be miserable if you didn't," Miranda told him.

He turned away. "Huh," he said.

Miranda tugged on his elbow. "You know," she said, "I love you. If ever you need anything…"

"Sure." He shrugged, and then looked at her and straightened to the height of his not-quite-five-feet yet. "I'm going to be a shipwright. So, later, when you need something, I'll be the one to provide it."

There were a thousand things she wanted to say to him, as he took his satchel to the door. *Don't get in trouble. Don't drink gin. Try not to do anything stupid.*

Instead, she reached into her pocket and retrieved a handkerchief. "Here," she said, handing it over. "You forgot to pack one."

He rammed it into his pocket and then left with the courier. While she waited, Miranda piled her own things into the valise that the runner had brought. She finished packing before the courier returned; there wasn't much to take. But a scant hour later, she left her garret room for good.

The runner conducted her across the water, past the cathedral and up a slope. Halfway up the hill, he turned onto a street overshadowed by trees. The bare limbs moved slightly in a breeze that brought with it only the smell of fallen leaves—no sewage, no starch. A row of houses, several stories high, rose on one side of the street. On the other was a park and a large stone building.

She had no time to explore her environs before she was ushered into the house.

She'd imagined Turner would obtain something for her along the lines of his own residence—a few rooms, perhaps smaller. But this was a lavish affair. The entry opened on a wide staircase, spiraling up two stories. A housekeeper—she introduced herself as Mrs. Tiggard—greeted Miranda, and she presented a cook and a pair of maids. She'd scarcely had a chance to get an impression of richly-papered walls and dark polished wood in the entry, before she was whisked on a tour of the house: parlor, pantry, dining room, all on the ground floor; then, up a flight of stairs, a sitting room, a morning-room, and a library. On the floor above that there was a dressing room and several bedchambers. The largest had been furnished for her.

The bed had four solid posts, and was covered in ivory linen sheets and a heavy gold coverlet. It seemed far too large for one person—or, for that matter, for two. Tonight, he'd come to her. There. Her skin tingled. Oh, God. She was really going to do this.

Before she had a chance to think matters through, however, a dressmaker was announced, along with three assistants. They'd brought with them a handful of mostly-finished gowns. Satins and silks and fine merino wools in browns and greens and blues— terribly impractical attire if one were to go walking down Temple Street. She caught a glimpse of herself in the mirror as they tried them on her, pinning and basting in place. It was as if she were dressing up again as a lady. This time, the charade would last not for an afternoon, but for a month. This time, *she* was being paid to have the gowns, instead of paying for their use.

The dressmaker clucked at the light stays she was wearing, frowned at her chemise, and sent one of her assistants out with a list of items to be purchased.

She was pinned and measured and prodded; the assistants made adjustments, and no sooner was one dress fitted than it was whisked away and another put on in its place.

A brief respite was allowed for tea in the afternoon. Miranda took the opportunity to corner one of the maids and to ask her to obtain a few items for her bedchamber. She was about to manufacture an explanation for why she needed them—a perfectly reasonable explanation, of course—when the woman simply curtsied and left.

Apparently, she didn't need to explain herself any longer. She just needed to ask.

And her time away from the dressmaker didn't last long. No sooner had she drained her cup than one of the assistants returned, laden with packages. Her personal maid stripped her down to her skin, and everything was tried on to test the fit—fine linen shifts and drawers and petticoats, followed by knee-high silk stockings held in place with garter-ribbons. She caught another glimpse of herself in the mirror as they fastened the corset for her. The seamstress grumbled about the fit, but it seemed finer than any of the ill-fitting secondhand garments Miranda had ever tried.

She was surrounded by feminine bustle, but she could not help but dwell on the masculine. *He* was going to see her like this tonight. He'd see her in far less. Tonight, he'd be the one undoing those laces. She found herself flushing.

She wasn't finished, not even when the dressmaker departed for the evening. Miranda's maids drew her a bath. They scrubbed her hair with something soft and floral-smelling, and dumped warm water over her when she stood. Afterward, they wrapped her in thick, warm towels and dried her hair by the fire. She had almost drifted off to sleep before they intruded again, this time to dress her in a cream-and-green striped silk gown. The smooth fabric spilled over petticoats that swished when she walked. Her clothing seemed to belong to another woman.

No, she corrected herself. *Another man. Who was going to take it off—every last inch of it.*

The thought should have horrified her. Instead, it sent tendrils of heat sifting through her. When she sent her maids away, she pulled out the parcel she'd had them obtain. A bit of sea sponge, a bottle of vinegar, and some silk thread. The simplest of the prophylactics she knew. Somehow, readying herself in that final way brought home the fact that she stood on the verge of something irrevocable. His body would fit where her fingers dipped. That sponge, soaked in vinegar, was lodged inside her because he was going to have her.

She could scarcely wait.

A scratch sounded at her door. She jumped to her feet, patting her skirts back into place, and rushed to open it. The maid blinked in surprise when Miranda threw it open herself; apparently, that had been the wrong thing to do, too.

But all the maid said was, "Supper is ready."

Supper, when she'd had tea just three hours past? She could scarcely touch the soup or the meat pie or the roasted beetroot. The repast was whisked away, and Miranda was left alone in the library, with tea and a tray of small, delectable lemon cakes. They were too good not to eat, even though she was full beyond belief.

"I could grow used to this," she remarked aloud. The books had nothing to say in response.

Easy to grow used to something when she hadn't yet paid the price for any of it. Tonight, she'd have to surrender herself to him. If she'd had any proper sensibilities, she should have been trembling in fear. But it was distinctly not fear that had her thumbs pricking. She wandered from shelf to shelf, glancing at titles of books that she couldn't bring herself to read, and reliving the feel of his hands on her skin, his mouth on her. She couldn't feel the sponge inside her, but she was aware of its secret promise. *Tonight.* It was going to happen tonight.

Finally, the housemaid ducked in once more.

"Mr. Turner to see you," she said.

He stood behind the maid, and her heart stopped beating.

Miranda had been so engrossed in her thoughts that she'd not heard him arrive. He waved the maid away—she wondered, briefly, what the servants said amongst themselves about this arrangement—and leaned against the doorway. His eyes met hers, smoldering with barely suppressed intent.

"Everything to your liking?" he asked.

He was damnably handsome. He was tall and imposing, topping her by more than half a head. There was something sharp about his features, true, but he was saved from severeness by the small smile he gave her. Her gaze dropped to contemplate his long fingers. He'd stroked her with those; he was going to do it again.

She was going to know all of him, and by the way he looked at her, she was going to enjoy it. He was dressed in dark wool; his white shirt and a green silk waistcoat gleamed in contrast. His cravat was tied neatly.

There were no diamond stickpins, no cuff links made of precious stones. She'd known he was a duke's brother. But somehow, she'd not quite comprehended what that meant. He lived by himself in a tiny house. How was she to have expected this luxury? And what did it mean that he'd casually lodged her here and promised her a thousand pounds without even flinching?

It means he has more money than you can comprehend, she told herself fiercely. *It's his to spend as he wants. And if he's eccentric enough to want you to enjoy yourself, it's because he expects to enjoy you, too.*

Her whole body tensed at the thought. His eyes wandered down her form, newly clad in silk, and then up to the neckline of her dress. The corset they'd fit her into had shaped her body. It had given her bosom curves and definition that Miranda hadn't known she'd possessed. His eyes rested there, briefly, before returning to her face.

"Everything is lovely." She took a lemon cake off the tray beside her, and crossed the room to him. "Especially these. They're delicious." She held out the cake, feeling utterly brazen. "Try one."

Slowly, he slid his fingers around her hand. He brought it up to his mouth, and took the cake from her, his lips brushing her fingers.

He held her gaze as he chewed. Swallowed.

"Let's see if we can discover what else is to your liking." His hand tightened around hers and he drew her close, until she could smell the lemon on his breath. And then he dipped his head and kissed her.

He tasted of sweetness and citrus, but there was nothing sweet about his kiss. It was hard and demanding.

Oh, God. This really was going to happen. Tonight. This very hour. She'd not imagined he would be the sort to dilly-dally, but his kiss left no doubt. There would be no waiting. Her body sang with anticipation. Her hands clenched in his lapels, and she kissed him back.

He lifted his head. "I've been thinking of you all day." He twined his fingers in the sash of her gown with deliberate, possessive intent. "I've been thinking of this all day."

She swallowed. He drew her to him, leaving little doubt as to what he meant by *this*.

"Tell me, have you been thinking of anything else?"

She could feel the tense muscles of his arms beneath her hands. She shook her head. "No. It's all been you."

"Good."

There was no preamble. No small talk about the weather. Just the intense flare of satisfaction in his eyes, and then his mouth, hot and possessive, over hers. She should have known that he'd be direct about it. He wanted her, and he was going to have her. It was that simple.

It wasn't just the slide of his tongue against hers. It wasn't the way he pushed her against the wall, pressing the full length of his hard, slim body against hers. It wasn't even the way he took hold of her skirts, gathering them up in his hands until she felt the cool air against her ankles.

It was something about the way he held her. As if kissing her had become as vital as breath. As if he couldn't have stopped except by conscious effort—and then only for a short space of time. He had taken his time with their kisses before now—progressing slowly from kiss to caress, until she burned for more. But tonight he hiked her skirts to her knees and pushed her firmly against the wall.

It felt fabulous. It felt wonderful. He parted her legs, slid his fingers between them. Cool air touched her thighs, and then her waist. His hands followed in sure, steady strokes, outlining her knees, her hips. He set his thumb on the cleft between her legs. And when he sank into her warmth... She let out a breath of air that she hadn't realized she'd been holding. She was on fire for him.

"Oh. You're definitely ready for me," he murmured. "Miranda Darling, you'll forgive me this first time, won't you? I promise I'll make it up to you."

It was only when he reached for the placket of his breeches that she realized that if she said nothing, he'd be inside her in seconds.

She'd agreed to it. Her body thrummed for that completion.

And still... "Wait." She put her hands over his.

He stopped. His breathing labored. He had her against the wall, and his chest pressed against hers. His hand rose to tangle in her hair. "Wait," he gritted out. "You want me to wait. How long?"

"I—there's no good way to say it. You've obviously done this before. It's just...I haven't."

He let out a disbelieving puff of air. "You're a virgin?"

She nodded.

He had a handful of her skirts in his hand. He let them fall. "I wasn't expecting that. From a sheltered society debutante, perhaps. Or a manufacturer's daughter, raised to middle-class pretensions. But from a woman who told me she was raised by actors? No."

"You don't believe me."

He met her eyes. "There'd be little point in manufacturing such a story now."

"Does it...does it change anything?"

"It changes a great deal." He stepped back from her, and held out his hand.

A dark sort of horror filled her. "You...you're one of those men who doesn't debauch innocents, aren't you? If you'd known, you would have never entered into this arrangement." She swallowed hard. "For what it's worth, I don't consider myself very innocent."

He watched her intently.

"Also," she finished quietly, "I had rather looked forward to being debauched. By you." She set her hand in his.

His fingers closed around hers. "Let me explain what has changed: I want to have you very, very badly. But as this is your first time, I'll have you very well instead. It would hardly be in my best interest to put you off the activity for any length of time."

Her mouth went dry.

"Don't look so worried. I'll have you against a wall eventually." Her whole body flushed, and he gave her a sly smile. "For now..." He gave her a look. "For now, we do this right."

He pulled her hand, reeling her in until she was tangled up in his embrace. And then, without any warning, he hefted her in the air. He didn't seem to strain under her weight. Instead he left the library and started up the stairs.

What would the maids say if they saw them? But there were no servants about—they'd disappeared belowstairs, leaving him with her.

He paused midway between the floors. "I didn't worry you when I mentioned the wall, did I?"

"I've seen alleys enough near the Floating Harbour. I have some idea what can be done with a wall." The thought sent desire spiraling through her. She was almost giddy with the feel of his hands on her.

But he simply shook his head. "If your point of reference is a glimpse you've caught of a business transaction conducted in an alley, I'd venture that you have no idea what *I* can do with a wall."

Oh God. She almost wanted him to stop and show her. Instead she grinned up at him. "Are you boasting?"

He kicked open the door to the bedchamber. "I don't boast. I merely state facts." He walked her to her bed and tossed her on the gold coverlet, letting her fall in a puddle of her skirts. He slid behind her. She couldn't see him there, could only feel his hands around her. One rested against her belly. His lips breathed heat against her spine; his other hand undid the hooks at the back of her neck. He slid the sleeves down her shoulders, and then peeled the gown to her waist. He kissed the side of her neck.

"What do I do?" she asked.

"For now?" His voice rasped. "Whatever you wish." His hand slid up the fabric of her corset to cup the curve of her breast. The touch sent a stab of pleasure through her, and she gasped. His thumb circled, idly, and she made another noise.

"Enjoy that, do you?"

"Yes."

But he took his hands away. She could feel him tracing the eyelets of her corset behind her. And then he undid the knot and her laces loosened. She took a deep breath, and he slid the corset away to thumb her nipples through her shift. He held her from behind; she couldn't see him at all. But the absence of sight only heightened her anticipation. She didn't know where he might touch next, what he might do to her. She knew only that his arms were around her, that his hands thrummed her like some instrument. And like that instrument, he pulled breathy gasps from her. She could think of nothing but his touch, could want nothing but the fierceness of his desire. Her body felt soft all over—soft and ready. And damn him, he took nothing.

He moved away suddenly. Before she could protest, he'd pulled her upright, and eased her gown over her head. He undid her petticoats, and these joined her gown on the floor. She had on nothing but her chemise.

He stood. He kicked off his shoes, sent them to lie next to the heap of her gown. His coat followed, and then his waistcoat. He undid his cuffs, and then pulled his shirt over his head.

He looked slim in his clothing; when he was divested of those layers, she could see that it wasn't scrawniness, but lean muscle. But she had no time to think of it. He undid his trousers and slid them off alongside his small clothes—revealing a nest of dark hair, and jutting from that, his hard erection.

She'd never seen one so close. He looked up, met her eyes. He must have seen her curiosity, because his eyes narrowed and he gave her a short, swift smile. "Indeed," he said. He came to stand before her.

Miranda knew the mechanics of what was about to happen. She even had a good notion as to the naked male form. But knowledge could not compare to reality: the long, hard length of him, ending in a dark head, almost purple in color. Knowledge had not encompassed the feel of his skin, soft and hard at the same time. She set her hand against his thigh. The sparse black hair was coarse to the touch; muscle rippled beneath her palm.

He didn't say anything, didn't move. He simply allowed her to explore him with her touch. She traced her hand down to his knee, and then up to his hips. And then, before her courage failed her, she ran her fingers down the length of his erection. His cock was firm under her questing fingers. Firm and hot. She brushed the head and he hissed, his member twitching in her hands.

This was going inside her. She already ached for it, a deep throbbing want. And by the way he set his teeth as she stroked down that hard length, he ached for it, too.

One didn't live in a traveling troupe of players without learning *something* about men. She leaned forward and placed a kiss on the tip. His hands fell on her shoulders, but he didn't say anything. Encouraged, she licked him. His fingers bit into her, and he gave a small growl.

She took the tip of his erection in her mouth. He tasted of mild soap, and he pushed his hips forward. Her tongue traced him, touched the slit at the head of his penis. If she'd had any sense at all, she'd have been horrified at her boldness. She should have been frightened: he'd paid for this home and her gowns and even her body. He could do anything to her, and nobody would gainsay him. But in that moment, she felt as if she had taken ownership of him. It didn't matter that he'd bought her; she'd taken herself back.

His cock hardened even more under her ministrations, grew longer and thicker and warmer. The knowledge that she was doing that to him only increased her own want.

He pulled away when she moaned around him. He said nothing. But he simply reached down and lifted her to her feet. In one smooth motion, he pulled off her chemise, and then he pushed her back onto the bed.

Now. He was going to have her now. But even though he got on top of her—even though his chest brushed hers, and his hard erection nestled against her hip—he didn't push inside her. Instead, he kissed her. His tongue darted into her mouth, more urgent than ever. He rocked her body with his, setting an insistent rhythm. It ought to have soothed her. Instead, it made her clench her eyes shut.

"More," she told him. It was the first word either one of them had said, and he lifted his head and gave her a wicked smile.

"Like this?" he asked, and leaned over and brushed his mouth against the tip of her nipple. A warm rush of pleasure shot through her, and Miranda gasped. This was new, but she'd lost all sense of shyness. She simply arched into him. She pushed up, hard, feeling his tongue circle her.

"More," she demanded.

His hand crept between her legs. And oh, it felt so good when his fingers brushed her sensitive flesh. So good when he drew a tight circle there. So much so that when he withdrew—but no, she wasn't letting him withdraw. She reached down and took hold of his hand, pressing it back into place.

He dipped one finger inside of her, and the sensation transformed from exquisite to almost unbearable. She needed *that*. Precisely that, but...

"More," she said. She rose to meet him, but even though it sent pleasure shooting down her limbs, it wasn't enough.

It took her a moment to realize what she wanted. Not his hand. Not his mouth. *Him*. His whole body, pressing into hers. His cock, hard and thick, sliding inside her. *This* was what it meant to be ready—not just that her body was slick for him, but that she would lose her mind if he didn't take her. She pushed his hand away and met his eyes.

"Now," she said. "Don't make me wait, Turner. *Now.*"

He gave her a fierce smile, as if he'd been waiting for only that. He adjusted himself against her. The hard ridge of his member pushed against her most private parts. He moved again, and it sent a delicious friction where they joined. It was so, so good to feel him, hard and thick, right where she wanted him most. Almost.

He made a scalded sound. She arched up into him. And like that, he slid into her.

It didn't feel good. It stung, a hard pinch that stole her breath away. He tensed above her, holding still.

"Is that acceptable?" His hand came up to the side of her face. He stroked down her cheek, finding a little tendril of hair. Not hard and demanding, like his member inside her, but soft. Sweet. Almost…affectionate, and he'd said that wouldn't happen.

She shook her head. He was such a rotten liar.

"It's all right." She moved underneath him. "It's…it's actually getting better."

"Good." His voice was hoarse. "Now let's try this." He took one of her legs and wrapped it about his hip. Just that little movement shifted him deeper inside her, so deep that his groin met hers. And then he withdrew.

She'd understood what was to happen. One couldn't grow up with actors and retain any degree of innocence. But she hadn't known it would feel so *good,* hadn't known that when he slid his hands under her bottom and angled her up, that change in elevation would send him sliding inside her in a way that made her shudder. She hadn't understood how powerful it could be to clasp him tight with her inner muscles and hear him gasp, to run her hands down his chest and feel his thrusts grow tighter, more controlled.

She hadn't realized he would touch the deepest part of her, that he would slide up on his forearms and touch *her* between her legs. She hadn't known that his fingers could make a counterpoint to his thrusts. She threw her head back and reached for his hips. Something vital coiled up inside her just as his thrusts grew more insistent. Her body was just as demanding. More. Harder. She could think of nothing but the pleasure of their joining. The sheer perfection of it had her digging her nails into his backside. Her inner muscles clamped around him hard—and then she cried out.

No words. There were no words she could use.

The pleasure passed through her like a wave, crashing over her head and tumbling her over and over until she couldn't tell up from down, couldn't draw breath. She was only vaguely aware when it spat her out, her legs clamped around his hips.

"Oh, my." She smiled up at him in a haze. He was panting, his hair wet with his exertions. She'd known it could be good. But she hadn't known it could be *that* good. Oh, *God*. She was going to get a month of this, and he was paying her for it? She wanted to laugh. She wanted to kiss him.

She did both. "Now what happens?" she asked.

His forearms tensed and he gave her a grim smile. "Now it's my turn," he said. He started moving again. The rhythm that had seemed powerful before, rocking her into ecstasy, became harder, more savage—like a drumbeat counting out its strokes against her body. His hands clenched on her hips, pulling her to him. He thrust inside her, hard and powerful.

It was different than before. He'd been holding back. The pace he set this time was as demanding as he was, a relentless master that insisted on more from her. More, when she was convinced she'd given him her last breath. Still, his every stroke sent pleasure rippling through her. He grew harder inside her, hotter. And when he finally pounded into her, she gasped as pleasure overtook her once more.

His hands tangled in her hair. The pads of his fingers were rough against her cheeks; his nose nuzzled the side of her face. He breathed against her neck.

"My God, Miranda," he whispered. "God." His fingers brushed through her hair, the movement almost wistful. As if for the first time that evening, he was unsure of his reception. Foolish of him, of course, when they'd just shared *that*.

She reached up and laid her hand against his face.

He froze.

Slowly she let her fingers trail down his cheek in a slow caress, saying with her fingertips what she was almost afraid to whisper aloud.

I care for you.

But something was wrong. Horribly wrong. He'd not relaxed against her, as she'd hoped. Instead, he pushed himself up on his forearms. His every muscle had tensed.

"What the devil are you doing?" There was no warmth in his words. She didn't know where that uncertain affection had gone, but it had vanished in an instant.

Her hand faltered against his cheek. Still, she pressed on. "What do you suppose?" She dropped her voice to a sultry whisper. "I'm caressing you."

He wrapped his wrist around her hand and pushed it into the mattress. His fingers bit into her—not ungentle, but so changed from the way he'd touched her before that she looked up at him in confusion.

"We agreed I wasn't paying you for that." His voice had gone hard.

For a second, Miranda almost doubted her judgment. He'd never *said* he cared for her. He'd never claimed to be kind. In fact, he'd insisted on almost the opposite. She'd presumed to know better, on the basis of evidence that was beginning to seem a bit thin in the face of his fierceness. He'd as much as said it was an act of commerce. Maybe…

But no. She was sure of this. She was sure of *him,* him and his lemon cakes and the cats that he'd fed in the alleyway. "We agreed that you couldn't buy my affection. But that's only because…" She choked. He'd offered her so much; she'd wanted to hold something back. Something valuable and precious, so she'd have something… She looked up at him. "I wanted to give it to you. As a gift."

He didn't release her hand. His chest heaved above her. She was beginning to feel trapped underneath him. Then he disengaged himself from her and pushed off.

"I told you." His voice was as cold as steel in winter. "I'm not looking for affection. Damn it." He started to sort through the pile of their clothing.

"I don't believe you. Everyone wants—"

"I don't." Fabric rustled. "I told you already, and I meant it. That is the last thing I wanted from you."

A slap on the face would have hurt less. She suddenly felt young and painfully inexperienced. He *was* older. How many women had he had? How foolish she was, to think that just because they'd shared that, it had meant something.

She should have known better. She sat up and brought her knees to her chest. He pulled on his trousers and then his shirt.

"That," he continued haughtily, "was not what I wanted from you at all."

She had agreed to an entire month of this. Those days seemed to stretch in front of her like an endless burden. She leaned her forehead against her knees and listened to him dress. She'd thought he would spend the night. She'd thought she was getting a lover, not a...not a *procurer*.

"Next time, then, I'll make sure to conform to your expectations, Your Worship."

He sighed, and wood scraped against the floor. The bed felt suddenly cold, no matter the softness of the coverlet that she pulled around her. It no longer seemed a soft, sensual place, this bed, a place to be wooed and won. It seemed a prison of linen and wool. And she'd agreed to it.

She was aware of all her muscles—the deep, strange soreness, pulsing inside of her. Her body seemed to stretch out in satisfied lassitude.

She'd had intercourse with him, and now she couldn't even remember why it had seemed so beautiful. She'd made a mistake, a dreadful mistake.

She bit her lip, but a tear escaped anyway. She turned away so he wouldn't see it trace down her cheek. She willed herself not to sniff. She wouldn't give him that satisfaction.

Fabric rustled again, and his steps neared her. His hand fell on her shoulder. "Miranda..."

She lifted her head haughtily. "I don't believe I'm paying you for affection, either." She was proud that her voice didn't waver once.

His hand fell away. "Very well, then." He turned and left.

The click of his shoes against the floor made a cruel sound. He shut the door behind him. She could hear him descending the stairs.

He'd been quite clear as to his expectations. She'd made up the rest herself—told herself a fairy tale of affection, based on evidence that now seemed utterly scanty. Attila the Hun probably liked cats. Attila the Hun could probably laugh at a woman's jokes, up until he'd had his turn at her.

And Turner wanted that from her again—forty-something more times. Forty more times, she'd have to welcome him inside her, pretend that nothing was wrong. She didn't even want to *look* at him right now. She wanted to screw her eyes shut and avoid everything.

She'd wanted *him,* and he'd only wanted to slake his lust. But she couldn't call him a liar. She had lied to herself. She'd been so eager to give herself to him that she'd invented affection out of what was merely physical passion. She'd been rapturously silly about everything about him. He just wanted her body.

She curled into a little ball on the bed. The sheets still smelled like him. And even if she rang the bell and demanded that her housekeeper change the linen, it wouldn't alter the dreadful truth.

He'd purchased everything in this house. Including her.

"Remember this," she said aloud into the night. The tears began to come then—not just for him, nor for her misplaced affection, but for the lonely month ahead of her.

She'd thought this would mean something. And it did: it meant a thousand pounds and cold sheets.

Chapter Twelve

"MIRANDA."

She opened her eyes. It was not yet morning. Little crystals of salt clung to her eyelashes, the remnants of last night's emotional outburst. She looked around her blearily, the world fuzzy and black in her first blinking awakening.

"Miranda." The voice came again. Turner was sitting next to her on the bed. His form was a dark, warm silhouette. He must have seen her turn her head, because he took something from his pocket and set it on the bedside table next to her.

A watch.

It was early morning, and the memory of the last evening swept over her like a breath of cold air.

He'd had her. He'd hurt her. And now he wanted to do it again. Miranda clutched her rumpled chemise to her. If there could be anything less romantic than awakening to this, she didn't know. When he'd talked in the churchyard about having her forty times, it had seemed utterly thrilling. Right now, doing it even once more would chafe.

He must have sensed that something was wrong, because he leaned over and took her hand. She sat up, groggily. Before she quite understood what was happening, he wrapped her fingers around something, holding it in place until she was awake enough to understand that it was a clay mug, warm, and filled three-quarters with a hot liquid.

She took a sip. It was warm, spiced milk. The gesture confused her. If he didn't want her affection, why bother with such trivialities?

"Turner?" She managed to keep the quaver from the word.

"Last night ended badly." His voice was quiet and sharp. "I didn't say what I should have. You took me quite by surprise."

She took another sip. It heated her.

"I told you when we entered this arrangement that I didn't want your affection, but I don't believe I told you what I wanted you for."

Her eyes shut. "No need to belabor the point. You've made your intentions perfectly clear."

"No. If you'd understood, you'd not have cried yourself to sleep." He paused, cleared his throat, and she felt a stab of embarrassment that he'd understood that. It was monstrously unfair that she'd given him everything, and he'd stolen her vulnerability, too.

"Let me tell you what I want you for, so that we are not laboring under any misapprehensions."

"Intercourse," she said.

He set his hand over her lips. "Let me finish, before you start scrapping at me. You don't let me frighten you. You're not afraid to disagree with me. From the first, you made me feel warm in a world where I often feel alone. I've reposed confidences in you that I've scarcely told another soul. And if you must know why I want you near, it's because I don't like to think of you too far away."

She let out a gasp. There was nothing to say to that. She simply sat up and clutched the mug to her chest, trying to make out his expression in the predawn light.

"I like you," he said. "I like you very well. I don't think I've ever been as desperate for a woman—for all of a woman, not just her body—as I am for you. And that, I suppose, is what I should have told you."

She simply stared at him, wondering if this was a dream. If she'd invented this to comfort herself in the middle of the night. But when she pinched herself, she didn't wake.

"My God," she said into that silence. "You *are* direct."

"I did not want there to be any chance of your misunderstanding me. And after last night, I very much feared you had."

She contemplated his silhouette. "No," she said. "I do not think I misunderstood what happened last night. I offered you a little affection, and you stormed off into the night. You can't come back and ply me with hot milk and compliments and expect me to understand. Your explanation does not make sense."

"Indeed," he said. "There is one other thing. It is a little thing that perhaps I should have mentioned before now." He sat back and folded his arms.

She waited. She waited a very long time, before she realized he was not cold, but uneasy.

"Don't touch my face," he said.

She waited even longer. She could hear his watch ticking steadily away, until finally he spoke again.

"You recall my mother locked me in the cellar," he said. "And it flooded. When the waters were at their worst, she came back. I was huddled on the ladder. The waters had stolen all the warmth from me, and my eyes had seen nothing but darkness for days. I was almost blinded when she opened the cellar door."

Miranda set her mug on the bedside table.

"She reached for me. I thought she'd come to her senses. She said, 'Oh, my poor, beautiful boy.' And she smoothed my hair back."

His breathing had become harsher.

"I had almost no strength in my grip, but I took her arm. She leaned down and stroked my face with her other hand. I wasn't holding on to anything except her; I was scarcely keeping myself upright on the ladder. And then..." He took a deep breath. "And then," he said, his voice getting harder, "she pushed me into the water. It came up over my head, and for a second I didn't think I'd have the strength to kick my way to the surface. When I did, she was gone.

"She hadn't come to save me. She'd come to say farewell. Since then, I can't bear to have my face touched. Everything else, I can manage. When you touched my face, it brought me back to that moment. Vividly. Never mind that it was decades in the past."

Oh, she was dreaming this. This kind of thing didn't happen to brothers of dukes.

"Don't." He set his hand over hers. "Don't feel sorry for me. Just accept my apology. And...don't touch my face."

It was awful. She wanted to touch his face *now*, to hold him against her and let him know that he was safe. What a horrible mess.

Instead, she simply let out her breath. "You should have told me that before we started. It would have saved us both a bit of grief."

"So noted." Another pause. "Although I believe that if I had simply forbidden it, like Bluebeard, you'd have given it a try. Besides, you fed me that line about not giving me affection. I thought I was quite safe."

Safe, because he'd thought nobody cared for him? She felt a lump in her throat. She didn't think he would appreciate the observation, though.

She let out a breath. "Is there anything else I ought to know?"

He sighed. "I'm sure there is. I've been by myself for so long, I forget these little things until they crop up. I've been told I'm not the easiest individual to care for."

"And who told you that? A former mistress?"

"My brother. Mark." He twined his hand with hers. "There is no former mistress, Miranda Darling. There have been affairs, mind, but they never lasted long. Usually, she decides I'm stoic and cold only because I have been unlucky in love. She thinks she'll be the one to melt through my defenses. She thinks that she can fix everything that is wrong with me by simply weeping over me. It lasts until she realizes I won't spend the night, she can't touch my face, and I despise women who weep for no reason. I have no tolerance for maudlin affection, and less for women who want to fix me."

"Fix you?" Miranda said. "Why would anyone need to fix you? You're not broken."

"That's precisely what I've always said." He slid down to lie next to her. "Oddly, few people ever believe me."

"I know what broken is," Miranda said. "My father was broken, after my mother died. He just stopped working. He wouldn't sleep. Wouldn't eat. Wouldn't even get out of bed. He just lay there and cried."

"Good heavens. How long did it last?"

"Three years."

"Three…three years." He shifted to face her. "Three years."

"I told you I know what broken is. That is broken—staring at the wall and weeping, while creditors hammer on the door and your troupe slowly slips away, stealing the best costumes in lieu of wages. When your friends leave you and you still cannot move, and nothing your daughter says can break you out of the spell. No man is broken because bad things happen to him. He's broken because he doesn't keep going after those things happen. When you told me about your mother, and how it made you resolve to be the person you are… What I thought was, 'Yes, please, I'll take *him.'* Because you didn't break."

There was a pause. He propped himself up on one elbow and then picked up the watch he'd left on the bedside table.

"Would you know," he said, his tone a bit more businesslike, "this conversation has officially exceeded my daily quota for mawkish sentimentality. That's it, then."

"Quota?" she said. "What are you talking about?"

"My sentimentality quota. There's a limit as to how much sentiment I will tolerate in a day. I've just reached it."

"It's not—" she glanced at the watch in his hands "—not yet three in the morning. And this is…a special occasion."

"Nevertheless, we're done. As much as my pride loves to be puffed up, I'd appreciate it if you could refrain from further compliments. And definitely no protestations of love—that would put me off for a good long while."

She might have argued. But then…a man who thought of drowning when a woman caressed his face might have reason to shy from sentiment.

This month no longer seemed dreadful. But it was not going to be simple, either. There was nothing easy about Turner. He'd fashioned himself into one hard edge. He was all blade and no handle. If she held him close, she'd risk being cut.

If she wanted proof that he cared for her, she knew how difficult he'd found this conversation. The surprise was not that he'd needed to end it; it was that he'd started to talk in the first place.

"I do have one question," she said.

"I'm sure it's more than one."

"When you call me Miranda Darling, are you calling me Miranda Darling as my name, or are you saying Miranda, comma, darling?"

His hand slid down her hair. "I don't believe I can answer that question without endangering the sentimentality quota beyond all hope of repair."

Which was, in its own way, an answer. A good answer. Miranda smiled, feeling suddenly giddy. He didn't have to say it for her to know it was true. He might not admit to being kind to cats, but if he fed them and petted them and smiled when they purred, she could trust in the strength of her own conclusions.

"Have it your way, then," she said airily. "I'm profoundly grateful that your skills in bed are passable. I'll enjoy spending your money, Smite."

"You know I hate that name."

"I do. I figured I'd best call you by it, to make sure we didn't risk your quota. Otherwise I might have to invent a pet name for you, and we should be finished with each other before the day even started."

He leaned into her. His mouth brushed hers in a kiss, startling in its sweetness.

"Ah. Miranda-no-comma-Darling," he said, "I knew there was a reason I wanted you to fill my days with an absence of sentiment. Thank you."

Chapter Thirteen

SMITE SHOULD HAVE SENT a gift instead.

The thought occurred to him only after he'd entered Miranda's home. It was half past four, almost dark. Scarcely a day had passed since he'd installed her in this house, and already he found himself far out of his depths.

He'd left in a panic last night, scarcely able to suppress his reaction. But when he'd awoken later, it hadn't been a nightmare that roused him, but a memory. He'd remembered that half-choke in her voice when he'd walked away. And he'd wanted to make it better.

The usual etiquette, when one offended one's mistress, was that one sent over some glittering bauble. If he'd been accustomed to this sort of affair, he'd have arranged for that. Instead, he'd risked real intimacy.

The warm, polished entry of Miranda's home smelled of some savory roast. The furniture in the parlor was soft and comfortable. It seemed a beguilement: a promise that he, too, might have these luxuries. Food. Warmth. Companionship.

The only companion he'd had over the last few years was his dog. Dogs didn't feel pity. Dogs didn't make plans to fix one, except by repeated application of tongue to face. No matter how much weakness one showed a dog, it still depended on you for food and exercise. As if to emphasize that, Ghost sat in the entry next to Smite, and looked up at him.

He'd let himself believe that he might share an easy affair with Miranda, one that didn't engage his emotions. Perhaps he'd convinced himself that she'd be so grateful for the largesse he'd thrown her way that she wouldn't ask any questions.

Any hope of that had gone up in smoke the instant she'd fed him the cake. There was nothing easy about any of this. One night, and she'd wormed her way beneath his skin.

Her tread sounded on the stairs overhead. He'd betrayed too much of himself to her already. She would—

For a second, he had a moment of melting panic. Then she came round the bend in the staircase and saw him standing there. He was *dithering,* and damn it, he hated dithering.

She broke into a smile at the sight of him.

Oh. Hell. He felt all tangled inside. She was wearing a blue-green satin. The sleeves of her gown scarcely skimmed her shoulders.

There'd been too many shared confidences between them. He scarcely knew how to greet a woman who knew so much of him.

"Turner," she said. She descended the last few stairs to him, holding out her hands.

He turned abruptly from her. He took off his greatcoat and handed it to the maid who had materialized at his side. She disappeared, leaving them intimately—awkwardly—alone.

When he turned around, she set her hand on her hip. She gave him a rueful glance, and contemplated him with lips pressed together.

Smite looked away from her. "If you don't mind, I'd like to let Ghost loose."

"Please."

He leaned down and fumbled with the lead. The knot wasn't difficult, but he lingered over it. From the corner of his vision he could see her hands, encased in delicate lace gloves. They clenched once and then relaxed. Once Ghost was freed, he walked about the entry, sniffed idly at Miranda, and then curled up on the floor where he could keep an eye on his master.

She watched him. "Would you care for supper," she asked, "or..."

"Or would I prefer to slake another appetite?"

She colored at that.

"Are you sore?" he asked bluntly.

That pink flush grew until it encompassed the skin of her neck. "I...I could manage. If you wanted."

"There's no need to be so damned solicitous of me." He reached up and loosened his cravat. "You sound as if you have to do everything I wish."

"Isn't—" She paused, shook her head. "I had rather assumed that's what you were paying me to do."

"Yes," Smite said. "You've nailed it precisely. I wanted you for your docile nature."

He remembered too late that she might not be used to his peculiar brand of sarcasm. But Miranda, thankfully, gave him a canny smile.

"I care about what you want," he said awkwardly.

"Then come here and greet me properly." She curled her index finger at him.

He drifted over to stand before her. She watched him with a little smile on her face, and he found himself leaning into her, setting his palm against her face. She smelt of something subtly sweet and calming—mint, maybe, or chamomile. His tangled insides unclenched.

Oh, hell. This was bad—worse than lust, worse than intimacy. He'd missed her. He wasn't used to missing anyone.

But he traced his fingertips down her cheekbone, followed the curve of her jaw until he touched her chin. He tipped up her face to his, and then he kissed her.

Her lips were soft and welcoming. Kissing was *different* with real intimacy present. He didn't have to think about where she was putting her hands; he knew she'd not touch his face. He could lose himself completely in the taste of her, the scent of her. The feel of her body, melting into his.

It was the first time he'd kissed a woman without feeling wary.

And then her stomach growled. He pulled away.

"I'm starving," she said apologetically. "There's roast pheasant. I've been smelling it the entire afternoon. Did you know I've never had pheasant?"

"Good. We'll eat, then."

Her cheeks pinked. "I asked them to lay the covers in the bedchamber. It's not the usual arrangement, but—"

"Usual arrangement." He met her eyes. "I don't have usual arrangements, Miranda. I just have you."

If she heard what he'd betrayed there, she let no sign of it show. Instead, she took his arm and they walked slowly up the stairs.

A small table before the window had been set for an intimate meal. From this high, they had an extraordinary view of the city. Evening was coming, and Bristol was doused in the hard reds and dusky pinks of sunset. Streetlamps sprang to life like glowing jewels. At the base of the hill, the graceful arches of the Bristol Cathedral were scarcely visible. Beyond it, a forest of masts from the Floating Harbour disappeared into the oncoming gloom.

He seated Miranda, and then sank into the chair across from hers. Cucumber soup came first. She chattered away about her day, asked him questions about his. She knew what spoon to reach for.

After they'd exchanged a few sentences and the soup had been cleared, he set his hand atop hers. "You didn't grow up in the bad part of Bristol," he remarked.

She slanted a glance at him.

"In fact," he continued, "I'm not sure you were raised in the bad part of anywhere. The finishing-school accent is quite convincing. I would say you have a hint of Oxford in your tone. And your manners are flawless."

"I should be convincing," she said. "I've been practicing since I was a child." She put a bite of pheasant into her mouth and closed her eyes.

"Good?"

She chewed thoughtfully and then swallowed. "It tastes like chicken. I feel disappointed."

He tried again. "So you were raised in a family that spoke the King's English and used proper etiquette. Just like me. How did you end up alone in Bristol?"

As he spoke, he took a small plate from the table and filled it with scraps of pheasant. She made no comment when he set this on the floor for Ghost.

"My parents were always terribly busy. During the day, they handed off care of me to the rest of the troupe. Everyone had a hand in my upbringing, but I was mostly raised by Jasper and Jonas. Jasper was from Yorkshire, and he was our lead actor. He was very handsome, very debonair and very good with accents. The ladies were constantly showering him with flowers. He taught me to read so that I could help him practice his lines."

"I can't believe a Yorkshire man taught you your accent."

"No. That was Jonas. Jonas was… He wasn't an actor, actually. He helped us put together our scenery, moved heavy boxes, that sort of thing." She frowned, and chewed more pheasant. "He also argued with Papa about what the plays really meant."

"Your porter taught you your accent?"

"Jonas wasn't a porter." Miranda had a dreamy little smile on her face. She looked up and away, as if recalling that happy time. "It happened before I was born, but Jonas used to be a fellow at Oxford before he ran off with my father's troupe. I gather it was quite the scandal. His family disowned him. He used to study classics. In any event, *he* taught me how to speak this way."

"You had an Oxford fellow moving your scenery?" Smite asked in disbelief. "Wait—you cannot mean *Jonas Standish?*"

Her eyes widened. "You know him?"

"By reputation only. He was well before my time. Jonas Standish," he repeated, feeling slightly dazed. "But he's brilliant. I saw some of his work when I was there. No wonder you've heard of *Antigone*. I can't believe he walked away from everything to join a traveling troupe. Your father must have been quite persuasive."

"Not my father," Miranda replied. "They quarreled over everything. My father only tolerated him because Jasper would have walked off, had he sent Jonas on his way. I followed Jasper and Jonas everywhere from the moment I could walk. They taught me half the accents I know how to do."

"Did Jonas also teach you proper deportment?"

Miranda shook her head. "That was Mama. She said if anything ever happened to her, I'd need to take her place. She and my father had this act they would put on whenever there was a disagreement with anyone outside the troupe. He would bluster and shout about aesthetics; she would timidly explain that my father was a temperamental man of art, and couldn't be made to see reason. So perhaps the theater owner would just consider a small, tiny alteration…?"

"Putting on an act—that worked well, did it?"

She must not have heard the hint of disapproval in his voice, because she grinned. "Like a charm. They would laugh and toast each other with cheap wine every time they succeeded."

He might have criticized, but her eyes were alight, and he couldn't bring himself to do it. "You had a happy childhood," he remarked instead. He couldn't imagine what that would be like.

"I'm sure someone could point out the many imperfections of my childhood, but I loved it. I loved it all."

In fact, her eyes seemed suspiciously bright. He remembered what she'd told him last night about her father. "So when the troupe fell apart, you lost everyone. Not just your mother."

"Yes," she said softly. And then after a pause, "Well, no. Jasper and Jonas had already left a few years back. Father found a patron, and so we'd been in London for a good space of time, see." She looked to the window, dark as it was. "They didn't like staying in one place too long. People talked. The last I'd heard, they were in Bristol. It's why I came here with Robbie—I'd been hoping to find the two of them. But they'd moved on, and I've never had the means to search them out."

He'd never wondered why she was alone with Robbie. Perhaps he should have. But he was so solitary by nature; it often slipped his mind that others naturally were not.

"Besides," she continued, "Robbie was ship-mad. And when I thought of him crawling about some mine in Yorkshire..." She shook her head. "But enough of me. Tell me more of you."

"I've talked of myself enough for today." He gave her his most repressive cold glance.

His most repressive cold glance bounced ineffectually off her sunny smile. She helped herself to a second serving of carrots and said, "No, you haven't. Tell me about your brothers. There are three of you in your family, are there not?"

Four.

But he didn't correct her. "Ash," he said. "The eldest. He's a damned nuisance." But he could feel himself smiling despite his words. "I would say that he's like Midas, turning every enterprise he touches to gold, but it's not that. He's just one of those men that brings out the best in everyone."

"Everyone except—I am guessing—you." Miranda took a bite of carrots.

"Except me. I *am* his brother, after all. He went to India at the age of fourteen. Five years later, he returned, conversant in several languages and with a fortune in the thousands of pounds. Which has only grown since. He has some of the most incredible stories."

He shook his head. "Then there's Mark, my younger brother. For a while, he was the most popular fellow in all of London. He wrote a book, for which the Queen knighted him."

"Mark Turner," she said. "Sir Mark is your brother?"

Smite gave her a repressive nod.

"Sir Mark of the *Practical Gentleman's Guide to Chastity?*"

"Yes," he growled.

"Oh, you do have disagreements with him, then."

"No. We are in perfect accord." He glanced at her. "Mostly because my letters to him have made no mention of you."

In any event, he suspected that even Mark might thank the Lord if he found out about Miranda. *You're too solitary,* Mark had said a few months ago. Smite shook his head.

What he said instead was, "Mark makes no mention of my affairs. I believe he harbors hopes that one day I'll fall in love. Always the damned optimist."

The tiniest intake of breath across the table betrayed what Miranda thought of that disclosure.

She held the fork too tightly and didn't look him in the eye. If she'd burst into tears or leveled accusations, it would only have annoyed him. But her stoic acceptance of his cavalier words—that he was never going to love her—befuddled him more than any overt emotional display.

But Smite suffered from no illusions about himself. It was best that she avoid them, too.

He chose his next words carefully. "I suspect he thinks that the cure for all my troubles is the love of a good woman."

She speared a piece of turnip, none too gently.

Smite continued. "He thinks that I need only meet The One, and all my little foibles will be cast aside, healed by the magic of her pearly white hands."

"I don't believe in magic," Miranda said. But her gaze cut away from his.

For all the faults of her upbringing, she'd grown up around love. She'd spoken of a sunny, effervescent companionability that he could never give her.

He couldn't bring himself to smile. "As you may recall, I'm already married to Lady Justice. There's little room in my life for anything else."

Her lips pressed whitely together. But she lifted her gaze to his and gave him a nod of understanding. "So I'm just your bit o' muslin on the side."

"Yes." And she was: a departure from duty, a holiday from his responsibilities. He was cheating on sobriety with her. The thought should have filled him with horror.

One month of companionship. One month of warmth. One month of her smiles. A one-month vacation from the coldness of his solitary existence. That was all he could let her be to him. Any longer than that, and he'd never give her up.

"Well, then," she said, extending her hand. Her smile was brilliant and harshly beautiful. "I'd best make use of you while I still can."

THE NEXT DAY, SMITE did, in fact, send a gift.

It wasn't emeralds. It wasn't pearls. It wasn't any sort of jewelry—just a few sheets of paper, folded, and his note scrawled across the bottom: *I'm sorry.*

After what that report indicated, sending jewelry would be a travesty.

When he entered her home a few hours after he'd sent that message, he didn't know what to expect. But what he heard surprised him: voices drifted from the parlor in the back. Their murmur made a gentle, reverent noise. He walked back and peered into the room.

Miranda sat on the sofa next to another man. The fellow was handsome and young—close in age to Miranda, Smite would have guessed, although he looked youthful to Smite's eye. Miranda was holding his hands.

If Smite had happened on her cuddling with another man on any other day, he might have reacted differently. But then, he knew what he'd sent her about George Patten, and it didn't take much to tell that Miranda wasn't flirting with another man. She was in need of comfort.

Nothing wrong with that. Still, his hand formed an involuntary fist at his side.

"I can't believe it," the man was saying. "I just can't believe it. I can't bring myself to believe that this is true."

"Oh, Jeremy." She rubbed his arm. "I know it's hard to comprehend."

"Impossible." The other man—Jeremy—pulled his hands from hers and shook them out. "It's impossible to comprehend, not *hard*. George is out there somewhere. And maybe we don't know where he is, but I refuse to believe that he could have died in so senseless a fashion." His gaze was trained inward; his eyes rested on some far-off point. "Miranda," he said slowly, "am I a terrible person if I refuse to honor my mother's dying wishes?"

Miranda did not seem to think this last question a complete non sequitur. "What, because you're thinking of George instead of contemplating marriage?"

The other man folded his arms about himself. "What she wants me to do is utterly foreign to my character." And then his voice did crack. "Oh, George. What am I going to do? It's my fault. I did this to him."

"It's nobody's fault. You can't blame yourself. It could have happened to anyone." She leaned toward him.

Jeremy made a rude noise. "The man who claimed to know what transpired said that George took a knife to the gut the night before his release. But no body was ever found, and the murder was not reported in any of the official proceedings." Jeremy shook his head. "If you think that could happen to anyone, you are sorely mistaken."

Smite had harbored similar doubts about the matter.

But Miranda reached out. "A fight in gaol. A gaoler who didn't want to admit he'd been remiss in his duties, and so hid the matter. George was in the wrong place at the wrong time."

Jeremy shook his head, and Miranda didn't say anything in response. Instead, she looked up—and as she did so, she caught sight of Smite, standing in the doorway of the room. She didn't startle. She didn't let go of her friend.

Smite knew damned well that nothing untoward was happening.

He was an ass. Not because he believed she had been unfaithful; there was no hint of lust in their embrace. Besides, Miranda had been anything but casual about their lovemaking. No; he was jealous for the most petty of reasons. He envied their rapport, their intimacy. He wanted her to turn to him for support, not this other fellow.

He was being fist-clenchingly irrational.

"Jeremy," Miranda said slowly. "I ought to introduce you to someone."

Jeremy looked up. He took in Smite, and his eyes widened.

Beside him, Miranda was still speaking. "Jeremy Blasseur, this is Smite Turner. Turner, this is Jeremy—he's one of my best friends."

"Lord Justice," Jeremy said dazedly, scrambling to his feet. "You're Lord Justice. Miranda, you little devil, you never told me the man in question was *Lord Justice.*"

A small smile curled the corner of her lip. "Yes. I rather wanted to see your response the first time you met him."

She'd wanted to introduce him to her friends?

"This was *not* the sort of person I expected you to—" Jeremy stopped abruptly.

"Do you know something about Mr. Patten's death?" Smite heard himself ask. "Something not in those papers?"

Jeremy took a long moment to shake his head—perhaps too long a moment. One couldn't enlarge on the length of a second, Smite told himself. And if this Jeremy didn't seem overly upset, grief took different people in different ways. Jeremy didn't hold Smite's gaze. He looked at the floor instead. "I just heard this story half an hour ago," he mumbled. "How would I know anything about it?"

"If you think of anything that might assist the authorities in finding out who killed him—any enemies he might have, any rumors that come to your ears—justice might be served."

Mr. Blasseur shook his head. "No," he said in subdued tones. "I don't believe there can be justice. Not for this."

AFTER JEREMY LEFT, MIRANDA wasn't sure what to say. Turner hadn't pushed Jeremy out or made him feel unwelcome. Nonetheless, he stood now and looked out the window of her parlor. She stayed seated on the sofa, watching him.

He turned his head slightly. "I suppose you'd prefer to be alone?"

Miranda shook her head. She almost never preferred to be alone.

He didn't move toward her. "Do you…you don't want to *talk,* do you?" He made no effort to hide the unsubtle horror in his voice.

Miranda shook her head once more. Her grief was rolled up inside her—more for Jeremy than herself. It was Jeremy, after all, who grieved most for George. It was Jeremy who hadn't yet comprehended that one of his best friends was gone forever. Miranda had known George only through his friendship with Jeremy.

Still, young people weren't supposed to die.

"Smite," she asked softly, "do you have any idea what to say to me in a situation like this?"

"Of course I do," he retorted. "I have plenty of ideas." He met her gaze ruefully. "Of course, they're all wrong, and so I'm totally at sea."

She patted the cushion next to her. He crossed the room and lowered himself down. And then, because he didn't seem inclined to do it himself, she picked up his hand and slid it around her shoulders. His muscles stiffened for a moment, but she leaned her head against his chest and he relaxed. His other hand came up to stroke her shoulder in a light caress, and Miranda shut her eyes and melted into him.

"I feel cold," she said.

It wasn't a cold that could be driven away by fire. The only warmth she found was in the butterfly-light touch of his fingers. He seemed hesitant to hold her, as if afraid she might break. But when she leaned into him, he grew bolder. Tiny caresses gave way to broad strokes of his hand, covering her arm from shoulder to elbow. After long minutes of that, she looked up at him.

He was watching her intently. She gave him a tentative smile, but he didn't return it. Instead, he shifted. His breath touched her cheek. His hands continued to stroke her arms, and Miranda let herself fall back onto the cushions of the sofa. When he paused, she pulled him atop her. He levered himself over her gingerly, his weight neither heavy nor stifling, but comforting. The warmth of his breath touched her cheek.

If death had its opposite, it was this. She came to life for him, her whole body tingling. Her breasts awakened. Her thighs parted. She fairly sizzled. And when he leaned in and captured her lips, it sent a shot of vitality through her being.

She didn't wait for him to take the lead. Miranda slid her hands down his hips of her own accord. She found the hard ridge of his erection in his trousers.

He froze and pushed away from her. "I'm not so ruled by my lusts that I must consort with you, even under these trying circumstances."

"I don't want you to consort with me. I want…" Miranda lifted her head and looked into the blue of his eyes. "I need you to touch me. To hold me. To remind me I'm still living."

He focused on her intently. Then slowly, slowly, he leaned back into her. He set his lips against hers, light at first.

This was what it meant to be alive—to conjure his want from kisses, to have her breath stolen with desire. She kicked her skirts up to her knee, and he obliged her by pushing up onto his forearms and then sliding the material farther up, parting her legs as he did so.

She spread herself out for him, and he slid to the floor beside her. Her drawers slid off, and he parted her folds with his thumbs. Before she could quite comprehend what was happening, he leaned over her and set his mouth on her sex.

He was the most determined, intense man she'd ever met. Small surprise that when he brought that intensity to bear on her, she exploded. His tongue slid down the length of her slit and then up, up, to swirl around the button of her sex. He slipped a finger inside her, and then another.

"Oh God," she heard herself moan. "God, Smite. Do that again."

He did. He did it harder and faster, until the heat pulsed around them in waves, until she felt elevated on high. Her orgasm passed through her, tearing her to pieces. Her fists clenched in her skirts, and she screamed. It wasn't just a release. It was a vindication of sorts.

He pulled away an inch and reached for his own trousers. Miranda had a moment of dim comprehension, before she set her hands atop his.

"Wait. I don't have my sponge in."

He paused for only the briefest of moments. "Where is it?"

"Upstairs. My bedchamber."

He slipped one arm under her knees and the other about her shoulders. Before she quite knew what was happening, he lifted her in the air. Her hand slid across the straining muscles in his back. "What are you doing?"

"Taking you upstairs."

He did. She never would have imagined that it might feel so lovely to be held. He cradled her close, up the two flights of stairs. When he arrived in her bedchamber, he set her on her bed, and then crossed to her chest of drawers. He pulled the stopper on the vial of vinegar and a sweetly sour scent filled the room; glass clinked, and he turned back to her.

She held out her hand, but he didn't give the sponge to her. Instead, he climbed beside her. He pulled up her skirts and parted her legs. The sponge was cold for one second against her flesh—but he pushed it inside her, trailing both heat and cold in his wake.

"Is that right?" he asked, his fingers still lodged inside her.

"Yes."

He curled his finger inside her passage. "And that?"

"God," she breathed. "Yes."

"What about this?" His thumb ran along her.

"Too much. Not enough." She pulled his hands away from her, sat up, and reached for his trousers. This time, the buttons came undone easily. His member sprang out, hot and hard.

"I want you," she said.

He made a deep noise in his throat, almost a growl. He kicked off his trousers and knelt before her. "Say it again."

His hands found her thighs.

"I want you," she repeated.

He pushed inside her, stretching her. "God. You're so good."

She gripped his arms and watched his face. His thrusts were hard and impatient; he bit his lip in concentration. His breath grew ragged. He was warm, so warm, and so alive. His hands found hers and clenched tightly around her fingers. And she was connected to him—deeply, intimately, perfectly. He drove away the last cold threads of fear from her, replacing them with life. He came hard inside her in a burst of heat.

He collapsed on top of her. They didn't speak for long minutes. He played his hand through her hair, twirling it about his fingers casually.

This was the point where she would have reached up and caressed his jaw. She would have run her fingers down the bridge of his nose and cupped his cheek in her palm. Instead, she took his hand in hers. She spread his fingers across her own cheek, guided him to stroke the side of her face.

"This is what I'd give you," she whispered. If she could.

His eyes drifted shut. She maneuvered his hand along her jaw; his fingers trailed along her lips. She couldn't touch his face, but she could still touch *him*. She could feel him relaxing against her, all that residual awareness seeping away. She entangled his fingers in hers.

"Stay with me," she heard herself whisper. *Stay all night.*

He must have known what she was asking. His arm curled around her. He inclined his head to hers.

"Miranda," he murmured. "Darling."

There had been a space between the words, a single breath. He hadn't stayed with her before, but tonight...tonight was different. Tonight she needed to be held. She needed someone warm and vital to remind her that not all youth ended in death.

"I can't," he said.

"Can't?"

He let out another breath. "Won't," he clarified.

He didn't apologize. He didn't explain. Miranda had never expected to have all of him, and so no matter how she yearned to hold him, she opened her hands and let him go.

SMITE HAD SET THE term of his arrangement with Miranda at one month because he'd thought it just short enough that they'd both avoid unnecessary emotional entanglement.

As the curtain rose at the Theatre Royal six days into the affair, he was contemplating how enormously he'd mistaken the matter. He was entangled already.

Miranda sat beside him, her gloved hands folded in her lap. Her attention was fixed on the stage before them. Her eyes were bright and she leaned forward eagerly.

They had taken seats in the pit of the theater. Both of them had dressed in plainer, simpler clothing, so as to not draw attention to themselves. It had been a tactical decision on his part to sit among the common folk. In a box, dressed in finery, everyone would see them. And everyone would talk.

Smite had enough ribald jokes to contend with from his fellow magistrates; he didn't want them to add Miranda to their repertoire.

Normally, he'd have kept Miranda in seclusion. But when she talked of the theater, her eyes lit. Her voice grew animated. And maybe—just maybe—he'd wanted to see them light more.

He was definitely in danger.

But Miranda's eyes were not alight with pleasure now. They were narrowed on the stage in front of her, and she sat back in her seat.

"Oh dear," she whispered.

"What is it?"

"If they brush that castle wall the wrong way, it's going to topple over," she said under her breath.

He followed where she gestured with her chin. He hadn't noticed it himself. But now that she mentioned it…the wall swayed in a light draft. He raised an eyebrow at her, and she shrugged. It had never occurred to him that she might criticize the theater.

It should have.

As the first act proceeded, she muttered about the acting, the execution of stage directions, the costumes. Miranda apparently took the business of putting on a play quite seriously.

If she'd been writing scathing commentary for the *Bristol Mercury,* she'd have had an adoring readership.

"It's a ghost," she muttered. "You're scared! You're acting as if you're speaking to a passing dairyman."

Then, a moment later: "Oh, no wonder. That has to be the least frightening ghost in all of England. Could he deliver his lines with any less feeling? 'Avenge me. Has the post arrived yet? Pass the saltcellar.'"

Smite choked back an outraged laugh.

Not so successfully. The man next to him nudged him with his elbow and glared at him pointedly. "Shhh!" he warned.

The other man hadn't noticed Miranda's commentary. Indeed, Smite could scarcely hear her himself. It was Smite's poorly-suppressed response that he was condemning. But Miranda didn't stop, and the theater seemed more and more absurd with every whispered remark. She drew his attention to people walking in before their time, lines got wrong, speeches mangled. She mocked costumes. He actually did laugh out loud. Twice.

Perhaps that was why, as the curtain fell on the first act, the man beside him jostled his shoulder. Smite turned, and found himself looking up and up into the narrowed eyes of a behemoth of a man. He was burly and dressed in laborer's clothing.

"That's the Bard you're laughing at," the man rumbled.

Smite considered explaining that he was, in fact, laughing at the woman who sat next to him, but something about the glint in the man's dark eyes made him hold his tongue.

"I saved my wages for a month to come," the behemoth continued. He flexed his arms; beneath the dirt of his coat, heavy muscles rippled. "And I'm not going to have my play ruined by some frivolous fleabite of a man. Get out now, or I'll throw you out. Quick, before the next act comes on."

There were a great many things that had never happened to Smite in his life. Getting into a brawl in a theater was one of them. If the man had known who he was—if he'd been sitting in a box overlooking the stage—he would never have interfered. But for tonight, Smite had chosen to be as close to anonymous as possible. He wasn't worried that the man could do him any harm: big men hit hard, but they moved slowly. Still...

"Oh, dear," Miranda was saying, looking as if she were truly sorry. "I do beg your pardon." She'd matched her accent to the man's—broad and ponderous. "My man, he's a little thick sometimes. Can't appreciate good Shakespeare. I'll take him off, and no more trouble to you."

The man touched his head. "Sorry, little miss," he said. "I could tell you were enjoying it. Paying close attention, you were. If you want me to send him off, I'll see you home."

He'd never found himself in a brawl over a woman, either, but Smite felt his fists clench.

But Miranda's eyes simply danced as she stood up. "No need to worry yourself. I'll take him out of your way, then." She gathered up her things, and Smite trailed after her in bemusement. She whispered to him the entire way, but he couldn't make out her words until they slipped through the double doors into the vestibule.

"...cardinal sin," she was saying. "It doesn't matter how bad it is, I shouldn't have disrupted the proceedings. If others are enjoying themselves, who am I to cause trouble?" She sighed and looked forlorn.

"Did I hear you right?" Smite echoed. "You think that interfering with someone's enjoyment of a play is a cardinal sin?"

"Yes," she said, with no indication that she exaggerated. "And we deserve to have been tossed out. Although I do wish we could see the rest."

"You want to see the rest?" he asked. "I had the distinct impression that you thought the players were inept."

Miranda shrugged. "Even so. I was enjoying myself. It was that kind of awful." Her face lit. "Oh, I know. There was a box upstairs that was empty," she said. "We could sneak in."

Smite simply stared at her. "You think that disrupting someone's enjoyment of a play is a cardinal sin, but have no qualms about sneaking into a box that we didn't pay for?"

She gave him a saucy smile and turned to head up the stairs for the boxes.

He lunged after her, grabbed hold of her hand. "I mean it. *No.* That would be wrong. I won't be party to that."

"Nobody's using it. Where's the harm?"

"Maybe someone *is* using it. Maybe he's just late to the theater."

She took another few steps up the stairs, and looked back at him. "Then he can oust us when he arrives. We've already been pushed out once; what's a second time? Besides, whoever he is, he deserves it. What kind of booby is *late* to the theater?" She spoke the last in scathing tones, as if she could think of no greater failing.

As if to answer her question, a man turned the corner and started up the staircase. "Pardon," he said, as he brushed past Smite and Miranda.

Just that one word, and Smite knew who he was. He froze, willing the fellow not to stop. Not to turn around.

Too late. The man halted two steps above them, as if registering what he'd seen. He turned around. And then, ever so slowly, Richard Dalrymple's jaw went slack at the sight of Smite with his arms halfway round a woman.

"I see," he said slowly. "So when I sent round that note yesterday afternoon, you really weren't just putting me off. You *have* been busy."

Smite had not wanted to think of the man.

Dalrymple gave a wave of his hand. "I know what that stubborn set of your chin means," he said. "It means you're planning to tell me to go to the devil. If you want to put me off, put me off. Nevertheless, I don't suppose you'd care to join me?" He cast a glance at Miranda—a glance that bespoke a certain curiosity. Smite wanted to strike that look off his face. "I have a box tonight, and I'm the only one in it."

"Ah, so that empty box is occupied, then." Smite glanced at Miranda beside him.

Miranda met his censorious gaze with doe-eyed innocence. "I repent," she said. "It would have been utterly unforgivable if we had been caught out in your—" She paused, looking at Dalrymple, and Smite realized he'd not introduced them.

"His brother-in-law," Dalrymple supplied. His eyes had grown large at this exchange.

"This is my...brother-in-law, Richard Dalrymple," he said. "Dalrymple, Miss Miranda Darling."

Dalrymple's eyes widened further at the *Miss,* but he said nothing more.

"Pleased to make your acquaintance," Miranda said. "I'll be even more pleased to sit in your box, as Mr. Turner here has got us cast out of our own seats."

Dalrymple glanced again at Smite, an utterly befuddled look on his face. And when Smite did not bother to contradict this particular tale—it *was* true, after all, if not precisely the way she'd laid it out—Dalrymple shook his head. "Miss Darling," he said slowly. "I fear that you are not a good influence on our upright friend. I'm not sure what to say."

Miranda gave Dalrymple a beatific smile. " *I* know what you should say: 'Thank you' comes to mind."

Dalrymple gave a surprised snort of laughter.

"You see?" Smite said. "That is precisely how we came to be arguing in the hall and not watching the play."

"Well. Then. Turner, if you please? I can conduct Miss Darling up, if you're worried about your upright reputation." Dalrymple smiled slightly. "It would probably be as good for my reputation as it would be for yours, if you're thinking about being observed."

Before he could answer—before he could even think of how he *should* answer—Miranda stepped forward and threaded her arm through Dalrymple's.

"We would love to," she said.

Chapter Fourteen

MIRANDA WAS BEGINNING TO understand precisely who Richard Dalrymple was—or, rather, who he *wasn't*—by the end of the play. She'd had few enough clues. Smite had maneuvered Miranda to sit between the two of them, effectively forestalling any opportunity for him to converse with the man. That knocked out the possibility that they'd had any pretension to friendliness.

But she didn't think it was a case of simple indifference, either.

Dalrymple kept casting glances at Smite throughout the play. Smite, in turn, studiously avoided the other man's gaze. When the curtain fell at the end, they all stood. Smite reached over and gave the man his fingers in the barest of handshakes. And Dalrymple looked…annoyed.

No, they were definitely not friends. But they weren't quite enemies, either. Was Dalrymple some sort of hanger-on, then?

"Look, Turner," she heard him murmur, "at least you could assuage my feelings by pretending to accept my apology."

"I took notice of your apology on the previous occasion when it was offered," Smite said. "I'm considering it."

"I was wrong," Dalrymple said. "But can't you consider that maybe you were not entirely in the right, either?"

Smite's jaw set. She didn't know what had transpired between these two, but there was murder in his look.

"Ah." Dalrymple turned away. "I forgot. How foolish of me. You're never wrong."

"On the contrary. I am daily reminded of my own fallibility. Having come to a decision, however, I choose not to doubt it."

She'd heard that tone of finality from him before. He'd spoken so to Billy Croggins in his hearing room all those weeks ago, when he'd had him charged with arson. He'd used it on her not an hour in the past, when she'd suggested that they steal into this box unattended.

"Smite," she ventured, "don't you think you could hear him out?"

He cast one glance at her and then looked away. "No."

"What could it hurt?"

"Nothing," he said, "but—"

"Then I'll hear you," she said to Dalrymple directly. "Would you care to take brandy with us this evening?"

Beside her, Smite drew in breath. But he said nothing to her—at least not with words. His hand came around her wrist in a grip that was not hard, yet still disapproving.

Let him disapprove. She raised her chin.

"Please," Miranda said.

Richard Dalrymple gave her a soft smile. "I'm too ill-bred to turn you down."

Turner had nothing to say to that. He gave Miranda his arm as they descended the staircase. But beneath the wool of his coat, his muscles were tense. Dalrymple had his own carriage to contend with, and after tersely communicating the direction to his brother-in-law, Smite handed Miranda into the hired cab that he'd had waiting.

He sat on the squabs opposite her and folded his arms. "What in blazes do you think you're doing?" he demanded the instant they were off.

"Isn't that what a mistress *does?*" she shot back. "She holds salons. She entertains a man and his friends."

"You're too intelligent to imagine that Dalrymple is a friend of mine. It was perfectly clear that I had no desire for his company."

"True. But I desired it, and you said I wasn't to think of what you wanted. That I should act upon my preferences."

His eyes blazed at that. "You prefer to infuriate me?"

"One day," she snapped, "that is going to be me—the person who so offends you that you won't even look in my direction. I know who I am, and *what* I am. Sneaking into empty boxes is the least of my sins. I hope to God that when I beg you to listen, as that man did just now, you'll do so."

He raised his eyes to hers. "Unlikely," he said, and cut his gaze away.

That stung so hard it stole her breath.

He looked up at her gasp and frowned. "Unlikely, I mean, that you will offend me as Dalrymple has. Or that I would fail to hear you out. When have I ever done such a thing to you?"

"To me? Never. Yet." She set her hand against her face, pressing her eyelids. "But... I tell myself that you are a good man. A kind man. Mostly, I have been proven right. But sometimes, there is a coldness in you. It scares me." She pressed harder. "What do you think I did in the slums to survive as I did? I didn't manage to keep my virginity intact because angels intervened at every turn."

She was falling in love with a man, and she wasn't certain who he was. He surely didn't know her—not her history, nor the full truth of what she'd done in Temple Parish.

"It's not coldness," he said quietly. "It's decisiveness. When I make up my mind, I don't look to change it. It would be cruel to allow someone to believe otherwise."

"But why don't you consider changing your mind? You're not one of those crabbed, angry fellows who abhors all alteration."

"Because no good can come of it." He looked away. "I deal in irrevocabilities, Miranda. If I issue a warrant for a man's arrest, he may be swinging on the end of a noose two weeks later. If I fail to do it, he may murder a good man. If a baker makes an error, his bread fails to rise. If I do, men die." He spread his hands. "Often there is no right answer. The law demands that a man must be sentenced to transportation—there is no room for mercy, no space for adjustment. And yet, if I act as the law demands, his children will be thrown on the parish, and into the workhouse."

She leaned across the carriage to set her hand atop his. He turned his hand up and clasped her fingers. His grip was cold in hers.

"It is a responsibility that every magistrate shares. So far as I can tell, there are only three ways to shoulder that burden. My way is this: even though I may be in error, I never allow myself to doubt what I have done. That way lies endless recrimination."

"What are the other two ways?"

"Pretend the people before you aren't human," he responded smoothly. "Then it doesn't matter if you make a muck of things."

"Or?"

"Or you can go stark raving mad. Neither of those last two options appeals to me."

She drew breath. "But this is not part of your responsibility as magistrate, Turner. This is life, not duty."

A longer pause, and the carriage came to a halt. "I see very little difference," he finally said into the quiet. "My life *is* duty. Essentially."

Miranda wasn't certain if she hurt more for him or for herself. "What part of your duty am I?"

He squeezed her hand. "You're the ray of sun at the center of the storm."

It choked her up, that image. A shaft of sunlight would be welcome, true, but the storm would pass on. His life was duty; and he had as good as said she was no part of his life. She focused on the squabs in front of her and let out a long, slow breath, hoping the tightness in her chest would ease. It didn't.

Instead, the hired cab drew to a halt outside her home. He jumped down, paid the driver, and helped her out. The night air was cold against her skin.

"Come," he told her. "I've forgiven you for drawing Dalrymple in already. You could hardly do much worse."

She drew a shaky breath. She'd *done* worse. The door opened; her home awaited, warm and inviting. She could put her past behind her.

Maybe Temple Parish was nothing but a memory to be left behind. What had happened there…it was a belated shiver running up her spine. She could pack those memories away and never speak of them again. She'd escaped it all.

She pulled her cloak around her and followed him to her door. On the threshold, she stopped, her gaze caught. There, next to the door, sat a small, smooth rock. She bent and picked it up. It was dark—almost black—and the underside was dribbled with red wax.

The Patron's sigil. He wanted a meeting with her. She almost dropped it.

"What is that?" Smite asked.

No. There were some things he didn't need to know about her past. Her hand clenched around the rock and she slipped it into her pocket.

"Nothing," she said. And then, because that seemed too suspicious, she added, "Just a rock."

He was too distracted to think more of it. Instead, he stepped inside. "Come. Let's ready ourselves for your guest."

MIRANDA WAS CHANGING TOO much about Smite's life.

It wasn't just the sweet cakes and brandy that she'd called for when they arrived at her home. It wasn't simply the comforting smell of wax and lemon and polish that pervaded the atmosphere, or the soft cushions of the sofa where he sat. It wasn't even the luxury of physical intimacy.

No. It was Richard Dalrymple leaning back against his chair, stiff and uncertain. It was Miranda's smile as she settled on the cushion near Smite. She drew him in, reminding him of a time when he and Dalrymple had been friends. A time when he'd been lulled into complacency.

Miranda took up her own glass of brandy and took a sip.

"Do you enjoy the theater?" she asked. Her gestures were delicate, even if the spirits she imbibed were not.

Smite knew he was being rude, retreating from the conversation as he was. But he had little truck with easy conversation. Nothing about him was easy; why should he pretend otherwise?

Dalrymple waved his hand back and forth. "I take some pleasure in it." He shrugged. "But I like boxing equally well. Fencing. Opera. My tastes are…"

"Unformed," Smite supplied.

Miranda cast him a pointed, sidewise glance. "Broad," she said instead. "What sort of opera do you like?"

Smite had lost the habit of conversing over polite nothings. Or maybe he'd neglected to learn it in the first place. Instead, he stared at the coals in the grate. The conversation flowed around him like the tide—always moving, never going anywhere.

"So what was it like being raised by actors?" Dalrymple was asking.

Smite looked up from the coals to see Miranda watching him. She'd spoken so freely with Dalrymple. They were on the verge of friendship, and once again, Smite felt that touch of uneasy jealousy. Miranda could make even Smite feel welcome; naturally, a charming fellow like Dalrymple would win her over.

He'd set the term of their liaison at one month. The time was supposed to be sufficiently short that she'd not grow disappointed with him.

Apparently, he'd misjudged. He could almost feel her approval of him fading. It made him feel utterly savage inside. Smite stood and walked away from their charming conversation. He turned to the fire, the better to stab it with a poker.

Miranda didn't even track him with her gaze. Instead, she was still conversing with Richard.

"Nobody ever believes me," she was saying, "but I had the most marvelous childhood. Jonas and Jasper took over the primary responsibility of looking after me." She was looking off into the fire as she spoke, a soft smile on her face. "Jasper was sporting-mad. He took me to every prizefight, every horse race that occurred within any county where we traveled. He'd put me on his shoulders and explain how to place a bet. Jonas would come along and shake his head in horror. I always supposed that's what fathers *did.*"

Dalrymple shook his head. "Not mine. Mine took me to a brothel when I was thirteen." A grimace. "That did not go so well."

As a stratagem to involve Smite in the conversation, it was too obvious to work. Smite didn't care about Dalrymple's revelations. He didn't want to think about any of it.

"But then," Dalrymple was saying, "they weren't your parents. They were just employees."

"Not just!" Miranda protested. "And besides, my parents weren't neglectful. They were just busy. I had supper with them every evening, and Mama always tucked me into bed. It was Mama who insisted that Papa find a patron when I was ten. She said we'd been bouncing about long enough. And so we moved to London."

"Did you enjoy settling down?" Dalrymple asked.

"No." Miranda scowled. "Jonas and Jasper left. Permanence wasn't to their taste. I wept for days."

Smite had never noticed it before, but there was something about the rhythm of that pairing. *Jonas and Jasper.* As if she'd often said those names coupled together in that particular singsong rhythm. Dalrymple's hand clenched at his side. He looked up, his gaze sharp, as if he'd heard it too. Like that, the conversation lost its easy feel. Somehow, they'd drifted far out to sea.

"Tell me," Dalrymple whispered, his voice suddenly hoarse. "This Jonas. This Jasper. They were…"

"They were good people," Miranda said sharply. "Very good. They practically raised me."

"They left *together?*" Dalrymple echoed.

"Ah," Smite heard himself interject from his vantage point by the fire. "Miranda. You should know something. Of the many unforgivable things that Dalrymple has done, the worst was this: he started a rumor a few years back, claiming that I preferred men."

Miranda's spine straightened, not in haughty dignity, but as if she were a cat, drawing herself up and puffing her fur out in rage. She let out a scalded breath and hopped to her feet.

"You did *what?*" she demanded of Dalrymple.

"I can explain!" Dalrymple brought up his hands.

But Miranda bounded across the room to him. She was far shorter than Dalrymple was; still, she managed to loom. "I don't care to hear your explanation. Do you know what they do to men like that?"

While Dalrymple was still sputtering for an answer, she slammed the ball of her hand against his shoulder.

"They hang them," Miranda said. "And it doesn't matter how good the men are, or how much they keep to themselves, or how kind they are to inquiring children." Her voice trembled. "It doesn't matter if they can translate ancient Greek into the most beautiful thing you've ever heard in English. They hang men like that. Do you know what it is like to live in fear of one whisper, one rumor, one false step? Do you know what it is like to fear love, because it will get you killed?" She punched his other shoulder. "Do you know what it is like to never stay in one place, just so nobody becomes suspicious of you?"

Dalrymple looked up at her. There was a long silence, broken only by the rasp of the other man's breath.

And then... "Yes," Dalrymple whispered. "I know precisely how that feels."

Miranda took one step back. She raised her hand to her mouth.

Dalrymple dropped his eyes. "I know what it is like to live under threat. For many years, the only person who knew of my proclivities was Turner here. And he suggested that if I took one wrong step, he would reveal everything."

"I did not," Smite said, annoyed all over again. "I promised you I'd hold your secrets in confidence. You should have known that I would keep that vow."

"Oh, yes. Lovely for me, that I should be forced to put my life in the keeping of a man who despised me."

They faced each other directly for the first time that evening. Smite found himself growling. "Have you any idea how much of an insult it was when you believed that I would be so cavalier with my promises?"

"Why must it always be about you?" Dalrymple demanded. "I have been trying to be civil. How much must I abase myself before you, before you'll deign to treat me as human? Why am I always the one who must put forth the effort?"

"Because you were the only one in the wrong," Smite snapped.

Dalrymple turned white. "Is that what you think?"

"I never accused you of crimes. I never spread innuendo blackening your character. Yes, it *is* what I think. It also happens to be the truth."

Dalrymple stood up. "Well. Fuck you, Turner. You could have stopped it at any time. For years, I begged you to tell me that you'd keep quiet. For years, you said nothing."

"You should have known I would keep my promise."

"Oh, I should simply have known without your saying so. I beg your pardon," Dalrymple said icily. "When I weigh your scarcely-wounded vanity against my very real fear that I would face the gallows, you come up rather short."

Smite caught his breath. He felt as if he'd had his legs swept out from under him, that he'd landed in an ignominious heap upon the ground. It made all his righteous anger seem…slightly less righteous. It made him even angrier that Dalrymple appeared to have an actual point.

Miranda had stepped away from them both, and she was watching with something akin to horror. For the first time, he saw himself through her eyes—cold, unforgiving, and in pursuit of principle to the point of pettiness.

"Just once," Dalrymple said. "Once, over the last twenty years, you could have said, 'Oy, Dalrymple, old chap, I'm not going to have you killed.' It would have cost you nothing—nothing but a tiny, wounded portion of your pride. It would have meant that I could breathe easily instead of watching over my shoulder. I know I shouldn't have done any of the things I did. But when your elder brother ferreted out the truth of my bastardy, I thought you had told him. That you were finally going for my throat. That summer before Ash married Margaret… I said and did a lot of things I regret now. I was wrong. I'm sorry."

Dalrymple held out his right hand, palm up.

Smite wanted to turn from it all. But there was nothing righteous in his anger now. It had turned black and unyielding. He wanted to walk away, to lick his wounds and mull all this over. He wanted this great, trembling uncertainty to dissipate like so much smoke.

"I hate having second thoughts," he muttered.

"Necessary, for second chances," Dalrymple put in.

"Pithy," he responded. "That doesn't make it right."

He should say the words Dalrymple had said. *I was wrong. I'm sorry.* He couldn't bring himself to do so. Instead, he reached out and took Dalrymple's hand. "For what it's worth," he said, "I never wanted you dead."

The other man's grip was firm and solid. His fingers convulsed, though, and his eyes squeezed shut.

And then because, damn it, his duty demanded it of him, Smite managed more. "You're right. I was an ass." He grimaced. "Is that all you require?"

Dalrymple's eyes flew open. "You—"

"Don't think anything of that," Miranda said, coming to stand by Smite. "For him, that was an apology on bended knee. Anything more than he just managed, and he'll overload his sentimentality quota."

Smite felt a touch of annoyance, and he yanked his hand away.

But Richard Dalrymple gasped. "Never tell me he still has the sentimentality quota."

Miranda's look of surprise mirrored his. "Never tell me that the sentimentality quota truly exists." The two of them exchanged shocked glances, and Smite found himself folding his arms across his chest.

"Oh, yes," Dalrymple breathed. "He's had a sentimentality quota since he was thirteen."

"Good heavens." Miranda looked up at Smite.

Smite pressed his lips together and gave her a repressive shake of the head. She ignored it and turned to Dalrymple. "I assumed he'd made it up to put me off."

"You thought I was lying to you?" Smite growled. "That was a poor guess on your part. Why would I invent such a thing?"

"Hmm. Why *did* you invent such a thing?"

"Sheer perversity." Dalrymple stood and walked to the sideboard, where he poured himself a tumbler of brandy. "But—ah—rather, I suppose I should leave the story for Turner to tell."

"No, go on," Smite said. "You've been telling my secrets for years. Why stop now?"

Dalrymple flushed. "God, one mistake, and you make me pay for it—"

"What he meant by that," Miranda interrupted, "was 'I'd rather not speak of it myself, and so if you would be so good as to explain, you would be doing me a great favor.'"

Smite felt a rueful smile tug at his lips. "I might have so meant," he muttered.

"He has a politeness quota in effect, too," Miranda said, looking toward Dalrymple with excessive earnestness. "He used up the sum total on the greetings this evening."

In response, Smite raised an eyebrow at her. "I would implement a quota on cheekiness, if I thought I had any hope of enforcing it."

Miranda smiled outright at that. "In other words," Miranda said, turning to Richard, "ignore his glower and satisfy my curiosity, please."

"Turner, are you sure you want me to tell the story?"

He shrugged. "Go ahead."

"So, when Turner first came to Eton, he was a bit behind the other boys in his schooling. His tutoring hadn't been quite up to par."

"Ha," Smite said.

"And he was rather upset for a variety of reasons."

Smite folded his arms. "No need to delve into those. She's heard most of it anyway."

Dalrymple accepted this. "In any event, Turner decided that...dealing with the aftermath of his tragedy was all well and good, but he needed to concentrate on his Latin. So he gave himself a sentimentality quota—thirty minutes a day to think of all those things, so long as he worked the rest of the time."

"Thirty entire minutes?" Miranda said. "Goodness. I'm so glad you've ceased to be so self-indulgent." She looked at Dalrymple. "He's down to twenty now."

Dalrymple was just beginning to warm to his subject. "You have no idea how irritating it was. I would repose the greatest confidences in him. He'd listen intently, kindly even—up until the minute he'd interrupt me mid-sentence to inform me that we'd reached our sentimentality quota for the day, and it was back to Virgil with us."

Miranda let out a delighted laugh.

"It's not the least bit amusing," Dalrymple said. " *I* didn't have a sentimentality quota, and I resented being subject to his. In any event, he passed me up in Latin in a few months, and had mastered Greek entirely by the end of the year. So maybe it had some utility."

"Of course it did," Smite put in. "My studies benefited, and I limited my indulgence in sentimentality, which is a particularly useless waste of time."

Miranda laughed. "I like you better and better the more I learn of you," she said to Smite. "If I could have subjected some of the actresses in my father's troupe to a sentimentality quota, oh, how easy things would have been."

That was not how things were supposed to be. After what had been said this evening, she was supposed to shrink from him. Instead, there was a playful lilt to her words, but no smile lingering on her face. He didn't even need to search his memory to understand. After all, it wasn't an actress's temper that came to mind. It was her father who'd needed to limit his sentiment.

She sighed in memory, and Smite reached out and took her hand in his.

"There," Dalrymple said, pointing. "What's that? That's *sentiment.* I can't believe I'm seeing this."

Smite looked at her hand, intertwined with his. He turned it in his grip. "I have no idea what you're speaking of."

"Hush," Miranda said to Dalrymple. "I've found that if you don't speak of them, he doesn't count gestures against the quota."

Smite met her eyes. Quite deliberately, he folded his other hand about hers. "You've both got it entirely wrong," he said. "The sentimentality quota only forbids the tired relation of mawkish particulars. It has never forbidden action. That is the point of it: to channel what would otherwise be endless yammering into firm resolve."

"Resolve," Miranda said thoughtfully. "Is that what you're calling that particular firmness?"

Dalrymple was overtaken by a coughing fit. When he recovered, he said, "I see I'm about to become extraneous."

"Indeed," Smite agreed. "Shall I show you out?"

Dalrymple smiled. "Don't be so eager, Turner." But this time, there was no insult in his words.

"I DON'T BELIEVE IN doubts."

Miranda pulled up her knees beside her on the bed. Richard Dalrymple had left hours before; Smite stood at the window looking out over the city. He'd said very little, but by the twitch of his jaw, he seemed at war with himself.

"Everything fits in its place," he said to the window. "Things are right or they are wrong; and even when matters are confused, there is a thread I can tug on to unravel the entire mess."

He was arguing with himself, not with her.

Miranda weighed responses and fingered the dark rock weighing down her pocket. "Not everything is courtroom-simple," she finally said. "Sometimes you tangle yourself. Sometimes you don't even know you've done it until it's too late. At that point, yanking strings only serves to tighten the noose."

She could feel the wax against her fingers.

He turned back to her, a quizzical expression on his face. "The noose?"

"The knots," she amended.

He turned away, not noticing her own confusion. "But if I have to imagine how Richard Dalrymple felt all those years, must I also think like a drunkard? A murderer? Am I supposed to find compassion in me for every benighted criminal?"

She was marked as one herself. She'd never stolen, never killed anyone. She'd never done anything truly criminal at the Patron's behest. Still, she didn't think he'd muster up any great respect for her past life.

But he shook his head, rejecting her argument before she could form it. "No," he said. "That would make a hash of morality. We'd excuse murder and mayhem. There must be a limit."

"You are very good at drawing limits," Miranda said.

He must have caught that hint of bitterness in her tone because he stopped mid-pace and cocked his head. "What is it?"

"Nothing."

"It's not nothing."

She let out a breath. "Only this, then. One day I'll be wrong. I don't know when it will be. But it will happen. And when it does, I don't think you'll have any warmth for me."

He didn't contradict her. She'd been half hoping for that.

"Miranda Darling," he said. The words came out slowly.

"Is that Miranda, comma, darling, or—"

"Miranda Darling," he repeated without clarification, "I wish I could tell you otherwise. But I am not a warm person. I'm not the sort who dithers."

"If it were me, wouldn't you dither just a little bit?"

He didn't even have to think. "No." But then he laid his hand on her cheek. "I don't dither for myself, if it makes you feel any better."

"Not even for Richard Dalrymple?"

He gave her a grim smile. "You may not believe this, but we were once good friends. I met him when I first came to Eton, which was not the easiest time in my life."

"Jonas didn't much like Eton, either," Miranda offered.

Smite paused. "Actually," he continued in more normal tones, "that was precisely the problem. Eton *was* the easiest time in my life. I had survived my mother's madness. From there, I'd run to the streets of Bristol. Then my eldest brother came home, fabulously wealthy, and all at once, instead of scraping for bread and fighting for my younger brother's virtue, my challenges were reduced to the conjugation of verbs. I had been too busy surviving to actually take notice of how horrid things were. At Eton, it all caught up with me. I..." He took a deep breath, looked away from Miranda. "I had nightmares. Horrible nightmares. And inexplicable fits of weeping. It was awful."

"It couldn't have been as bad as all that."

He exhaled. "It was," he said bluntly. "Nobody needed me for anything any longer, and so I fell apart. That's when I met Dalrymple. He had just discovered that he was...different. He needed someone to lean on. So I came up with a sentimentality quota. There isn't any need for doubt. There isn't any room for dithering. I don't like this fussing about."

She could think of a hundred responses to that. But he was arguing with himself more effectively than she ever could.

"For one second, tonight," he said, "I saw how things must have seemed to him. He wasn't right. He was completely wrong.

There was no excuse for the things he did..." Smite sighed, staring off into the distance. "No. Enough with this dithering. I'm not doubting; I'm being too kind to myself. He would not have done those things if I'd had an ounce of compassion for his situation." He grimaced. "I *knew* he thought I'd tell. I didn't bother to correct him."

"Are you sorry I asked him back here?" Miranda asked.

He didn't answer that. He simply turned from the window to look at her. "Miranda Darling," he said. And then he crossed the room and sat beside her.

There had been a comma-like pause between *Miranda* and *Darling*—the closest he ever came to an endearment. She wasn't sure why a hint of bittersweet invaded his voice at that, why his breath grew just a little ragged. She only knew that he pulled her close, that she felt the whisper of warm air against her forehead.

He held her for a few moments longer, his arms tight bands around her. And then he disengaged, turning from her.

She didn't know what men typically did with their mistresses, but she wanted to hold him longer. To feel the warmth of him next to her throughout the night. She didn't want him going home alone to a cold bed.

But he never stayed.

"Smite," she said softly. She reached for his hand. The grip of her fingers about his was all the entreaty she dared to make.

His other hand found hers. He squeezed her fingers—not hard, but just enough to communicate. When he let go and moved away, it was all the answer she needed.

No.

Miranda wasn't foolish. She had more of him than any woman had in the past. Quite possibly more than any woman ever would. He gave a part of himself over to her that he didn't show to anyone else, and she treasured it. Nonetheless, it hurt to have so little. A few hours every day; not even a night's worth. It was foolish to want more when he'd told her that was all he could give.

He'd also told her he would have her for a month. The days were slipping past too quickly. What would happen when he came to the end of her? Perhaps that month he'd allotted had not been some initial period to determine if they'd suit. Maybe he'd simply given himself a Miranda quota. When he came to the end of those days, would he cut her off as ruthlessly as he cut off all other sentiment?

No use getting exercised over something that hadn't yet happened. She stared at his silhouette.

No, she vowed. He wouldn't set her aside so easily. She wouldn't let him.

Chapter Fifteen

THERE WAS NO ROOM for doubt in Smite's duties. But his arrangement with Miranda had infected him with uncertainty. Last night's questions had followed him into today's hearing room. He sat, arrayed in black under an itchy wig, and stared in front of him in dismay.

The defendant, a hard-eyed woman with stringy blond hair, was charged with public obscenity. Specifically, Mrs. Grimson had been accused of shouting, "I hope your stones shrivel up and rot off, you bloody bastard," in a public square.

There was no question as to her guilt. Everyone had heard her, and she'd admitted to uttering the words in question. It should have been a five-second discussion.

And yet, when he thought of Dalrymple, what had once been simple became all too complex.

"Why?" he asked. "Why did you do it?"

There was no element of *why* in the inquiry.

Mrs. Grimson scowled at him. "Are you simple?" she demanded. "I said it 'cause I hoped his stones would—"

"No need to repeat it," the mayor interjected hastily. "Really. Does it matter?"

Not to the law, it didn't. But now that Smite had found doubt, he could not dispel it. Every crime, even one as simple as this, seemed suddenly shaded about by circumstance. What if she'd been provoked? What if the man had groped her? It wouldn't excuse the conduct—the law was clear on that point. No matter how angry she'd been, she couldn't utter obscenities so blithely in a public place.

He found himself persisting. "Why did you hope it?"

"Because he ran into me," Mrs. Grimson said sullenly. "And because he had an ugly face."

Smite let out a breath he hadn't known he'd been holding. "Guilty," he said.

But even that didn't stop his mind running. When the day's work was over, he followed his fellow magistrates into the back room.

"You're getting even more particular," the mayor said. "Asking questions. Wanting to know details that can't possibly matter. What's got into you, then?"

Smite handed his robes off to Palter. "It's a passing fancy."

"Lady Justice must be giving you quite the ride." A raised, leering eyebrow shaded the otherwise innocent statement with something sordid.

Smite gritted his teeth and turned away.

"Something's putting color in your cheeks," the mayor continued. "And here I'd thought that if you ever took a mistress, it would make you *more* willing to skip over details, so that you could run back and ride her once more."

Smite moved in front of the man so quickly, he wasn't even sure what he was doing. He held his hand up, and the other man stopped and took a step back.

"Never talk about her that way again," he heard himself growling.

"What? There *is* someone?" The mayor let out a loud guffaw. "Oh, that's famous. It explains your extra attention today. You don't want Lady Justice getting jealous, so you're sending her extra trinkets. This other woman… When you're done with her, let me know. She must be—" the man mimed bosoms, melon-large, with his hands "—if she's distracting even you."

Smite reached out, and tangled his hands in the other man's lapels. "Don't talk about her that way," he repeated.

The mayor stopped, looked down at Smite's grip on his shirt. He took a deep breath. "Ahh," he said. "I see. A lady, then."

She wasn't, not in any usual sense of the word. Still, he found himself nodding in agreement. He was finding doubts everywhere these days.

"That's difficult," the mayor said, giving him a condescending pat on the shoulder.

Smite jerked away.

IT WAS NOT YET six when Miranda heard the door open several floors beneath her.

Smite was earlier than usual. In fact, in the first week of their arrangement, he'd never been so early. Her maid was still dressing her for his arrival. When she pulled away, Betsy murmured in protest.

Light footsteps ascended the stairs—too light to be his, and besides, Ghost had taken to bounding up before his master and greeting her, and she didn't hear the click of his claws against the wood floors.

A scratch on her door, and the housekeeper ducked her head in. "There's a man here."

"A man? You can't mean Mr. Turner, then?"

"No, it's not His Worship. But he's asking for the master of the house. I didn't know what to tell him."

"Did he give you a card? Is he waiting outside?"

Behind her, Betsy gave a final tug on the laces of her gown, and Miranda turned.

"He's waiting in the parlor." Mrs. Tiggard gave her an apologetic look. "He just... I opened the door, and he walked in as if he owned the place. He doesn't look like the sort of man who would easily shoo."

A brief panic took Miranda. The Patron would not so brazenly send someone to confront her, would he? No—not and ask for the master of the house. And besides, the sort of man connected with the Patron wouldn't have been able to cow Mrs. Tiggard.

"Maybe he knew the previous owner."

By Mrs. Tiggard's sheepish look, she obviously hoped Miranda would oust the man.

Miranda shook her head. "Betsy, are we done?"

"Not quite, ma'am."

Miranda needed her sash tied and a few errant curls tucked away. Betsy found her a shawl for her shoulders—"Makes you look more imposing, miss," she explained.

But even those tasks took only a few minutes. No more delay was possible. Miranda left her dressing room, walked down two flights of stairs, and entered the parlor. The man had his back to her; he was tall and broad. He was wearing a thick, sable topcoat, and his boots were polished to a shine. *Not* an emissary from the Patron, but almost as frightening. This man was wealthy and important, and no doubt he could cause her trouble.

He must have heard her footsteps, but he didn't turn. Instead, he was examining the wall-clock.

"Took you long enough," he said. "You never used to take so long to dress."

There was something wrong with his accent. It was *almost* right—like a piano that had only one note out of tune. She could usually hear Eton or Harrow or Rugby on most wealthy men's tongues. That subtle boyhood influence left its mark like indelible ink. But this man wasn't marked. He hadn't gone to public school.

He sighed. "And that's the welcome I get, is it?" He turned around, and then stopped when he saw her. His eyes widened. There was something familiar in his features—that dark hair, that nose...

But all he said was: "Oh." He took in her gown—turquoise silk with seed pearls tucked into the seams where the fabric gathered, and matching lace gloves. His eyebrows beetled together in puzzlement.

"The house has newly changed ownership," Miranda said. "I collect I am not who you expected."

But the man didn't make his apologies. "I know," he said. "About the house. And the ownership. That's why I came." He gave her another curious look. "This is a devil of an awkward question. But...are you by any chance married to my brother?"

Miranda felt her mouth dry.

"You see, my solicitor sent me a note that after nearly a decade of Spartan quarters, my brother had finally purchased a house that was suitable to his station. I decided to investigate forthwith. I had thought—"

Somewhere, some book of etiquette dealt with this situation—what to do when your lover's brother asked if you'd recently married. But if it did, Miranda had never seen it. She choked back nervous laughter.

"I think we'd better start this again." He gave her a bow. "If you're married to my brother, you'd better call me Ash."

If he could have seen the stockings she wore under her gown, the improper red ribbons she'd tied as garters, he'd have known instantly. "I'd better call you 'Your Grace,'" Miranda said, as calmly as she dared.

"Ah." He looked down. "Well. This is even more awkward." He didn't seem discomfited. He strolled to a chair and stood behind it, as if waiting for an invitation to make himself at home.

Miranda frowned. "Do you really think your brother would get married and not inform you?"

"Yes," he said instantly. "How well do you know him?"

"Well enough to know he wouldn't." She paused, waited for him to open his mouth to argue, before she spoke again. "He wouldn't marry at all," she added.

"True. So you're his mistress, then?"

Of course a duke would be comfortable with the notion.

No point in dissembling. "Yes."

He sat down. "Is he well? Is he happy? What *is* he doing these days?"

"I don't know that he would want me giving out private information."

The Duke of Parford winced. "Damn. He's already infected you with his peculiar brand of reticence."

"Reticent?" she said in surprise. "I don't know what you mean. I've found him extraordinarily forthcoming."

"Really? Are you...no. You're not joking." He stared at her as if she were some kind of a strange beast, and she found herself bristling.

"You'd better call me Ash in any event," he finally said. "And now I can't decide if I was right to leave my wife behind for this interview or not." He studied her face for a moment and then shook his head. "Next you'll be telling me that pigs fly, and he has Richard Dalrymple over for tea."

"Brandy," Miranda replied. "It was brandy, not tea."

The duke's countenance shifted. "Was it, then?" That last came out quietly, but his face darkened.

Before he could say anything else, the door opened once more. This time, claws skittered against the floor. Ghost bounded in and barked at Miranda; he made a second circuit about the Duke of Parford and barked again. She reached down to pet him, just as Smite walked into the room.

The two brothers ought to have embraced, or at least clasped hands. Instead, they simply stared at one another.

"Ash," Smite finally said. "I see you've acquainted yourself with Miss Darling. What are you doing here? And why didn't you let me know you were coming?"

"Oh, I have to hire criers to get any sort of welcome?" Parford rubbed his forehead. "Have it your way. I'll be off. I can see when I'm unwanted."

Smite frowned in puzzlement. "I implied you were unannounced. I did not say you were unwanted."

The duke turned to him. "You don't need to *say* it. All this time, you've told me that you won't come to Parford Manor when my brother-in-law is about because the two of you have some quarrel you can't sort out. But now I hear that you took brandy with *Richard,* of all people. Was it all just a ruse, then?"

"Oh, I objected to Dalrymple's company," Smite snapped, drawing himself up. "But what the devil do you mean, complaining of that? You're always harping on me to give him a chance."

"Couldn't you have given him a chance *last summer,* when all the family was together?" The duke's knuckles clenched. "I've been telling myself that it means nothing when you decline my invitations, that it isn't me, it's your quarrel with Richard. Obviously, that tale you gave me was a pack of lies."

Miranda winced, and Smite stiffened. "I don't lie."

Parford must have sensed that he'd gone too far. He sighed. "You could try explaining matters to me. I have to hear everything from Mark. It...it hurts, a little, that you can tell Mark what the matter is and not mention it to me. I'm your brother, too."

Smite shoved his hands in his pockets. "I don't tell Mark. I never have to explain anything to Mark. He, unlike you, was present when everything relevant occurred."

Parford flinched. "It's down to that again? Will you ever forgive me for absenting myself when you needed me?"

"Needed you?" Smite snapped. "That's always the problem. I've never needed you."

"Oh, bollocks. You just shove everything I try to give you back in my face. All I want is to be a brother to you. Is it so hard?"

They'd forgot about her. They circled each other now, tense and wary as wolves, looking for a weakness in the other.

"You want me to be dependent on you," Smite said. "You've always resented that Mark comes to me first when something is wrong."

"I do not!"

"You do. When we were young, Mark would always go to you, and you would make things right."

The duke paused. "I'd forgot that."

"Then Hope died, and you left. And *I* became the one who protected Mark. I made sure he had enough to eat. I kept Mother's eye from falling on him. I took it upon myself to make sure that she never, ever hurt him the way she hurt us. It was too late when you returned. Mark is mine, and there is nothing you can do about it. Don't pretend this is about my failings, Ash. You've resented me since Mark first turned to me instead of you. You can't stand that I took your place."

There was a long pause. Then: "Mark is yours?" the duke asked.

There was a pregnant silence. Smite put his hand over his face and shook his head.

Miranda didn't understand any of what she'd just heard. But there was one thing she especially didn't understand. "Who is Hope?" she asked.

The way the two looked to each other, she feared the worst. He'd had a wife, or a sweetheart—but no. He'd been eight years old when his brother left. Far too young to be considering such matters.

Parford was the one who answered. "Hasn't he mentioned her, then? Hope is—was—our sister. She passed away decades ago."

Smite turned away. "Hope is *your* sister." His voice shook. "She's *my* twin."

And on that pronouncement, he left the room.

"Well," Miranda said. "That went..." She couldn't think of a word sufficiently calamitous.

Parford stared after his brother. "It always does," he sighed. "Tell him—no, never mind supper tomorrow; Richard will be over. And the day after, I've a meeting..." The man sighed and scrubbed his hands through his hair. The gesture looked so akin to something Smite might do, she frowned at him. "Tell him that I'd love to have his company two days from now. For tea. Conversation. Surely he can manage a few hours." He glanced at her. "I wish to God he'd married you."

"He would be ostracized," she said in shock.

"Indeed." Parford shrugged, and that faint hint of sarcasm in his voice seemed like a pale echo of Smite. "Because he isn't now."

SMITE COULD HEAR HIS brother leave, could hear Miranda's soft footsteps trudging up the stairs. His head pounded. He didn't know what to say to her.

So, he imagined her saying, *you have a dead twin sister. Odd that you never mentioned her before now.*

So. Care to explain why you claimed ownership of your younger brother?

Instead, she entered the room quietly and came to stand next to him by the window. She didn't touch him, which almost made him cringe more—she'd learned that when he was upset, he couldn't bear to have skin-to-skin contact.

"So," she said softly.

He flinched.

"Did your mother kill Hope the way she almost killed you?"

He shook his head. "Different. Infected rat bite." That was all he could manage. He took another deep breath. "My mother wouldn't let her be treated. She told Hope when she became ill that the heat of her fever was the fires of hell, come to claim her."

"What a terrible thing to say to her own daughter. If Hope was anything like you—"

"She wasn't," Smite interrupted. "She was a hellion. In her own way, she was worse than Ash. She was forever getting me into trouble. I was forever holding her back. Don't give me that look. You're giving me that look that says, 'Oh, a twin.' I know what people say about twins. She wasn't the other half of my soul or any other such ridiculous claptrap. We were never in perfect sympathy. We had the most magnificent rows. The only time we weren't fighting with each other was when we were fighting with someone who was trying to separate us. We never shared a secret language. Hell. Sometimes I wondered if we both spoke English, as I never understood her." He glanced at Miranda. "If she'd lived, I would never have introduced the two of you. It would have been a disaster. She wouldn't have simply stolen into the box at the opera with you; she'd have convinced you to do some other horrific thing to draw attention." He sighed. "After she died, nothing ever seemed fun again."

"Shocking," Miranda said. "After that, you had only to keep your brother safe from your mother's madness, escape a cellar, dodge a few floods, and frolic about the streets of Bristol. What could be more amusing?"

She soothed some deep, wary part of him. He reached out and took her hand. "I don't believe I would like you half so well if you weren't sarcastic."

"Nonsense," she said. "You don't like by halves. You don't have casual acquaintances and people you hold in mild distaste; you have best friends and bitter enemies. You don't have an occupation that takes up the daylight hours; you have a calling that requires that you devote your entire life to it."

"True," he said.

"Have you ever considered doing things in smaller portions? You don't have to give your brother your undying and unconditional affection; you just have to enjoy his company from time to time. You don't have to exonerate your brother-in-law of all harm. You just have to tolerate his presence."

"You make it all sound so reasonable."

"Only because you're unreasonable in the first place."

"I am not," he protested.

She folded her arms around him. "Yes, you are. You can't even be sentimental by quarters, and so you've apportioned it off to a specific time. You're utterly unreasonable."

He was silent for a little while longer. "Are you…are you doing me by quarters, then?" He spoke in a casual tone of voice, as if the question were scarcely of interest. Still, he felt himself holding his breath.

"No," she said. "You know I'm not. I don't believe anyone can do you by quarters, no matter how hard she might try."

"Good." He leaned into her and inhaled her scent. In truth, he feared he'd taken on too much of her.

But she gave him a brilliant smile. "I'm giving you at least thirty-seven percent."

Chapter Sixteen

"APPARENTLY," MRS. TIGGARD SAID on the next morning, "there's a new fashion in mystery. Last night it was an unannounced gentleman. Today, a boy brought this by."

Miranda turned to see her housekeeper holding out a single envelope.

There was no name stamped on the paper, no card attached, and no return direction. She took the envelope, turned it over, and then tore it open.

A sheet of paper was inside. The writing on it was thin and spidery. Portions had been crossed out, but the import was clear enough.

The Patron is pleased to hear that you have influence over Lord Justice. He imagines Lord Justice would be simmarlly interested in your prior activities. If you want to keep your seeckrits, you know what you must do. Our arranjemint is not over.

Miranda hadn't responded to the stone left on her doorstep. She'd been trying not to think of it ever since. But now the threat had grown to include blackmail. Miranda didn't know what Smite would do if he heard about the three years of favors she'd granted the Patron—guards she'd flirted with, constables she'd distracted so that the Patron's men might evade detection.

Mrs. Tiggard was watching her, so she flipped the paper closed.

"It's from an old friend," Miranda said. "One I haven't heard from in a good long while. She wants me to do her a favor."

Mrs. Tiggard sighed. "Isn't that always the way? You never hear from them except when they need you."

Turner no doubt suspected she'd not kept her hands entirely clean, but he'd hardly want to be confronted with a detailed list of her crimes. She knew how straitlaced he could be about such matters—and how unforgiving he was. She didn't want to see the light fade from his eyes when he looked at her.

She could manage this on her own. It would be simple. She'd go to Temple Church… She'd find out what the Patron wanted. Maybe she'd even do it. Smite would be gone all day. He would never have to know.

Unbidden, the memory returned of her last time in Temple Church. The Patron had wanted information. He'd obtained it; he'd discovered that she cared enough for Robbie that she'd revisit the rules she'd originally set. The Patron might not be angling after control over Lord Justice. But information?

The Patron wanted to know if he could make her do his bidding.

Miranda hadn't so much as thought of gruel since she came here. Robbie was happy, situated in his new apprenticeship. She'd seen him on his half-day, and they'd not even argued once.

She'd forgotten the weight of her responsibilities. But she hadn't rid herself of them. She'd only misplaced them.

She could take care of this on her own.

She shut her eyes and imagined what Jeremy would say. *You are going to get yourself killed.* Smite had asked for very little in exchange for this bargain, but he'd wanted honesty and fidelity. She suspected he would rather she engaged in intimacies with another man than perform a favor, however innocent, for a known criminal.

If she were someone else… But no. She wasn't.

Smite had bought her gowns and paid for lemon cakes, but she'd bargained for those things. She'd not bargained for his forbearance. She couldn't pay him for it, and she didn't know if she could ask for a favor she couldn't repay.

Her hands trembled, and she stared blankly at the wall.

Independence was all well and good when it was only dinner on the line. But if she didn't learn to live with this, it would surely kill her. And so, instead of dashing off to Temple Church, she went to her desk and wrote a single word. She sanded the paper, tucked it into an envelope, and addressed it. After some thought, she searched until she found the dark stone that had been left on her doorstep a few nights past. These things she handed to her maid, to be delivered to Temple Church.

IT HAD BECOME A foregone conclusion that, instead of heading to his own home after work, Smite would go to Miranda's. It was a foregone conclusion that he'd spend the evening in her company—reading, talking…making love to her. It was almost enough to make a man think sentimental thoughts.

Almost.

He smiled privately at that, and tried not to think of the passage of time. Surely, by the end of the month…

No. No. He was definitely better off not thinking about it.

He let himself in by means of the front door. One of the maids was dusting bric-a-brac on the curio shelf in the parlor. She ducked her head at him. Miranda didn't call out in greeting, though. He let Ghost off his lead.

"Well," he said softly. "What are you waiting for? Go find her."

The dog looked up at him, sniffed the ground, and then trotted off. After a few false starts, Ghost clambered up the stairs. But the dog barely sniffed at the door of the sitting room. Smite was just beginning to wonder if she was out—but surely the maid would have said something?—when Ghost paused at the threshold of the library and waved his tail happily. Smite peered around the door.

Miranda was poring intently over a book, making notes on a sheet of paper as she read. She was wearing a light green gown of muslin, embroidered in little white flowers. She'd managed to spatter droplets of ink on the lace of the cuffs, though, and her fingertips were stained black. Rationally, she hadn't become prettier over the course of their arrangement. Subjectively…well.

She leaned forward and scratched something on a piece of paper, and then gingerly turned the page of the book. Ghost chose that moment to scamper toward her and thrust his nose in her lap. She reached down, idly, to pat Ghost—using the flat of her palm to avoid getting ink on him. Then she set down her pen and looked up.

As always, he realized how much he'd missed her when she lit up at his presence. Her eyes were green and mobile, and filled with a spark that made him think she was amused.

But he didn't say anything so ridiculously maudlin.

"What is it that has you so engrossed?" He walked forward and tipped back the book so he could read the spine. " *Investment on*

Real Securities," he read in bemusement. "I didn't know you invested."

She rubbed her ink-stained fingers against a cloth. "I don't. Not yet. But…after, I won't be able to return to Temple Parish. I'll need to find some way to get a decent return on my investment."

"After," he repeated stupidly.

"I don't think I can stay in Bristol, either," she was saying. "I'm not sure where I'll go. Up north is too cold. Bath is too close. But—here—" She thrust a piece of paper at him. "There's this scheme for transporting coal from the midlands via canal."

"Miranda, what are you talking about?"

"After you're done with me," she replied matter-of-factly. "I can't stay here. You see, I received this piece of blackmail today, and it got me thinking about what I was to do. I have to take care of myself, so—"

"Wait." Smite set his hands on her shoulders and leaned in. "What the devil do you mean, you received a piece of blackmail today? I should think that you ought to lead with that, and not babble on about shares in some canal venture and how I'm going to be done with you."

She looked up into his eyes, her own sparkling brilliantly up at him. "Yes," she said, her voice almost breathy. "Do that again?"

"Do what?"

"That—that *thing*. With your eyebrows. And leaning over me, your voice cold as stone. I love it when you try to intimidate me."

"I'm not—damn it, Miranda. Stop trying to distract me. The blackmail."

She gave him a negligent wave of her hand. "Well, that's important, too. Still, if you insist." She sounded grudging, as if the matter of blackmail were a mere trifle. "I was sent a threatening little note today, saying that he would tell you about all the things I had done if I did not agree to meet with him."

"He." Smite rubbed at his forehead. "When you say 'he,' you are referring to the Patron?"

Her breath sucked in. "You know of him?"

He knew only what he'd overheard of her conversation with Robbie. But he waved his hand at her. "Obviously, you've not done anything that you need to be concerned about."

"Oh," she said. "Obviously." She glanced at him and he realized that beneath her airy demeanor, she was on edge. "Why is it obvious again? Because, actually, if you recall the initial circumstances of our encountering one another—"

He sat down next to her. "Are you telling me that you performed tasks for this…this *Patron* that were illegal?"

"Oh, no. I never stole anything. Or hurt anyone. There might have been a time or two when I distracted a constable while someone *else* did something, but I personally never did anything wrong." Her tone seemed easy, but she watched him carefully.

He winced. "I don't think I wanted to know that. I suppose now is not the time to acquaint you with the complicated doctrine of vicarious criminal liability?"

She frowned. "No. No, it is not." She twirled her hair around her finger. "I assumed I would be better off telling you about this, rather than waiting for the entire thing to blow up in my face. You did ask for honesty, after all. It seemed to be a matter of basic common sense. When one is threatened by a shadowy criminal figure, one goes to the magistrate that shares one's bed rather than the shadowy criminal figure."

By her voice, he might have thought her without a care in the world. By her hands… It suddenly all made sense. The investment. The nervousness.

She thought he was done with her. He should have been. A few weeks ago, he'd have been coldly annoyed at her declaration. But…but, God, he felt sick at heart just thinking of walking away from her. This wasn't a hearing room, and she wasn't accused of any crime.

She'd flat out admitted that she'd been involved in one. There was no excuse for what she'd done.

Was there?

He sat down next to her. "Tell me, Miranda. Why did you go to the Patron in the first place?"

"You don't want to hear my excuses," she said. "I'm sure it was all the usual reasons. I was scared. I needed money." She didn't meet his eyes. "I had no choice."

"You had a choice," he said. "But maybe I want to know how you came to make it."

She looked away. "I was seventeen when I first went to the Patron. I'd been in Bristol for a few months. And…and if you want to understand this, you need to know something about me."

"I'm listening." He pulled a seat from the wall and sat next to her.

She swallowed. "I enjoy a little bit of danger. I suppose I got the taste for it from my father. My parents always lived one step from ruin. Even when we were at our best, we had little money. If my father had a windfall, he tossed it away. If he found an extra sixpence, he bought me ice cream. If he got an extra ten pounds, we'd travel to London and see the circus. If he received fifty, there would be silks and cashmere as gifts, and extravagant lodgings. My father used to say that money was meant to be spent, not kept."

"That sounds a precarious way to live."

She shrugged again. "Perhaps. But when you're a child and it's all you've known, it doesn't seem unusual. My mother always laughed at the worst of it. We would play this one game when I was younger. She called it 'How Many Landlords,' and we'd have to guess how many people my father would have to visit until he could talk someone into giving us a place to stay." Miranda sighed. "Sometimes I think my father would talk to people he had no hope of convincing, just so I could win.

"In any event, you know how I came to Bristol. I was young and naive and friendless. I know I say that I was raised by actors, but they knew so much of the world that they managed to shelter me from the worst of it. And they did all that while leading me to believe that I was wise and prepared. My first months here were my initiation into a world I'd only heard whispered about."

"Poverty?" Smite asked.

"No. Men. For the first time, men didn't see me as my father's child. They treated me like an adult. And they very much wanted to be treated as adults, too. There were some good ones—solid fellows who had steady work and decent prospects. I suppose if I had been a clever girl I would have married one of them."

She glanced up at him. He should have felt the faint stirrings of jealousy, but something in her posture made him hold back.

"Naturally, I didn't. The man I chose was utterly beautiful. He was dark and swarthy and muscular, and quite a bit older than I was. I was doing piecework at the time for a seamstress. He was the man all the girls whispered about. He was wicked, everyone said. No decent girl would want anything to do with him." She gave a tight little smile. "Naturally, I wanted him. It was rumored that he'd committed dark deeds—that he'd nearly beaten another man to death. I was convinced that I would be the woman who would change him. I would heal the horrible darkness inside him, and reform him completely."

"I take it that didn't happen."

"At first, it seemed to. He wanted me. For a few weeks, he was utterly sweet. We kissed. We did a great deal more than kiss, actually, all leading up to that one thing—the one thing he most wanted. I knew that all I had to do was give it to him, and he would be mine. Love would transform him forever."

Her voice had taken on a mocking tone.

"We came very, very close one evening. I pulled away. I wish I could say that it was some degree of common sense finally coming to life in me, but it wasn't. I just wanted him to pursue me more." She pressed her lips together. "Instead, he backhanded me and told me that he'd had enough of my teasing. I was his and he was going to roger me as he pleased, and nobody would stop him. He only left then because Robbie walked in."

She was still smiling, but there was a bit more tension in her face.

"Of course, I told him I never wanted to see him again. But after that, he was everywhere. He waited outside the seamstress where I worked all day. He would walk beneath my window, whistling, at two in the morning. He'd try to break down the door to my room; I'd lie in bed, praying that the trunks I'd piled in front would keep him out. Robbie didn't understand what was happening, and I couldn't bear to explain. That's when I realized that dangerous is not always thrilling. Sometimes, it is just frightening. One day, one day soon, I was going to make a mistake and he was going to have me."

She looked up at him. "So there you have it. That's my excuse. I needed someone bigger and stronger. I crept out to visit the Patron's men in the wee hours before dawn. I demonstrated my facility with accents and costumery, and explained how I could be of use. By afternoon, the news was everywhere: Marcus had been badly beaten in a public house. When he'd staggered outside, all doors had been closed to him, and his old friends had turned their backs. He was knocked over the head and stripped of his purse and his shoes. When he awoke and limped back to his quarters, those had been stripped bare of everything, too. Everything except a railway ticket to London and a man who issued him a warning. He left town that very day."

Smite let out a long breath. There was a sort of rough justice to her tale. It painted both Miranda and the Patron in a more sympathetic light than he'd imagined. What she'd done was wrong; the law would have labeled it conspiracy to commit assault. But there was nothing simple about her story. What else was she to have done? Complained to the constables about a man whistling beneath her window? He knew the help she'd have received: they'd have said she deserved whatever befell her, and sent her on her way.

"There," she said. "I arranged for a man to be beaten and robbed. I didn't hold the stick, but I asked for it. *Now* are you going to lecture me on the complicated rules of vicarious criminal liability?"

He took a deep breath. "No," he said.

She gave him a swift, bloodthirsty smile. "Good. Working for the Patron... It wasn't right, I'm sure. But he was the only one who kept order in Temple Parish. He cared about justice, about what was right. Women could go to him, and receive help they'd not find anywhere else. I know it wasn't right." She made a faint noise. "But it wasn't always *wrong,* either."

He didn't know how to think of something that was neither right nor wrong. "Well," he heard himself say stupidly. "I suppose that explains why you were still a virgin."

"Yes," she said simply. "It made me rather careful of men afterward. You see, I never lost my taste for dangerous men. I just realized that I needed to look for a man who wasn't dangerous to *me.*"

So. She was biding her time. Still looking. He didn't care. He had only so long with her, and he knew this wasn't permanent.

"And that's how I found myself here," she said softly. "With the most coldly intimidating man I have ever met. He's so good, that for a woman like me, he might as well be forbidden." Miranda smiled up at him, almost sad. "I have always had a taste for the forbidden."

"Do you, now." His heart was pounding.

"When I got this—" she held up a scrap of paper "—I nearly ran to Temple Church. I wanted to do it all by myself, to prove that I could handle it on my own." She handed him the note. "I can't."

It wasn't just a piece of paper she gave him, or even a story. It was a piece of herself, complicated and confusing. She'd trusted him to listen. In return, he trusted that no matter what had transpired in her past, she would turn to him first. If someone had told him he'd find this kind of mutual reliance with a woman who'd associated with criminals, he'd have scoffed.

He glanced over the paper and then folded it and set it back on her desk. "Well. There's no need to worry. Right, wrong, whatever he is—the Patron cannot threaten you with me." He leaned close to her. "You've forgiven enough of my faults. I can overlook this little thing." He paused. "I'm not even sure if you've described a fault or a strength. You survived. I cannot quarrel with that."

She let out her breath and looked up to him, not quite believing what he was saying. He wasn't sure what he was saying, either, but he felt as if he were slipping into some dangerous world—one where answers ceased to be easy.

He had only a couple of weeks left with her. He brushed a piece of hair from her mouth. "Come with me to the opera." It was the stupidest whim, especially after the debacle they'd made of the theater.

"What?"

"The opera," he repeated. "Don't let this bother you." He set the paper back on the desk. "Come with me to the opera tomorrow, and show the Patron that you won't be moved."

He intended to show her more than that. Maybe it was selfish, but he wanted to mark her every bit as much as she'd marked him.

EVER SINCE HER CONFESSION, Miranda had felt out of kilter—waiting for Smite to realize what she'd said, waiting for him to walk away from her.

The opera only heightened her sense of confusion. She didn't know why he'd suggested it—surely not just because she'd enjoy it. And he'd seemed uneasy through the entire performance. No; not uneasy. Tense. As if he waited for a particular moment. When the opera was almost over, that moment came.

He leaned over. "We're leaving now," he murmured.

"Leaving? Why are we…" She glanced up at his face. "Oh." There was no mistaking why they were leaving. There was a hot need in his eyes, something dark and deep and roiling. He wanted her. And he wanted her now.

She took his arm as they slid out of their seats and picked their way to the back of the hall. It was dark, and the soprano had started in on the final aria. Nobody could see the way her fingers dug into his arm. Only she was close enough to sense his urgency. He practically dragged her into the empty entry. The marble pillars echoed with their footsteps; behind her, the soaring song climbed high, and then higher.

"In return for making me miss the aria," she said, "I'm going to torment you the entire way home." She pulled off her glove and ran her finger down his chest. "Think you can stand twenty minutes of me, Turner?"

He turned and took her hands in his. "You're not missing the aria." He spun her around to face the wall and his voice dropped a few dangerous notes. "We're not going anywhere, either." He raised her hands and set them against the wall, and Miranda shivered.

"Anyone might come out of those doors," he said. His hands settled themselves at her waist, and he stepped up against her skirts. His body formed a warm, solid mass behind her. "Anyone at all. And if they do, they'll see me doing this."

His gloved hands slid up the stiff fabric of her bodice to cup her breasts. His thumbs circled her nipples. The material of her corset diffused the feel, spreading it out. But it did not mute the sharp spark of pleasure that shot through her.

"If that door opens now, of course," he murmured in her ear, "I can step away and only the flush in your cheeks will raise suspicion." His hands continued to chart a dangerous course over her body. He stroked her, caressed her, until she strained against him. He kissed the back of her neck. "So I think we should remove any doubt as to what is happening."

At first she had no inkling what he meant. But he braced her waist. She pushed against the wall, the palms of her hands hot against the cool stone. And then she felt air against her ankles. Her calves. Her thighs.

He was going to have her *here*. Now. Like this.

"Anyone might see us," she protested halfheartedly. But her pulse was already racing, and she found herself wet for him.

He didn't flinch. "That is rather the point."

Fabric rustled and he stepped closer. She could feel his frame, hot and muscular and hard behind her own. She was on fire for him—for *this*. Anyone might see. It scared her. It thrilled her. She felt as if she'd been brought to the climbing heights of the aria. His hands left her, briefly; she heard a rustle, and smelled a hint of vinegar.

"First," he said, and slid what must have been a sponge inside her. His fingers were sure and steady. Miranda bit down on a moan.

"Now this," he continued.

He shifted against her, and she felt the hard ridge of his erection naked against her skin.

She was wet and ready for him. He nudged her opening; she spread her legs as best as she could from that position. His entry wasn't smooth or easy, but it was *good*. When he was finally seated inside her, she felt an impossible thrill.

She had no notion how much time was left in the opera. By the libretto she'd been watching, not much. Only a few minutes until the curtain fell, and the audience stood to leave. Their discovery wasn't just a possibility; it was practically a given.

But there was no sense of hurry in his deliberate thrusts. He didn't use his fingers to aid her along. There was nothing but the slow, slick feel of him, taking her in a leisurely rhythm.

"Hurry," she said.

"Not a chance." He sounded amused, not transported by passion. "If you think I'll let you go before you explode, you are vastly mistaken."

"Everyone will find us."

"Then they'll see this." His hand pinched her nipple.

The soprano started one last, desperate climb into the heights. The music swelled over them. Their surroundings couldn't disappear—they wouldn't. She felt not just the need rising up in her, but that growing crescendo of music, the swelling sounds of the orchestra. Her pleasure wrapped around her, taking her higher. And then it hit, hard, just as the singer hit that final, clear lingering note. She heard herself call out.

Surely someone must have heard. But no; her cry was muffled in the roar of applause that followed.

His hands closed on her hips in grim satisfaction. His thrusts came harder and harder. And then he stiffened behind her. His teeth grazed the back of her neck. He came as the audience began the rustling murmur that presaged an immediate exodus. One last lingering kiss against the back of her neck, and then he disengaged.

He should have been flustered. It would be mere seconds before their privacy was invaded. She turned. He was as calm and unruffled as a windless lake. He adjusted his trousers. She must have been positively disheveled in contrast. He'd reduced her to a panting heat. At the very least, her hair must have fallen from her chignon. But he patted her skirts back into place and gave her a long, slow smile.

" *Now* we're going home," he said.

They said little as the hired hack brought them around. He stroked her hands, kissed her lips. He held her close, and she basked in the warm glow that came after intimacy. It took her almost a quarter of an hour to realize that something was wrong.

"There's something I don't understand," she said finally. "I hadn't thought you would be the sort to get excited by the threat of discovery."

"Did you like it?" he asked simply.

"I loved it."

He smiled in response and looked away.

And that was when she finally understood. He *wasn't* the sort to become aroused by the thought that their tryst might be discovered. No. He'd listened to what she told him earlier. She liked danger.

So he'd created it for her.

"Turner. I don't know what to say."

He made an embarrassed motion with his hand. "Pray don't say anything at all." He set his hand on her shoulder, and let it slide down her side.

She let out a shaky breath. He'd satisfied her, and not just physically. He'd filled that part of her that yearned for danger. He didn't talk of affection, but beneath the gruff exterior, he was tender. And he didn't need to say he cared to make her understand.

She'd worried about not being able to pay him back for his forbearance in the matter of the Patron. But this… Her left hand couldn't repay her right. There was nothing of commerce to their arrangement any longer. He'd done something that she suspected was deeply, deeply contrary to his own nature. And he'd done it to let her know that he accepted her. All of her.

Falling in love with a man who'd declared the relationship to be a month long, who'd warned her he would never love her, was all kinds of reckless. He wouldn't even share a night with her after intercourse; he was never going to share her life. And yet he made her feel safer and more in peril all at once.

It was dangerous to entrust him with anything besides the month he'd asked for. But then, her tastes ran to danger. Perhaps that was why she tossed her heart his way without a protest.

"You did that for me," she said, as he handed her out of the carriage.

"If you think I put you up against a wall and had you without my own self-interest being engaged, you've a great deal to learn about men." He opened her front door.

He made it sound almost vulgar. But he'd thought about her. About what she wanted. What she *needed*. It wasn't the act itself that made her heart feel so tender; it was the care he'd put into it. As if she were somehow precious to him.

"It wouldn't mean the same thing if you did it here," she said.

"We can test that."

She swatted at his hand. "Don't. Don't try to make something sweet and beautiful into something tawdry."

Silence. Then: "There's nothing tawdry about you, Miranda." He paused, just that tiny amount. "Darling." His arms came around her in the dark. It was an embrace—one without heat or want, just care. Affection. *Love,* even if he wouldn't say it, and wouldn't want it said. She wrapped her arms around him, holding him close. She held that fluttering sense of new emotion close as well.

She loved him. How could she not?

And then she heard a rustle down the hall. The parlor door opened, and a small head poked out from behind it.

"Miranda?" The voice was rough with sleep, but shaking with terror.

"Robbie." She let go of Smite. "Robbie, what are you doing here?"

He stepped out into the dim light of the entry and looked up at her. He had dark circles under his eyes. "Miranda," he said, "I think someone is trying to kill me."

Chapter Seventeen

"KILL YOU?" MIRANDA SAID. "What makes you think that?"

Robbie hunched. The bony points of his shoulders jutted out beneath his coat, an eloquent statement of his discomfort. But as eloquent as his expression was, it still was not an answer to her question.

"Robbie, please," she said. "I want to help. Just talk to me." *And consider using actual words.*

Beside her, Smite gave her a short shake of his head, and a look. She was probably doing everything wrong again—and here she'd thought, over the last two Sabbaths when he'd visited, that they were getting beyond that—but at least Robbie had come to her when he needed help. That counted for something, did it not?

Smite rang the bell, and when the maid came, he called for a blanket, a glass of warm milk, and a plate of sweet biscuits. While he did so, Miranda bustled them all back into the parlor to sit by the fire.

The maid didn't ask what Robbie was doing there. It occurred to Miranda, rather belatedly, that she didn't need to explain herself to the servants. The woman came back in short order with a tray.

Smite gestured. "Those ones, with the sugar on top—they're quite good."

Robbie needed no further encouragement. He reached out and took one in each hand. Before she could protest—or even convince him to chew—he'd inhaled first one, and then the other, and was eyeing the still-full plate with zeal.

"Hard to gather thoughts on an empty stomach," Smite said. "Don't worry about how you say things, or what order you tell the story in. If I don't understand something, I'll ask questions. Just tell us what you know."

He was watching Robbie carefully. It was easy to forget that he did this sort of thing on a regular basis: asked questions, and tried to piece together what had happened. She hadn't imagined that Smite was the sort of person who could put anyone at ease. But Robbie slouched into the cushions of the sofa and took another biscuit.

"I want you to think back. When was the first time you realized that something might be amiss?"

"This afternoon, when—no." Robbie stopped. "Mid-morning, Mr. Allen said his ring had gone missing."

"What sort of ring was it?"

Robbie frowned. "Gold?"

"A wedding band?"

"I guess." Robbie frowned. "He wore it here." He pointed to his ring finger. "Except when he worked. He takes it off to work. He asked us to keep an eye out for it, but I forgot about that, because somebody dropped a hammer on my head."

Miranda winced. But Smite simply reached forward and rubbed his hand in Robbie's hair. "You've a bit of a lump," he reported. "Nothing serious."

Miranda resisted the urge to report that men had been known to keel over after simple blows to the head. By the look on Robbie's face, it wouldn't have helped.

"Who dropped the hammer?"

"Don't know." Robbie shrugged. "It hurt too much at first to look."

"Can you make a guess?"

"Could have been almost anyone. There was a crew working above me." He cast Smite a defiant glance. "Besides, I didn't want to fuss over it like a baby."

"Naturally." Smite waited, and Robbie took another biscuit. It vanished as swiftly as its predecessors; Robbie washed it down with a hefty swallow of milk.

"Half an hour before the dinner bell, a crane came loose. It swung across the deck. Knocked me clean off my feet and into the water."

Beside her Smite had tensed. "How far above the water was the deck?"

Robbie shrugged. "Twenty feet?"

"You...you *can* swim, can't you?"

"A little. Hard part was getting out of the water. The nearest stairs were on the north wall, and when you're neck-deep in water you can't see them." Robbie's nose wrinkled. "They had to send a boat for me."

Smite stood. He picked up a biscuit himself and passed it from hand to hand. His breath was a bit ragged, and Miranda suspected that he had his own memories of water to contend with. But after a few minutes he turned back to Robbie.

"I hope you weren't too cold," was all he said.

"Freezing," Robbie reported. "And everyone ribbed me." He frowned, as if that was more disturbing than attempted murder. "They sent me back to my bunk to change into something dry." Robbie reached into his pocket and pulled out a crumpled twist of paper. "That's when I found this."

He passed it over to Smite, who untwisted the paper. As he did, a worn gold ring fell out. Smite caught it midair, and then glanced at the containing foolscap. His eyebrow raised, and he handed the message to Miranda.

The paper held words written in a spidery hand—one that she recognized from the last note she'd received. And the message... *Tell her that it will be you innstead,* it said. *She needs to come speak with me.*

"The Patron is a poor speller," Smite noted.

Miranda lifted the paper to her nose and inhaled. There was a faint scent of stale tobacco smoke. It could have meant anything, but... "The Patron smokes a pipe," she said. "But no. It's possible the Patron didn't write this himself."

"If they thought I stole the ring, they'd hang me, wouldn't they?" Robbie whispered.

Smite gave a slight shrug of his shoulder.

"You're staying with me," Miranda said flatly. "You're not to leave this house, hear?"

"I have to leave." Robbie hunched deeper into the cushions. "It's a crime to desert an apprenticeship. Besides, I can hardly stay here forever."

"You can't go back out there." Miranda stared at the paper. "Or I have to—" Her eyes darted away and met Smite's briefly.

His expression was frozen in hard contemplation. "It's not any kind of life either of you will live, hidden away inside a building." He frowned. "Robbie, how *did* you get in here? I sincerely doubt the maids would have let you simply take up residence in the parlor upon application."

Robbie looked sheepish. "I, uh, I picked the lock. It's easy enough. You just need a hairpin, and you slide the tumblers up and to the right."

"Don't tell me where you learned that." Miranda put her head in her hands.

"Joey," Robbie offered anyway.

"This doesn't make sense," Miranda said. "I'm not worth the bother. The Patron has plenty of other minions. He's going to extraordinary lengths to get my attention. Why?"

Smite stalked across the room to the window. They'd not lit any lamps in the room, but he pulled the curtains shut, regardless. "Does it matter? You're not safe here." His gaze swept the room, encompassing both Miranda and Robbie in that sweeping statement.

Robbie spoke first. "So what do we do?"

Smite looked at Robbie. "You'll have to leave Bristol."

Robbie's eyes jerked down. "Why?" He swallowed. "By *myself?* Am I…am I going to another apprenticeship? Because I don't really mind when Mr. Allen clouts me over the head. Aren't they going to force me to come back?"

"No," Smite said. "It's only a crime to leave when you abscond without permission. That can be obtained easily enough. This will be somewhere temporary. Secure."

"A prison?" Robbie gulped.

"A home in the country." Smite turned.

"It's an orphanage." Robbie stared at the wall, his spine rigid. "A place for unwanted children."

"No," Smite said softly. "Not an orphanage. I'm taking you to my brother. He'll enjoy having you. He might not want you to leave."

"Likely, I'll have to fight him to give you up," Miranda added.

Robbie lowered his head.

"Can you consent to that?" Smite asked.

There was a long pause. And then, Robbie gave a bit of a shrug. "I guess," he said.

Smite took this equivocation in stride. He simply nodded. "We'll leave in the morning." He glanced at the curtained windows. "I'll be here all night, to make sure you're safe."

"You're...you're staying the night?" Miranda asked.

He glanced at her, perhaps understanding what she was intimating. He gave her a slow shake of his head. "Not as you might think. I won't be sleeping."

THE FIRST FEW HOURS were not so awful. Smite called for pen and paper and sent off a series of instructions—a long one to his solicitor, a shorter note to his clerk, and a brief query to the shipwright to whom Robbie was apprenticed. But he hesitated a good long while before he started the last communication.

Ash—

I will be unable to attend you tomorrow evening. I have been called out of town on urgent business.

He found himself drawing in the margins and staring at the still mostly blank sheet of paper, not knowing how to go on without making things worse between them.

Undoubtedly, you will hear that my urgent business is with Mark. I can only imagine how that will seem to you—my abandoning our time together, in favor of visiting him. I beg you not to enlarge upon it.

I will return the day after tomorrow, and if it is convenient, I will wait upon you at noon.

He paused once more. In years past, he'd received letters from his brother. They had all been written entirely in his secretary's hand, save for the complimentary closing. That alone had been scrawled in Ash's scarcely intelligible script. When he'd been younger, he'd thought it had been negligence on his brother's part—that he'd been too busy to even compose his own letters. He'd only learned what those additions had meant to his brother years later. Writing did not come easily to Ash.

Sometimes, he felt that the gulf between him and Ash was unbridgeable. But if it could be spanned by anything, maybe it was those few words Ash had always offered in closing.

And so now, he finished as carefully as possible.

All my love,

Smite.

He blotted the ink dry and then passed this, too, to the maid to seal and deliver.

Responses started to return to his inquiries. Some were long; others were quite short. It was hours before Ash's reply arrived.

Be well.

—Ash

He'd written it out entirely by himself. He wouldn't have taken that trouble if he were irreparably angry. Smite drew a deep sigh of relief.

He imagined that Miranda must have gone to bed by now. But when he wandered down the hall to her room, he found her oil lamp burning at the dimmest setting. She sat on the edge of the lace coverlet and stared at the wall.

"Miranda Darling," he said, as sternly as he could manage. "You ought to be asleep."

He ought to be watching her.

She turned to him and gave him a wan smile. "Do you suppose I'll see Robbie again?"

"I'm sure of it." He sat next to her on the bed and pulled her into his embrace.

He didn't think she had followed what he had said to its logical conclusion. If Robbie had to be sent away from Bristol, so did Miranda. And if Miranda went...

This had been inevitable, since the day he'd kissed her.

He could recall that moment now. The luminous look of her eyes. The quiver in her voice. *Kiss me,* he'd said, *and make it worse.*

He'd not realized then how bad it was going to be. When Miranda left, he would be alone. He had known this was coming. He hadn't expected it to be so soon.

"He needs to know that I'm not leaving him," Miranda said. "He's been left so many times. I've never been a parent to him, but I'm all that he has."

"He'll know," Smite said. "He'll know because you'll tell him. And then you'll write to him, and when it's safe, you'll come and get him."

Smite felt a tug of wistful envy. She'd come back to Bristol to see Robbie; of course she would. Maybe he could get Robbie to tell him how she fared over the years. *Years.* Robbie would meet her husband. Her children.

His fist clenched around the coverlet.

"Will you take me to visit him?" Miranda asked. "While he's there."

It took Smite a moment to realize that she was still talking about Robbie. His fist clenched even further and he looked away. "No."

Her breath rushed in.

"I don't go to Shepton Mallet," he finally offered.

"You're going tomorrow, are you not?"

He shut his eyes. He hadn't been back to Shepton Mallet since he and Mark had escaped, all those years ago. It had been decades, now, and still he felt that cold chill creep over him.

"Tomorrow," he said more to himself than to her, "it can't be helped. What can't be helped must be tolerated."

He didn't know whether seeing Miranda in his childhood home would make the place bearable, or if it would taint his memories of her forever.

"That hardly sounds auspicious," she said. "And you're doing it for me. I might almost think that you tolerated me, too." She was looking directly in his eyes as she spoke.

"Would you know," he finally said, "I've hit the end of my sentimentality quota for the day."

"How can that be? That's the first remotely sentimental thing I've said tonight."

"Yes, but…" But he'd been wallowing in sentiment all evening. "I've spent the last minutes memorizing you," he finally said. He didn't think that memory could capture the bright color of her hair, though, or the intelligent light in her eyes. Memory would never quite capture the luminous look she'd given him on the carriage ride home after the opera. Even a memory as clear as his couldn't call back the precise feel of her seated next to him, or the texture of her fingers against his. And he never could recall scents once they'd gone.

He folded his arms and set aside the inevitability of the future. There was only the present. In the present, Miranda was here. Solid. Touchable. He held her close, breathing her in. She smelled like mint tea—sweet and cool. Calming.

He wouldn't be able to hold the feel of her in his memory after she'd gone. Still, he could try.

SMITE HADN'T THOUGHT THROUGH what would happen when he arrived on his brother's doorstep after a lengthy journey. His brother must have seen him arrive from the upstairs window, because instead of waiting for him to be announced like a rational human being, Mark crashed through the door, his face utterly white. He grabbed hold of Smite's arms before he'd had a chance to properly step down from the phaeton.

"Oh, God," Mark said in urgent tones. "It's Ash, isn't it?"

"What about Ash?"

Mark shook him. "What's wrong with Ash? Why are you here?"

Smite stared at his brother in confusion. His brother's fingers gripped his arms all the more tightly. His blond hair seemed wild on the top of his head. His bare hands were stained in ink.

In fact, he'd smeared ink on Smite's cuff.

It was easier to concentrate on his younger brother than to pay attention to his surroundings. Behind him, he could see the entryway of his childhood home. The door was clean and new, painted a bright blue in color. Mark had replaced the older front windows with clear, smooth glass, so that the entry shone with sunlight. It wasn't the same house, he told himself.

But beneath the fading scent of the lavender that had been planted by the front entry, the house smelled the same. There was something about that peculiar combination of wood and stone that brought to mind old memories—as if the unquiet ghost of his mother still lingered.

"What the devil are you talking about?" he finally asked. "Nothing's wrong with Ash. He was the picture of health, last I saw him."

Mark let out a deep breath. He let go of Smite, but only long enough to punch his shoulder. "What were you thinking, scaring me like that? You *never* come here. Why else would you come, except to bear—oh."

His gaze shifted behind Smite, landing on Robbie, who had climbed out of the hired phaeton.

"Oh," he repeated, more stupidly this time. "I'd best get Jessica."

Smite reached out and grabbed Mark's cuff. "Wait."

Miranda followed Robbie out of the conveyance. She adjusted the dark brown fabric of her traveling gown, and then glanced at Mark.

"You'll never understand this," Smite said his voice low, pitched for Mark's ears only. "And you'll never see the two of us together again. I want to introduce you."

Mark gave Smite a long, measuring look, and then walked forward to greet his guests.

"Robbie Barnstable," Smite said. "This is Sir Mark Turner."

Robbie looked up at Mark. "He didn't say you were a sir."

"Just call me Mark. I was knighted a handful of years past. I keep hoping everyone will forget it, but alas."

Smite drew a deep breath. "And Miss Miranda Darling. This is my brother. Mark, this is..." He paused, not knowing how to go forward. He didn't think Mark would be shocked if he introduced her as his mistress. Still...

Mark solved the dilemma of his introduction by taking Miranda's hand and shaking it. "I'm delighted to meet you," he said.

"Miranda has been caring for Robbie," Smite said. "But he'll need somewhere safe to stay temporarily. I thought of you."

"Welcome," Mark said simply, and that was that. He glanced at Smite. "Are you coming in? Jessica will be furious if I let you run off without saying a word to her." He glanced around. "But it's a fine day. We could stay outside."

It wasn't. It was gray and cloudy. "It looks about to drizzle," Smite said. "I won't perish if I enter. Besides, I would hate to interfere with your marital tranquility. We can come in for a short space of time."

"Ha!" Mark said. "She'd be angry at *you*, not me, for dashing off. First order of business." Mark took Robbie by the arm. "I'll take you upstairs and introduce you to my wife. Lady Turner is a lovely woman, and she'll get the servants started on obtaining you a bath."

"A bath?" Robbie said scornfully. "I just fell in the Floating Harbour yesterday. I don't need a bath."

Mark wrinkled his nose. "Ah, so that smell is algae." He turned to go in the house.

"I'll—I'll just stay out here, then," Miranda said.

Mark swiveled back and took Miranda's arm. "No," he said cheerfully. "You'll come inside. Jessica would have my head if I left Smite's..." He paused and glanced at Smite—just long enough for Smite to know that he'd heard every word that he hadn't said. "Smite's friend outside. Come, now, Smite. Did you not prepare her for anything?"

Smite shook his head and watched his brother bend his blond head close to Miranda's fire-orange hair. He whispered something; she laughed in response.

In the end, it was Smite who held back, watching from a distance as his brother introduced Jessica to Miranda. It was Smite who concentrated on his breathing. He'd wanted Mark to know Miranda, if only for a few seconds. Mark knew everything important to him, even if he never spoke of it. But this house...it overwhelmed him. He focused on the window to the yard outside, ignoring the cellar that lurked beneath.

The two women exchanged greetings and then took Robbie upstairs, leaving Mark and Smite alone. The smile slowly slid off Mark's face, and he turned to his brother. "Come," Mark said. "Let's go for a walk in the back garden before you cast up your accounts in the house."

Chapter Eighteen

MIRANDA WATCHED ROBBIE DISAPPEAR behind a door, half-dragged by an upstairs maid.

"There," Lady Turner said beside her, brushing her hands. "The servants will see to his bath." She sighed. "I have to admit, I have always hoped that Smite would fall in love, but you are not what I expected."

Miranda choked. "Pardon?"

"I've never been certain he would marry. He's rather odd," Lady Turner was saying. "Once you get past his frightening exterior, he's actually quite kind. But I suspect you know that."

"He feeds stray cats in Bristol," Miranda heard herself offering.

"Of course he does." Lady Turner pinched her lips together. "He's very sweet, no matter how he tries to hide it. He never doubted me—not once—and I daresay my past is more checkered than yours." She looked down and drew in a deep breath. "They've managed to obscure the matter quite a bit, but I was a courtesan for years before I met Sir Mark. The Turners are something out of the ordinary. All of them. It has taken me some time to grow accustomed to the fact that I am not the oddest one in the room when they're around. You'll begin to understand, eventually."

"You shouldn't imagine this is anything other than temporary."

Lady Turner's eyes met hers. "Nonsense. Smite hasn't been back to Shepton Mallet in twenty years. Mark goes to Bristol to see him because he won't come here. Smite knows perfectly well that bringing you here is tantamount to a declaration."

"No." Miranda stared at the wallpaper. "He's quite precise in everything he does. I have no doubt that he cares for me. He may even love me. But he sees what is between us as fleeting."

"I've never known him to be fickle."

Miranda shook her head. "It's not that. I know when a man is saying good-bye." She thought of the way he'd held her last night, and the dire look in his eyes in the phaeton this morning. "Even if he doesn't say it directly, Smite is most assuredly telling me farewell."

Lady Turner gave her a long, level look. "That, I can believe. He scarcely lets Mark close. I was so hoping…"

"What? That he'd fall in love and turn into an ordinary man?" Miranda choked on the words. "Anyone who loved him would never want that. It would be like loving the ocean, but wishing it would change into a glass of water."

"No. I rather think it would be like loving the ocean and wishing it could feel a little sunlight." Lady Turner adjusted a vase on a shelf. "When I first met Mark, he told me that I reminded him of his brother. At the time, I didn't realize what a compliment he was paying me. He was saying I was difficult, but worth the trouble."

It had never occurred to Miranda that Smite was on good terms with anyone in his family. He was so extraordinarily solitary, and he'd argued so ferociously with his brother, the duke. She'd supposed that his relationship with his siblings was as fraught as his time with his mother. But that wasn't so. He was loved.

It made his solitary life seem all the starker.

"Come," Lady Turner said. "They'll be in the garden. Let's go find them." She led Miranda downstairs and out the front. But Smite and his brother were nowhere to be seen; Lady Turner frowned and then took Miranda along a path of slate stones along the side of the house. Miranda heard male voices before Smite came into view.

"Aren't you going to lecture me?" Smite was saying.

"What about?"

"Chastity." Leaves rustled. "Miss Darling. I know what you must be thinking."

"I'm thinking that there's no need for me to lecture you, as you appear to be lecturing yourself quite effectively." Smite's younger brother spoke with an easy air.

"Did you know she was a virgin when I met her?" Smite threw out. Miranda knew that tone of voice; he was daring his brother to quarrel with him.

"Tsk, tsk." Sir Mark didn't sound disappointed in the least. "You terrible man, seducing an innocent young lady. Is that what you want me to say?"

"Say something. Say anything. I can't argue with you if you won't even put up a good show."

"I refuse to quarrel with someone who wins arguments by profession. It seems rather imprudent."

"Ha," Smite replied grimly. "It's never stopped you before."

There was a long pause. Then, in a low voice, Mark spoke again. "Is it so bad, then?"

Lady Turner rounded the corner just ahead of Miranda. At the rustling of the underbrush, the two men looked up. They were seated facing one another on a bench. Smite looked up at Miranda. His eyes caught hers, darted to Jessica, and then he looked back at Mark.

"No," he said. "Which makes it utterly impossible."

Sir Mark seemed to think that this answer made perfect sense. He rose from his seat and smiled cheerfully. When Miranda held back, he cocked his head at her. "Smite surely didn't tell you that we're sticklers for propriety. It's rather misleading, that Ash ended up a duke. We've been anywhere and everywhere between. Ash says that the notion of social class is a delusion. At some point, someone will figure out that he really means that."

She'd never thought about what it meant, that Parford had left home at fourteen, that Smite and this man had ended up on the streets of Bristol as children. She'd never thought about the bewildering change of events that had struck them. And Sir Mark had married a courtesan.

"What does it mean, then?"

"It means," Sir Mark said, "that I'm quite pleased with you. I consider it my personal mission as younger brother to keep my elders out of sorts. You've been doing a beautiful job of it."

"Nonsense." Miranda drew herself up. "I do nothing of the kind. Smite keeps himself out of sorts all on his own."

Sir Mark let out a sharp crack of laughter, and behind him, a rueful grin spread across Smite's face.

"Tell me," Miranda said, "how do you handle his sentimentality quota?"

"That?" An airy wave of Sir Mark's hand. "I simply refuse to acknowledge its existence."

"You can do that?"

"Of course I can. I'm his younger brother. I can do anything I wish."

It had never occurred to Miranda that Smite was so well loved. He'd spoken to her of horrors in his past. He'd mentioned his brothers in warm tones once or twice. But she'd never believed that he might have this teasing friendship available to him—and that he might nonetheless turn away from it.

It wasn't the only thing he rejected. He could obtain a luxuriously furnished house on a few hours' notice without blinking about the cost, and yet he himself lived in a few austere rooms. He chose not to spend nights with her. She'd been harboring—somewhere deep inside her—the hope that if she offered him the warmth and care that he'd lacked all these years, that he'd decide he couldn't do without her.

But this destroyed all her illusions. She wasn't the first person to care for him. She wasn't special at all. And if he could walk away from the brother who so clearly adored him, whom he had known from infancy, a few weeks with her would prove no impediment at all. Her last, foolish hope crumbled under the crushing weight of reality.

"Come, Miranda," Smite said, standing. "We'll need to say our farewell to Robbie and get on the road."

Sir Mark stepped forward. "It will be dark in a few hours. Won't you at least—"

"Stay the night?" Smite asked, raising his eyebrow. "Come, Mark. You know there isn't the least chance of that happening."

Sir Mark shook his head and shrugged. "Well. I had to offer."

Chapter Nineteen

THE JOURNEY FROM BRISTOL to Shepton Mallet in a phaeton had taken half the day. On horseback, Smite might have managed the return in one single, tiring afternoon. But they'd gone no more than eight miles down the road before dusk crept up on them.

Had these been ordinary circumstances, he might have pushed through, even with a team of horses. But he was exhausted, having not slept the night before. And Miranda slumped next to him. Her hands were entangled around his arm; her head leaned against his shoulder.

Somehow, he was supposed to give her up.

Ahead, he could see the lights from a posting inn. He sighed and tapped Miranda on the shoulder.

"Mmm?" came her sleepy response.

"We'll be staying at the inn ahead for the night," he informed her.

She straightened, rubbing at her eyes. "We?" she repeated? " *Staying?*"

He took a deep breath. "With you here, I likely won't strike out in my sleep, as nightmares will be less probable." There. That sounded plain. Unemotional. "Still, you should consider whether you'll take the risk and share a bed with me. There is always some danger." His fingers clenched about the reins as he waited for the questions to come. *You still have nightmares? You poor thing.* If he'd wanted her pity, he'd have mentioned his dreams earlier.

Instead, Miranda pulled off her gloves and fumbled with the little silk bag she'd brought with her. "There," she finally said in satisfaction. He had no idea what she'd found; he couldn't see it.

It was almost worse to have her not comment on what he'd said. But she tied up the strings of her bag, and then slipped her gloves back on. She was close enough, and there was just light enough, that he could see the intense expression in her eyes.

"There is no chance I would forgo the opportunity to share your bed," she said quietly. "But then, you had already guessed that."

He gave her one painful nod. One night with her—it could not hurt so much, could it?

"I don't believe it is your intention to be so secretive," she continued. "But you are not much in the habit of explaining yourself to others. I had already guessed you were afflicted with nightmares."

He drew a breath in. "You did?"

"You mentioned them before."

He rummaged back through their conversations, brought up those words. "In the past tense."

She shrugged. "You're not a very good liar."

"Ah." He turned the reins over in his hands.

"I had assumed it was simple pride that kept you away for the night. You don't like being fussed over, and I suppose others might feel pity if you woke in the middle of the night. But I've learned better than to do any of that."

"Indeed," was his stellar contribution to this conversation, which was not going as he'd envisioned it at all. "You are quite acute."

"Don't fob me off with false compliments, Smite. Just now, you implied your nightmares are less likely to happen if I am present. What the devil did you mean by that?"

The air against his face was bitter cold. They had drawn near enough to the inn that he could see white walls rising up, overgrown with some creeping vine. Light seeped from the windows. He could catch the savory smoke from some roasting meat.

"There are some things that help alleviate the nightmares," he said, as he drew the phaeton to a halt. "Companionship. Comfort. If I lived the life of luxury my eldest brother wished for me, my dreams would probably dwindle to once-a-year occurrences."

She sat in silence, digesting this, as he tied up the reins. "You *want* to have nightmares."

"They serve as a reminder of why I am needed. What will happen to others if I fail. It's nothing to lose a few moments of sleep on occasion."

She made no response for a few moments, and rubbed her hands together. "That's bloody stupid," she finally offered.

"Why? I do not fear what comes at night. I dread its absence. I fear being caged by luxury. I fear that one day I will no longer understand desperation, and with that, I will slowly stop listening to what others have to say." He pulled on the reins, bringing the phaeton to a halt just outside the inn. "I don't regret what circumstances have made of me, inconvenient though they may be. I make a difference." His breath was growing harsh. "If I made myself like everyone else, I would fail. This way—" He stopped, choking on the words. "If you put it all together, it sounds so awful. The nightmares. Not being able to bear it when someone touches my face. If I tried to be like everyone else, I would be nothing more than a broken failure. This way, it means something."

"You purposefully push others away so that you'll have nightmares."

"I did tell you I was wed to my duties." He sighed. "Although it is an annoyance when I wake half the inn, shouting."

"Is that likely tonight?"

"I just came from my mother's house. It's a possibility. Otherwise, I wouldn't have mentioned it." He shrugged. He didn't think that show of indifference convinced her.

She pulled her coat more snugly about her. He stepped down from the phaeton; she gave him her hand. His hand clenched around hers through her gloves. But the only comment she made in passing was, "Lady Justice is a lucky woman."

If there was a hint of bitterness in her voice, it did not show in her face when they entered the lamp-lit entryway of the inn.

The proprietress had roused herself from the kitchen; she ran her gaze over them with a sharply trained eye. No doubt she was considering the fine cut of Smite's coat, the smooth wool of Miranda's traveling habit. The ostler had likely whispered a word about the phaeton—hired from Bristol, but well-made. This, she weighed against the lack of servants traveling with them.

"Welcome," she said, with a hint of curtsy that suggested she'd totted up the sums and decided the two of them ranked just above poor gentry. "Might I be having your names for the register?"

It was at that moment that Smite realized he'd made a tremendous miscalculation. He'd been so preoccupied with the prospect of going to his mother's house—and then the necessity of staying in an inn—that he'd simply not considered how they were to present themselves.

He cast Miranda a pained look—one that the sharp-eyed woman detected instantly. One hand shot to her hip and her lips narrowed. But if Miranda noticed this, she paid it no attention. Instead, she gave Smite a brilliant smile—one that seemed to slice deep into his belly. "May I do it, dearest?" she asked.

"Do what?"

"Sign the inn's register." Miranda beamed at the innkeeper's wife.

The woman's face was still frozen in a mask of suspicion.

But Miranda simply removed her gloves and set them on the counter. "I can't get enough of it."

Smite made a gesture, which Miranda seemed to take as permission. She swept forward, took hold of the barrel of the pen, and spoke as she signed. "Mr. and *Mrs.* Dashwood. I just adore the sound of that. It never grows old."

Miranda was wearing a ring made of simple gold on her finger. It looked the sort of thing that impoverished gentry might use as a wedding band. She must have slipped it on in the phaeton. Smite shook his head. She'd come prepared to tell a story.

The scowl on the woman's face began to melt away. "You're newlyweds, are you?"

"Oh, no," Miranda said earnestly. "We're not new at all. It's been all of…two months, one week, and three days. Isn't that right, dearest?"

"Mmmm." It was fascinating to watch her spin the tale. She'd adjusted her accent yet again, adding just a twitch of country. She looked up at him with just the right amount of girlish adoration. As if they were deeply in love and barely beginning to discover one another.

He couldn't help looking back with the same expression. He wasn't dissembling.

"Well, go on," Miranda said. "You *are* going to tell her, are you not? About the, um, the other thing."

He had no idea what she might be alluding to. She didn't expect him to *participate* in this lie, did she? He raised an eyebrow at her repressively.

"We don't want a repeat of two nights ago," she admonished him, and then turned to the woman. "The proprietor of the hotel…well, he broke into our room. At two in the morning, no less."

"Of all things!" said the woman in front of her. "Why would he do that?"

Miranda flushed a dainty pink. "It's—it's a bit delicate, you understand? He heard shouts. He thought I was being hurt. I can understand his concern. It was entirely laudable, but so, *so* embarrassing." She made a little motion with her hand, so adorably coy that he almost believed her himself.

"I wasn't," she said, looking down. "Hurt, I mean." She lowered her voice to a conspiratorial whisper. "I can't imagine what the innkeeper was thinking—I wasn't even the one making noises. It was dreadfully embarrassing."

"At two in the morning?" the innkeeper's wife repeated in fainter tones.

Miranda blushed deeper. "I know. What would my mother say? But…he always does make it worth my while. And I never can say no."

Smite heard himself make a strangled noise in his throat.

The woman gave him a sharper appraising glance. "Doesn't talk much, does he?"

Miranda leaned in. "Doesn't need to," she whispered, just loud enough for Smite to hear.

The innkeeper's wife smiled at Miranda, coming to some feminine understanding. "You have him wrapped around your little finger, don't you?"

"She does," Smite said, finally able to contribute something truthful to the conversation.

The woman met Miranda's eyes. "We'll be sure to give you two your privacy, then. There aren't many guests here tonight, and the upper floor will be all yours. I'll just send Mary, the maid, to sleep downstairs. She won't mind."

"Thank you so much," Miranda said. And then, as the woman gathered her keys and bustled down the hall, she looked up at Smite and winked.

THEY SETTLED IN A small room upstairs. The wood floors were covered over with plain rag rugs; the walls were recently whitewashed. The room was clean and cozy. A boy brought up their single valise, and departed after Smite threw him a penny.

Smite had not yet been able to meet Miranda's eyes. He puttered about, washing with cold water from the single metal basin. He focused on the details of the present: unpacking his bag, although there was hardly anything to set in order. Nonetheless, he laid out the sparse collection of soap and shaving materials next to the basin.

He could hardly ignore Miranda when she came to stand beside him. She slid her arms around his waist. He set his hand atop hers, but couldn't bring himself to push her away.

"I know what you're thinking," she said.

Ha. "I'll wager a shilling you're wrong."

"You're berating yourself because you let that little white lie I told stand. Now you're wondering if you must go and correct my perfidy, and never mind that it will get us tossed out of the inn."

He turned to her. "Hardly. I win."

For so long, his wishes had harmonized. He wanted to introduce a certain amount of discomfort into his life. He wanted to avoid the pity of others. That had all amounted to a simple directive: avoid those who fussed over him—namely, everyone.

But Miranda never fussed. And just now, with a handful of smiles, she'd rearranged his life so that he did not need to be an object of pity. He could imagine the future spread before him. The two of them could live in a proper house with a flock of servants poised to wash Ghost when he nosed about in unsavory messes. They would hold doors and make lemon cakes. His bed would always be turned down. On cold nights, hot bricks would appear. He might live like anyone else—so long as Miranda was there to smooth the way.

She'd told him once about her parents, presenting a facade to the outside world and then laughing together when it succeeded. They'd been liars, yes… but they'd faced everything together.

Without even trying, Miranda had just made him part of a team. He wanted to grab hold of the chance that she offered.

And yet he held back.

The thought that he might one day transform himself into one of the fat, complacent burghers who sat in judgment alongside him was intolerable.

He'd been staring at the hard gray lump of his soap for too long. He set it down and turned to Miranda. "It's like this," he heard himself say. "When you leave, I will wish you well. I'll watch you go, and I won't make a fuss, because I know what lies ahead of you will be better and more satisfying than anything I can give."

Her chin rose. "That's terribly kind of you. Hopefully, I'll have left you with a penchant for company, and you'll replace me soon enough."

He had a penchant for her. "Hardly," he heard himself say.

"Shall we be clear?" Miranda said.

"By all means."

"We are not talking about some hypothetical future," she said. "You are talking about when our month is up."

He was talking about tomorrow morning.

"I'll be miserable without you," she continued. "And don't pretend you'll be happy to be rid of me, either. I know you better than that."

He turned away from her and wandered to the window. "I'm sure you'll find happiness eventually."

She followed to stand shoulder-to-shoulder with him. "I notice you make no protestations on your own behalf. I expected you'd at least make some cutting remark in a flat tone of voice. Something like, 'I suppose I'll survive.'"

He flipped her to face him, pushed her back against the wall. "Is that what you think? That I shall simply survive?"

She stared at him. And then she slowly rose onto her toes and kissed him.

He should have stepped away. He should have remained still when her lips touched his. But he might never have this chance again. He might never hold her this close, might never sink his hands into her hair.

And so instead he kissed her back out of deep, dark desperation. He worshipped her mouth. And when her hands untucked his shirt, slid up underneath the linen to reveal his bare chest, he didn't bother to restrain himself. He picked her up and tossed her onto the bed.

The sheets were soft against his touch, but not as soft as her skin. The warmth of her breath as she pulled him down to her only reminded him of the cold future that awaited.

But no matter the desperate urgency he felt rising in him, he took his time to strip her bare: unbuttoning her habit and peeling it away, unlacing her corset, freeing the small, firm mounds of her breasts. He untied her garters and slid her stockings down slim legs. As he removed her petticoats one by one, she undid his cravat, and then removed his waistcoat. She pulled his shirt from his head and undid the buttons of his fall.

She sat up, just long enough for him to pull the chemise from her head, long enough to kick out of his unwanted trousers. Then he pushed her back into the bed. She was wet for him; he slid inside her with one sharp thrust. And this time, he held nothing back. He set his hands on her and took her, claiming every inch of her. Her tight, hot passage clenched around his cock. Her nipples, tipped in coral, offered themselves to his mouth. She dug her nails into his backside.

Dimly, he was aware that the headboard of the bed thumped into the wall, that the boards beneath them squeaked in time to his thrusts. He didn't care; didn't care about anything but Miranda beneath him, Miranda's hands on him. For now, for these last few hours, Miranda was still his. She was hot, and a tight, sharp pleasure gathered in his groin. Her breath stuttered against his cheek. She made a strangled sound, and her hips rose to his. He could feel her pulsing about him. Waves of heat surrounded him, and he drove into her hard, until his own desire overtook him.

He came inside her, hard and savage and satisfying.

When they'd both caught their breaths, she met his eyes. She didn't say anything. She didn't need to. He could see the satisfied set of her lips.

See? You can't survive without me.

"You're perfectly right," he said, in answer to the sentiment she hadn't voiced. "There's no two ways about it. When you leave, it will slay me."

IN THE END, SMITE slept without dreams, and the remainder of the journey back to Bristol passed unremarkably. They arrived at Miranda's house shortly before noon. When Smite pulled the team up, he could tell immediately that the instructions he had left behind had been followed. They were met there by a groom and a cart containing three trunks and a bandbox.

Smite jumped down from the phaeton and spoke with the man in a low voice. He almost wished that something had gone awry, anything to turn him away from the awful inevitability of this moment. But the man handed him an envelope and then went to the seat of the cart.

Smite turned to Miranda. She had followed him; her face seemed utterly blank. Perhaps she could sense his unease.

This was never going to get any easier. He strode forward and handed her the envelope. He couldn't let her see any doubt, not now. Not after last night.

"You'll be going with Dryfuss here," he said.

"Dryfuss? Who is Dryfuss?"

"The cart driver."

She stared at the envelope in her hands.

He continued on. "Your railway ticket is in there. You're headed to London. You'll be met at the station."

"London? But why am I going to London?"

"Because that is where I have another house. I promised you a house for a month, and I do keep my promises."

She let out a gasp and tried to shove the ticket back in his hands. "You're sending me away *now?* I had thought—but there's at least two weeks left."

"I haven't time to argue. I've an appointment to see my brother at noon, and you've a train to catch at two this afternoon. Think on it: if it's not safe for Robbie to stay in Bristol, how could it be safe for you? You're at even greater risk."

She looked at him. Her eyes grew wide, and her fingers clenched around the envelope. "But it will be safe for me to return, some day." She gulped; she must have seen his expression grow darker. "Perhaps in a month. You'll send for me then."

He met her eyes and did not flinch. "No, Miranda," he said softly.

"Because I'll come back." Her voice withered away in the starkness of the look he gave her. "Or you'll come visit."

"No," he repeated. "It's best that we don't." He reached out and touched her cheek. "This was going to end, in any event."

She shook her head.

"One day, you were going to realize precisely what you'd saddled yourself with. You don't need me." He gave her a little smile. "You can do a great deal better than an obstinate—"

"You're going to tell me what I want?"

"I'm not trying to put words in your mouth," Smite tried again. "But I do think, that given some time—"

"Time? You think time will change what I want? Maybe," she said, "I want a man who takes what should be an unbearable weakness and forges it into strength. Maybe I want a man who will be loyal to me with his dying breath."

"And maybe, when you've had a little time to think it through, you'll want a man who can sleep through the nights, and who doesn't flinch at the thought of hiring servants. Maybe you'll want a man who can stand to have his face touched in affection. Someone who can make you a part of his life instead of shunting you off to one side. What you feel now...it'll fade, Miranda, and when it does, you'll not want to be stuck with me."

"Don't be ridiculous," she said. "I love you."

"I know." He turned away so she wouldn't see his face. "I know. But—I have always been wedded to Lady Justice. And if you think that I will be loyal to you above the demands of my work, you are mistaken." His own voice was breaking. He took a deep breath. "With me, you would always be second. You deserve to be first with whomever you find." Smite hated him already. "I will never come to get you. I will not be waiting for your return. If you come back to me, I will turn from you. This is over."

"So I was right," she said. "You were rationing me. Allowing yourself only a small space of time with me, before returning to your solitary existence."

He gave a nod. "Precisely."

"In a few years, will you forget me altogether, or will you take out the memory of me on occasion, for your few minutes of sentimentality?" There was a hint of belligerence in her tone; she looked up at him with one eyebrow raised.

He'd hold the memories dear and deep, no matter how bittersweet they became. His free hand lifted to her cheek. A wisp of her hair was falling out of her chignon. He reached to tuck it back behind her ear, but when he did, he noticed that the hairpin that had held it in place was loose. Instead of pushing it back, he found himself pulling the metal from her hair. The piece pressed hard into his palm.

"You'd best be leaving," he said. "You'll want time to make sure you're settled on the train."

Her eyes widened, but she turned away from him and swept to where Dryfuss awaited. He followed her; he was helpless not to. And he handed her into the cart. But she didn't let go of his fingers when she'd found her seat. "If this were a play," she said, "this is the point where you'd realize that you can't possibly allow me to leave." Her eyes were suspiciously shiny; her voice quivered. Her fingers lingered on his.

But even the sight of her obvious distress could not break him. "No," he said quietly, disentangling himself from her. "This is the point where I wish you Godspeed."

He gave Dryfuss a nod, and the man shook the reins.

After she left, he stood as still as he dared, listening to the sound of the cart recede into the distance. Listening, past all hope of hearing her. He wasn't even conscious of breathing, and yet his lungs ached fiercely.

He had been wrong. It would have been easier if it *had* slain him. But he was still standing. Still cogent. And that meant he was all too aware of how badly it hurt. He clutched her hairpin until the metal cut into the palm of his hand, unable to let even that much go.

Chapter Twenty

SMITE ARRIVED AT THE hotel where his brother was staying just as the clock struck one. He found Ash pacing before the mantel, shaking his head.

"You're late," Ash said, turning around as he entered the room.

"My apologies. The delay was…" He stopped, catching himself on the lie. Those last minutes with Miranda hadn't been *unavoidable.* They'd merely been vital.

"You're so rarely late." Ash dropped the watch he'd been holding into his waistcoat pocket. "I was beginning to worry. And wonder that I'd done something wrong. Again."

"You didn't do anything wrong," Smite said. "Not everything I do is about you, you realize. You can't fix everything."

Ash's forehead crunched, developing parallel sets of grim lines.

"In any event," Smite added, "nothing needs to be fixed."

Ash grimaced.

They had had some variant of this conversation a hundred times over the last decades. Ash apologized, and tried to ply Smite with things to salve his conscience; Smite refused, and tried to convince Ash he truly preferred not to be cosseted. Somehow, Smite's insistence that nothing was amiss had turned into a cycle of accusation and recrimination.

Smite was too bone-deep tired to try to fend off such well-meaning attacks. He sat down wearily.

"Let me explain," he said. "I don't need anything from you. It doesn't mean I don't care about you, or that I wish you ill. It doesn't mean that I'm rejecting your offers. It simply means that I don't need or want anything."

Ash didn't respond to this. He simply wandered over to the fireplace and looked up at the ceiling, as if wondering what he had ever done wrong.

"You act as if I'm damaged," Smite continued. "As if one foot put wrong will cause me to collapse. But nothing is wrong."

Silence stretched. Ash set his hands on the mantel. Finally, he spoke. "I see. You live in cramped quarters on your own, eschewing all servants, when I know damned well I've given you enough money that you could afford an entire estate. You do that all for the fun of it?"

Smite stared straight ahead.

"You scarcely visit, and you never spend the night. That's because you're just an ordinary fellow? And you harbor no resentment toward me at all."

"I never said I was *ordinary*. Just that I wasn't…wrong." He was feeling more and more wrong now. As if he'd given away his center. As if he'd sent it via train to London.

"Oh, no." Ash rolled his eyes. "You're not wrong. You're *never* wrong—always damnably precise, you are. Still, I must wonder— why are you always so angry at me?"

"I'm not angry!" Smite growled. "I just don't need you to do anything for me. How can I make you understand that?"

Ash threw up his hands. "How am I supposed to believe that nothing is wrong? I remember when I first found you on the streets of Bristol. My God, Smite. I left you and Mark with Mother at her worst. You won't even tell me what happened. How can you *not* hate me for that? I can scarcely stand to think of it myself."

Smite spread his hands. "It was noth—"

"It's always nothing with you. I don't believe you."

Smite could almost hear Miranda, could almost see that resigned smile on her face. *You are the worst liar.* But that unbidden memory nearly overwhelmed him. He shut his eyes and turned away. It was almost a physical pain, that tearing in his gut.

He took a deep breath and thought of the only thing that could dislodge that wave of sorrow.

"She locked me in the cellar," he said flatly. "It flooded. I nearly drowned. I have nightmares about it still, and I can't bear to be around other people. I hold no grudge against you specifically. It's everyone."

Close enough to the truth.

"I'm so sorry," his brother began.

Smite slapped his fist into his palm so hard that it stung. "Don't be. It made me who I am. I don't wish what happened to me undone. And when you do, you wish me less of a person."

Ash crossed the room to him. He lifted one hand a few inches at his side, and then let it drop. "Very well," he finally said. "If you say you're not angry with me, that there's nothing you wish I had done…"

"I didn't say that," Smite heard himself rasp out. He didn't know where the next words came from. He surely hadn't thought them out. But still they spilled out of him. "You should have saved Hope."

It was an ugly thing to say. Ash's face grew pale. It was entirely unfair. Ash had been little more than a boy when their sister had died. What he could have done to combat that ugly fever, Smite didn't know. And yet, cruel as those words had been, they felt *right*. True.

"You should have saved Hope," he repeated. His voice shook. "You were older. You were stronger. You always knew how to do everything. You should have found a way to save her. But you didn't, and I had to face the fact that my big brother was human. That you made mistakes."

"Oh, Smite." Now Ash did set his hand on Smite's shoulder. "I'm sorry."

Smite shrugged the touch off. "I'm not finished yet. You should have saved Mark. When Mother truly began to go mad, you should never have left. You have no idea what I had to go through, keeping him fed, keeping him safe. Keeping him away from her notice when she was at her worst. You should have been there. You should have saved him."

He hadn't even known he felt this way—black and ugly and unforgiving. But he couldn't hold back the tide of his anger, now that he'd given it voice.

"You should have been a god. I've never forgiven you for being merely mortal."

Ash shook his head. "Why don't you say what you really mean? I should have saved you."

For a second, Smite felt choked by floodwaters. He could feel his hands numbing, beginning to lose their grip no matter how hard he held on. But what brought him back to the here-and-now wasn't his brother's concern, but the sharp feel of metal cutting into his skin. Miranda's hairpin was in his pocket. That much of the present, he could hold on to.

"There you're wrong," he said. "I don't need saving. Nothing is wrong with me." He took a deep gulp of breath. He didn't need saving, damn it. And yet...

"Still," he found himself whispering, "sometimes I wish that this quest had not come to me. Justice is an impossible beast to track. The trail is lonely, and she offers no reward when she's caught but the promise of another hunt."

Until today, he'd not minded so much. He'd given up a great deal over the years. It had never seemed so much, compared to what he could have lost. But now that he'd had Miranda... No. He wasn't going to think of her. If he did, he might do something foolish. He might demand a horse and ride for the railway station. He still had a quarter of an hour before her train departed.

Ash laid a hand on his shoulder. Smite flinched, and his brother took a step back, stricken. "Don't touch me unaware," Smite heard himself mutter. "One time, Mother—never mind why. Just... don't."

"God, Smite."

"Don't feel sorry for me. Don't fuss over me. I'm not broken," he heard himself say.

Ash nodded, but he looked so damned concerned. The room smelled of wood and wax, with the faint, lingering scent of astringent black tea. Black tea, not mint.

He couldn't call to mind the scent of mint, that sweet calming scent that Miranda always seemed to carry about her. His memory of Miranda had gone cold already, devoid of the animating spark that he'd most cherished. That, more than anything, nearly overset his emotions.

"I'm not broken," he repeated. "Although at the moment..." This was what came of violating the sentimentality quota. Everything he kept bottled inside him came out. He shut his eyes and pinched the bridge of his nose. "At the moment," he muttered numbly, "I may be coming a bit unraveled."

Ash let this pronouncement sit. He didn't say anything as Smite gasped for air. And maybe this was what they'd always needed—the chance to be silent with each other. This time, when Ash reached out, he paused, waiting before he took his brother's hand. Smite took his palm and clutched it hard. It was just a little touch, but he was almost undone by it.

The clock ticked, counting past Smite's allotted sentimentality. It counted the minutes while Miranda sat and waited onboard some railway car. Smite didn't trust himself to speak until she had gone.

"I did save Mark," Ash finally said.

"Oh?"

"I left him with you."

It was too much. Smite felt his throat close up.

"I mean it. When I found the two of you in Bristol, you were shadowed. Mark...Mark was just *hungry.*"

Smite nodded.

"I have never wanted to think about what you must have done to keep Mother's madness from falling on him. But you must have done *something.* Just look at him. How he can stand to live in that house, I don't know."

Smite found himself smiling through a shudder. "It gave me the cold sweats, just being there for a few hours yesterday."

Another pause. "Why did you go? When you said you went to Mark, I knew it had to be dire. Neither of us would go into that house otherwise."

Smite shrugged. "It was for Miranda," he finally said.

"Miranda." There was a subtle change in Ash's voice. "And what can you tell me about Miranda?"

Her train was pulling away, right at this moment. He thought of her looking up at him and saying that she loved him. He thought of her leaving. Her hairpin bit into the flesh of his palm.

He thought of her finding someone else, and he let out a little breath of air. Finally, he managed a small half-smile and he looked his brother in the eye. "I saved her, too."

THE ROAD MIRANDA TOOK to the railway station was all too familiar. And yet to Miranda's eye, it seemed entirely different. After the long weeks of her absence, Temple Street had altered. Now, it seemed forlorn and dirty. She'd never noticed the refuse that spilled onto the streets when she lived here. She must have blocked from memory the blackening muck that was never swept from the cobblestones. The smells of manufacturing were thick about her: the scent of vinegar from the foundry warred with tar from the shipyards. The splitting shriek of a steam engine cut through the clatter of horses' hooves.

Strange, that this neighborhood had changed so much in just a few weeks. The cart she was in rumbled past taverns she had visited, fishmongers she had argued with, shops she had patronized...

Better to concentrate on all that she passed, than to think about— "Stop!" she said.

The cart came to a halt. Dryfuss peered at her. "I'm not supposed to stop," he said. "My orders are—"

"New orders," Miranda said briskly. "I'll only be a few minutes."

"But, Miss..." This protest came from the maid Smite had insisted should accompany her for good measure. It had seemed so excessive; Miranda had never needed a chaperone in Temple Parish. "We were told to take you straight there."

"I need to say farewell to someone." She hopped down out of the cart. She was too visible on the street now. Even though she'd donned a traveling habit, a dull brown high-necked gown designed to hide the dirt of a journey, passersby glanced at her. The gown was tailored to her form, leaving no room for the bending and moving that a working woman required. The bustle and petticoats were too wide. And even though the material was plain brown, it was well-made and lustrous. People watched her idly. Speculatively.

And then someone knocked into her from the side. Gray fabric flew everywhere. Miranda turned, catching herself before she fell. Dryfuss stepped forward.

"Oh, dearie me," said a familiar voice.

"Mrs. Blasseur!" Miranda said. "I'm so sorry. I was just standing here, looking around—I didn't even see you coming."

Mrs. Blasseur began to pick up the laundry that had spilled from her basket. The tips of her fingers were blue, her movements slow. Miranda knelt beside her as best as she could in her stiff corset, and helped her collect towels.

When they'd finished, Mrs. Blasseur looked up. "Well, look at you." She paused, took a step back. "You look well. Very well. I haven't seen you in an age." She wrinkled her brow. "When you said your father had left you a bit of money, I hadn't realized it was quite so much."

Miranda simply shook her head and picked up the basket. "You've never been stupid, Mrs. Blasseur," she said. "You know quite well how I came by this."

The woman gave her a small, pained smile. "Indeed." She coughed heavily into a handkerchief and looked away.

"I've come…I need to talk to Jeremy, actually. Is he in?"

Mrs. Blasseur gestured in front of her. Miranda opened the door, and then held the basket for the other woman.

Once inside, she turned to her. "Do you need—"

Mrs. Blasseur rescued her load of laundry. "Shoo," she commanded with a shake of her head. "Go talk to Jeremy."

Miranda smiled. The store was like Temple Street itself: the same as always, and yet substantially dingier. The bolts of fabric looked cheap to her eyes, the ribbons pale and faded. She was almost afraid as she made her way to the back of the shop. Afraid that she herself would have altered so much that…

But no. Jeremy sat in his usual spot on a stool, mending a seam on a pair of trousers with infinite patience. He didn't look sullen or scuffed to her eye. He still looked utterly dear.

"Jeremy," she breathed.

"Miranda!" He stood up, smiling. "Oh, you look fabulous. What are you doing here?"

She crossed over to him and put her arms around him. He stiffened slightly, but hugged her back. "I've come to say farewell," she whispered. "I'll be leaving soon—leaving Bristol. Possibly forever."

He nodded sagely. "Going with your protector?"

"No." She took a deep breath, and dropped her voice. "It's not safe for me here. I have to leave. The Patron threatened Robbie— set him up for a hanging offense. I don't want to be next."

Jeremy turned utterly white. "Robbie? The Patron threatened *Robbie?* Who—no—why—" He took a breath. "How do you know?"

"He sent a note, mentioning me. The Patron wants something. I can't fathom it, either, but I don't intend to wait around to find out what it is." When the danger had passed, of course…

"Ah," Jeremy muttered. "God. Not again. This isn't happening again." He set his needle down and looked across the room, his eyes shadowed.

"I don't know what he wants," Miranda said, "but the Patron has proven that he'll pursue the ones I care about. Jeremy, I'm worried about what he might do to you."

Jeremy didn't look at her. "I'm not in any danger from the Patron."

"I don't care if you've paid for protection. Something different is going on. The normal rules are suspended." Miranda looked away. "Assume the Patron knows everything. He knows we're friends. He knows I'd want you to stay safe. Maybe you should…"

But of course Jeremy wouldn't come with her, not with his mother in such straits.

Her eyes fell on a display of top hats—rat-eaten, battered, and coming apart at the seams. So limp, they'd scarcely stay on a head. They were in a bin next to some shabby coats. Someone had pinned a label to one of them: " *Old hatts for the Guy.* 2d."

It was close to the Fifth of November. But the possibility of buying a hat wasn't what caught her attention. She reached and picked up the foolscap label. That handwriting… That spelling. It couldn't be.

Her world swirled around her.

"Trust me," Jeremy said behind her. "I'm not in any danger from the Patron. I'm certain of it."

She *knew* that hand.

"I see," she heard herself say. Someone from the shop must be working with the Patron. Closely. She'd received letters from him.

Could it be Jeremy himself? No; she knew how he spent his days. She knew his writing, too.

But that left…

The smell of tobacco smoke wafted into the room. Up front, Old Blazer had lit his pipe. She'd smelled that scent before—that exact same smell, that same dreadful blend. It had come drifting to her through a rosewood screen once. And…and on the two days when she'd visited the Patron, Old Blazer hadn't been in the shop. He'd been out—sick, Jeremy had said, but how was he to know? Jeremy had been left alone. Old Blazer hadn't been in.

The writing, the tobacco smoke…none of those things added up to proof. But she knew Old Blazer. He was canny: he saw too much, bargained too well. He was reasonable—until he was crossed, and then his temper could not be controlled. The man had little love for the law. She'd heard his diatribe about the magistrates. He blamed them for the death of his only son.

She spoke very softly. "So. One of the Patron's trusted workers is in this room."

Jeremy grimaced. "Not quite. The Patron wants...damn, there's no good way to say this."

Miranda sucked her breath in on a sudden, cold certainty. How would Jeremy know what the Patron wanted, if he wasn't working with him? How would Jeremy be so certain of his own safety?

There was only one way. Old Blazer wasn't *working* with the Patron. He *was* the Patron.

Miranda unpinned the note from the hat and slipped it into her skirt pocket.

"Tell me, Jeremy. What is it that the Patron wants with me?"

He looked around and then leaned in. "The Patron," he whispered in low tones, "is planning to step down. The Patron will do whatever it takes to win the compliance of the heir apparent." There was a bitter hint to his words. "Why do you think George disappeared? Of course the Patron wants to talk to you. He needs a replacement. George is just leverage. As was Robbie."

It would have made just as much sense if Jeremy had told her that the Rat-King of Andor had chosen her as his successor. She could think of absolutely no reason that the Patron would have picked her to take her place. "I don't understand. That doesn't make any sense." But then, it didn't make any sense to threaten Robbie. And senseless as it seemed, it fit the evidence. The Patron was desperate to talk to her.

Jeremy gave her a grim smile. "The only thing you need to understand is that I'm the one person the Patron won't endanger. How do you think I've felt, all these weeks?"

She knew how Old Blazer looked at his only grandson. The old man adored him.

Across the room, Old Blazer puffed on his pipe. He watched her so idly, she never would have guessed his interest. He saw her looking at him, and slowly he raised his hand. The greeting seemed all the more sinister for its nonchalant friendliness.

"Get out of here, Miranda," Jeremy said softly. "Don't worry about me. Just get out."

She nodded. "Farewell."

"Maybe, in a few years…" He trailed off.

She didn't know what to say. It was too much, to lose Jeremy and Smite and Robbie, all within the space of twenty-four hours. She felt as if she might be losing herself. *All* of her friends…

But she hadn't lost Smite. Not if she knew who the Patron was. It was her *duty* to tell him, no matter how that recounting might affect Jeremy and his family. She simply had to walk out of here as if this were one last good-bye. She embraced Jeremy again and slipped out the door.

But outside posed a greater problem. The cart had disappeared. Dryfuss had vanished. Her maid was nowhere to be seen. Miranda was utterly alone in Temple Parish—a wealthy-looking woman without luggage. Without protection. For the first time, as she looked around streets that had once been familiar to her, she felt truly unsafe.

She swallowed and started up the street toward the bridge. Even though the insistent beat of fear in her throat suggested otherwise, she had to hope they'd gone to the station to load her luggage. Once she found Smite, all would be well once more.

But the passersby brushed against her. The shoves grew more aggressive the farther she walked. Her heeled boots hadn't been made for long journeys. She'd never been so glad to turn the final corner, to see the gray stones of the Bristol Bridge in front of her. Even without her driver, she'd made it.

The blue uniforms of several constables, waiting at the gate, seemed even more welcome. She raised her head and strode forward.

One of the constables stepped in her way. "Your pardon," he said. "But we're looking for a woman answering to your description."

The first thought that went through her was that Smite had changed his mind. A bolt of hope shot through her. He'd not given up on her—on *them*. But then the constable put his hand about her wrist and held her tightly.

"We're told you've got something that doesn't belong to you," he said. Behind him, his companion reached out and put his hands into her skirt pocket. He rummaged about, and then pulled out a watch. It was tarnished and battered, but it ticked complicitly in the man's hands.

She stared at it blankly. "That's not mine," she protested.

"We know." The grip on her wrist tightened. "Make a note of it. She admits it."

"No! I mean I don't know how it got there."

"They never know, do they, James?"

"Oh, no. It's always planted there. You're all innocent—the lot of you."

"I *am* innocent!" she protested.

"Tell that to the judge," James said sarcastically.

But it was the officer who held her who truly made her shiver. Because he leaned in and whispered in her ear what she had just begun to fear: "Tell that to the Patron."

Chapter Twenty-one

AFTER MIDNIGHT, MIRANDA GAVE up trying to sleep. Her cell was cold; the cot impossibly hard.

When she lay down, her corset cut into her waist. She couldn't reach behind her to loosen the laces of her gown. Instead, she listened to the guards that patrolled the area.

They hadn't brought her to the gaol; that was for convicted criminals. She was in a small holding cell at the police station. The only window was a small square hole cut in the door. Closed, only a faint trickle of gray seeped around the edges. She could see nothing. Her other senses brought her little information, too. There was the regular sound of booted feet as the guard crossed the hall and stood, not ten feet away, as part of his rounds. When he stood close by, the dimmest hint of light shafted into her cell from his lantern. He stayed for a few minutes. Then his footsteps started once more, and he disappeared down the hall. She counted past two thousand in impenetrable blackness before he appeared again.

Over and over, the patrol repeated, until her head began to spin.

The pattern altered sometime after a clock somewhere struck three. The rhythm of the footfalls that drew near seemed more complicated—the sound of two people walking, not just one. Miranda sat up, clutching her blanket. The patrol stopped in front of her cell. This time, metal jingled and a key scraped in the lock. The door opened.

Two lanterns shed light, turning the people outside into black silhouettes.

Miranda shrank back against the wall. One dark, cloaked figure strode in, and set a lantern by the door.

"Who are you?" Miranda's voice shook.

No answer came. The wooden door thudded shut, but the figure did not move. Miranda's breathing grew shallow. She held still, as if somehow, if she didn't move, he wouldn't see her. Outside, the footfalls moved onward. The officer had left her alone with…with whomever this was.

Still, the figure didn't speak. Instead, he advanced toward Miranda.

"I'll scream," she choked out. She looked around wildly for a weapon, but the only thing within reach was a tattered blanket.

"Go ahead." The answering voice was raspy, and not at all what she'd expected. It was a woman. An older woman.

"You're with the Patron."

The woman didn't bother denying the charge. She reached out and grabbed hold of Miranda's shoulder. Her grip was surprisingly strong, her arm muscular. She brought her other hand up, and a glint of light caught a metal blade.

Miranda did scream then, and she kicked out hard. But the woman simply grunted, absorbing the blow, and pressed Miranda against the wall.

"Shut up," she said, holding the knife up near Miranda's throat. "This is what your life is worth—five seconds and a scream in the dark that nobody hears."

Her assailant grabbed a hank of Miranda's hair and jerked her forward. Her scalp stung; the knife flashed. Miranda bit back another scream.

But the woman had done no more than cut off a lock of her hair. She stepped back, putting her knife away. Miranda became aware of the rapid beat of her heart, the shallow rasp of her breathing.

"I thought the Patron wanted a replacement," Miranda gasped. "How could this convince me to support his cause?"

A snort came in the dark. "The Patron decides matters of justice. If *someone* doesn't like the Patron's version of justice, well… you can just tell that *someone* to construct his own version in its place. This is a warning, dearie. Count yourself lucky. You could have ended up like George." Another chuckle. "You still might. This—" the figure held up the hank of hair "—is just a token of the Patron's good will."

"An arrest and a cold cell is a token of good will?" Miranda muttered. "I'd hate to see him angry."

"Your name will be on the list distributed to the magistrates tomorrow morning. Lord Justice will free you before seven of the clock. You won't even have to wait for the hearing." The woman turned, and then threw over her shoulder. "Tell him that, when next you see him. Tell him that you're here on sufferance. Next time..."

Miranda shivered. None of it made sense. Why would the Patron want *her*, of all people, as a replacement? A reluctant replacement would hardly do any good. And Miranda had shown little talent for running criminal enterprises. She could drive a hard bargain; that was it. All those days in Old Blazer's shop—had he been watching her then?

She curled into a ball. Her hands were trembling. "If the Patron doesn't want to harm me, why threaten me? Why threaten *Robbie?*"

There was a long pause. "The Patron wants what every man wants," the woman finally said. "He wants to leave a legacy."

Miranda rubbed her forehead. Her head was beginning to ache with the dull throb of sleeplessness. She could hear the sound of boots tramping down the corridor once again—hard slaps against the stone floors.

"Why me?" She'd meant those words as a pure whine—the sort of thing that Smite would have immediately dismissed as self-indulgent rubbish.

She received no answer.

The guard returned and opened the cell door. The figure leaned down to recapture her lantern and slipped away. The lock clicked behind her. Once again, footfalls traversed the station. Five minutes, that had taken. It felt like hours. Miranda sat in shaking silence, her mind awhirl.

If sleep had been unattainable before, it was unthinkable now. Every tread of the guard's passing reminded her of the nightmare she'd just gone through. Her hands shook. She could not find warmth, no matter how tightly she curled up. She didn't escape that sense of terror until black night turned to dark gray, and gray turned to dawn.

Dawn brought her the first ray of hope.

Sounds of activity rose around her: the indistinct murmur of conversation in some other room, and the clop of hooves, filtered through the one high window in her cell.

A clock tower eventually chimed seven. Miranda imagined the lists going out to the magistrates. Smite might not look at his immediately. He had other duties, after all.

He might first read the paper. He'd surely look over the accounts of the more violent crimes first. Or...

With each passing quarter hour, she invented a new duty for him to perform. But each chime of the bells brought a fresh wave of anxiety. When eight o'clock came, a new fear ascended: he wasn't coming.

That possibility had never occurred to her, not once during that foul nightmare of an evening. But he'd remarked before about the use of public power for personal gain.

At eleven, a constable unlocked her cell and escorted her to the hearing room. It was every bit as dingy as it had been when she'd stood here all those weeks ago. But the faces that watched her seemed harsher, less forgiving. And the magistrates...

There were four this time, all dressed in a somber black. Two of them scarcely glanced at her. One frowned—a frown that said he had every intention of punishing her to the fullest sense of the law. And the last...oh, the last was Smite.

She might have collapsed with relief, seeing him there.

Yet when his eyes met hers, he showed no sign of recognition. No widening of the eyes. No smile. No shake of the head. It was as if she simply didn't exist, except as another prisoner to be judged.

Her knees almost gave way. If he had been anyone else, she might have thought that he was acting indifferent so as best to help her during the hearing. But she knew Smite. It was no pretense when his gaze slipped over hers. He didn't have it in him to lie that well.

No. She had to face the simple truth. He had well and truly set her to the side.

She'd forgotten what he sounded like on the bench. He was incisive and clear. He ferreted out answers. He did his *duty*, without regard to the person who was before him. It was going to be awful to have him do his duty toward her.

Maybe it would be worse if he did not. The other magistrates were scarcely even attending to the other prisoners. Long ago, she'd told him that magistrates and constables saw the poor as guilty before the law, no matter what had actually happened. He was the sole exception to prove that rule.

She sat through three convictions before her case was called. She struggled to her feet and half stumbled on her way to the front. Her limbs were all pins and needles. But before anyone could speak, Smite stood.

Thank God.

He did not look her way. "Gentlemen," he said to his fellow magistrates. "This lady is known to me. I cannot grant impartial judgment in her case. It is my duty, therefore, to recuse myself."

Her head felt light. She reached out to take the arm of the constable who'd conducted her in. She wasn't going to faint. Damn it, she was *not*.

"If you must, Turner," one of his fellow magistrates said. "Always were a bit too nice about these matters."

The voice seemed to come from very far away.

Even in her worst imaginings, she'd supposed he would be there. It had broken her heart to imagine him treating her with indifferent, sterile fairness. But it broke her courage to not have him at all. At least he would have listened.

"Smite." His name crept out. He must have heard her entreaty, but he didn't flinch. He didn't even turn around.

"I cannot hear this case," he repeated. There was no hint of regret in his voice. Just steel.

He walked to the door without a further backward glance. He was simply going to leave her to the mercy of his fellow magistrates—and from what he'd told her, they didn't have anything like mercy.

She stared after him, too stunned to even make a sound.

He stopped in the doorway. His hand rested on the frame. He turned and finally, finally, he regarded her. She thought that he might apologize then, or at least offer her a smile in comfort— something so that she would know that he still cared. But there was no warmth to his gaze.

"One last thing, gentlemen." His voice was quiet, but the hearing room was so silent she could almost hear the frightened slam of her own heartbeat.

His gaze locked with hers. "When I said that this lady was known to me, I meant that I esteem her more than anyone else on this earth."

The bottom dropped out of her stomach. If the room had been silent before, it was death now, everyone straining to hear his words.

"If I can do my duty and walk away from my best beloved," he said, "you can all do yours and listen to what she has to say."

The hearing room erupted in babble. But even though shouts and questions emerged, Smite turned and let the door shut behind him.

The other magistrates *didn't* listen to her, of course. After that, they were beside themselves with apologies. The mayor seemed to believe she was some sort of a lady. It took scarcely a minute for them to let her loose. All the while, they gawked at her as if she were a rare specimen.

"Didn't know he had—" she heard one of them muttering.

"Where is she from?" someone else was asking.

She was nearly as confused herself. But they freed her, nonetheless.

He was waiting for her in the anteroom. He stood silently at the far end, his figure stiff and unmoving. He had the most intensely solemn expression on his face. She wasn't even sure he was breathing, so still did he seem. Somehow, Miranda put one foot in front of the other, willing her legs not to wobble.

She was all too aware of the crowd behind them, gawking eagerly. There would be no privacy here, not for this conversation. She couldn't throw herself at him. She didn't even know if that was what she wanted.

"If you'd been Miss Daisy Whitaker," he said, softly enough that only she could hear, "we'd have met here long before, and I would have walked you back through the market."

"If I had been Miss Daisy Whitaker, it would have been a damned dull walk." She took another step forward.

"You'll note," he said warily, "that nothing has changed since last we spoke. I'm still not sure—"

She reached out and touched his arm. "Smite, I have spent almost a full day in custody. I have not slept or eaten. I'm sore and scared and the only good thing that has happened to me in the last two days is that you called me your beloved. Don't you dare take that away."

His hands slid to her waist and he pulled her close, nestling her against his chest. "I couldn't take it away even if I wanted to do so. You *are* my best beloved."

She felt tears form at the corner of her eyes. Much more, and she might not actually be able to hold her emotions in. "Be careful. Your sentimentality quota…"

"Suspended for the moment, I'm afraid." He leaned down and touched his forehead to hers. "Beloved," he whispered. "Miranda, comma."

She didn't know how long they stood there, his arms about her, she leaning against him, their breaths trading back and forth. They didn't kiss. They were in public, after all, and the embrace was scandalous enough. Besides, it seemed vital that he simply *hold* her.

When the crowd had begun to dissipate, he spoke again. "This is what it means to be my beloved. If it comes down to a question of you or my duty, I must put my duty first. You have no idea. When I saw your name on the list, and surmised what must have happened…" He pulled away from her. "I hadn't time to do more than fetch an attorney to speak on your behalf. I take it he wasn't even needed. I can't even beg your forgiveness for not doing more. That is what it means to be me. My duty *must* come first."

It had been distressing. But it had passed. She wouldn't—couldn't—ask him to give up his honor to save herself from a few hours of dismay.

"Do you understand?" he was saying. "I had the ability to order you released at any time. Why are you still near me?"

She had always thought that she wanted someone to love her beyond all reason. Someone who would slay a regiment of knights to save her the slightest inconvenience.

She'd been wrong. That sort of fool left nothing but a swath of bloody knights in his wake.

"You will always put your duty first," she said.

He nodded.

"So long as you put me best, I shall be satisfied."

"I'm not the easiest man," he replied warily.

Miranda smothered a smile. "You sound as if you fear this might come as a sad shock to me. And yet, over the course of our acquaintance, I *had* noticed that. Nonetheless, despite all sense and rational argument, you are my favorite."

His lip quirked up in a smile. It lasted but briefly, before he was serious once again.

"Miranda, nothing has changed. The reasons I sent you away—"

"But everything has changed," Miranda whispered. "I know who the Patron is. It's my friend Jeremy Blasseur's grandfather. They call him Old Blazer."

Chapter Twenty-two

AFTER THEY LEFT THE Council House, Smite didn't conduct Miranda back to her home. Instead, he led her toward the heart of town, and finally to the Royal Western Hotel. The walk there wasn't too long, but a sleepless night spent in a cold room without supper or breakfast had robbed Miranda of most of her strength.

The building was a newly constructed spectacle of modern architecture: four stories high, with stone columns dominating the entryway. Inside, the paintings were bright and new; the cushions on the chairs seemed as if they'd never been used. A waft of some delicious, savory scent drifted through the foyer, and her empty stomach growled. But Smite didn't conduct her into the salon for a meal. Alas. Instead, he motioned a footman over.

Miranda ran her hand along the carved wainscoting while Smite murmured something to the fellow. The man bowed to him, then turned and spoke to another man, who turned and ducked through a door. A few minutes later, the fellow returned, this time followed by a man in gray-and-maroon livery.

Neither man was carrying a tray of food, which was rather depressing. Both servants bowed to Smite—and flicked glances toward Miranda.

They no doubt took in her wrinkled traveling habit, the frightful disarray of her hair. She had no hat, no gloves, and no cloak. Her mouth felt like cotton. When Smite held out his arm for her, she clung to it. Touching him, even just his elbow, seemed the key to safe passage through these perilous halls.

If she held on too tightly, he made no mention of it. Not as they ascended the wide, polished wood of the stairs. Instead, he set his hand—his *gloved* hand—over hers. When they reached the next floor, he paused briefly and turned to her. "We must have a few words," he said, motioning to the servant ahead of them. The man simply nodded, and ducked through a door.

For a moment, they were alone in the hall, with nothing but the shining crystals of the lamps to keep them company.

"Only words? That's rather stingy of you."

His lips twitched in a smile. "Granted," he said smoothly. "This is the safest place I can imagine, without sending you out of town once more." He cast her another look. "Or trying to, at any rate."

Her fingers twitched convulsively at that.

But he made no other attempt to soothe her. Since he'd sent her away, she had touched him. Held his hand. Miranda had even embraced him—and in public, no less. He had called her his best beloved.

But he hadn't tried to kiss her. He'd walked away from her once. He could do it again.

When she shifted close to him now, he stepped away. It was so smoothly done that it might not even have been a rejection.

"I've taken you to my brother, the Duke of Parford. He's staying here." He paused, looked at Miranda, and added, "Don't worry. They're all good sorts." Without any further explanation, he opened the door the servant had entered earlier.

Here seemed oppressively foreign. The home Smite had obtained for Miranda had been impossibly luxurious; by comparison to this hotel, however, it seemed a hovel. The room before her seemed both palatial and austere at once. The ceilings seemed too high overhead. The floor was marble, and covered with carpets that positively gleamed with wealth. The room was so massive, and the illumination so bright, that for one second, she thought Smite must have opened up a passage to the outdoors.

But outdoors did not have embroidered silks hanging on the walls. Today, it was cloudy and gray, in sharp contrast to the bucolic autumn scene depicted on the nearby wall. And gentlemen wore hats and the ladies bonnets outdoors. The two men who struggled to their feet at their entrance were both hatless.

Miranda had no time to balk. Smite pressed his hand into the small of her back, and she stepped into the room.

It was the biggest parlor she had ever seen. The mural on the wall was not just an autumn scene, but a harvest scene. Sheaves of grains rested against beets and turnips... She could eat a raw turnip. She could eat a raw, painted turnip.

She knew both of the men. Richard Dalrymple had just stood up from his seat in one of the chairs. By the corner of the sofa was the Duke of Parford, Smite's brother. Still seated on the sofa... The woman was dark-haired and pretty. She was dressed in an exquisite silk morning dress. It was a deep, dark purple—the color of a bunch of grapes. Miranda swallowed hungrily. Her metaphors were running toward meals.

The servant who had entered before them spoke. "Mr. Smite Turner. Miss Miranda Darling."

The woman's expression seemed to freeze in place.

Dalrymple's mouth dropped open, and he glanced over at the sofa. She had to be the duke's wife—and therefore Dalrymple's sister, the Duchess of Parford.

Miranda winced and slid her ungloved hands into her skirt pockets. It was one thing for Smite to introduce his mistress to an older male acquaintance from his school days. It was another to bring her into a duke's hotel rooms when said duke's wife was in residence. It was still another to do all of that, and not give said mistress sufficient time to change into a gown that wouldn't embarrass her.

The duchess was eyeing her with frank curiosity. Her gaze dropped to Miranda's skirts. The gown had been serviceable when clean, but it was dusty and wrinkled now. Her hem was torn, and Miranda felt a well of resentment. The duchess had likely never worried about whether her wigs would sell. All that purple silk wouldn't have lasted a night in a cell. And she wouldn't look nearly so serene if she hadn't eaten in over a day.

"Smite," the duchess said. "You have yet to perform a proper introduction."

"Of course. Margaret," and Smite sounded almost bored as he spoke, "this is Miss Miranda Darling. Miranda, Her Grace the Duchess of Parford, my sister-in-law. I believe you are already acquainted with my brother." He glanced once at Dalrymple, and then looked away. "Brothers."

"I say, Turner," Dalrymple muttered, looking away. But if he had been about to object to Smite's introducing Miranda to his sister, he chose not to do so. He didn't grumble when Smite conducted Miranda to a seat. Miranda sank into the cushions gratefully; Smite stood by her side and folded his arms.

The duchess's impassive mask did not alter in the slightest during all of this. "A curious introduction, Smite." She had not taken her eyes from the other woman. "And precisely who is Miss Darling to you?"

"A witness to an ongoing criminal endeavor."

"And?" Parford prompted.

Smite didn't respond. He simply tapped his foot and waited.

The duchess sighed and looked upward. "A witness," she said. "Ash, you have done a very poor job convincing your brothers to involve themselves with suitable women."

Parford shrugged. "How was I to accomplish that? Mark is the only person who has ever convinced Smite to go to a ball, and even then he nearly asphyxiated within the first few minutes."

Miranda converted a surprised laugh into a cough.

The duke grinned down on his wife. "I've long accepted that I'm the only one of us who would have a suitable wife. And that was rather an accident on my part."

The woman frowned at her husband, and then glanced up at Miranda. "Well, then, Miss Darling," she said. "Six years ago, I believe I would have had you thrown out. Beware the Turners. They'll upend your life." There was no rancor in her voice, and Miranda noticed that she was holding the duke's hand. Still, she gave Smite a level look. "At least Mark gave me a chance to collect myself so I could plan what I was going to say. If you don't give me any notice, I fear I might say something uncivil."

"Ah, yes," Dalrymple mused. "Turner propriety. Satisfied so long as everyone has something to say. I've almost accustomed myself to the prospect."

Smite glared at Dalrymple, who held up his hands.

"Don't pounce on me now," Dalrymple said. "I'm Margaret's bastard brother, in more than one sense of the word. I'm the beneficiary of Turner propriety, and hardly one to criticize. I know I might have, in the past. But, ah…" He looked up. "I'm talking too much, then. Why are we talking about this in the first place? Smite was always the formal one anyway."

"Indeed." Smite leaned back casually. "There's no reason to talk of it at all. It's well known that I can do no wrong."

The duke simply nodded.

"What!" Dalrymple said. "But—he—I—" He glanced at Smite again, and then frowned. "Oh. You're joking."

"It is equally well-known," Smite said, "that I am a humorless barbarian."

"Who is never wrong," Parford added.

The room was beginning to swim around Miranda. Their words were blurring together.

"I believe," the duchess said, "that we're beginning to overwhelm Miss Darling. It's easy to forget that the family can be a bit much gathered *en masse.*"

"In any quantity," Dalrymple muttered.

'You have to understand," the duchess continued, "we so rarely see Smite. We wouldn't throw him out, even if he showed up with five baboons and a leper in tow."

Smite crossed his arms. "If you're comparing Miranda to baboons..."

"True. You're more of a leper than she is." The duke grinned at Smite, and then turned to Miranda. "This makes it all the easier to tease him. I don't suppose Smite ever told you about the time he locked himself in the bell tower, did he?"

Miranda managed a shake of her head. Her stomach gurgled.

Parford gave her a brilliant smile. "Oh, lovely. He was seven, and—"

Smite turned around, quite abruptly, and without saying a word, left the room.

Everyone stared after him—his brother, the duchess, Dalrymple, and especially Miranda herself, who swallowed the faint meep of protest when the door closed behind him.

"Was it something I said?" the duke was muttering. "It was in good fun. He was teasing me back."

"It will all make perfect sense in a few hours," Miranda ventured. "It always does, your Grace."

This made the duke examine her more directly. "No," he contradicted. "It does not. Damn it. He is so bloody impossible."

"Speaking of impossibilities." This not-quite-casual comment came from the duchess. "Who are your people, Miss Darling?"

It was turning into a regular interrogation without Smite around. Miranda gripped the arms of her chair. "My father was Jeremiah Darling. He owned the Darling Players. You might, perhaps, have seen them in London many years ago." Blank looks

surrounded her. "No? Well. Then. My mother was born Eliza
Scripling. She was a scullery maid for about two months, before she
quit to tread the boards. That she did for almost ten years before
she met my father, had me, and was married." She glanced at the
duchess. "I have never inquired as to the order of those events."

"Of course." The duchess rubbed her forehead. "Mark and
Jessica have evaded censure by staying in the country, where there's
little chance of the truth coming out. But there's no chance of
Smite quitting Bristol."

If her head had been spinning before, it positively whirled now.
"I wasn't aware there were social requirements to being a man's
mistress. It won't help, but after my father's death, Jonas Standish
was appointed my guardian. He was of good family, until they
disowned him."

Perhaps she should not have said that. She scarcely knew them,
after all. But hunger bred familiarity. The duke and duchess
exchanged glances over her head.

"Believe you me," Miranda said, aware that perhaps it would
make more sense to keep quiet, "he's still trying to figure out how
to rid himself of me. It only makes it *worse* that he cares for me."

The door opened and Smite came back inside. He was closely
followed by a footman bearing a tray. At the first waft of the scent
rising off it, a wave of hunger assailed Miranda. She was instantly
salivating.

The servant set the tray on the table in front of her—a wide
bowl of soup and an array of delicate sandwiches.

Smite sat down beside her.

"You'd mentioned not eating anything in the last day," he said.
"Your stomach was growling."

She could have kissed him. She took a sandwich instead, only
to look up and see everyone staring at him once more. It was as if
they had no notion that he could be kind under that gruff exterior.
Smite shifted uneasily in his seat.

"Don't mind him," Miranda said airily. "He only needs to
question me. He can't if I keel over from hunger. He's just
being…efficient."

He met her eyes with rueful humor. "Precisely. I'm nothing if
not efficient."

Miranda took a bite of sandwich.

In a voice that was not quite soft enough, the duchess said, "I think that may be one of the sweetest things I've ever seen. Either that or the strangest."

The tips of Smite's ears turned pink, but he handed Miranda another sandwich. The first had disappeared with remarkable speed, and the second didn't take much longer.

"When you're ready," Smite told her, "I'd like to hear what happened since last I saw you."

None of the others made any move to leave, and after a moment, Miranda began to speak. She described leaving the Blasseurs' shop to find the cart missing. She told them how she had walked on her own, how the constables had found her along the way.

She told them about the visit she'd received in the dark of night, and Smite's visage grew more serious.

Finally, she recounted what Jeremy had told her. As she spoke, she reached into her pocket and took out a piece of paper and handed it to Smite.

"Hatts for the Guy," he read.

"We still have the other notes. There was one that I received, and then the one that Robbie got. I think they were all written by the same person."

"Likely." Smite stared at the paper, and then looked off. "It's the same sort of paper as well." He tapped his fingers against the leg of his trousers. "It's possibly enough to issue a warrant for Old Blazer's arrest. But an arrest is only the beginning. I am trying to decide if we have enough evidence to sustain a conviction. You know the shop well. Did you see any signs that a criminal enterprise was conducted on the premises? Shady characters coming and going, shipments that were hidden... Even something as simple as goods being displayed that you thought might not have been purchased."

Miranda shook her head. "Nothing. I know you won't believe this, but my friend Jeremy would never stand for that sort of thing. He's terribly straitlaced."

"Then this is simple." Smite drummed his fingers on the table. "We only need to ask your friend to testify."

Miranda gasped. "You can't ask Jeremy to testify against his own grandfather!"

"On the contrary," Smite rumbled. "It's perfectly within my powers to issue a subpoena—"

"Of course you're capable of it. But it wouldn't be right to force him to tell tales about the man who raised him."

"I still beg to differ. If your friend is so upright, he should jump at the chance. One can frown on snitches in the schoolyard when the consequences rise to skinned knees and hurt feelings. When we are talking murder, however, every right-thinking man will speak out rather than let the guilty go free."

"Oh, I suppose *technically* you are right," Miranda muttered. "But don't expect anyone to agree with you." She glanced up at the watching faces. "I doubt that the Duke of Parford, for one, would be willing to betray you. Even if you had murdered someone. You can't hang your hopes of a conviction on the belief that Jeremy will betray his own grandfather. He won't do it."

Smite simply regarded her for a few moments, and then closed his eyes with a sigh. "Well, then. We'll surround the building with constables dressed in street clothing—"

"No constables," Miranda said.

"No constables?"

"One of the men who arrested me yesterday mentioned the Patron. The man on patrol let a woman into my cell at the station. There may be more. Bring the constables in, and the Patron will know before you arrive, and he'll disappear."

He accepted this with a slight tightening of his mouth. "What of using hired men?"

"Hired from where? Robbie's shipwright must employ men loyal to the Patron; they threatened him there. Half of the workforce of Bristol lives in Temple Parish. Do you have any idea how many people's lives the Patron has touched? You can't organize an expedition of any kind without the Patron catching wind of it."

"So what am I supposed to do?" Smite asked. "Attempt to uncover the truth by myself? With you? That would hardly be safe. No; nothing is without risk, this least of all. But I'd rather risk the possibility of losing secrecy than doing this alone. I'd need at least two others—"

"Let's see if I have this right," Dalrymple said. "You're facing a crazed criminal, the risk of death, and a police force that might not be on your side. It's lovely being a magistrate." He tensed. "Useless people rarely face risk."

"Speaking from experience?" Smite snapped.

Dalrymple gave him a pale smile. "Speaking from stupidity, I'm afraid. I volunteer."

THE NEXT TEN HOURS passed with far too little to occupy Smite. He had only to sit by and watch as Miranda sent a note to Temple Church in the hopes that it would find its way into the hands of the Patron.

He hated the thought of using her in that way. Unfortunately, they'd not come up with a better plan. After they'd hashed out the details, Smite paced uselessly in the room while Miranda had a bath and then a nap. Under the interfering auspices of his sister-in-law, he couldn't even watch her sleep. He had a brief moment of activity, when Ash had a drawing of plans for Temple Church sent up, and they'd squabbled companionably over their respective roles. But after that, there was nothing to do but wander uselessly about the room.

Half an hour before they were to leave, Miranda finally came out, dressed and scrubbed and clean. He walked over to her. But Margaret didn't leave the room, and so Smite could do very little more than bow over Miranda's hand and conduct her to the sofa. He sat next to her, feeling rather out of sorts.

The muffled sound of his eldest brother dictating instructions in the next room formed a murmured, calm counterpoint to his frustration. Smite didn't even know what to say to Miranda. Instead, he simply contemplated her.

The corners of her lips twitched into the semblance of a smile. "I'll wager that sometimes you wish you'd never come after me that day," she said.

He met her eyes. "Do you, then?"

A few feet away, the duchess grimaced. She glanced once at Miranda, and then looked away.

"No," Miranda said thoughtfully. "I suppose not."

"There you are," he said. "I make it a habit not to harbor regrets." A small smile touched his lips. "I'm especially particular about the matter when regrets would be unwarranted."

"Flatterer," Miranda said calmly.

Margaret was trying valiantly to appear uninterested in their conversation.

But Miranda leaned over to the other woman. "Despite his apparent fluency in the English language," she said earnestly, "Smite lacks the capacity to express some very basic thoughts. Compliments that other people manage quite easily, like 'My, you look lovely,' or 'I hope you don't die tonight' are quite difficult."

God. How had he ever thought he would be able to send her away? He still had her hairpin in his pocket. It made no substitute for her.

"You look lovely," Smite repeated. "I'd rather you didn't die. Don't believe a word Miss Darling says, Margaret. I can express any concept I wish. I merely prefer not to."

"Oh?" Margaret's gaze dipped down to their fingers. Smite's hand lay close to Miranda's on the sofa. They were mere inches apart.

In the other room, Ash's voice trailed off. Margaret glanced over. "I'll wager you ten pounds you can't go tell my husband that you love him."

Smite shifted back in his chair. His breath caught in his lungs. And then Margaret met his eyes, and he realized that she was in dead earnest. How many years had it been since he'd said the words?

All his vaunted memory, and he couldn't call up a single instance. It had seemed a given. They'd had their share of anger and resentment, he and Ash. But love was still the bedrock of their relationship. Ash knew that. Didn't he?

He stood and crossed over to the open doorway.

"Ash," he said.

An indistinct murmur came back. Smite put one arm behind his back. His hand formed a fist, and then he drew himself up. "Are you ready? It's almost time."

"Yes." The duke's response was barely audible. "I just need to—"

"Because I wouldn't want to be late. We need to be there before Miranda arrives on the scene." Smite's fist clenched just a little bit more.

Ash frowned at him. "Anything amiss?"

He felt his face growing hot. "Where in God's name is Dalrymple?" Smite turned swiftly away. He couldn't avoid Margaret's eye as he turned. She didn't shake her head or otherwise indicate her disapproval. He'd had every intention of saying it.

Maybe the words had gone rusty from disuse. Nothing else could explain it.

He walked over to his sister-in-law, and after examining the contents of his pockets very carefully, handed over a banknote. He didn't dare look Miranda in the eye as he did.

THE PLAN HAD SEEMED so simple earlier: they had to catch Old Blazer in the act of being the Patron.

It had been easy enough to answer his request for an audience. Miranda had agreed to come speak with the Patron, but only if he came in person. Given what Jeremy had implied, she thought he might come. If he did, he'd prove his own guilt.

Simple.

But as Miranda crept down Temple Street after dark, the prospect seemed fraught with difficulty. Ensconced in the warm, bright hotel room, everything had seemed possible. Now, she felt uncomfortable and out of place. Her cloak was too good, her boots were too new for this part of town. She'd never felt the need to hide on a busy street before. But now, the crowds seemed subtly hostile.

As she came up on the little lane that led to the church, she repeated to herself the arguments she'd made earlier. So far, the Patron had only asked to see her. His representative had spoken of good will. If Old Blazer wanted her dead, he could have ordered it already.

He was looking for a replacement, after all. That made her safe.

It was one thing, though, to talk of safety while surrounded by friends. Here…

She ducked into the dark lane that led to the church and clutched her cloak tightly. She was still surrounded by friends.

That dim figure, leaning against a far-away building—that was the Duke of Parford himself, keeping watch over the front entrance. Smite and Richard Dalrymple stood guard at the back doors. They'd argued for what had felt like hours about whether they needed to bring more men. In the end, they'd decided that secrecy was preferable to a show of force.

But close as the men were to her, nobody walked beside Miranda into the church. The evening service had ended hours past, and the place was deserted. Only softly guttering candles, burnt almost to the stub, lit her way as she walked down the aisle to the confessional.

She pushed aside dusty curtains and took her seat on the stool.

Even through her gloves, her hands were cold. When the curtains stopped swaying, they cut off even the hint of faintly flickering candlelight. She'd started the day cocooned in the darkness of her cell; her memory stirred uneasily in these close, dark quarters.

She smelled wood and soap and wax. But her ears brought her no sound—nothing but the faint creaks of the building around her. No footsteps. No breath.

Each minute seemed to stretch into forever. The darkness slowed time.

There was no warning when things changed—no announcement, no sound except the sudden, sharp crack of the rosewood screen one second, and the whistle of falling wood the next. Miranda scarcely had a chance to lift her hands to shield her head before the wood struck her, hard.

She was too scared to scream. She scrambled backward through the curtains, tripping over her own skirt. Even the dim light in the chapel seemed blinding. Her heart pounded. She launched to her feet and dashed down the aisle.

Her eyes had scarcely adjusted when she caught sight of a silhouetted figure in front of her. She tried to stop but couldn't. Strong arms grabbed her shoulders.

"Miranda."

She let out a gasp of relief. It was Parford.

"Tell me they have Old Blazer," Miranda said.

"No." She was now beginning to make out features. Parford's face was set in a grim mask. "They're gone. Smite and Richard. They've vanished." The duke ran his hands through his hair. "God *damn* it," he swore. "I shouldn't have let him do this."

"What are we going to do about it?"

"Rouse the constables," Parford rumbled. "Rouse every able-bodied man I can find. Muster the militia, if I have to, and tear this city apart brick by brick until I find them."

"Do you know what will happen if the militia comes after the Patron?" Miranda demanded. "Here? The Patron has been all that's kept us safe. It will be like the Riots of '31 again, except this time, the other side will be organized. It will be war."

"The Patron grabbed a magistrate off the streets." Parford glared at her. "The Patron took my brother. It already *is* war. I walked away from him once before. I don't care if it takes a riot to get him back. I am *not* leaving him on the streets of Bristol again." He bristled in fury. "As it is, it'll take 'til dawn to get everything in readiness. There isn't any time to spare."

He turned and strode off, obviously expecting her to follow. She did—but she could scarcely keep pace with him. And when he turned on to Temple Street…

There was almost nobody about at all now. The shops stood silent and closed. Only a hint of music in the distance suggested life. Miranda slowed; Parford hadn't noticed yet that she'd dropped back.

If the Patron was confronted with force and backed into a corner, who knew what he might do with his hostages?

Parford didn't realize when they passed Blasseur's Trade Goods & More, but Miranda surely did. There had to be a better way.

She was going to have to find it herself. Before Parford noticed her absence, Miranda slipped into an alley and stole away.

Chapter Twenty-three

MIRANDA GAVE UP AFTER a few seconds of tossing pebbles at Jeremy's window. The tiny stones weren't drawing attention. Instead, she searched in the rubble against the building for a rock. She had just found a likely candidate when the scrape of wood against wood sounded above her. She looked up. Jeremy leaned out over the sill.

"Miranda, what are you *doing* here?" Jeremy asked.

What she could see of his hair was tousled; most of it was hidden under a voluminous nightcap. A heavy nightshirt covered his torso.

"Where is Old Blazer?" Miranda hissed.

Jeremy frowned down at her from his window, rubbing his eyes. "God, Miranda. That's all you have to say? Last I saw you, you said you were leaving town. After—" He looked about. "I heard you were set free. Why in God's name did you stay, when you'd had the dangers spelled out so clearly?" He frowned down at her. "It's not safe out. I'll go down and let you in."

"No, I—"

But he'd already ducked back into his room, and her words were swallowed in the screech of his window closing.

She waited at the back door. A few infinitely long minutes passed before Jeremy opened the door. He'd pulled on trousers and a shirt, but his feet were bare. He folded his arms about him against the cold, and jerked his head, indicating that she should come inside.

She tapped her toes stubbornly on the doorstep. "Where is Old Blazer?"

"Asleep. Listen—you can hear him snoring."

She could, very distantly. Miranda shook her head. "Then I'm not going in. It's not safe. He's got to be furious at me right now. Jeremy, we need to do something."

Jeremy rubbed his chin. "Furious? Why would Old Blazer be furious?"

"This whole thing…" She blew out her breath furiously. "God. I wish I'd never been involved. I wish I'd kept my mouth shut. Everything I do just digs me deeper, and now—"

Jeremy caught hold of her shoulders and pulled her inside. He shut the door quietly behind her. "Calm down. Take a breath. What has you so upset?"

"Smite," she said. Just saying his name brought to mind her deepest fears. What if he'd already been killed? What if his throat was slit, and he'd been tossed—but no. She couldn't think that. She couldn't let herself.

"Lord Justice?"

She nodded. "There's no good way to say this, Jeremy. The Patron had his men arrest me after I left your shop the other day."

"I know," he interjected. "I thought you'd had the good sense to leave town after you got free."

She took a deep breath. "Lord Justice didn't think much of the Patron using his constables and his court for personal gain. And so he came up with a plan to…to, um, to, um…"

"To bring the Patron to justice?" Jeremy's voice grew a hint chillier. "That would comport with what I have seen on this end. Don't tell me: it didn't work as planned."

She nodded. "The Patron took Lord Justice."

Jeremy scrunched his hair with one hand and screwed up his face. "Damn it."

"It's worse than damning. His brother, the Duke of Parford, is threatening to turn Bristol upside down in the search."

"Of course he is," Jeremy muttered. "It wanted only that— she's holding the entire *city* hostage now. I'll get the message shortly." He blew out his breath. "Miranda, I wish you weren't here. But it is so good to have even one person to turn to. I can't do this." He began to pace the floor. "But I have to. But I *can't*. I couldn't do it even for George."

"We can stop it," Miranda said. "While all his men are busy with Lord Justice. Jeremy, I know he's your grandfather, but the two of us could tie Old Blazer up, take him in right now. We could avert the entire crisis."

Jeremy stopped mid-pace and cocked his head. "Old Blazer?" he asked. "What does *Old Blazer* have to do with any of this?"

There were no words to describe the feeling of sick, sinking vertigo that assailed Miranda. "What do you mean?" she whispered.

"You think *Old Blazer* is the Patron?" Jeremy asked.

All of Miranda's certainty came to a tumbling halt. There had been that letter, written in the same hand as those prices. Jeremy had told her the Patron was Old Blazer. Hadn't he?

Miranda shut her eyes, and an image drifted to her mind: Mrs. Blasseur, seated on a stool, cutting foolscap into strips.

Her heart stopped. "Oh, no," she moaned. "I thought—"

"No," Jeremy snapped. "You didn't. You didn't think at all. Old Blazer has no sense of discretion. Have you ever known him to keep his mouth shut?"

"Well, no, but—"

"He's forever talking to people. And he won't even do his part in the shop if he feels the slightest ache in his little toe. Do you really think he'd be the sort to work long hours on a thankless endeavor?"

"I hadn't thought of that."

"More to the point," Jeremy said softly, "Old Blazer isn't in dire need of a replacement. My mother—" His voice cracked.

"Your mother can't be the Patron." Miranda shook her head. "Why would she want me to replace her? It doesn't make any..."

She trailed off once more at the dire look in Jeremy's eyes.

"Oh," she said stupidly.

"Miranda," Jeremy said gently, "you haven't any sense of discretion either. You haven't any training. You haven't any claim to the enterprise." Jeremy reached into his pocket and fished a hank of hair, gleaming dully copper in the moonlight that filtered through the windows.

Miranda shivered, remembering the knife that had removed that.

"That lock of hair," Jeremy said, "was delivered to me as a warning. My mother thinks I'm in love with you, after all. And she thinks that George is my friend—she had him arrested, too, and when he was about to be released, had him secreted away as a hostage. This isn't about you." He gave her a sad smile. "It's about my refusal to take up the family business."

A knock sounded at the front door—two blows, a pause, and then three short raps.

"There," Jeremy said. "That will be my invitation. All I have to do is go with whomever she's sent, and I can avert this whole crisis. There's an initiation ceremony." His lip curled in distaste. "If I'm supposed to take up the Patron's mantle, I have to administer the Patron's justice. It...it proved to be a sticking point before."

His tone had grown harder as he spoke.

"What kind of..." Miranda stopped, not willing to go forward. She knew what the Patron's justice was like. The man who'd threatened her all those years ago had been driven out of town— and that, just for a threat. Men had died for the Patron's justice— died and disappeared. If Jeremy was supposed to become the Patron...

His skin was the color of cold wax. "I can do it," Jeremy was saying, more to himself than to her. "If I agree to take her place, I can find out where he's held. Have him released. The stakes this time...there could be riots. I can kill one man to save the city."

Miranda wasn't sure she believed him. Moreover, she wasn't sure what it would do to him, to commit murder.

"If I knew where my mother kept prisoners," he was muttering, "perhaps I could... But no. No. There is no other way."

Miranda caught his arm.

"Actually," she said. "I have an idea. I know how to find them, without going through the initiation first."

Jeremy glanced at the front door.

"Quickly," Miranda said. "If we go out the back way, you won't have to talk to him at all."

IT WAS COLD AND lightless when Smite awoke. He was slumped against some hard surface. He twitched; even that slight movement sent a scatter of pain through his head. No sun played against the lids of his eyes; no lantern-light danced nearby.

It made no difference when he cautiously opened his eyes. It was still black. The floor under him was hard and cold, and a series of curiously regular bumps jutted into his skin. Even breathing hurt.

It took him a moment to orient himself. Last he'd known, he'd been standing behind Temple Church, pretending to smoke a pipe and watching the church. He'd had his back to the wall.

Someone had hit him from the side. He had a vague, troubled recollection of movement, but no memory of how he came to be *here*. Wherever here was.

There was no movement to the air; it hung about him, close and still. The setting almost felt like one of his nightmares, yet it seemed curiously tactile for a dream. He could make out the odor of metal and grease, and he could never smell in dreams. And in his dreams, he always heard the babble of the passing millrace, growing to a crescendo.

Here, silence engulfed him. Only a faint sound—an almost liquid burble—hovered at the edge of his hearing. It made him uneasy.

He put his hand out. Cold metal met his fingertips, and he found a hard edge in the floor next to him. A moment's exploration brought the surface to life.

It wasn't a ridge, and he wasn't asleep. It was a seam, and those bumps marching alongside the hard metal edge were rivets. He was enclosed in a box made of iron.

Don't think of it, Turner. If you don't think of it, it needn't affect you.

"Turner?" It was a familiar voice. "Is that you?"

"Dalrymple." Smite felt an unreasonable sense of relief at finding himself not alone. The man's voice brought back everything—the plan, the church, the Patron… "Tell me Miranda's not here," he said.

"If she is, I've not encountered her."

"Ash?"

"Not him, either."

No point in thinking of them now. He hoped they were safe. Instead, he ran his hand along the metal beneath him. "Where are we?"

"I'm not certain. I only saw a bit near the end, when the scarf binding my eyes slipped. They took us aboard a ship. I only got a glimpse before they slammed the door shut."

"Ah," Smite muttered. A simple word, to hide the unbidden nausea that rose in his gorge. There was only one deserted ship in the Floating Harbour. He was aboard the *Great Britain*. Buried deep in her bowels. That noise he heard—that was the flow of liquid around the hull. His hand trembled against the cold floor.

He pressed it flat.

Stop fussing over yourself.

"Are you well?" Dalrymple asked. "You couldn't even bring yourself to swim at Eton, not without becoming ill. And now we're surrounded by water. It's all around us. I think—are you shaking?"

"Shut up, Winnie." Smite drew a deep breath. The pain in his side was receding, but it still hurt. "If you don't mention it, I don't have to think of it." If he didn't think of it, he might be able to keep his old memories from devouring him alive.

"Oh. Sorry." A pause. "It's been ages since anyone called me 'Winnie.'"

"A deplorable lapse on my part," Smite said.

Dalrymple had been the Marquess of Winchester, back when they'd been boys—back when almost everyone had believed him to be the heir to a dukedom. The title had been shortened to just Winnie amongst his intimates.

"You're right," Dalrymple said presently. "I am a coward. They simply pointed a pistol at me and told me not to make a fuss. That was all that was needed. I didn't fight. I didn't scream." He made a disgusted sound. "Even girls can scream. Ash would have punched them."

"At least they didn't shoot you," Smite said. "I count that a positive. As I told you before, I'd rather you didn't die."

"Ha."

Despite himself, Smite smiled. "How long have we been here?"

"An hour? Maybe two."

"If we've been here an hour, you've used up the sentimentality quota." Smite rubbed his forehead. "So stop telling me what you should have done, and start thinking about what we will do instead."

That comment brought only silence. And with the silence came that sound again, the noise at the edge of hearing that made him think of water rushing in.

He was outright grateful when Dalrymple spoke again. "It's like Eton all over," the man muttered. "I whine to you; you tell me to keep quiet and do something instead. Every day I was convinced you'd discover what a little sniveler I was. Every day for two bloody years."

"Still too much sentiment," Smite said. But at least Dalrymple's voice drowned out the sound of water.

"When you finally did discover it, I hated you for it."

"My head is splitting." Smite moved, and winced again. "We're in captivity. I believe I can weather your hatred for a few hours longer."

Dalrymple gave a shaking laugh in response. "I know what these early friendships mean. There was no reason our friendship should have survived adolescence." A heavy sigh followed. "But unlike you, I didn't have a brother who worshipped me. I didn't have a family that stood behind me no matter what. For me, there was only you. And you were cold and brilliant and fascinating. You could always set the other boys aback with an insult so exact that it cut precisely to the bone and no further."

There was no way to answer that.

"In return, I was just...me. I could never figure out why you chose me as your friend, other than the fact that we shared a birthday. You were brilliant and perfect, and I was *me.*"

"I wasn't perfect," Smite said slowly. "I was...harsh." He blew his breath out. "I still am."

He heard Dalrymple struggle to his feet, and take a few steps away. "You were indifferent. To you, it was just the kind of friendship that boys have at Eton. It was a passing thing. For me, it was everything."

Smite looked up into the darkness. His head throbbed. His side twinged. If he thought of where he was for too long—enclosed in darkness, with that quiet sloshing of water all around him—he might lose his mind.

"I need something to do," he commented. "Soon would be good. Now would be better."

"It makes it worse, you know," Dalrymple was saying. "Carrying a grudge when the other man doesn't even give a damn. When he scarcely even knows you exist."

"I knew you existed," Smite said simply. He set his hand gingerly to his head and probed the sore area.

"You scarcely noticed when I stopped talking to you."

"Mmm. When I fall to pieces, I tend to do so by myself. After you walked away, nobody needed me for anything. It was a bad few years."

"Really?" Dalrymple snorted. " *How* bad?"

Smite paused. "There was laudanum," he finally answered. He didn't like to think of those years much. "The details aren't relevant. It took me years to find my feet properly."

There was a longer pause. "Does it make me a bad person that I rejoice in your suffering?" Dalrymple asked.

Smite laughed. It hurt, but he laughed. "No," he finally managed, "but it leaves us both still in captivity. I need something to do."

"About that," Dalrymple said, a touch too casually. "If we do what they say, they won't kill us. Right?"

The Patron had already committed hanging offenses. At this point, Smite would call in the dragoons rather than allow the man to walk free. The man might sometimes take action that was close kin to justice, but he was too cavalier with assault and imprisonment for Smite to overlook his crimes.

"They haven't killed us yet," he said carefully. "Maybe the Patron hasn't the stomach for outright murder."

"Oh," Dalrymple said. "Good." There was a bit of silence. "Are you just saying that to make me feel better?"

"Yes," Smite admitted. "I suspect the only reason we're alive is that the Patron may be wanted elsewhere. The instant we have his personal attention, he'll have us murdered, and the bodies hidden. He hasn't any choice."

A grim silence fell after that.

No. It was never silent down here. The faint lapping of water came to him once more. "Say something," Smite said. His voice sounded harsh. "Say anything."

"I was thinking that it's a shame that neither of us knows how to pick locks."

Smite looked up into the darkness. "You need a thin, flexible piece of metal. A hairpin will suffice. This, you slip into the keyhole. You use it to turn the pins to one side, whatever that means."

There was a long silence. "How did you know that?" Dalrymple asked. "Oh—never mind. I had forgotten how disconcerting your memory could be."

"I owe the knowledge to Robbie Barnstable." Smite scrubbed his hand over his face. "I owe him a debt of thanks, it appears."

"Why?" A glum sigh came from the other side of the room. "We don't have a hairpin."

Smite's hand slid to his waistcoat pocket. He cleared his throat. "Actually," he said. "I do."

"You use hairpins?" The disbelief was apparent in Dalrymple's voice.

Smite pulled the piece of metal out. "Of course not. This one belongs to Miss Darling."

He stood and shuffled forward, finding the wall with his hands.

"You have Miss Darling's hairpin in your pocket? What an astonishingly fortuitous coincidence."

Smite continued his search for the door in the dark. "As it turns out, I've been carrying it for two days."

"Two days? How does that happen?"

Smite sighed and looked up at the dark ceiling. "Little fairies hide it on my person when I'm not looking," he snapped.

"Um. Truly?"

"Of course not." He found the edge of the door. Felt for the handle, the keyhole. It seemed a staggeringly small thing upon which to rest his hopes. But he straightened the pin. "I have it on me because I put it in my pocket this morning," he said.

He slid the metal into the lock and felt around gently. There were supposed to be...pins. Or tumblers. Something like that. He prodded about.

"But *why* do you put it in your pocket?" Dalrymple persisted.

"Pure sentimentality, I'm afraid." He felt a resistance against the metal in his hand. He pushed gently, and then a tiny click sounded. A shot of jubilation ran through him. So that was what Robbie had meant by pins.

"Sentimentality? You?" Dalrymple sounded surprised.

Smite maneuvered the pin in the lock, and heard a depressing clunk as the pin he'd moved fell back into place. "Damn."

"Truly," Dalrymple persisted behind him. "That's...downright romantic. I'm astonished."

"Why?" Smite prodded the lock and found the ridge of the pins once more—one, two, three, four of them. This was going to be harder than he'd thought. "I'm human, same as you."

The first pin slipped before he could get the second one down. Smite scowled at the door and ignored Dalrymple's latest sally in favor of the lock. There was nothing but the metal, the hunch of his back as he leaned against the door. He moved one pin, and then another. He was working on the third when—

"You admit that you're human?"

Clunk-clunk. The pins slipped once more. Smite rested his head against the wall, gritting his teeth in frustration. "Winnie," he said, "really. Shut up."

"Oh. Am I distracting you?"

"No, but it's convenient to lay the blame at your door." Smite bent down to the lock once more. He had no sense of the passage of time in that dark room. It took long enough that his hands cramped. His back ached from stooping. The pins slipped again and again. Finally, he managed to trigger them all together. The lock clicked, and Smite let out a breath and opened the door.

A faint, pearly gray light filtered ahead of him. He turned to Dalrymple. The man was looking at him, his head cocked to one side.

"What the devil are you looking at?"

Dalrymple gestured at the hairpin in Smite's hand. Smite followed his gaze. In the faint light, Smite could make out the two metal prongs, one bent now, both held together by a bit of wrought metal.

"You're carrying a flowered hair pin," Dalrymple whispered. "It's like you're positively replete with sentiment. I can't make you out."

"Can't you?" Smite slipped the bent object back into his pocket. "I wouldn't need a sentimentality quota if I had no sentiment to begin with."

"You just like appearing omniscient." Dalrymple stumbled forward.

Smite followed him. They found themselves in another, larger room. The faint light they had detected trickled out in a thin line in front of them. Smite fumbled forward. "There's another door," he reported. "It's locked, too."

"Damn it." Then, louder: "Damn me. Turner, there's someone else in here."

Smite could hear the sound of breathing now that Dalrymple mentioned it. He'd been trying not to think of sounds; when he did, he noticed that added to the murmured noise of water rising was the soft patter of falling raindrops. He felt faintly uneasy.

"You there. Are you awake?" Dalrymple spoke loudly.

There was a long pause. The breathing hitched.

"Turner, who is he? Why isn't he answering us?"

Smite tamped down his uneasiness. "We come across a strange person on a ship I've never set foot upon. It's too dark to see a hand's breadth beyond my face. You must really believe in my omniscience to direct such a question to me."

Dalrymple let out an exasperated sigh. "Did you ever consider saying 'I don't know' in response, or would that have been too polite?"

"It would have been untruthful," Smite said. "I *do* know who this is. This is George Patten."

A gasp escaped the man, and Smite knew that he'd guessed aright.

IT TOOK MIRANDA FAR too long to travel across town to Smite's home, and more valuable minutes trying to pick the lock to his house. After a few haphazard tries, Jeremy pushed Miranda aside and managed it with a little too much finesse.

Ghost greeted them at the door. If he had been a proper sort of watchdog, he would have barked his head off and bitten them. Instead, he was delighted to see Miranda, whom he knew quite well—and equally happy to see Jeremy, whom he had never met. Miranda found his lead and took him outside. Together, they walked quickly to the alley where she had last seen Smite waiting with Dalrymple. Ghost snuffled around happily. Getting the scent, Miranda supposed, although the behavior seemed indistinguishable from anything else she had ever seen him do before.

"Find him," Miranda commanded Ghost. "Find your master."

It seemed like a good idea. He'd done it before, hadn't he?

"Are you serious?" Jeremy demanded.

"Completely."

As if to utterly undermine her claim to authority, Ghost raised his leg against a building. If this had been a story, Miranda thought, Ghost would have sensed their worry. His doggy ears would have perked up. And his paws would have eaten the pavement as he unerringly tracked down Smite.

But it wasn't a story, and Ghost wasn't that dog. Instead, the animal led them on a roundabout path from the alley, stopping to sniff here and there—and once to snag some unknown treat, which he crunched noisily between his jaws. He brought them down alleys, behind buildings, and went twice around one great square, before trotting off down a street.

"Are you sure he knows what he's doing?" Jeremy asked.

She frowned. "He's done it before." He seemed to be doing it, however, on his own schedule. "Ghost, do you know what you're doing?"

The dog's ears flicked back. It might have been a yes. It might have been a no. She sighed. It was probably the doggy equivalent of "I don't speak English."

"Lord." Jeremy gave a disapproving shake of his head. "Relying on a dog."

Still, they moved slowly toward the Floating Harbour, and then over the Prince Street Bridge. Ghost snuffled his way around one of the dry docks, happily—obliviously—bounding along while Miranda's worry ate at her insides. She could sense the minutes slipping past. Every quarter-hour was a risk. Every time she heard clock-bells strike in the distance, the possibility that she might not see Smite alive again grew. How long would it take Parford to raise a militia?

For Ghost, it was nothing but a game. Surely he would sense if his master was hurt. Surely, through some sort of canine magic...

But no. This was Ghost. He didn't have canine magic. Right now, he was more interested in leaving his mark on a lamppost along the water's edge.

"Go," Miranda said, a lot more forcefully this time.

Ghost ignored her. He sniffed once, and then turned in a lazy circle to face the other direction.

The dog was looking straight at the docks, so fixedly that Miranda was certain she would see a squirrel scampering along the stone walls that bordered the harbor. But no. There was only a ship that seemed all too familiar. The *Great Britain* loomed before them.

It was at that moment that it began to rain. It had been cold before, but the rain brought with it a chill from on high. Every drop felt like ice against her skin.

Ghost whined and lowered himself to the ground, where he gave a lazy yawn.

Miranda exhaled. Angry, frustrated tears threatened to well out. The wind whipped around her, driving cold droplets of rain into her face. She balled her fists. It *couldn't* end like this.

Jeremy tapped her shoulder.

"What?" The word snapped out more harshly than she intended.

He set his finger to his lips lightly and then pointed. High on the deck of the *Great Britain,* a dark figure paced to the edge and looked over.

"A night watchman," she said.

He shook his head. "Not with that lantern."

"What lantern?"

"Precisely. That hood hides it, except when you see it directly on. Watch, and you'll see the flash when he turns. A night watchman wants to be seen. He doesn't."

"But why would there be someone on the...ooh." The answer was too obvious. If she needed to keep someone in private, where would she go? People in the slums were too close-packed; the Patron could never keep the location secret. Too many people would have known they were about. But where could one hide a prisoner?

Aboard a ship that was abandoned because it was too large to fit out of the locks.

"What do we do now?" Miranda asked.

"What do you think? I march on board and act like I know what I'm doing." Jeremy strode forward.

Miranda followed. A rope ladder had been cast over the side of the ship. Jeremy caught one end and scampered up. Miranda climbed after him more slowly. When she reached the top, instead of starting down the middle of the deck as Jeremy did, she crouched off to the side.

The deck of the ship was punctuated by six great masts. In the middle, the dark, silent chimney of the funnel rose. And all around them were...were those things called hatches on a ship? Robbie would have known. Miranda shook her head.

There were two men on board, not just the one she'd seen earlier. Their burly forms huddled together; they watched Jeremy's approach in tense anticipation.

Jeremy had a confident swagger to his step, and a commanding, cheerful ring to his voice.

"You've been expecting me, I imagine."

"Sir."

"Where are they, then?"

A murmured answer, too indistinct for Miranda to make out. Then Jeremy's response floated back to her. "No. No need for any of that. Leave me the keys and get on with you. I'll take it from here."

Miranda held her breath and shrank back into the darkness on the edge of the ship. The men glanced at one another. Surely they had to hear the beating of her heart. But Jeremy betrayed not the slightest uneasiness. He held out his hand.

"The keys," he said. "And the lantern. You know the Patron's always intended to let them go. There will be riots if we don't."

Slowly the man extended his arm. Miranda heard a jingle of metal.

"Now away with you. You don't want Lord Justice seeing your faces. He has a memory like a steel trap. He'll never forget you."

The watchman shook his head hastily, and the men decamped. Jeremy stood in the center of the ship, waiting, tossing the keys in the air. After the other men had disappeared, Miranda crept out to join him. The rain had turned to freezing slush. She could scarcely feel her hands through her gloves.

"Come on," Jeremy said. "We haven't much time."

Chapter Twenty-four

THE SECOND LOCK AT the end of the room where Smite had found Patten proved harder to undo. The dim hint of light that filtered under the doorway made it all the more difficult. It made Smite want to rely on his eyes, when all he could see was shadow. Trapped with water nearby—he was glad to have something to do, just to distract himself.

He'd bent, crouching at the door, for the better part of half an hour. But it wasn't the sound of pins falling into place that made him straighten and swear under his breath. It was the soft rhythmic tread of footfalls.

Beside him Dalrymple reached out and tapped his shoulder.

"We need to take them together," Dalrymple whispered. "They won't expect us to be here. The instant the door opens, we jump on them."

Smite nodded.

"Patten," Dalrymple whispered.

"Mmm." The man, it turned out, was in chains. He could scarcely hobble.

"Stay back. If anything goes wrong, you'll be able to claim you had nothing to do with this."

"As if I would do anything so cowardly," came the scornful response.

A key scraped in the lock. Smite's muscles tensed, waiting. The door opened.

Dalrymple jumped ahead of him, screaming and flailing wildly. Smite couldn't see anything—just a mess of tangled limbs, illuminated in the faint moonlight that spilled into the room.

He could see two silhouettes, and beyond them, a ladder leading up to salvation.

"Wait!" a familiar voice was saying.

"Smite!" called someone else. Miranda's voice. It brought on a moment of panicked unreason, where he imagined the worst thing in the world—that he was trapped under rising water, and Miranda was with him. There were voices all about, people surrounding him. The incipient panic that he'd been suppressing broke, and he struck out wildly around him.

He had no notion of anything except that he must be choking on water. He was being restrained. Hands caught at his wrists. He fought back.

"Don't touch him!" Miranda's voice again.

He whirled about, but all was still.

"Good God, Turner," Dalrymple said nearby. "What the hell was that?"

His knuckles hurt. For a moment there... They'd been in close quarters. He'd glanced ahead, and seen steep stairs leading up. So much like that cellar ladder. He took a deep breath.

"Everyone has moments of irrationality," he said into the silence.

"You're well?" That was Dalrymple's dubious comment.

"I'll feel substantially more at ease once I'm off this vessel."

"Amen," said a voice. It took Smite a few seconds to place it. Jeremy Blasseur. Miranda's friend; the grandson of the Patron. He didn't want to think what it meant, that her friend had been able to find them. He heard the sound of metal clinking.

Mr. Blasseur, apparently, had the keys to Patten's chains.

"George," he was saying, "I'm so sorry. It's my fault. I didn't know what to do."

Patten made an indistinct answer. In the dim light, Smite could barely see the man struggle to his feet. Mr. Blasseur reached out to help him up, and when Patten stumbled, took his arm to steady him.

As they made their way to the staircase, Miranda appeared by Smite's side. She didn't reach out and touch him. She just stood— near enough to comfort him with her presence, but not so close as to overwhelm him.

"Miranda," he said.

"Yes?"

He reached out at the foot of the ladder and took her hand. Her fingers were cold. His own were trembling. It was this secret he entrusted to her—the shameful prize of his weakness.

"I suppose," he heard himself say, "I should tell you it's not safe to be here."

Her fingers curled in his. "You never make it safe to be by your side," she answered. "This one might be a little extreme even for you." The low teasing lilt of her voice robbed her words of any sting they might otherwise have carried.

"But then," she continued, "I always did fancy dangerous men."

"Get on up." He watched her ascend, then started up the ladder behind her. Everyone was quiet above him. He reached the top. The rain he'd heard had turned to snow, flakes melting into grayness as they struck the deck. Just as he reached the top, though, Miranda let out a short, pained burst of air. She stepped protectively in front of him. Strangely, Mr. Blasseur did the same thing—moving in front of George Patten, who was still limping from the chains they'd unlocked.

Men were scrambling onto the deck. Two. Three. Four. Five. The count hit seven, and then the last man reached down his hand and pulled up one more person.

It was a woman. Smite hadn't been expecting a woman.

Beside him, Miranda stiffened. "There's no time to explain," she said hastily. "She's the Patron—Jeremy's mother, Mrs. Blasseur. She wanted him to take her place. That's what it has all been about."

The Patron didn't look like the sort of person who ran a criminal enterprise. Her face was pleasant, if gaunt and sallow. She walked slowly: not shakily, as if she were elderly, but each step was a heavy trudge. Smite could hear her breathing. She heaved as if she'd been running for hours.

"Jeremy," she said in tones of motherly exasperation. "Why do you always have to make things so difficult?"

"It's too late," Jeremy said. "It's all too late. The Duke of Parford is raising the militia as we speak. You have only a matter of hours until he comes after you."

The woman sat down heavily. "Really, Jeremy. I have only a matter of days. It's not the militia I fear." She gave him a sad smile. But her gaze shifted beyond Jeremy, and she caught sight of Smite.

"Ah. Your Worship." She graced him with a disconcertingly friendly smile. "I have so wanted to speak with you. I feel that we could have been very great friends. It's a shame that only one of us will come out of this encounter alive. That seems professionally discourteous, after all. We're in the same business."

"We are?"

"Of course we are. We both deal justice. Only this time, it's your life in my hands. What is it that you'll offer me for it, I wonder?"

"Nothing," Smite said.

Beside him, Dalrymple twitched.

Mrs. Blasseur took a handkerchief and coughed into it delicately. "You value yourself highly." She cast her gaze about. "And your compatriots."

"You misunderstand. If you have to purchase it, you cannot call it justice."

Mrs. Blasseur curled her lip. But what would have been a cold, cutting silence was broken up by her ragged cough. Her frame bent over; Jeremy, standing next to George Patten, took one step forward.

She held up a hand. "Lord Justice, do you know why I began doing this? It was because *your* court paid little heed to crimes committed in Temple Parish. Rob a merchant, and you'll hang; but let a man beat his poor neighbor half to death, and the constables are nowhere to be found. Ask Miranda where she went when she needed help. What would your constables have done with a seventeen-year-old girl who was threatened by an older man? I do good things for the people you scorn. If *your* justice isn't paid for, why is nobody in Temple Parish rich enough to avail themselves of it?"

She coughed again.

Smite bit his lip. "I admit to some imperfections with my model. I've been doing my best to alleviate that."

"Ah," she said. "I know what you'll say next. You're going to remind me that I killed people. You might mention a few threats I've made. But I've seen men hanged in the name of the Queen. I saw you on the bench, once, issuing threats to others should they not stay honest. So tell me again, how are you different?"

Smite glanced back toward George Patten, still unsteady on his feet.

She caught the direction of his thoughts. "Yes. I imprisoned an innocent man. Are you so certain you've never done that?" She gave him a tight smile.

"This is sophistry," Smite responded. "Let us be clear. I want you not to kill me—or anyone here. You know that your time has come. You've been discovered, and it's only a matter of time until you and your organization are brought down. If I don't do it personally, someone else will complete the task. You're not here to mete out justice to me. You've come to beg for mercy."

"I have not." She had a sad smile on her face.

"No use denying it. And there's no use pretending I can give it. There will be none for you. I have some discretion in the performance of my duties; I have none where murder has been committed. You have, by your own admission, killed."

Mrs. Blasseur shook her head. "Oh, dearie me. You *are* serious, aren't you? I'm not here to beg for my life." She gave him another tight, sad smile. "I could scarcely walk here. In a few days, I doubt I'll be able to stand. Even speaking winds me. The doctor says I simply can't take in enough air to survive. You don't have to hang me. My body is suffocating of its own accord."

The Patron with nothing to lose... It didn't bear thinking about. "What do you want, then?"

"I want you to let Jeremy take charge." There was a low ferocity in her voice. "I've made my peace with death, but I want what I have built to live on. I want a legacy."

"Mama," Jeremy said.

"No, listen. He's trained for this. He's a good boy—he *listens* to people, and they like talking to him. He won't do anything lightly. Agree not to interfere with him and I'll let you go. After all we've suffered through, Temple Parish deserves justice. Don't let it die with me."

A few months ago, Smite would have suppressed the flash of unwilling compassion he felt at those words. There was only one answer to be made: there could be no other justice. His duty required him to eradicate the whole scheme, root and branch.

"Mother," Jeremy said, his voice low. "I can't do this. Don't ask it of me. Please."

"You can. I believe in you." She smiled at her son, as if she were encouraging him to persevere in a difficult set of lessons. It was morbidly touching. "Everything's already in place. If someone needs help, they know who to go to. All you need to do is respond."

"What you do is not justice," Smite heard himself say. "When I step down, my replacement will be chosen openly by Queen Victoria. I may have, by mistake, sentenced an innocent man to prison in the past. But I've never purposefully held a man who has done no wrong in an attempt to coerce my chosen replacement."

Jeremy bit his lip and glanced at Patten.

"When I order you to be held, it will be because I have a reasonable suspicion that you have committed a crime. A grand jury will hear the evidence against you and charge you. Should you live long enough, you'll have the opportunity to rebut that evidence at an open trial. This system is funded by the open and equal administration of taxes and duties, rather than robbery and blackmail. I cannot claim that the rule of law is perfect. But it is not hidden. Its flaws can be examined by all, and changes made. Justice that shrinks from the light of examination is nothing more than vengeance. I cannot let your organization persist."

Mrs. Blasseur shook her head sadly. "Then our conversation is over." She raised her hand, and the men she'd brought with her started forward.

Smite met her eyes. "It doesn't need to be. If I am not found, my brother will tear apart Temple Parish looking for me. What you have accomplished will be destroyed. There will be nothing to pass on at all. I have a better idea."

Mrs. Blasseur cocked her head and slowly lowered her hand.

"Jeremy," Smite said. "You were unwilling to serve as your mother's replacement. I have another position in mind."

"What?"

Smite rubbed his hand along his chin and found unruly stubble. "I became a magistrate because I wanted to help those who most needed it. Over the years, I've needed to remind myself of the cost of justice. I have used the…memory of my own experiences."

He'd held onto them with both hands.

"But my own experiences are limited. There is much that I haven't seen or understood. And that is where you will come in. People, I am told, talk to you. Tell me what they say. Bring the good in your mother's organization out into the open. Rid yourself of the need for threats and false imprisonments."

Mrs. Blasseur frowned at that. "How?"

"Start by choosing a new set of constables, intended for Temple Parish alone. Find new men, who can serve as magistrates—men who really will listen. Take what is good from what the Patron offers. Do you think you could help with that?"

Jeremy gave a short, jerky nod.

"There we are, then." Smite raised his eyes to Mrs. Blasseur. "There *has* been some good in what you've done. I shouldn't want to see it discarded entirely. But the days of justice funded through burglary and enforced by murder are over."

His hands were growing cold. If he was beginning to go numb, Mrs. Blasseur, frail as she was, must be freezing. But she made no sign that she felt the cold. Her eyes simply bored into his, knowing what he had not yet said.

"Can it be that easy?" Jeremy asked, his voice shaking.

That hint of compassion touched Smite again, fleeting as butterfly wings. He shut his eyes. "No," he said softly. "It won't be easy."

"What do you mean?"

That was Jeremy's question, but it wasn't Jeremy that Smite faced. It was Mrs. Blasseur. "You are hereby placed under arrest." He spoke softly, but his words seemed to expand to fill the vast open space of the Floating Harbour. The snow was beginning to stick on the ground, and it blanketed everything he said with chill. "You will be held in custody until such time as the numerous charges are laid against you. If charged—and you will be charged— you will be held in a cell alone, isolated from those you care for." He paused. "It *is* consumption that afflicts you, is it not?"

She nodded.

"Then I doubt you'll live to see the Quarter Sessions. In all probability, you'll die alone in a cold cell. That is the price you must pay. Your organization will survive in some form; you cannot."

"Can there not be the smallest bit of mercy for her, then?" Jeremy asked.

"No dear," his mother answered. "There is no room for mercy. That is what it means to take charge. You can show no weakness, no compassion. I know what it means to fill your shoes, Lord Justice. If you have any sense at all, you'll bind my wrists and march me to the station at this moment."

"March you?" Jeremy said, anguished. "You can scarcely walk!"

Mrs. Blasseur was taken by another fit of coughing. When she finished, she looked up with a resigned smile. "Don't you see? He can't show any mercy for me, or nobody will believe me defeated. He needs to drive me before him in the snow to *prove* I'm no longer a threat. That his...his regime will replace mine."

Jeremy shook his head.

"He's right." There was a bitterness to her voice. "Only one of us will survive this night. And if I try to make it me..."

Jeremy choked. "There has to be a better answer."

"There cannot be. There is no escape for me. If this is the way I get what I've built to survive in some manner... I haven't long to live, in any event. Promise me that you won't make a fuss. Whatever he has to do—promise you won't interfere. Don't help me if I fall. Don't—"

He felt a curious kinship with the woman. She didn't deal justice—not truly. But like him, she'd tinkered with the machineries of death. She saw the people she helped as human and real. Maybe, without the benefit of the law behind her, she had gone just a little mad.

"Mrs. Blasseur," Smite said. "I had not thought to drive you to the station like cattle."

She stopped and frowned at him. "No? Well, I suppose it might turn ugly if I couldn't make it."

Smite didn't push aside that moment of sympathy now. He embraced it, let himself feel the sorrow that Jeremy did. And then—because it had to be done, because there truly was no other choice...he let that moment of wistful regret dissipate and he met Mrs. Blasseur's eyes. "Under the circumstances," he said, "I had rather thought I would carry you."

"Carry me?"

"It turns out," he said, "that my duty dictates only *what* I must do. There is no mercy in the what. But there is room for it in the how."

THEY MADE A SOLEMN, silent procession as they made their way to the city center in a column. The men Mrs. Blasseur had brought with her had vanished into the night. Ghost trailed the remaining folk almost somberly. Mrs. Blasseur weighed almost nothing in Smite's arms. She didn't tremble. She didn't fight. She scarcely even breathed.

Halfway through the walk, the snow turned back to slush, and from there to a hard, cold rain that drummed against him relentlessly. The streets were deserted.

But when they arrived at the station, it was lit brightly. Smite pushed open the door to see a throng of blue-uniformed police officers standing near the front. A corporal was giving out orders; to his side stood Ash, watching the proceedings with a grim determination.

"We have reason to believe," the corporal was saying, "there is a large group of armed men there. Do not hesitate to use force if it should prove warranted. Assume that nobody means you well—not women, not even children."

Smite gently let Mrs. Blasseur down on her feet. Ash hadn't seen them enter yet; he was watching the corporal with a hard, fierce look in his eyes.

"This is an insult to the city of Bristol that must be answered with force," the corporal said.

"On the contrary," Smite called out. "Force will not be necessary."

As he spoke, Ash turned to him. A spectrum of emotions played across his brother's face—fear changed to surprise, followed by a heart-stopping emotion that Smite could put no words to.

It took a few minutes to calm the crowd and to allay their worries. It took another few moments for Mrs. Blasseur to vanish into the holding cells. Ash slowly drifted across the room to him.

"Smite." Ash reached out and clasped his hand. His brother's fingers were warm against Smite's chilled flesh.

"Yes?"

"I had this notion for years that I would need to be the Duke of Parford to make things right for you. I thought—" he choked, then stopped. "Damn you, Smite. I must have aged ten years tonight."

He grabbed Smite's shoulder with his free arm and then pulled him into a fierce hug. Smite only stiffened for a second before he hugged him back.

"You know, Ash," he said, before he could lose his nerve, "I love you."

Ash pulled back and looked at him quizzically.

"And you will need to be the duke for me," he said. "I made some rather egregious promises tonight. We're going to need more constables—and you're just the man to fund their salaries. Not to mention that we'll need more magistrates; I'm weary of being the only one here who listens." Smite gave his brother a tired smile.

"Parliament will have to handle that. I'm hoping you'll help me out."

Someone else might have blinked an eye at that. But Ash simply shrugged his shoulders. "There," he said. "You see? I was just saying that I needed to consider more charity."

IT WAS ALMOST DAWN by the time Smite brought Miranda home— *home* to the house he'd bought for her. The rooms seemed too quiet to her; the servants, not expecting her to return, were in bed for the evening.

He brought her up to her bedchamber, helped her strip off clothing made sodden and cold. They rubbed each other dry with towels, then slipped into wrappers that should have been warm.

They weren't.

A fire in the bedchamber upstairs didn't help. Huddling under the covers brought no warmth. The rain beat against the roof, hard at first, and then more softly. It was only when he drew her to him that Miranda stopped shaking. He pressed his body full-length against hers, and Miranda began to warm.

But even though he stroked her skin, he did not attempt anything so tame as a kiss. It was just warmth they shared: nothing more. He'd not tried anything *more* since…since that night in the inn. It seemed so long in the past. It was the only time he'd actually spent the night with her.

Through her window, the gray sky tinted first pink, then orange. The rain stopped and the clouds drifted apart, letting through ragged strains of early morning sunlight.

Smite sat up beside her. His gaze focused on some far vista. Just beyond the flotilla of masts on the Floating Harbour she saw a rainbow. It glimmered ephemerally, and then disappeared.

"You know," Smite said softly beside her, "even in the Bible, there was just that one flood."

"One seems more than enough."

He stood. "Mine comes back. It's a recurrent promise, one that I've held to all these years. It wasn't the flood that drove away every living thing. It was me, afterward."

She sat very still, but her heart thundered inside her. He turned to her. He seemed so solemn. "I don't know how to do anything by halves, Miranda."

He was going to send her away after all. She could scarcely breathe.

"So," he concluded, "you're going to have to marry me."

She choked. "What?"

"Marry me," he repeated.

She stared at him. He sounded perfectly rational. His hair was disordered, true, and he needed to shave. But there was no outward indication that he'd gone mad.

"You can't marry me," she said finally. "I'm your mistress. Nobody in polite society will ever see you again."

He blinked at her for a few moments, and then drew a deep breath. "That possibility had never occurred to me," he said stiffly. "In that case, I retract my offer. My overcrowded social calendar must be protected at all costs."

She stifled a grin.

"Give over, Miranda," he said. "That's not a serious objection."

"You still can't marry me," she told him. "There's no need. We can continue on—"

He set his hand over her lips, stopping her words. "I sent you away once." His fingers trailed down her cheek. "There are some things that cannot be made right by simple apology. It's not simply marriage I intend. It's a promise. I will never be without you again."

Her heart thudded wildly in her chest.

"I was hoping I could avoid the bit in the proposal where I lay out all the advantages of the match to you. There aren't nearly enough of them. The truth is simply this: you can find a better man than I. God knows you wouldn't have to look very hard. But I don't believe you can find one who loves you more."

She sucked in her breath.

"Love will never magically make me whole. It won't heal old wounds. But when I'm around you, I do not feel as if I must be alone. I smile when you're in the room and I laugh when you're happy. I feel as if I've come home to you." He slid his fingers up her arm, around her back. "There isn't one part of me that you've flinched from. I don't know why you'd marry me, but I know why I'm desperate for you. Nobody else on earth would bring me to myself as you have."

"Oh, don't you know why I love you?"

He turned to her. His hands closed roughly about her wrists. "Say it again."

"You anchor me without holding me down. You frighten me without threatening my future. You're unflinchingly devoted. I love you."

It had been *days* since he'd so much as kissed her. He made up for that now, with a hard, demanding possession. But his kiss was belied by the soft touch of his hands on her, stroking her arms, then her ribs. His fingers trailed up her sides as he kissed her, sliding up until he cupped her face.

"How will we live? What will we tell people?" she asked.

"I don't know. As long as it's with you…" He kissed her again. "If it matters, I can—"

"We," she corrected. "When it matters, *we* will find a way." She gave him a long, slow smile.

He echoed it back at her.

"And we'll start right here. With this." She leaned in and slowly, tenderly, kissed his shoulder, and then down his neck.

After a moment, his arms came around her. "Yes," he murmured, pulling her close and slowly peeling back her wrapper. "This is an excellent place to start."

Epilogue

ALMOST EVERYONE IN MIRANDA'S new family had gathered at Parford Manor on the day before Christmas—two weeks after their marriage. The thought of these people as *family* was still foreign to her. Like the ring Smite had put on her finger, she was still too aware of them—not uncomfortable, nor unwelcome, but still all too conscious of their newness.

Lady Turner's sisters had arrived in the early morning. They sat before the fireplace with Margaret, and played with Lady Rosa, the duke's daughter. Rosa had just learned to pull herself up on the furniture. She stood on chubby, wobbly legs and grinned at the adulation this garnered.

The room was hung with holly, and the scent of pine boughs was heavy in the air, mixing with the hint of smoke from the crackling fire. Snow was thick on the ground outside, but the sun was out, and light glinted off the surface, brightening everything.

On the long divan, Smite, Ash, and Richard Dalrymple were arguing companionably about some item in the newspaper. Every so often, Smite would glance up and meet her eyes.

The low, private smile he gave her curled her toes. He'd been hers for every night of their honeymoon.

They'd settled into her house in Bristol, with Mrs. Tiggard staying on as housekeeper. They'd hired a manservant—but only the one, and he didn't live in. They'd started a quiet, private life. When the New Year came, Robbie would join them. Smite would return to his duties. And Miranda would announce that she was home to visitors. Everything would change, and they'd have to make everything work once more. But for this short space of time, he was all hers.

Through the window, she caught a flash of brown.

Smite stood, dropping the paper, and cutting off the friendly back-and-forth with two words. "Mark's here," he announced.

Before anyone could say anything else, he darted away, opening the front door in a flurry of bells. Miranda followed with the rest of the family—everyone came except Margaret, who stayed back, bundling Rosa into warmer things.

Smite reached the carriage first, just as Mark was stepping down.

"Mark." His pause was perceptible to her eyes only; he caught his brother in a hug after only that one bare second of hesitation.

"Where's Ash?" Mark said. "Not hanging back, I hope."

"Oh no," Smite said slyly. "He has other plans."

Mark frowned. "Other plans?" He peered around dubiously. "I can't bring myself to believe that, on Christmas Eve of all times. After all, I—"

He was cut off by a snowball thudding into his chest.

"Guess again," Ash called out cheerfully. "I'm fortified."

"You distracted me." Mark stared at Smite. "You distracted me *intentionally* so that Ash could get me."

Smite laughed and ran away, just as his younger brother ducked behind the wheel of the carriage and scooped up snow. Robbie tumbled out of the conveyance. But instead of going to greet Miranda—he'd been visiting Mark for the duration of their honeymoon—he exclaimed, "Brilliant!" and joined the battle.

The war was fierce but short; it ended when Lady Turner sneaked up behind Ash and dumped a bucket of slush down his neck.

She was declared the victor.

Miranda was picking snow out of her husband's collar—and wishing she'd joined Lady Turner's initiative—when a second carriage topped the rise.

"I thought everyone was here," she said.

"Did you?" Smite's answer was a little too nonchalant. "Perhaps you've forgotten someone."

Everyone else was waiting with avid interest. A cousin, perhaps? The duchess's other brother?

As the carriage pulled around the drive, Smite found his way to her side. He slid his arm about her and then leaned down to whisper in her ear.

"I've owed you a wedding present all these weeks," he said. "This is it."

She had one moment to wonder what he could possibly mean when the door opened. It had been years since she last saw them, but she could never have forgotten. She started forward. "Jasper?"

The man who stepped out saw her, and a brilliant grin lit his face. She ran across the snow, skidding into his arms. Jonas was next out.

"Look at you," Jasper said. "You're all grown." He held her close, and then murmured into her hair, "You'd best tell us what the jig is quickly, so we don't put the lie to anything you've said."

"No lies," Miranda retorted happily. "He knows everything."

"And he invited us anyway?" Jonas came up behind them, enveloping her in a hug.

Smite was already coming forward. "Smite Turner." He held out his hand. "It's good to have the two of you here. Standish, I hear you've got a translation of *Antigone*. My brother Mark and I would love to hear what you've got."

"Oh, no," said Jonas. "I must hear this story first. Miranda, how in God's name did you end up *here?*"

"Well," Miranda said. "It's a sweet tale, about kittens and puppies and rainbows and love."

Smite gave her that low, private smile again, and she warmed even in the cold air and bit her lip.

"Especially love," she said, linking her arm with Jonas's. "Now shall we all go in?"

Thank you!

Thanks so much for reading. I hope you enjoyed *Unraveled*. If you did, I hope that you:

Check out the rest of the series. *Unraveled* is the last book in the Turner series. The other books are *Unlocked, Unveiled,* and *Unclaimed.* You can find out more about the series at http://www.courtneymilan.com/turner/.

Check out my other books. A full list of my available titles, sorted by series order, is at http://www.courtneymilan.com/byseries.php.

What's next? If you want to know when my next book is out, you can sign up for my new releases e-mail at http://www.courtneymilan.com.

Author's Note

THREE YEARS AGO, I wanted to write a series about an insane mother who had a powerful effect on all three of her children—but a different effect on each one. I got the first hint of where Smite had come from when I read *Asylum Denied* by David Ngaruri Kenney. In that book, Kenney describes some of his experiences in his home country of Kenya. A particularly vivid image was his description of standing in solitary confinement in water. When I read that, I set the book down and said aloud, "That's Smite."

The rest of the Turner series formed itself around that moment. I had known that I wanted Smite to be a magistrate in Bristol; he must therefore have grown up in Somerset. I found Shepton Mallet by searching for floods in Somerset, and Mark's book was born from that. Ash became the brother who escaped the worst of the torment and who felt the weight of survivor's guilt.

But Bristol lent a dimension to this book that it would not have had in the abstract.

The Bristol Riots that Old Blazer describes in 1831 were the result of a large number of disenfranchised citizens who became very angry when a bill that would have increased the number of eligible voters was scotched in Parliament. The result of the riots, and similar unrest throughout Britain, was a series of changes affecting Britain's government from the local to the national level. The Reform Bill passed Parliament the next year. Increased scrutiny into Bristol's governance over the next years yielded some embarrassing results. For a lengthier account, including some indications that Bristol's ruling class had been embezzling from charitable institutions prior to reform, Graham Bush's *Bristol and its Municipal Government* is excellent.

Parliament passed the Municipal Corporations Act, which was supposed to be a major reform. In truth, however, many of the same people who had been running the show before were simply put in charge once more. The result was a ruling class who cared a great deal about the few enfranchised voters (still not a large proportion of the population) and not at all about the working poor.

At the beginning of this book, Miranda notes that in the years before Smite sat as magistrate, only one person had been found innocent in the petty sessions. I know this sounds unbelievable, but it's exactly what I discovered when I visited the Bristol Records Office and examined the notes from the petty sessions from that time period. I saw conviction after conviction after conviction. The only people who weren't convicted were those who had some strong indicia of wealth—for instance, a person could afford to hire a lawyer, or who owned substantial property. In all the records I examined, I found precisely one person who was not convicted and who appeared to be poor. In that case, the court reporter was so sure of a conviction that he had actually written down that he was convicted before the verdict was handed down—and had to cross off the erroneous result and write in the acquittal.

But I did take a bit of a liberty with regard to other actions by magistrates. In *Unraveled,* the other magistrates essentially rubber-stamp police requests for warrants and the like. In reality, my trip to the records office suggests that the magistrates did exert at least a modicum of real oversight on these questions.

The ending is a bit of a fairytale, I'm afraid; I'd love to fantasize about a version of Bristol where the constables served the entire population, not just the wealthy and middle-class citizens as early as the 1840s. But history suggests that just wasn't so. I prefer my version.

Richard Dalrymple, in the first handful of chapters, gets the 1840s version of a parking ticket. Those really did exist; you can find a picture of an early-Victorian parking ticket on my website.

The *SS Great Britain* was one of the first iron steamships constructed. It really was docked for months after its launch in the Floating Harbour because its hull was unable to fit through the locks. Eventually, the harbormaster agreed to enlarge the locks and, almost a year after it was officially launched, the *Great Britain* finally sailed. The *Great Britain* has been restored to its original condition; if you visit Bristol, you can (and should!) visit it.

I took a few liberties with regards to the interior of the *Great Britain*; I invented an interior for Temple Church and another for the Royal Western Hotel and the theater. There is no opera house in Bristol. I suppose an opera could have played in the theater. Since the theater wouldn't have been officially opened in November, in this book it could have been hired out for a short space of time.

Astute readers with legal backgrounds might wonder about two elements of law in this book. The first is this: would it not be a violation of principles of double jeopardy for Smite to charge Billy Croggins with arson after he had already been charged with another offense based on the same underlying conduct? The answer is that in England in that era, double jeopardy didn't attach to non-felonies, and it didn't attach preconviction.

Readers might also wonder about Smite's refusal to hear cases in which he had an interest. The concept of recusal existed at the time period, but the principles that Smite applies to himself are substantially more strict than the historical norm. Justices were supposed to act impartially, but the procedure by which that impartiality was procured is described, for instance, in George Oke's *The Magisterial Synopsis*: "Cases also frequently arise to which...local circumstances...attach a fictitious or imaginary importance, which renders them fit to be discussed in the presence of several magistrates, in order that their administration of justice may not only be impartial, but beyond suspicion." In other words, if there was the possibility of a suspected interest, the solution was typically to have many magistrates decide together, not to have one magistrate walk away. *Blackstone* is even clearer on the question: "The law will not suppose a possibility of bias or favor in a judge, who is already sworn to administer impartial justice."

The modern, more familiar, American standard, which says that judges should avoid even the appearance of impropriety is significantly stricter.

Nonetheless, recusal was not an impossibility. A judge's statement that he could not administer impartial justice in a case would have been given extraordinary weight. Smite's principles are without a doubt a great deal nicer than the British historical norm—but his objection was grounded in the oath of office that he swore, and while it was out of the ordinary, it was not unheard of.

It doesn't surprise me that on this point, as in all others, Smite holds himself to a higher standard than those around him.

The Patron is, of course, my own invention.

Acknowledgments

AS I WRITE THIS, the floor of the room where I am sitting is strewn several inches thick with the paper detritus from the last drafts of this book. I'm fairly certain that under some of those layers of paper, I will be able to find pens, clothing, and perhaps small cities.

I'd like to thank my husband for not complaining about this exciting archaeological feature over the dinners I didn't cook, or while putting away the dishes I didn't do, or while shelving the groceries I didn't buy. I'd especially like to thank him for putting up with my inability to talk about anything except this book during many long walks that were supposed to be just about "us" and ended up being brainstorming sessions. Mr. Milan also provided needed medical advice—without him, I'd not have known how to describe Mrs. Blasseur's end-stage lung cancer.

As I mention in the Author's Note, this book started with a simple image from *Asylum Denied* by David Ngaruri Kenney. I also drew on Charles Dickens's descriptions of legal matters in *Bleak House* and *Oliver Twist*—and I explicitly drew on Dickens's hapless Jo, the street-sweeper, from Bleak House, in portraying Widdy.

I also drew on materials from a visit to Bristol. In particular, I'd like to thank the staff at the Bristol Records Room, who retrieved numerous important historical documents that helped shape this book, ranging from postcards that showed the layout of the gaol to the parchment paper that contained the oath of office that Smite would have taken. I also am indebted to the staff at The Georgian House. Miranda's home was patterned after this historic home.

As always, I have to thank Tessa Dare, Carey Baldwin, and Leigh Dennis for (a) listening to me talk about this book, and (b) putting up with me when we met for a weekend, and I did nothing but work on it. As always, my enormous thanks to Franzeca

Drouin, Robin Harders, and Martha Trachtenberg for editing. Lynn Funk, Nicholas Ambrose, and Anne Victory did wonderful proofreading work. My agent, Kristin Nelson, has been relentlessly supportive.

I have a lot of people who help talk me down from various ledges: the Vanettes, the Peeners, and the Pixies. The Vanettes in particular helped me write cover copy for this book, which I doubt I could have managed on my own.

And thanks most of all to SOC, without whom this book would have looked very different. I love you.

Most of all, I want to thank all the many readers who I've found over the course of writing the Turner series. The extraordinary response that you've had has made a huge difference in my life. Thank you all so much for reading, for engaging, for talking about these books with friends and even with random strangers on the internet. I could not be where I was today without you.

CPSIA information can be obtained at www.ICGtesting.com
Printed in the USA
LVOW06s1803250713

344649LV00007B/849/P